DI Gus McGuire Book 4

By

Liz Mistry

Copyright © 2018 Liz Mistry

The right of Liz Mistry to be identified as the Author of the Work has been asserted by her in accordance Copyright, Designs and Patents Act 1988.

First published in 2018 by Bloodhound Books

Apart from any use permitted under UK copyright law, this publication may only be reproduced, stored, or transmitted, in any form, or by any means, with prior permission in writing of the publisher or, in the case of reprographic production, in accordance with the terms of licences issued by the Copyright Licensing Agency.

All characters in this publication are fictitious and any resemblance to real persons, living or dead, is purely coincidental.

www.bloodhoundbooks.com

Print ISBN: 978-1-912604-08-1

Also by Liz Mistry

DI Gus McGuire Series

Unquiet Souls (Book 1)

Uncoiled Lies (Book 2)

Untainted Blood (Book 3)

Praise For Liz Mistry

"I cannot wait to read more by this author. This book is perfect for readers who enjoy an outstanding crime, suspense and mystery rolled into one full plot."
Gemma Myers - Between The Pages Book Club

"What a fantastic story which is full of twists and turns whilst being sensitively written about an absolute horrendous subject!"
Clair Boor - Have Books Will Read

"It is a very complex story with many strands intertwined to make up a very gripping, adrenaline filled book that has the reader turning page after page well into the night."
Jill Burkinshaw - Books n All

"Omg what an excellent start to a brand new series.... Absolutely brilliant storytelling."
Livia Sbarbaro - Goodreads

"Another fantastic read from Liz. I loved unquiet Souls so I knew this would be just as good."
Susan Angela Wallace - Goodreads

"A gritty storyline, an excellent ending and very believable characters. A very well written book."
Misfits Farm - Goodreads

"Strong writing. Believable characters and a fast paced plot."
Owen Mullen - Author

"Another rollercoaster, action packed, murder Mistry! As enjoyable as book one with the

"Untainted Blood is yet another great book in an already gripping crime series. I have to admit to racing through the pages towards the end to what was an extremely satisfying climax."
Sarah Hardy - By The Letter Book Reviews

"I just loved Liz Mistry's writing style, there is such a simplicity about it that makes if very easy to follow, as all the characters are very distinctive."
Susan Hampson - Books From Dusk Till Dawn

"The writing style was spot on and it covered a controversial but highly relevant topic and boy it was done well."
Donna Maguire - Donnas Book Blog

"The book is well written and keeps you gripped throughout and has a few twists that made me gasp!"
Julie Lacey - Goodreads

For Nilesh, Ravi, Kasi and Jimi

Cruel minds take pleasure
In hedonistic pursuit
Forsaking all that's pure

Prologue

Leeds, 2012

Mushrooms of dense throat-clogging smoke hung in the air. Every breath was like sucking through cotton wool and, even after gargling with mouthfuls of cold water, Detective Inspector Sandy Panesar could still taste it; a coating of ash, sharp and acrid on her tongue.

'Have they got the child?' Her voice was shrill as she rushed forward towards the dark figure of a firefighter wearing breathing apparatus leaving the blaze.

The figure carried an amorphous bundle that was wrapped so completely in a blanket that it was impossible to tell if it was even human. With practised ease, the package was transferred onto a stretcher trolley, leaving Sandy to watch, her heart hammering in her chest as the paramedic unwrapped the small, still body. Her heart plummeted. The child's face, beneath its mucky streaks, was pale and its eyes remained closed, its body unmoving. Sandy focussed on the child's chest but could detect no movement as she willed the paramedics to make a miracle happen. Their examination seemed to take forever and Sandy's view was obstructed as they started chest compressions and fitted a drip. Their muttered words meant nothing to her as they worked with an economy of movement she would, in different circumstances, have admired. Just when she'd given up hope, one of the paramedics turned towards her with a smile and stepped away from the child; ten years old yet the size of a three-year-old, with an oxygen mask dwarfing its tiny face.

Sandy, realising she'd been holding her breath, took in a huge gulp of air and sent a quick prayer heavenward before bending down and gently ruffling the child's matted black hair. Two huge, unblinking eyes stared right through her, seemingly lost in whatever hell played out in its mind. Her heart almost broke. Surviving the fire was only half the battle for this little one. The biggest battle lay ahead. She patted the kid on the arm and stood back.

The paramedic smiled. 'It's the shock, that's all. It'll pass with a good night's rest and some food.'

Sandy wondered if he was referring to her or the child. Watching them take the child away, she thought, *Yeah, a good night's rest, some food and a lifetime of counselling.* Pulling herself together, she glanced through the darkness at the crowd. The tall distinctive figure of her detective sergeant, with his head of three-inch-long dreadlocks, rose like a sphinx above everyone else. He tilted his head to let her know he'd seen her and continued directing the uniformed officers to control the gathering crowd before striding over.

He pointed to the departing ambulance. 'Was that the kid, then?'

Sandy thrust her hands in her pockets, and glowered, 'Yep, uninjured bar some smoke inhalation and shock, according to the paramedics.'

DS Gus McGuire acknowledged her words. 'Yeah, although not unharmed.'

'No, not unharmed,' she agreed and kicked a loose stone towards the blazing house. 'When the fire service have left and their assessors are done, get the scene processed.'

'Sure thing.' He wiped the back of his hand over his streaming eyes, 'No news yet of the social worker, boss?'

She shook her head, knowing that the chances of finding Amina Rose alive decreased with every passing second. The heavy lump in her chest wasn't just anger at the situation: it was also personal worry. She'd worked with Amina before and knew her well. 'They're still looking for her.' She turned and glared at the four trollies situated outside one of the ambulances. Each one bore a body bag and Sandy's gaze was directed to the two largest ones. 'The firefighters said she wasn't anywhere near those bastards in the living room, so maybe she got lucky, like the child. Shame the other kids weren't so lucky.' She rubbed the back of her hand over her nose. 'Hell, we don't even know that the kid and Amina were together.'

Biting his lip, Gus spoke in a quiet voice. 'The boyfriend is waiting over there, boss.'

Sandy's shoulders slumped as she saw the man leaning against a police car at the periphery of the scene. She'd met him once at one of those inter-departmental Christmas parties that spouses were invited to. His name was Kyle and he'd had his face looked like a slapped arse all night, so presumably Amina had forced him to come. Not surprised she wanted back-up. Those does were always a trial in themselves. A scarf was tied round his nose, probably to block out the toxic smoke that was drifting in his direction. She sighed, and with a rueful glance at Gus, walked slowly over the grass verge to stand beside him. Kyle acknowledged her presence with a quick nod and then continued his silent vigil, until a flurry of activity near the front of the blazing house brought him lurching forward. A firefighter carrying an inert figure over his shoulder stumbled through the flames. Amina was the only other person unaccounted for, so this had to be her.

'Amina!' Kyle's voice cut through the smoke like a machete and he began to run, his movements uncoordinated. Sandy followed, catching hold of his arm as the firefighter passed the figure over to the paramedics. A frenzy of activity played out in slow motion as they approached. Twice, the screech of the defibrillator charging rent the thick air, followed by a thud as they tried to jump-start Amina's heart. Twice they failed. A quick shake of the head was enough to tell Kyle that his fiancée was dead. He flung himself towards her lifeless body and a high-pitched shriek splintered the heavy atmosphere, before two firefighters managed to pull him away. Sandy wrapped her arms round his shoulders and held on tight. As he collapsed, she fell onto the wet grass with him, holding him as he cried. Over his shoulder, she watched, tears in her eyes, as three firefighters removed their helmets respectfully and averted their gaze.

When she'd come on shift three hours ago, she'd had nothing more pressing on her plate than a teenager caught shoplifting. Until, out of nowhere, a hostage situation involving a social worker and at-risk children had erupted. Now, shift's end in sight, she'd chalked up five dead bodies and a traumatised child.

On days like this, Sandy Panesar could happily retire.

November 2017
Saturday

Chapter 1

20:30 Robin Hood's Bay

The rolling mist and drifting clouds cast eerie shadows over the coastline and the boats bobbing in the distance were becoming ever harder to see as night descended. The autumn chill made DI Gus McGuire glad that he'd worn his shabby fisherman's jacket over his jumper. He and his best friend, Mo, sat in companionable silence on a wooden seat at the top of the steep hill that wound down past shops and pubs to the bay. They were well used to this view for Gus' parents had brought them here often when they were boys; Gus and his two compadres. They'd had such fun, rock pooling and paddling and searching for fossils. An unlikely trio they were: the posh mixed-race kid with the Scottish parents and annoying sister, the working class white kid from a single-parent family and the Pakistani Muslim with a wicked sense of humour. Once, Gus had overheard one of his teachers referring to them as the 'united colours of Benetton'. At the time he hadn't understood what she was on about.

Now though, it was only him and Mo left. Greg, the third musketeer, had died when Gus stabbed him. Gus still struggled with that. Greg had been in the grips of a schizophrenic episode and had attacked his wife and young son. In the end, he'd attacked Gus, nearly killing him before he'd got the upper hand. However, he'd been too late to save Greg's wife and little Billy. How things had changed for the three boys from Bradford.

Greg, a talented artist, was gone. Mo owned a popular fast food samosa café. He'd settled down with his childhood sweetheart, Naila, and together they seemed to be working towards producing an all-woman football team. Gus, meanwhile, had headed off to university, got a psychology degree and become a detective inspector with Bradford Police.

Nearby, the sound of a badger snuffling its way in the shrubbery, seeking discarded fish and chip wrappers, held their attention. Its nose appeared, followed by its distinctive white stripe and then, as if it could sense their presence, it was off. A stone's throw away in The Smugglers cottage the voices of his parents, his ex-wife Gabriella, his sister Katie and Mo's family drifted up to them. They'd been playing a game of Monopoly round the kitchen table when Gus and Mo had escaped and, judging by the laughter, his dad was keeping them entertained as usual. He glanced back and saw his mother's head outlined against the light from the kitchen window as she pottered about. His heart contracted and the awareness of everything he had so nearly lost hit him like a cudgel. It did this sometimes – however, if he concentrated on his breathing, he could, more often than not, avoid a panic attack.

His mother had insisted the entire family come for a week. *Her* pretence was that she needed to get away to recuperate, although they'd all known that her main objective was to force a truce between Gus and his sister. Had it come six months earlier both siblings would have refused. However, Corrine McGuire had nearly died just a few months ago and neither Gus, nor Katie could refuse her anything. Of course, his mum was well aware of that and had, without shame, played on it.

It hadn't been so bad. After the initial awkwardness of seeing Katie and Gabriella together as a couple, things had eased. In fact, his current relationship with his ex-wife was less fraught than when they'd been married and as the week progressed they settled into some sort of normality. His reward was seeing the lines on his mother's face fade and hearing her laugh again. The attack had burst her bubble, although she seemed to be beginning to mend now. He could tell his dad was pleased, too. His gruff laugh was frequent and he looked less drawn. All in all, this family foray had been a roaring success.

Mo and his family had driven over from Bradford for the day, which had been spent crabbing, eating fish and chips and scoffing ice cream. Mo and Naila had a room in the hotel at the top and the girls were spending the night at The Smugglers with Gus and his family. A full house, what with five children, three dogs and five adults.

At last, Gus turned to Mo. 'Okay, big man, spit it out. What's up?'

Mo stretched up and, shoving his fingers into Gus' dreadlocks, pushed his head, like he used to do when they were kids. Gus shook his hand away. 'Come on, stop trying to distract me. Just spit it out.'

Mo exhaled. 'That obvious, is it?'

'It is to me, mind you, I've known you since we were kids.'

Mo pulled his coat a bit tighter round him and tucked his chin beneath the neckline. 'It's Zarqa.'

Gus waited. Mo would tell him more in his own time, however, he hoped to hell Zarqa wasn't in any trouble. She was Mo's eldest and was very intelligent. She was heading for A-stars in her GCSEs.

'She's asking questions.'

Not quite sure where Mo was going with this, Gus cast a sideways glance at his friend. Mo was gnawing at his lip; a habit left over from their childhood. *Okay, it must be bad.* 'About...?'

Mo shuffled his feet, 'Me and Naila.'

'Ah. What have you told her?'

'Nothing yet. We don't know what to say. How much to tell her? She's still just a kid. It might be too much for her to take in.' He sighed and took a bite of the chicken leg he'd brought from the house. 'What do you reckon, Gus?'

Gus had little experience of kids other than Mo's, and only ever as an honorary 'uncle'. He'd never had to consider making decisions for them. 'Mmm, don't know, to be honest, Mo. What does Naila say?'

Mo snorted. 'She thinks we should talk it through with her.' He made air quotes with his fingers. 'Be "transparent".'

Gus smothered a smile. It was clear that Naila and Mo disagreed on the subject. No way was he going to side with Mo against his wife. Hell, no! He knew how ferocious she could be. He sympathised with his mate, though. It was hard being dad to five girls, and *this* hurdle was never going to go away. Deep down, he suspected Naila's approach was the best way forwards, yet he couldn't say that to Mo. No, he'd leave them to sort this out on their own. 'I think you and Naila need to decide this together, Mo.' He punched his friend on the arm, 'It's not the end of the world, you know? Zarqa's a good girl. She'll understand.'

Mo picked at his cuticles, looking unconvinced. 'I'm not so sure, Gus. I'm not so sure.'

Sunday

Chapter 2

10:30 Cottingley

'Fuckin' hell, Jake, what're we gonna do?'
Standing in the middle of his smallish bedroom, Jake shrugged, head down, hands thrust deep into his pockets. He kicked the wooden bed leg repeatedly. With a scowl, he delivered a final kick and flung himself onto the chair in front of his desk where his computer flashed a rolling programme of photos of him and his mates doing stupid stuff. He didn't know what to do, but didn't want to admit it to Matty. Truth was, he was bricking it.

'How the fuck should I know?' He grimaced, grabbed a half-full bottle of Lucozade from the computer table and glugged. 'Fuckin' headache. Wait till I catch the bastard that spiked our drinks.'

Matty pulled a crumpled packet of Ibuprofen from his pocket and handed it to Jake, who popped two pills and downed them with another slug of Lucozade.

'Cheers.'

He threw the packet back to Matty, who was sprawled on Jake's bed, eyes bugged out of his head, bloodshot and swollen. Even under the angry pus-filled mountainous terrain that was his face his pallor was evident. With a sudden movement, Matty jerked upright and grabbed a plastic bucket from the floor. He barfed and the sweaty male hormonal stink was overpowered by the sweet sickly stench of regurgitated alcohol, coke and stomach acid.

Jake slapped one hand over his nose, jumped to his feet and with the other flung open the window. 'Fuck's sake, Matt! Empty that fuckin' thing before my mum comes up and gives us shit.'

Looking even paler than before, Matty, trailing a sicky smell in his wake, walked across the landing with the bucket and deposited its contents down the loo. Seconds later he was back. With a serious face, he sat down and repeated his earlier question. 'What are we gonna do, Jake?'

Jake shook his head. He was still thinking things through and nothing was making sense yet.

'What about Si? Where the hell is he?' Matty perched on the edge of Jake's bed, his fingernails worrying an angry pus bulb on his chin. 'You don't think…?' He hesitated and glanced at Jake.

Jake frowned at him. 'What the fuck! You don't think *he* did it, do you?'

Matty shrugged and blotted his burst spot with the edge of his sleeve. 'Nah, course not. It's just well… who *did* do it?'

Crossing one leg over the other, Jake cursed. 'God, coulda been anybody Matt. We didn't know half the idiots who were there. Don't even know who *she* was, do we?'

Matty kicked off his Vans and sat back with his legs dangling over the side of the bed and began work on another spot. 'He still not answering your texts?'

'Naw and it goes to voicemail when I ring.'

'I'm gonna text Tayyub, see if he's seen him.'

Jake snorted, 'That retard! He won't have seen Si. Too busy with that stupid fuckin' camera of his.'

'Aw, shut the fuck up, Jake. Tayyub's alright. Just a bit weird that's all.'

'Hmmph. If you say so. Go ahead, text him.'

> **Matty:** *WUU2?*
> **Tayyub:** *Working*
> **Matty:** *You alright mate?*
> **Tayyub:** *Yes*
> **Matty:** *You seen Si?*
> **Tayyub:** *No*
> **Matty:** *Sure?*
> **Tayyub:** *Yes.*
> **Matty:** *Safe, in a bit*
> **Tayyub:** *Yes goodbye. I will see you later*

Jake leaned over Matty's shoulder. 'See what I mean? The fucker don't even talk right.'

Matty raised an eyebrow and smirked. 'Nah you're right he *don't* talk right. Not like us, all posh 'n' that.'

'Tosser!'

Matty sat up. 'You worried 'bout Si?'

With a glance at his friend Jake said, 'Yeah, you?'

Matty snuffled and wiped his mucky sleeve across his eyes. 'Yeah.'

'Don't start fuckin' crying. Just stay cool, right.'

Matty wiped his arm over his eyes again.

Chapter 3

12:30 Manningham

Tracey knocked on the bedroom door. When there was no reply, she pushed it open and in the light from the hallway made her way across the carpet, avoiding the tangle of wires and connections hooked up to the complex computer system that took up an entire wall.

'Tayyub?'

From the single bed in the corner Tracey heard a low keening sound. *Oh no, what's happened now?* She took a deep breath, marched over to the bed and sat down on the edge. Placing her hand on the foetal shaped lump that rocked to and fro, she patted, slow and rhythmic until the rocking stopped and the keening abated. Leaning over, she switched on the bedside light before speaking in a matter of fact voice, her face displaying none of the anxiety she felt. 'Come on Tayyub, sit up and tell me what's got you in this state.'

She waited for a few seconds. No response. 'Oh Tay, come on, what's up?'

The teenage lad at last sat up on the bed, eyes wide and red rimmed. His slender frame all edges and elbows. He pulled a pair of ear plugs from his ears and sniffed.

Tracey shook her head and standing up she took his hand and pulled him to his feet. 'Bloody hell, Tayyub, you stink. First thing for you is a shower. Then I'll make us a cup of tea and you can tell me all about it.'

Tayyub lifted his arms one at a time and smelled his armpits. With a lopsided grin, he looked at Tracey.

'Sorry, Sis.' He wrapped his long arms round her petite frame pulling her to him in a cuddle that dwarfed her. Tracey savoured these moments of contact. It had taken years for Tayyub to respond in that way; and to do it voluntarily was a recent thing. He was high-functioning autistic and the human touches, the eye contact, the responding to her gentle humour were difficult for him. Struggling, she escaped with a laugh and waved him off to the bathroom.

Waiting for him downstairs, she wondered what had upset him so much. It had been ages since he'd taken to his room, rocking and keening like that.

Chapter 4

21:36 Cottingley

Jane Proctor didn't know what had possessed them. Pulling into the woods had been a complete act of madness. In some ways, the perfect end to their long weekend break. It was even less typical of James than it was of her. He'd always been the more prudish, so when he'd driven off the road and cut the lights, tingling anticipation made her pelvis contract.

Like teenagers, they'd dragged off garments, manoeuvred limbs and giggled over the obtrusive gear stick. Last time they'd done this, it was in her Fiesta nearly twenty years ago. Today, even though the car was bigger, there seemed to be less room and their shagging was a peremptory tribute to their old life... the one before Simon... before they got all boring and predictable. Ah well, at their age she was surprised they'd managed to manoeuvre, never mind complete the act. It had been fun, though short-lived. Who'd have thought James still had it in him?

Leaning back, knickers discarded in the depths of the foot well, Jane laughed. 'We should really share a joint now... just for old times' sake.'

James, still red in the face from his exertions, grinned. 'The most I'd manage these days would be a vape.'

Squeezing his arm, she grinned. 'We've still got it, haven't we?'

Eyes crinkling in that way she loved, James beamed, knocking ten years off his age as he shuffled back into his trousers. 'With bloody bells on!' He started the engine and reversed out of the snicket, still grinning.

Minutes later, driving into their quiet street, Jane leaned forward in her seat laughing. Their house stood like a beacon at the bottom of the cul-de-sac with every light on. 'Simon has either forgotten to turn every electrical item off at night *or* he's decided to illuminate the entire neighbourhood, so we don't get lost.'

James pulled into their drive, yanked the handbrake on and grimaced. 'Bloody boy! Bet the only thing he managed to switch off over the entire weekend was the fridge freezer. I warned you that this long weekend away wasn't a good idea. He may be sixteen, however, he's got all the maturity of a coked-up chicken.'

Jane punched him on the arm. 'What do *you* know about the maturity of chickens, coked-up or not? We've had a glorious weekend.'

He leaned over to kiss her. 'Yeah, we had a wonderful time and an extra few quid on the old electricity bill is a small price to pay for your undivided attention for four days.'

Grinning, Jane straightened her skirt. Her time away with James had been fantastic. Just enough to re-charge their batteries before autumn set in. They'd been so busy over the past few months and this time away had allowed them to reconnect as a couple rather than as business partners or parents. Thoughts of long walks along cold beaches faded as she opened the car door and she hoped her tone didn't betray her reluctance to get back to reality. 'Come on then, grab a bag and let's survey the damage.'

Overnight bag in hand, she paused to savour the view of Heaton Woods lit by the rest of the city. Lister Mills towered behind; a tall tribute to Bradford's textile history. Straight ahead was Saltaire village, rows of sandstone terraced houses, each one cleaned to within an inch of its life, were testament to Sir Titus Salt's benevolence in the area. To the left was Cottingley, with Bingley further afield. It was this panoramic view that had compelled them to buy this house when Simon arrived. A home on a hill for their new family in a quiet cul-de-sac. James came over to her and swung his arm round her shoulder. They stood together: two tall silhouettes against Bradford's backdrop.

She shivered and James pulled her tightly to him, whispering, 'That's what comes of leaving your knickers off.'

She punched him on the arm, 'Couldn't find them, could I? God knows where you threw them.' Linking arms, they walked towards the front door.

James blew out a puff of air that steamed in front of his face, 'Look at that, it's going to be a frosty night. Hope he's had the heating on.'

Jane tried to turn her key in the lock. 'Silly bugger hasn't even locked the door. Hmph, you can't trust him with—'

As she spoke, James pushed the door open. Her final words drifted away and her heart thudded in her chest. She struggled to make sense of the scene before her.

James brushed past, his breath a series of grating gasps. 'What the bloody hell has gone on here?'

Eyes wide and uncomprehending, Jane shook her head, speechless for a second, then, 'I'll bloody kill him!' Chest tight, she stepped into the hallway and yelled, 'Simon, get down here right now!' When there was no reply, she turned in a circle surveying the damage.

The small table at the bottom of the stairs where they all had, at one time or another, sat for lengthy phone conversations, lay smashed to bits, the phone lying broken amidst its ruins. The wallpaper was spattered with a brown sticky substance. Flung carelessly on the floor was the framed photo of the three of them at Harry Potter World. She lifted it up and turned it over only to find the glass was broken and the photo inside damaged. Stifling a sob, her eyes moved along the hallway. The kitchen door hung off its hinge and the glass panes were smashed. Beyond the door, broken crockery and furniture were scattered. God only knew the state her living room was in. She gagged as the acrid stench of vomit assaulted her nostrils. Vomit, stale booze and sweat. She retched again and a rush of foul liquid sprung into her mouth. She was going to be sick. Closing her eyes, she swallowed it down and breathed in through her mouth.

Her lips tightened and a tingle spread from the top of her nose back to her eyes. Blinking away the tears, she turned to James and as their eyes met, the tension she'd left behind on holiday surged into her shoulders. James moved to her side and took her hand, his grip strong and reassuring. Simon had promised no parties and, like fools, they'd believed him. He'd been so damn convincing. He hadn't even had the courtesy to clean up after himself. That's what really pissed her off. This was *his* mess and like the irresponsible teenager he was, he was either hiding at Matty or Jake's, hoping it would all blow over, or he was upstairs, sleeping it off. Oh, she could murder him!

'Simon!' Her voice reverberated round the hallway. there was only silence.

Jane took a step forward and gripped the bannister. 'Bet he's up there, drunk as a skunk.'

Placing a hand on her shoulder, James halted her. 'Maybe I should go, love. I think it'd be better for me to deal with this.'

Exhaling a long breath, she gave a curt nod. James was right. She'd lose it big-time and that would just set Simon off on one of his moods. It was so frustrating. They'd been through so much and things were looking rosy for them… now this. James was the calm one. The pragmatist. It was best if he made first contact with their son. 'Okay, you go. Just don't be soft on him. He'll be cleaning this mess up *and* paying for the damage.'

'Hell, yeah. This is his mess. He'll damn well fix it… when he's sober, okay?' James' smile was cheerless, 'Remember that party you had at your folks' house when you were seventeen? The whole neighbourhood could hear it and yet your parents never said a word.'

Her shoulders relaxed and her lips tugged up in a reluctant grin. James always knew exactly how to make her put things into perspective, 'Okay, okay, I get what you're saying. There wasn't this mess at my party, was there? Bloody teenagers, huh?'

'Wait here, I'll check upstairs.'

Swallowing hard, she agreed with him. One last tight hand squeeze and he was off up the stairs yelling, 'Simon', in the voice he reserved for mega misdemeanours.

Regardless of the sticky surface, Jane, legs like jelly, lowered herself onto the stairs. James banged through the upstairs rooms, yelling for Simon as he went. Spent, she rested her head in her hands and sobbed. By the sounds of it Simon wasn't upstairs which meant he was cowering away at his mates' houses. Not a smart move. He'd be better to 'fess up' and deal with the backlash now than allow her temper to fester.

Hearing James behind her on the stairs, she looked up. The brief moment of hope that flared in her eyes disappeared when she saw his face. His skin looked grey and in the last few minutes he had aged. She jumped to her feet, arms outstretched, 'What is it? What's wrong? Is Simon hurt?'

Shaking his head, he barged past her, hand over his mouth. He pushed open the front door, jumped the steps and fell to his knees on the crazy paving. Before she could reach him, he'd leaned over and puked into the flower beds.

'Christ, James! You're scaring me! What's wrong?'

He pulled out a Kleenex from his pocket, and wiped his mouth, pulled out his phone and dialled.

'Who are you calling? Are you phoning Simon?' Jane grabbed his arm and shook it hard.

James sighed. 'No, not Simon… the police.'

Before Jane could ask more, Simon turned and, his voice hoarse, spoke into his phone, 'I need to report a murder…'

Chapter 5

22:15 Cottingley Ridge

Getting out of his car, Gus took a brief moment to admire the sprinkle of lights that spread out like an ocean before him. It reminded him of the view he and Mo had shared at Robin Hood's Bay a few days ago. He and Gabriella used to spend time in his car, just watching the lights, chatting and snogging before they were married. Things had been simple then. Now he was visiting a crime scene not a stone's throw from here.

This little pocket of 'poshness' on a hill just outside Cottingley was in sharp contrast to many of the places he visited in Bradford. On the outskirts of the inner city, Cottingley Ridge was an anomaly of wealth against a backdrop of poverty and food banks. It was one of Bradford's more affluent areas and was the size of a postage stamp compared to some of the rougher estates that seemed to stretch for miles. As he entered the cul-de-sac, it was clear which of the eight detached houses was his crime scene. The area was alive with police, crime scene investigators and all the other houses had groups of observers hanging about in their drives, despite the chill nip in the air. The houses were well spaced out, each with a sizeable lawn to the front. The entrance to the street was almost hidden from the main road by a line of trees. They'd be in the highest council tax bracket. The houses were newish and had none of Bradford's characteristic yellow sandstone. According to his Google search, each house had four double bedrooms, all with ensuites, and two rooms as well as a kitchen downstairs.

Alice waved and Gus walked over to join her. 'What's the story so far?'

With her hands thrust into the pockets of a black full-length coat that seemed to weigh down her petite shoulders, Alice looked almost too fragile to be a police officer. However, her dark brown eyes, darkened by a thick kohl outline and heavy mascara, glinted with resolve. Pausing, she kicked at a loose stone. 'Looks to me like a house party gone tragically wrong. No sign of the sixteen-year-old son, Simon Proctor, who was left in charge for the weekend. First impressions show that the house is pretty much trashed; lots of empty alcohol bottles and cans, stinks like a mixture of a working men's pub prior to the smoking ban and a dopehead's bedroom on a bad day.'

She paused and stared straight at Gus. 'Then, of course there's the body. Young white girl, maybe sixteen years old or so. No ID yet. Upstairs front bedroom. The parents' room. Crime scene techs are in there now and we're waiting for the pathologist.' She took her hands from her pockets long enough to rub her cold nose. 'Uniforms started door-to-doors, cordon's established and I'd like to extend it to the entrance and the property boundary at the back.'

'Get that sorted and find out what the uniforms have got so far.'

A young PC he'd seen in passing at The Fort, walked over and stood beside him as he glanced around. With a grim smile, he noticed that the neighbours were being cooperative. Despite the lateness of the hour, they were distributing mugs of hot drinks and welcoming the interviewing officers into their homes.

'The middle class are being *awfully* British tonight, don't you think?'

Gus glanced at the officer, surprised by the bitterness in her tone. 'You don't think it's genuine?'

She shrugged. 'I wonder why none of them saw the need to contact us on Saturday. House parties, especially those that get out of hand, are usually loud.'

As she spoke, Gus studied her. She had her hair pulled back into a severe pony tail and looked to be in her early twenties. Her lips were tight and a frown pulled her sculpted brows together. He wondered at her attitude. 'Were you the first responder?'

'Yes sir, PC Iqrah Ali. I set up the initial cordon.'

'I see what you mean about the neighbours. In my experience, folk keep to themselves until their involvement's necessary… then they get out their tea pots and round up the troops. Too little too late, huh?' Gus didn't agree with the sentiment, nonetheless he was interested to hear what the officer had picked up on. Maybe she'd sensed or heard something 'off'. Often the first responders were at an advantage as they got the raw initial reactions, whereas he and his team arrived later when everyone had had a chance to 'adjust'.

'Yeah, pisses me off a bit. Surely they saw or heard something last night.' She rammed her hands into her pockets and shrugged. 'Oh, just ignore me. I'm never happy. If we were on Canterbury Estate, I'd be moaning at the racist abuse I'd be getting. It's just you somehow expect better from the educated middle classes.' She shrugged. 'A cup of tea will be nice, though.'

Alice returned with a mug of coffee for Gus and they watched Iqrah strutting off, her shoulders rigid. 'What's up with her?'

Gus stroked his chin thoughtfully. 'She's a bit pissed off at the tardiness of their middle-class solicitude.'

'What? Oh, I get it. You mean she wonders which hole their heads were buried in on Saturday night when their neighbour's house was being ransacked?'

Gus took a slurp of coffee welcoming it warming his throat on its way down. 'I must admit it'll be interesting to find out. Nice area like this, you'd expect a few calls, wouldn't you?'

'Maybe a case of just keeping themselves to themselves. Happened all the time when I was in London. Nobody was interested in their neighbours. Nobody wanted to get involved.'

Gus started to walk towards the house. 'Maybe she's right, maybe if they'd been a bit more neighbourly, a bit less up their own arses and reported the party, we wouldn't have a dead body and a missing teenager on our hands.'

'Er... well, hate to be the bearer of bad news... it's not *a* dead body. It's *two* dead bodies. They've just found another one in the living room – another girl. They were concentrating on the upstairs and have only just sent a crime scene team downstairs.'

'Fuck's sake, Al. What the hell's going on here, with the Stepford Wives on the one hand and house parties and dead bodies on the other?' He thrust his empty coffee cup at a passing PC and raked his fingers through his dreads. 'Let's see the crime scenes and then I want to see the parents. The dad phoned it in, didn't he?'

'Yes, I got onto family liaison as soon as I'd done a brief initial statement with them. When the FLO arrived, I got her to accompany them to a Mrs Owen's at number twenty-three. It wasn't healthy for them to stay at the scene. He'd already vomited on the azaleas, she'd stomped all over the montbretia. I was concerned about the fate of the dwarf pines and rose bushes if they'd stayed any longer.'

Gus laughed, appreciating her effort to lighten the mood. 'Very green-fingered of you, I'm sure.'

Together, they walked into the canvas porch. With its whiteness accentuated by the harsh spotlights it stood in front of the front door and stretched out to cover most of the front lawn and pathway, hiding some of the comings and goings from nosy onlookers. Gus thanked the officer who handed them crime suits and bootees. With the speed of one experienced in struggling into the cumbersome garments, Gus covered up before entering the tent with Alice. 'You did good work securing the scene, Al. Now all we need is the bloody pathologist. Where the hell is he and please tell me it's not–'

Before he'd finished his sentence, a huge hand with stubby fat fingers gripped the loose canvas doorway, pulling it to the side to admit a large turnip head adorned with a veritable brush of eyebrows above gregarious eyes and a bulbous nose.

'Yoohoo, all! I'm here.' Doctor McGuire tilted his head towards his son. 'Hope that wisnae you taking mah name in vain again, Angus?'

Gus closed his eyes and turned away from his father silently mouthing, 'Fuck!'

'I dinnae see why you're moaning, I've been interrupted from mah dance class, yet again.'

Gus groaned. *Oh, no, please say we're not getting a repeat performance of the damn kilt scenario.* Gus was still being ribbed about that even now and that incident had been nearly a year since.

A foot in a shiny patent shoe poked through the tent opening and Gus was relieved to see that the leg that accompanied the shoe was clothed. Tutting, he moved towards the door, ignoring Alice's, 'Aw, no kilt tonight, Doc?'

'Hmph, no, Alice, mah dear. Some mardy-bum takes objection to traditional dress. Sure, I could have him done for that.'

Chapter 6

22:30 Heaton

Matty couldn't settle. Every time his phone vibrated he jumped. This was crap. He'd had enough, so he grabbed his phone and dialled. 'Jake, that you? What the fuck's going on, bro? Simon's mum's been phoning me. What are we gonna do?'

'Fuck's sake, Matty, stop whimpering. She's been phoning me, too. Did you answer?'

'Nah, course I bloody didn't.'

'Good, good, neither did I. She left a message on the answer phone to call them. I deleted it.'

'Aw fuck, Jake, where *is* he?'

'Fucked if I know, but we better prepare for the police coming to see us.'

'Aw shit! My dad'll have a heart attack.'

'Yeah well, I'm more worried about Simon's state of health than your old man's. Just keep me informed; and Matty…'

'Yeah?'

'We can't tell them the truth. This is some really serious shit and we're in the middle, so we can't come clean in case we get blamed for that girl.'

'Aw fuck, we won't, will we?' Matty rubbed the length of his sleeve across his face.

'Not if we keep quiet.'

Chapter 7

22:30 Manningham

Shamila's phone vibrated by her leg as she lay flat on her tummy on her bed, arms bent and hands propping up her face. She tried to concentrate on her homework. She'd been glad to let her hair down after having it up all day and with the beginnings of a headache building, she'd thrown her scarf on the end of her bed.

'Shamila, it's me. I've seen Tayyub's stuff. He's done a really good job.'

Shamila, with a quick glance towards her closed bedroom door, sat up and dropped the physics text book. She swung her legs round and sat cross-legged, pushing her long black hair back from her face as she moved the phone to her other ear. Her heart beat fast, yet she kept her voice low. Her mum didn't like her speaking to boys at the best of times, although she had it in for Tariq in particular. Who knew why? 'Oh, wow! That's brill, Tariq, have you told the others?'

'Just about to. Can you meet at the mosque tomorrow night? The meeting room's free at six.'

'Yeah sure, can't wait. This is The Young Jihadists best plan yet.'

When she hung up, Shamila wrapped her arms round herself and rocked for a minute, her brain buzzing as she started to prepare in her mind what she would say to the committee the next evening.

Chapter 8

22:40 Cottingley Ridge

Gus and Alice entered the hallway, which was a hive of worker bees in crime scene suits, busy photographing, gathering and sifting through evidence, whilst sharing a raw humour that would seem out of place, perhaps even insulting, to the lay person.

Gus stood by the door, gloved hands clasped behind his back, taking in his surroundings. 'Fuck's sake! How many teenagers does it take to make a shithole like this?'

Alice glanced at him. 'Is that a joke, Gus?'

'Eh?'

'You know, along the lines of "How many detectives does it take to change a lightbulb?"'

'You're bloody warped, Al, mentally deranged.' And he stepped inside, Alice tagging behind. Surveying the scene, his covered foot nudged a broken picture frame and flipped it over. Family photo? 'By the way, how many elephants *do* fit in a Mini?'

'Duh? How am I supposed to know, *I'm* mentally deranged after all!'

Gus grinned at her. 'Ha, bloody, ha!' Then, feeling the stickiness of spilled beer on the carpet under his feet, he grimaced. 'Glad I've not got kids, if this is the shit they get up to.'

An androgynous figure in white approached, sounding like a blocked Jacuzzi behind the mask. 'Hi, Gus, Alice. Glad it's you two I'm dealing with and not your effing boss.

Last time *she* took off her damn mask to sneeze, took her hood down to scratch her head and forgot to wear gloves. Stupid cow, contaminated the entire effing crime scene.'

Gus was all too aware of his boss, DCI Nancy Chalmers' propensity to cock up a crime scene. That was why, on the rare occasions she expressed a desire to accompany them, Gus tended to divert her elsewhere. He raised his hand in acknowledgement. 'Hi Suse, got a cold again? We're too bloody scared of you to mess up a crime scene. Anything for me yet?'

'Two bodies not enough for you, Gus? Greedy bastard.'

Gus grinned behind his mask. Suse was Hissing Sid's sidekick and Gus liked her down-to-earth manner. 'Well, it was more clues than bodies I was after.'

Suse snorted. 'Humph! You'll be lucky to get any before the end of next century. The place is a cesspit of DNA. God knows what's relevant. Just sent your dad upstairs with Hissing Sid and body number one. Number two's in there, behind the couch.' Sniffing, she inclined her head towards the living room. 'Why don't you see what your dad's got first and then come back down to this one after we've had a chance to lift what we need... before the troops parade through like a bunch of majorettes in their size nines *and*...' She paused and winked at Gus. 'If I'm correctly informed, a pair of shiny dance shoes.' She poked Gus none too gently in the arm, flung her head back and let loose a guffaw that rattled the windows.

Gus shook his head. 'Ha, bloody, ha!' He pointed at the living room. 'What can you tell me about that body?'

'This one's another girl. Looks like the missing son might be your number one suspect.'

With Alice following, Gus walked back towards the stairs. 'Could be, Suse, or maybe victim number three. Best not jump to conclusions just yet, hmm?'

Suse snorted. 'I hope he's alive. We're backed up to the hilt as it is. Any more bodies and I'm going to have to ask Tesco if we can borrow their storage facilities! You know it doesn't go down well with the shoppers when they find Carte de Morgue next to their Ben and Jerry's cookie dough.' With a giggle and a wave, she was off.

Alice snorted. 'Bloody idiot!'

Reaching the top landing, Gus once more looked around. The smell of stale booze was fainter up here. Nevertheless, the paintings were askew on the wall and the pristine white carpet was speckled with stains. Cans were tossed across the landing, some with trails of beer staining the area around them. The bedroom doors were ajar, revealing similar scenes of destruction. 'Well, looks like the little bastards had a good time, doesn't it?'

'And, if my nose is correct – and it doesn't often let me down – I'd have to surmise that an overindulgence in a variety of guilty pleasures, some illegal, no doubt, has resulted in a veritable volcano of vomit. Or, in other words, they've been shagging, smoking dope and drinking themselves silly.'

'Such a way with words, Al. As if the stench wasn't bad enough on its own, you feel the need to embellish it.'

Alice leered and added with relish, 'Ah, but the other little titbit of info my nasal passages sense is…'

Gus turned and waited as she raised her nose in the air and sniffed, 'Alright, go on then, what else?'

'Blood!'

'Shit,' Gus tutted and began to breathe slowly through his mouth. Now she'd mentioned it, he could smell it too. His own blood drained from his face leaving him light-headed. He swallowed, concentrating on his breathing. *Should have brought my damn Vicks!* Why couldn't he have inherited his dad's constitution? No matter how often he came across blood in his line of work it was still a major trauma for him. Mind you, not as much of a trauma for him as for the dead girl behind the door. As he approached it, he tried to ignore the butterfly wings in his chest. If he just breathed through his mouth, he could get through this. He always had before.

Alice held out her hand, which was cupped round something. 'Go on. You might as well take it. Better than you puking all over the crime scene. Wouldn't want Suse on your back, now, would we?'

When he held out his hand, she dropped a small Vicks vial onto his palm. Gus slathered some onto his hankie and handed the bottle back to her. Straightening his shoulders, he ignored Alice's smirk. It was okay for her, taunting him. She didn't have to concentrate whilst trying to hold her stomach contents down with sheer force of will. 'Right, Sherlock, we already knew the body was in the main bedroom and, well,' he hooked his thumb towards the door, 'that *is* the main bedroom.'

He steeled himself, reached for the handle and opened the door. 'You get the low-down from the CSIs and get them to walk through the rest of the upstairs with them. I'll focus on the victim. Let's hope they've got something to give us.'

As he entered, Dr McGuire moved away from the double bed. Gus' eyes were immediately drawn, not to the bed, but to the wall behind it which had been defaced with large, red, block capital letters:

REDEEMED

He hadn't expected that. The word printed so boldly on the wall smacked of glee. It was a taunt, no doubt about it.

Whoever had done this was perverted. It made his skin crawl. When they'd got the call, he'd expected a tragic accident at a kid's party gone wrong. This flagrant taunt above one of the victims lifted a senseless tragedy into the realms of malicious intent. This was sinister and he doubted this case would be an easy one to solve. The stakes had increased and Gus was determined to catch this fucker. It was just a damn shame that Sebastian Carlton had shot over to liaise with the FBI in Quantico. He had a feeling that he may need some insight into the mind of this killer before too long. Engrossed in his own thoughts, Gus studied the word. Was this a religious connotation? A moral judgement?

The sound of someone clearing their throat distracted him. Followed by the word 'Lipstick' being uttered, his attention was diverted to the edge of the bed, where Sid was kneeling.

'Lipstick?' It took Gus a moment to realise that Sid referred to the word on the wall. *Not blood, lipstick.* That was a little better – not *quite* as much of a sadist as he'd first thought. He grimaced, as if he was talking in term of degrees of sadism.

Hissing Sid stood up. 'Yeah, whoever wrote it climbed onto the bed after she was dead. Look, you can see where they've stood in the pooled blood.' He pointed to a stain, dull against the cream carpet. 'Mind you, most of it's soaked in now.'

This was true, the carpet's thick pile made the blood appear gritty and there was only a thin patina where it had landed in denser puddles. Gus tried to pretend it didn't look like shreds of flesh, yet the image of offal was persistent. He held the hankie to his nose again and ignored Sid's knowing smirk as he continued to explain what had happened.

'The killer then stepped up onto the pillow and then here, look, back down to the carpet.'

Eager to divert his mind to less gory thoughts, Gus knelt down and studied the print on the floor. 'Got pictures, measurements, etc?'

'Yeah, we'll get them on the database as soon as we can.'

Gus stood up and approaching the bed, looked down at the girl for the first time. All the time he'd been talking to Sid, he'd been conscious of her presence. He'd wanted to wait till Sid has explained about the writing on the wall before looking at her, though. She deserved his full attention and that's what he would give her now.

Her arms and legs, like skinny pipe cleaners, flung out from her naked body, made a star shape half on, half off the bed. The blood on her chest and abdomen almost concealed her teenage breasts and made it difficult to identify her wounds. Blood had coagulated in her hair making it appear dark and matted in places, though, judging by her pubic hair she was a natural blonde. The girl was barely older than Mo's eldest girl, Zarqa. Gus quelled the comparison as soon as it had arisen. He had to retain objectivity if he was going to get the justice this girl deserved. Comparing this poor girl to his 'niece' would only make it harder. Christ, it was hard enough as it was! Aware that his dad was waiting next to him, giving him the time to process the scene, Gus continued his appraisal, then turned to Sid, 'Any thoughts on the attack, Sid... Doc?'

Sid scrunched up his face, 'When the doc examined her, there was blood underneath her. I reckon she was either moved after she died or she put up a struggle.'

'Hmm.' Doc McGuire shook his head. 'There's nae defence marks and the way her hands are flung wide isn't a natural position if ye've been stabbed. Yer instincts would be to curl up and cover yer head and chest, not offer a wider target.'

'So, you think it's been staged?'

Sid pointed. 'From the blood splatter, it looks like the girl was on her side when the first blow struck.'

Dr McGuire gestured to a barely visible stab wound just under her left breast, 'This was the first. You can see the spatter up the wall from when the killer pulled oot the knife from this first wound and retracted his hand ready tae deliver the rest. She rolled onto her back. That would have been instinct.' He pursed his lips together, 'Maybe he got in another stab before the wee soul went into self-protection mode. Probably this wound'. He pointed to an area between her breasts at the top of her abdomen. 'What do you think, Sid?'

'Yeah, doubt he'd have managed two, then again, he didn't need to, did he?'

'Hmph, no you're right. He didnae need to. This was probably the wound that killed the wee lassie. It would have been mere seconds. Yet, we have multiple stab wounds to the abdomen and chest. Possible serrated edge. The post-mortem will give us a better idea. I'd say they look quite deep and forcefully driven. Most will have been delivered post mortem, I suspect. We'll ken mair later.'

Sid pointed to a drag stain on the duvet. 'He's pulled her round and to the left so her legs dangled off the bed. He's pulled them apart, just like he did with her arms.'

For a second there was silence as the three men looked at the girl. The positioning of the body indicated that the killer had tried to have sex with her, either as she was dying, or after she was dead. This took things to a whole new level of depravity. Either way the killer would have been soaked in this girl's blood.

Gus wanted to back out of the room and down the stairs and away from this fucked-up crime scene. Their very presence there, looking at this anonymous girl at her most vulnerable, made Gus want to rage at the world. It was as if she was being violated in death as much as she had in life and she was only a child with her entire life snuffed out by some pervert.

Gus heard his dad swallow as if trying to dislodge something from his throat. The sound was deep and resonant and Gus was all too familiar with it; it was one of his old man's 'tells'. A murder so soon on the back of Gus' mum's ordeal was bound to have a profound effect on his old man. This sort of case wasn't easy for any of the people involved in investigating it. The fact was, when it became routine for any of them then it was time for them to retire. It was their humanity, their empathy with the victim that distanced themselves from the monsters they encountered and made them good at their jobs.

Dr McGuire rolled first one shoulder and then the other before speaking. 'There are signs of recent sexual activity. Lubricant, no semen.'

Gus' scowl deepened. He could feel the tension across his forehead and shoulders. He mimicked his dad's earlier movements. *The kid looks like she should be eating ice cream and watching* Frozen, *not bloody shagging in a friend's parents' bedroom.*

'Yeah, I get that, consensual or forced?'

Dr McGuire's shrug was non-committal. 'Hard to tell. The PM will tell us.' Gus lifted his gloved fingers to run them through his hair, and tutted when they encountered the hood of his bunny suit. 'He used a condom, so no DNA?'

'Not so far, but we'll comb the body and sheets. We may get lucky.'

Sid waved a baggie in front of Gus' face. '*Or…* we may *already* be lucky.'

Whilst Gus and his dad had been chatting, Sid had moved away to collect trace evidence from around the bed area. Gus looked at the clear evidence bag that Sid was dangling. If the CSI was bringing it to his attention with his eyes sparkling like that, then it must be good.

'Found it jammed down the back of the bed between the pillow and the headboard. It's a tissue covered in…'

In a move that made Gus' stomach roil, he pushed his nose towards the open bag and sniffed, '…semen by the smell of it. Maybe our boy took off his condom, wiped his dick with the tissue and pushed it down the back of the bed. Mucky bugger! I'll try and get the sample expedited – fingers crossed.'

Gus slapped him on the back. 'Good find, Sid. Did you find her clothes? Any ID or anything there?'

Sid shook his head, 'Yes, to the first, no to the second.' He pointed to a pile of brown paper bags that were used for dry clothes, 'I'm assuming these were hers. They were bundled up on that chair; black suede ankle boots à la Primark, size five, skinny jeans (red), size ten, tight T-shirt and a baggy overshirt again, size ten, black thong, no bra, however she didn't really need one, did she? I went through the pockets and we've looked on the floor, alas, no bag or ID. Nothing, so far.'

'Phone?'

'Nah, just her clothes.'

Where was her phone? Had her killer taken it with him? Maybe they'd come across it later. He hoped so. He wanted this girl identified as soon as possible. Surely someone had noticed her disappearance by now? As Alice walked back into the room, he turned to her. 'No young girls reported missing since yesterday?'

'No, I've put an alert out, so if any are reported, we'll be notified.'

Gus looked at his dad. 'Anything else?'

'Not a lot. Very young. I'd say between twelve and fifteen at most. I'll get her processed. I've been told I've got another visit to make before I'm done. This job just keeps on damn well giving!' Give me twenty minutes and then I'll let you know what number two has revealed.'

Now that his dad was gone, Gus took the time to look round the Proctors' bedroom. Despite the disarray, it was clear the family was well off. However, everything that had been matching and tasteful was now tainted by the presence of the dead girl. He doubted they'd ever live here again. Most victims of violent crime in the home moved within twelve months and it was hardly surprising. Who'd want to live with the constant reminder of the most traumatic time in your life? Like the other rooms, it had been trashed. Ornaments and make-up scattered the floor. The wardrobes were open and clothes had been dragged from hangers and tossed around the room. Mr Proctor's suits and shirts soaked up beer in one pile, whilst Mrs Proctor's dresses and underwear dotted the floor and bedside tables. Who knew whether this was the result of a drunken rampage by teenage kids or something far worse. Had the killer done this? Or had it been done earlier? Whichever it was, he was going to get to the bottom of it.

He looked at the girl for a last time before leaving the room. Someone somewhere was missing a daughter and they didn't even know it yet. Did they even care? Well, even if *they* didn't, *he* did.

Chapter 9

22:40 Heaton/Cottingley

Matty: *You hear the sirens?*
Jake: *Yeah, might be nowt.*
Matty: *It's gotta be that, Jake.*
Jake: *Calm down. We done nowt wrong. Stop being a wuss.*
Matty: *Where the hell is Si?*
Jake: *Go to fucking bed, Matty*

Chapter 10

23:10 Cottingley Ridge

By the time he came back downstairs, Gus was sticky, hot and bad tempered. His nostrils were clogged with the stench of alcohol, vomit and weed. He was sure the latter was having a mild effect on him as his head was full of sludge. Maybe he needed a caffeine hit. When they'd exchanged their bunny suits for fresh ones to avoid cross contamination between the two scenes, Gus glanced at Alice. 'Ready?'

She shrugged. 'As I'll ever be.'

Pushing open the door, Gus poked his head through. 'Hi Suse, you ready for us, now?'

Suse broke off her conversation with Gus' dad and beckoned them in. 'Yeah, stick to the blocks and make your way over.'

In single file, Gus and Alice made their way towards the massive leather couch, where Suse and the Doc stood. Before speaking to them, Gus looked round the room. It was open plan with an archway leading into the dining room which, in turn, had double doors going into the kitchen. The room was bigger than Gus' kitchen and living room put together. Apart from the oversize couch, two matching chairs and a coffee table, the only other item that stood intact in the room was a wall-mounted, widescreen TV. The carpet was covered with up-ended plant pots, broken photo frames and shattered ornaments. It was hard to get a feel for the room; nevertheless, the magnolia and white colour scheme had Gus veering towards a minimalist look.

In here, despite having become accustomed to the mixed smells throughout the rest of the house, Gus became aware of a heightened awareness of acrid filth and before speaking, he swallowed hard and took several slow shallow breaths.

'Fuck! The stink's worse in here.'

Suse looked at him with a puzzled frown. 'Is it?'

Alice snorted, 'Just a bit, Suse, just a bit.'

'Oh, okay, if you say so.' Suse gestured for them to follow her. 'She's here if you want to see her *in situ*, Gus.'

Gus walked round to the front of the settee. The girl lay with her head wedged into the corner of the couch. Her feet were sprawled at an angle as if she'd slouched down to rest her head, barely skimming the floor. She looked like a ragdoll in a giant's castle. Her short hair was dyed black and her T-shirt, jeans and knee-length boots were also black. Each finger and both thumbs were adorned with heavy silver-coloured rings. Her wrist was circled by a single, wide bangle which only partly concealed the serpentine tattoo which snaked from beneath the bracelet around her arm and undulated upwards till it disappeared beneath her jacket sleeve.

Gus bent down to see the girl's face. Her eyes stared at him, making him recoil. He steadied himself before looking back. Slathered over her chin and down the front of her T-shirt was a stream of alcohol-tinged vomit that had pooled in her lap, making Gus glad he still had his Vicks hankie at the ready. Underneath her intricate black liner and eye shadow, the whites of her eyes, red with petechiae, looked demonic. Her lips were blue-tinged except where her piercings glinted like snake fangs from her mouth.

Gus, his limbs leaden, stood up and sighed. *Another fucking waste. Two dead girls in the confines of one family home. Did they know each other?* Judging by their dress sense the two girls belonged to different 'clubs'. Maybe they went to school together, though. He turned to Dr McGuire, who looked more stooped than he had an hour earlier. *This must be getting to the old man, too.* The sparkle in his eyes had faded and they looked dull and determined. 'Asphyxiation?'

'Yes, that's right. Did you spot the petechiae?'

Gus gave an abrupt nod. Hell, even his dad's voice was flat. 'Suffocated on her own vomit, did she?'

'Hmm,' Doc McGuire lifted the girl's head. 'That's what I'm not so sure about. See those few faint marks on her neck? They *could* indicate a third party. She certainly wasn't here on her own. Suse and I found traces of what could be semen, here... and here.' He pointed to her trousers and the couch between her legs. 'And also, at the other end of the couch. Suse is on the case with that.'

'Any ID on this one, Suse?'

'Yeah, school bus pass.' She held out a clear cellophane bag containing a bus pass with a photo of an innocent-looking girl. 'It's her alright – prior to piercing, haircut and death. Jade Simmonds, no address. Metro will be able to supply that.'

Crouching before the girl, Alice tutted. 'What the fuck went on here last night?'

Fergus McGuire patted Alice gently on the shoulder. 'Ye'll get there in the end, Alice, hen. You always do. Noo, I'm done here, so I'll away off noo.' He straightened his huge lumbering frame, clicking his shoulder joints as he moved and turned to Gus. 'See ye the morra at the post-mortems?'

Gus gave an abrupt nod. Not that he was looking forward to it. The very thought of seeing these two young girls subjected to further indignities turned his stomach.

Packing his accoutrements into his bag, Dr McGuire continued, 'I'll start early, since we've two tae get tae grips wi'. Seven-thirty suit you?'

'Yeah, thanks, appreciate it.'

Robin Hood's Bay seemed a lifetime away. He sighed. At least the break appeared to have done his dad good. Despite the circumstances that had brought him down in February, over all, he was a little more like his usual jaunty self again.

Doc McGuire raised his hand in salute to the CSIs who still worked around the room and headed for the door. 'I'll see ye then, Angus. Must get off; lots tae do and I fancy a wee dram afore I retire for the night.'

Gus, relieved to see his dad finally departing, turned as Suse approached.

'Thought you'd want to see this. Loads of them were strewn around in the kitchen, hallway and living room.'

Gus reached out and took a rectangular business card from her. On one side there was a psychedelic image of a long lens camera and on the other the photographer's details:

Tayyub Images
Personalised photography for any occasion
Video Imaging
Personalised stationery.

Accompanied by contact details including home address, mobile and home phone numbers and email.

'Interesting. Wonder if he was at the party and decided to do a bit of self-promotion while he was here.'

Alice read the card. 'Looks like it, we'll follow up on that tomorrow.'

A CSI approached carrying a clear evidence bag with a phone inside. 'Found this in the shed, behind an old deck chair. Battery's dead. It fits the description of Simon Proctor's phone, given by his parents.' They began to move towards the kitchen until, hearing his name called, Gus stopped and turned impatiently to find his dad's head poking round the living room door like a floating pumpkin.

'Oh, one mair thing, Angus, I nearly forgot.'

Gus tapped his foot on the floor and sighed. 'Yes, what is it, Dad?'

'Your mother says you've to come for Sunday lunch. She's got a surprise for you.'

Gus' heart sank. He was all too familiar with the sort of surprises his mum produced. Ignoring Alice's chuckle, Gus glowered. '*Dad!* I'm working. How many times do I have to tell you, I don't mix work and family?' And trying to ignore the sniggers from the others, he turned on his heel and moved into the kitchen. Why the hell did his dad always have to make him the laughing stock? It was getting beyond a damn joke. At least he'd had the sense to change *out* of his kilt this time. Gus' mouth quirked. *Bloody 'dancing shoes' indeed. Who the hell does he think he is? Bloody Cinderella?*

Chapter 11

23:45 Cottingley Ridge

As they approached the neighbours' house, the door opened and Mrs Owen, a flamboyant woman in a scarlet kimono, gestured them through to the dimly-lit living room. Jane and James Proctor sat together on a red leather settee, faces pale and hands tightly clenched in their laps. The contrast between this home and the one they'd just left hit Gus in the gut. It wasn't just the calmness after the activity in the Proctors'. It was something deeper than that, something clean and pure... Innocence? Whatever it was, Gus breathed it in, savouring the cleanliness, whilst conscious that his clothes still carried the noxious odours from the Proctors' home. The family liaison officer sat opposite the worried couple on a matching chair.

When he saw which liaison officer had been assigned to Simon's parents, Gus' heart sank. If *he* found her irritating, he hated to think how the Proctors would react. He wished they'd sent Janine Roberts. She was unflappable and allowed the family space to breathe. This one, whose name he could never remember, was downright irritating. In-your-face the entire time; sugary sweet and overly solicitous. He could only hope that the Proctors wouldn't find her so. She jumped to her feet immediately and made the introductions. Gus managed a smile and then asked her to take Mrs Owen into the kitchen so they could have privacy.

Gus and Alice had just loosened their coats and sat down on the two chairs opposite the Proctors, when the door opened and kimono woman popped her head through. 'Cup of tea?'

Gus groaned. *Couldn't the damn FLO keep her away for two bloody seconds?* Hoping his grin was friendlier than it felt, Gus declined, ignoring the smirk on Alice's face that told him she'd seen his eye roll.

'Coffee…? No. Okay I'll let you get on with it. I'm just in the kitchen if you need anything.'

As the door shut, Gus turned to the Proctors, leaning forward, elbows on knees. 'I know this must be really hard for you, but we just need some information, then we'll get you settled into a hotel for the night. We'll take a proper statement tomorrow, okay?'

Mr Proctor's shoulders slumped and his wife looked in front of her, her mouth slack and her eyes vacant.

Gus turned to Alice. 'Al, book a double with breakfast at The Mansions, please.'

Mr Proctor ran his fingers through his hair and put his other arm round his wife's shoulders. 'Gemma offered to put us up here. To be honest, I don't think we'll sleep tonight although we could do with some privacy.' He glanced at his wife. 'Couldn't we, Jane?'

She started and looked up at him, her eyes glazed. 'What?'

He squeezed her shoulders tighter, his knuckles whitening with the pressure. 'Privacy. I'm just telling the detective inspector that we could do with some privacy.'

Jane glanced at Gus as if she'd only just noticed his presence. 'Have you found him yet? Simon? Have you found him?'

Gus gave his best comforting smile. He was sure it made him look manic, deranged. Unlike Alice, he'd never quite mastered the art of offering platitudes. It was too much like lying or offering false hope to people who'd grip onto any lifeline offered to them, even if it would ultimately sink them. Extracting information from parents like the Proctors entailed a fine balancing act. On the one hand, he was sympathetic to the fact that they had just suffered a great shock and were now fearing for their son Simon – who, he'd been told, was their only child. On the other, though, the case was time-sensitive and he needed to extract as much information as possible from the couple right now. He couldn't afford to give them the luxury of a night's rest and time to come to terms with the situation. He had to strike now.

A quick assessment of the two told him that whilst James Proctor gave an outward appearance of holding things together, he, too, was near breaking point. His face was grey and drawn and he kept clenching and unclenching his fists. Mrs Proctor, by contrast, looked like a zombie. An air of inertia hung over her. Even a simple hand movement seemed to drain her of what little reserves of energy she had.

'No, Mrs Proctor, not yet. We're doing our very best.'

Her striking blue eyes looked directly into Gus' for a second and then she nodded, as if reassured by whatever she saw there. When she spoke, her voice was slurred and slow. Gus knew she hadn't been medicated, so he put her delayed reactions down to shock.

'Call me Jane.' She lifted a hand to Gus and then, as if it was too much effort, she let it drift back down to rest on her thigh. Closing her eyes, she inhaled and drew away from her husband's arms, pulling her shoulders back and exhaling as she did so. Opening her eyes again, she linked the fingers of both hands together in her lap. Her entire body remained still, bar for the thumbs that twiddled circles around one another as she spoke. 'I suppose you've got things to ask, so please go ahead. Before you do, though, I want to make one thing clear, so you don't waste your time going off in the wrong direction.'

Her eyes, more focussed now, met first Gus' then Alice's. 'Simon... did not... touch that... poor girl,... you know?' Each word was punctuated by a pause.

Holding her gaze, Gus said, 'Jane, we're not suggesting he did. However, we *really* need to find him, so we know what went on at this party and to make sure that he's alright. Now, you've tried his phone, but it's switched off, is that right?'

'We've tried repeatedly since we got back. It goes straight to voicemail. Last time we spoke to him was about 8:30 on Saturday night.'

'How did he sound? Was he at home? Could you hear anything else in the background?'

Jane wiped her eyes with a ragged tissue. 'It was a short conversation. Just to touch base, you know? He said he was fine and at home watching telly.' Her twiddling thumbs increased in speed. 'We *trusted* him.'

Reaching over, James placed his hand over Jane's. The bulk of his frame emphasised how fragile his wife looked as he repositioned his arm around her shoulders and pulled her head to rest there, mumbling reassuring words that were inaudible to Gus and Alice.

Averting his eyes, Gus gave them a few seconds before asking, 'What about friends? Have you tried to contact them?'

Lifting her head from her husband's embrace, Jane swallowed hard. 'We've phoned *everyone*. No-one knows where he is. His two best friends are unobtainable and no-one else seems to have been at the party or they're not telling us, anyway.'

'Who are his best friends?'

'Jake Carpenter and Matthew Bates. We've tried their homes, too, and got the answer machine.'

'Give their numbers to DS Cooper and we'll follow it up. Addresses too, if you have them. We're going to have to ask you to write a list of all of Simon's friends.'

At least they'd feel like they were doing something if they did that.

'Did Simon have a girlfriend?'

Both parents shook their heads. Then Jane snorted 'Maybe he did and didn't tell us. You never know with sixteen-year-olds. I mean, he promised not to have a party or anything and look what happened. Who knows what other lies he's told us?' Her eyes filled with tears and she kneaded her knees with trembling hands.

'You're doing really well. Just a couple of other things and then we'll be on our way. Do you know a girl called Jade Simmonds?'

The pair looked at each other and then shook their heads. James swallowed, then in a quiet voice asked, 'Is she the girl in our bedroom?'

Gus shook his head. 'No, we haven't managed to identify her yet and you said you didn't recognise her at all?'

James' face paled and his hand shook as he lifted it to push his hair back from his forehead. 'No, never seen her before in my life.' His voice caught in his throat and he rubbed his arm across his eyes. 'Bloody tragic. Poor girl. How could this have happened? Who would have done something like this?'

'What about Tayyub Hussain? Do you know him?'

Jane's eyes lit up for a moment. 'Oh Tayyub, yes of course we know Tayyub. He's a friend of Si's. Don't know why I didn't think to try him. Simon's probably there.' With a smile, she withdrew her phone from her pocket, but Gus laid his hand on her arm. 'Wait a minute, Jane. Put it on speaker phone. Ask if Simon's there and nothing more. Don't give any details, okay?'

Taking a deep breath, Jane dialled Tayyub's number. The phone rang three times before going to voice mail. With a sigh, she hung up.

James patted her knee. 'He might still be there, Jane. He might.' The last was said as if he was trying to convince himself more than Jane.

'Or he might be lying dead in a damn gully somewhere, James. After everything he's been through too. It's not fair. It's just *not* fair.' Jane lifted her hands to her face, bowed her head and began to cry.

This was horrible. Gus' experience with his mum earlier in the year told him that not knowing was worse than anything. He would have given anything to be able to say, *'There, there, it's okay. Everything's going to be just fine.'* He couldn't, though. He, of all people, knew that life could be shite and that, just when you thought things couldn't get any worse, your life could take a nosedive into a cesspool without breathing apparatus.

He stood up and began to put his coat back on. 'Look, keep trying Tayyub and his other mates. If you get through, just find out if Si is there, or when they last saw him. Don't mention *anything* else and only phone when the family liaison officer is with you, okay?' Not that he held out much hope of her being any bloody use to the Proctors. He must have scowled because Alice nudged him and frowned. Taking the hint, he schooled the furrows in his forehead away and pasted on a smile.

'I think you've given us everything we need for now. I'll get somebody to take you to the hotel. Get that list of all his friends with addresses and contact phone numbers to us. Your family liaison officer here will make sure any information you need to give us gets to us and also that anything *we* find out gets to you. Please don't speak to the press. They're animals and will hound you given the chance. Again, your FLO can get rid of them for you.' Well, he hoped she could anyway.

Gus had turned to leave when Jane Proctor jumped to her feet, grabbing his arm. 'He's not dead, is he? You don't think he's dead?'

Gus patted her arm. 'Mrs Proctor, at this stage we don't know anything. His body wasn't found in the house, so the chances are he just got frightened and ran away.'

He turned to her husband. 'Do you need a doctor to prescribe something to help you sleep? It won't do anyone any good if you're exhausted, will it?'

James shook his head. 'We'll be fine, thanks, won't we, Jane?' And he put both arms round his wife and held her close.

Chapter 12

23:55 Heaton/Cottingley

> **Matty**: *Mrs P still ringing*
> **Jake**: *Me too*
> **Matty**: *What'll we do?*
> **Jake**: *Told you. Keep fuckin' shtum!*
> **Matty**: *They must've found her. Am brickin' it!*
> **Jake**: *Pussy! Fucking man up.*
> **Jake**: *… and go to fucking sleep, Tosser!*
> **Matty**: *You're the Tosser. Shouldn't have listened to you. Should've stayed like I wanted to.*
> **Jake**: *Shut up Matty. We're in this together now. Just keep fucking shtum or Si will kill us. You know what he's like!*
> **Matty**: *Maybe he's dead. Then none of it'll matter.*
> **Jake**: *Grow up… and shut up, ok?*

Monday

Chapter 13

00:30 Cottingley Ridge

When they reached the pavement, Gus breathed in the ice-cold air, pulled a bottle of Irn Bru from his pocket and took a deep slug. 'I hate these sorts of cases. Nowt good's gonna come of all this.'

Glancing over Gus's shoulder, Alice groaned. 'Talking of "nowt good". It looks like it's heading this way as we speak.'

Gus turned round and swore under his breath as a bull of a man strutted towards them, his pugnacious face set in an irritating sneer. This was the last person he wanted to see at his crime scene. The man was objectionable and downright obstructive. He'd tried his best to make Gus' life miserable on The Matchmaker case. 'I thought we'd seen the last of DS Knowles when DCI Hussain went. Thought the pillock had been transferred to Skipton.'

Alice turned her back on Knowles as he approached and muttered 'No such bloody luck by the looks of it.' She grinned. 'He's not a DS anymore, Gus. Got demoted. He's a bog-standard DC now.'

Knowles stopped just a little too close to Gus, invading his personal space. Recognising the tactic, Gus stepped even closer and straightened to full height, towering over the shorter man. 'Well?'

Knowles raised his eyebrows, his mouth curled and his arms held loosely by his sides. Gus recognised it as a fighter's stance and he recalled the other man was an amateur boxer.

When Knowles spoke, his tone was a hair's width away from insolence. 'Well, *what*?' He hesitated as Gus' eyebrows raised before adding, 'Sir.'

Gus glared at him. 'Watch yourself, Knowles. I'm not about to put up with your shit, not even for a short time. Give your report and then you get on back to headquarters. I don't want you anywhere near this enquiry. Understood?'

Knowles lowered his gaze, flicking a glance to his right, his face reddening as he did so. Gus realised then that a small group of officers had gathered within hearing. Seemed that Knowles hadn't made many friends in Bradford. 'Didn't know you were back, Knowles. What did you do to get kicked out of Skipton?'

Knowles' mouth tightened. 'I asked to be transferred back. Wanted to keep an eye on the likes of you.' He took a deep breath and then as DC Talvinder Bhandir approached, he snorted. 'I see you've kept your positive discrimination quota up... *sir*. Despite that Hussain bird dumping you.'

Gus' stomach clenched. Hearing Sadia's name on Knowles' lips had knocked him off kilter for a second. It didn't happen so often now; only when he was caught off guard. However, it wasn't the jibe about Sadia that pissed him off. It was the underlying venom in the other man's words. His racist intent was clear, yet he'd said nothing Gus could get him for.

Alice tutted and stared him out, whilst Gus prodded him on the shoulder. '*That's* where you're wrong, Knowles. I don't select my team on the basis of positive discrimination. I select them because they're the best investigative officers of their rank.' He leaned right into Knowles' face. '*That's* why *you'll* never make it onto my team. You're just. Not. Good. Enough.' Gus punctuated his final four words with additional prods to Knowles' shoulder. He stood back, and winked at Taffy and Alice, his tone containing no trace of its previous venom. 'Now let your *superior* officers hear your report and then bog off.'

Knowles glared in turn at all three of them and then spat a globule of phlegm on the ground, close to Alice's boot. She glowered, 'Uggh, you are a despicable little man, aren't you?'

He ignored her and looked at Gus. 'Nothing to report.'

Gus frowned. 'You've been here for almost three hours and you've *nothing* to report?' He folded his arms across his chest and shook his head slowly from side to side. 'It's that lack of precision that lets you down, Knowles. Let's see if I can help you out. Why don't you share some of your thoughts about the people you interviewed?'

Knowles' eyes flicked away as he shuffled the ground.

'You *did* interview some neighbours, didn't you? Or did you just eat biccies and drink coffee all evening, whilst we've got two dead bodies and a missing lad on our hands? Come on, tell us what you thought about them.'

Breathing deeply, fists clenched by his sides, Knowles swallowed before replying. 'I don't get paid to think.'

Taffy's gasp made a good job of drowning out Alice's snort. Raking his fingers through his hair, Gus took a deep breath. Officers like this were the bane of his life. Just as well there weren't too many of them left in Bradford. Knowles and officers like him had been weeded out. Their adherence to procedures was suspect and their methods downright appalling, so the powers that be had, when possible, rooted them out of the police altogether. However, the few that had slipped through the cracks for one reason or another had, on the whole, been diverted to areas where they could do little damage. Gus struggled to control his temper. Even so, his voice boomed through the night air when he spoke, 'That's fucking crap and you know it! Thinking is *exactly* what we all get paid for. You really are a useless article and

I'll certainly be passing my observations onto your new boss.'

Alice rested a hand on Gus' arm and, with a quick nod, he ran his fingers through his dreads again and reigned in his formidable temper. 'Just get off my crime scene, now.'

Knowles spun round on his heel and began to strut off, his walk unhurried, his stance arrogant. Then he turned back, his voice full of glee. 'Forgot to mention it, DS Cooper, your paparazzi friend was hanging around earlier. Probably waiting for you to leak a few crucial facts to him again like you did in Keighley.'

Gus, anticipating Alice's reaction, reached out to grab her, however he was too late to stop her marching over to Knowles and slapping him on the face. The unmistakeable sound of flesh hitting flesh with force hung in the air, causing an immediate silence as the officers nearby turned to look.

Knowles stroked his hand over the reddening mark and glared at her. 'You'll regret that, Cooper. I'm going to write this up when I get back. You won't get away with it. That's assault.'

Gus glanced round, seeing only a few officers nervously watching the scene. He, recognised them and knew that, like him, they'd have no sympathy for Knowles, who was well known as a lazy backstabbing piece of shit. He turned to Knowles. 'If you cause me or anyone on my team a *single* moment of discomfort, I promise you I'll come after you. You think your old buddies Alfie Redmond and Jazz Panesar will have your back? Well they won't. They rely on *me* now at The Fort. So, if I need any shit dealt on a little bulldog like you, I know where to go. Got it?'

Knowles held Gus' stare until his eyes flickered. He turned to Alice, eyes narrowed and pointed his finger as if it was a gun. 'Watch your back, darling!' Glaring at the group of officers, he walked away, his thick shoulders rolling as he ducked under the crime scene tape.

When he was out of earshot, Alice turned to Gus. Her face flushed and her eyes sparking, 'Fuck, Fuck fuckity fuck fuck fuck! I'm sorry. Shouldn't have done that.'

Gus shrugged. 'No harm done this time, Al. Just try to keep a hold on your temper. He's a sneaky bastard and he'll have his eye on you, now. You've got to let Keighley go. It was yonks ago and you've proved yourself ten times over since then.'

Alice cocked one eyebrow. 'Oh yeah, here speaks the master of letting things go.'

Taffy, grinning like the village idiot, lifted one hand and holding thumb and fingers together, flicked it, emitting a loud crack. 'Wow, that was some *beeeitch* slap, Alice. Wait till I tell Compo and Sampson. Bloody ace, that were.'

Gus snorted with sudden laughter. Taffy's enthusiasm, despite the American accent fading to Yorkshire by the end, had tickled him. After the night they'd had, they needed a laugh. Patting Alice on the back, he wiped the grin off his face. 'Tone it down a bit, Taffy. We need to down-play this, yeah?'

Taffy, still grinning, ran his fingers through his gelled hair. 'Oh yeah. Yeah, I got it, Gus.' He cast a sideways glance at Alice and lowered his voice. 'It were fucking sick, Al. Fucking sick.'

Gus rolled his eyes. What part of 'play it down' did the kid *not* get? 'Right, back to business now. Alice, I'd like you to interview Simon's friends Matty Bates and Jake Carpenter first thing tomorrow. Drop in on one at sevenish and try to get to the other before nine. I want both interviewed before they head off to school and I want the parents there, okay? Sampson can go with you. I think he's over there somewhere interviewing the neighbours.' He handed her a piece of paper with the addresses.

'Taffy and I will attend the PMs with my beloved father. Morning briefing at, say, 10:30, okay? You been to a PM before, Taff?'

'Eh, no.' Taffy's brow furrowed for a split second and then his usual grin was back in place. 'I'll be right, though, Gus. Don't worry about me.'

Alice laughed. 'It's more than likely you'll have to scrape Gus up from the floor, Taffy. He's a wuss when it comes to PMs.'

'Ignore her, Taffy. We'll be fine.' And he really hoped they would be. A thought struck him. 'Taff, have you done a notification of death?'

The younger man's face fell and his eyes went wide. 'No. I've not done that, either.'

Gus glanced at Alice who shrugged and said, 'Might work, Gus. Give it a go.'

Placing an arm on Taffy's shoulder, Gus squeezed. 'Look, Taff. PMs and death calls are crap. The worst job we have to do, okay?' At Taffy's nod, he continued, 'I reckon that if you come with me to do the death call for Jade Simmonds, it'll put the PM into perspective. Make it easier to bear, knowing what those parents are having to suffer. It's also useful to bear in mind that the PM is one of our most useful investigative tools. It's another way for us to stick up for the dead… to get them justice, if you like.' As he spoke he wished he could take the words to heart. It wasn't that he didn't believe what he was telling Taffy. That knowledge never made the PMs any easier for him. God knows why his dad's blood and gore tolerance had bypassed him and instead landed with his sister, who was a paediatric surgeon.

Chapter 14

01:05 Holmewood Estate

Gus pulled his jacket round him and gave Taffy, who stood on the doorstep with him, a reassuring smile. Together, they walked down the path. Gus' head was throbbing and he was drained. Nothing to what the family they'd just left were feeling. Notifying the parents of a teenage girl that she was dead was bad enough; to tell them in the middle of the night was the absolute pits. He noticed a single tear rolling from Taffy's eye and coughed. 'That went well, I thought.'

Taffy glanced at Gus, biting his lip. When he replied, Gus was pleased to note that his voice held only a slight wobble. 'Well, sir, if you call the mother falling in a dead faint and the drunken father calling you an effing Paki bastard and blaming us for not finding her sooner, instead of waking them up at this time of night, I'd tend to agree with you. It did go rather well.'

Smiling at him, Gus shrugged and took a slug from his Irn Bru bottle. 'I think you missed out "twat" and "prick". Other than that, well reported. How do you feel?'

Taffy grimaced. 'Like I've been hit by an express train? Was it obvious it was my first?'

Gus shook his head, 'Not at all, you remained calm and unflustered, which is all you can do in these circumstances. We're the lucky ones. When we walk out the door, it's over, yet for those poor sods, it's just beginning.'

They'd reached their cars before he spoke again. 'When they're interviewed again tomorrow, I want you there. It'll be less traumatic for them to have a familiar face there at the interviews, as well as the FLO. Think you're up to it?'

'After the PM tomorrow, that'll be a piece of cake. Thanks, sir, I'd like the opportunity.'

Lifting a hand, Gus slid into his car, turned on the engine and headed for home. He was proud of Taffy. The lad had remained calm despite the abuse flung at them by Jade Simmonds' drunk father. Mrs Simmonds had collapsed. Fortunately, the family liaison officer had taken over, coaxed her up to bed and called a doctor. God knows, Mr Simmonds was no use to her in the state he was in. No doubt that'd just add to the guilt he'd feel in the morning.

An hour later, Gus was laid out sound asleep on his battered old sofa with Bingo taking up more than his fair share of the room. Both snored loudly.

Chapter 15

03:55 Unknown Location

I open my eyes. Head's pounding like fuck! Mouth dry as a nun's cunt. Can't move, though. Not right now. Aw God, I'm dying! I open my eyes again, just a little bit this time. It's dark, the sort of dark that takes time to settle in your head. The sort of dark that makes you think you could be buried... alive?

What the fuck? Who's put the street lights out?

Fucking green dot over there, right high up, keeps flashing; One eyed alien? Smoke alarm?

Heart's hammering now and I raise my head just a fraction. It starts to thrum like a low volt electricity pylon. God, it hurts. When I lift my hand to touch my temple, it's like a fucking bear yanking it, pulling my shoulder out of the socket. It's like there's barbed wire burrowing and gnawing into my skull, gouging my brain. I want to be sick. This is the worst hangover I've had in ages. It's like I'm not really here. Maybe I'm not. That makes me laugh. If I'm not here, then where the fuck am I? I remember something for a nanosecond and then it's gone. What is it?

Closing my eyes, I try to focus. Something's not right. This isn't my bedroom at home. Then, I remember... the party, kids dancing, the girl on the table, Matty, Jake... the mess. The memory of overpowering alcohol and cloying weed makes my stomach lurch. Shouldn't have mixed the shots and the bud.

I lie motionless, hoping my head will stop spinning and I'll be able to sit up. It's freezing. I try to remember how I got here, that part is blurred, though. Not even sure how long I've been here. Despite the darkness, I know I'm alone. A groan slips from my lips, followed by a wracking shiver. I pull my other hand from under the coarse blanket and reach out to touch the canvas bed, but my fingers don't work. I flex them trying to work the numbness from them, but they're stiff and swollen. Vicious prickles spread to my fingertips like sheet lightening and my knuckles throb. This is bad... really bad. When was the last time I had a downer like this? Maybe that time with Matty and Jake on the Hill. Can't believe the folks never even noticed how gone I was.

I scrunch my toes and they're just as bad. How long have I been out? How long have I been here? I start to cough, and phlegm tinged with vomit fills my mouth. I force myself to swallow it. It's lumpy and tastes vile. I tuck the blanket under my back on both sides, creating a cocoon. Like that fucking Hungry Caterpillar book, *she'd* read to me when I was a kid. Thought she'd always be there for me. She promised!

No! No! I'm not going there. Not today!

So, I pull my hood up over my head, snuggle my chin into my neck and roll up like a baby, eyes screwed tight. Focussing on getting away is hard because of the cold and those other thoughts; the ones that won't let me go. At first, it's just Matty and Jake, the music, Tayyub being a div taking photos... then the bikers arrived–

No! Not going there either.

I delve deeper inside... Gotta reach my safe place right inside my head. No-one can reach me there, no-one can hurt me.

I'll think about what to do next when I feel better.

Chapter 16

06:25 The Fort

DC Sampson, Costa coffee in hand, looked at Alice's new car. She'd chosen a Mini Cooper again, yet that wasn't what Sampson was staring at. It was the colour of the car. It wasn't only that she'd opted for a particularly virulent shade of purple; it was that it was damn near fluorescent and reminiscent of puke after an evening of exotic cocktails and a beetroot binge. He glanced at his half-drunk coffee wondering if he really needed it now he'd been shocked into wakefulness. 'We could take my car, you know, Al?'

Chin jutting, Alice put her hands on her hips. 'And why would we do that?'

'It's just mine's a bit less, well…' He shrugged. '… noticeable, you know?' Apart from its toxic colour, the doors, bonnet and roof were covered by an intricate tangle of black flowers, some open-petalled, some closed, some elongated, some short and stubby. If anything, she'd gone for an even more detailed paintwork on this car than on her previous one. It was distinctive, to say the least. However, it wasn't the vehicle's décor that had Sampson hesitating. It was car's abhorrent lack of foot room, combined with Alice's erratic driving.

'So? We're not undercover or anything, are we?'

'Em, well… no.' Sampson had to concede that. He sighed, knowing that his next words would not be well received, yet he was determined to say them anyway. 'Minnie 2 is a beautiful vehicle. You know I love her to bits.

However…' He paused. 'She's just too damn small for my legs. Riding in her is like being squeezed into a bloody tin of peas, or being forced into a packing crate… or,' he strode round the car, his words spilling out fast and furious, 'one of those puppet's boxes where the doll's folded in half. Why don't you just bloody chop my legs off and be done with it?'

Alice opened her mouth, however Sampson held his hand up. 'Oh, yeah, it's okay for you. You're a bloody shortass. Hell, you need to sit on a damn *cushion* to see over the dash board.' He halted and spun round to face Alice. 'And there's another thing. You drive too fast and you talk all the damn time and you *never* concentrate. You're going to get us both bloody killed one of these days.'

Silence hung in the air between them for long seconds. Heat rushed to Sampson's cheeks and he knew he looked like a tomato. His sisters often teased him about that after he'd had a rant at them. He didn't regret his words, perhaps just the way he'd said them. The resentment about Alice and her precious Mini had been building up for months now. Getting it off his chest was well over-due. He risked a glance at Alice. Her pixie face was scrunched up as if she was concentrating. He waited for her to blow, bracing himself against the steaming geyser he was sure was heading his way.

Alice opened her mouth and then closed it again.

Shit, wish she'd just spit it out!

She put out her hand and patted Minnie on the roof as if soothing the car after Sampson's harsh words.

God, could it get any worse?

'Well, that was a bit of a turn-up, Sampson. Who'd have thought you had it in you?' She turned on her heel and strutted off.

Uh, uh! 'Wait, Al. Where are you going?'

'To get a bloody pool car, you big idiot. Where do you think? You should've just said it was cramped in Minnie. Now come on.'

Speechless, Sampson trailed behind feeling that somehow, yet again, Alice had got the upper hand. Despite having umpteen sisters, he reckoned he'd never understand women.

Chapter 17

06:45 Heaton/Cottingley

Matty: *You awake?*
Jake: *yeah. What's up?*
Matty: *Nowt. Just worried. You heard owt?*
Jake: *No. You?*
Matty: *No. Wonder where he is.*
Jake: *Me too. Just keep shtum, ok? It'll all blow over.*

Chapter 18

06:55 Ashwell Road, Heaton

Alice turned into Ashwell Road and parked near to number forty-six in front of the church. As she and Sampson got out, she studied the row of houses before them. She loved the terraced houses that typified Bradford. They were such a sharp contrast to the pokey Lego houses she'd lived in in Brent. It was early, and although most still had their lights on behind drawn curtains, there were a few vacant car spaces where a few had already left for work. She hoped Matty Bates' dad was still at home. Mum had died a few years previously.

Matthew Bates' house was snuggled between the end terrace and number forty-four, where a dog yapped at them from the window as they passed. A well-tended, if basic, patch of lawn with a small shed to one side took up most of the front garden. Unlike their neighbours, who had pots upon pots of shrubs, herbs and flowers, the Bateses had a solitary rose bush in the corner. Alice would have bet her soul that it was dedicated to Matty's dead mum.

As she locked the car, Sampson stamped his feet and blew on his hands. 'I hate knocking on doors before the street lights have gone off, don't you?'

'Yeah, soon as they see us they know it's not good news. At least we're not reporting a family death, this time.'

She crossed the road in the dull morning light and pushed open the creaking gate, before jogging up three steps and pressing the bell. Within seconds she heard the sound of activity inside. A shadow appeared behind the glass and the door opened a crack. A middle-aged man in a dressing gown peered out. Alice made the introductions, quickly explaining that no-one was hurt, and suggesting they move inside.

Mr Bates read their ID cards, and then opened the door, allowing them access to the warm house. Alice, curious as ever about how other people lived, stepped through into a worn, yet cared-for hallway. The carpet on the stairs to the right was threadbare although it had clearly been hoovered and the air smelled of a cooked breakfast in the making. Alice examined a series of mismatched framed photos depicting a happy family of four. In each picture the presence of a plumpish woman with a ready smile seemed to light the scene. In one a gap-toothed boy and a shy looking girl in swimsuits gazed up at her, unadulterated adoration shining from their eyes. In another scene, a younger Mr Bates stood, one arm round his wife, his other on the shoulder of a young lad, probably Matty, who in turn hugged his sister. All four faces were radiant. Similar scenes were repeated along the wall and the poignancy of the photos wasn't lost on Alice. She was in no doubt that the loss of the woman they all clearly adored must have been devastating for the family. She really hoped Matty hadn't done anything wrong.

'I was just getting the breakfast on the go. The kids are upstairs. It's school today.' Mr Bates yanked his dressing gown belt so tight around his middle that Alice was concerned he'd cut himself in two. He caught Alice's eye and a vein of red appeared high on each cheek. *Poor sod's embarrassed to be caught in his PJs.* Her smile bright, Alice said, 'Go and get dressed, Mr Bates. We'll wait in the living room.'

This option seemed to unsettle him even more as he shuffled from foot to foot, sending quick glances upstairs as he debated Alice's offer. 'I've got work at nine. What can I help you with?'

Realising Mr Bates wouldn't leave them unattended in his home, Alice gestured towards a half-open door. 'Shall we go in here and sit down, Mr Bates?' He bit his lip and glanced from Alice to Sampson before pushing the door fully open. Alice and Sampson followed him into a small front room with a comfortable if saggy leather suite and a super huge plasma telly that dwarfed the rest of the furniture.

Mr Bates gestured to the couch. 'Have a seat.'

Alice sat down on the couch, leaving the armchair nearest to the gas fire for him to sit on.

'What's all this about? Summat happened to my sister?'

Undoing her coat, Alice laid her gloves on the coffee table in front of her. 'No, no, nothing like that. As far as we know your sister's fine. We're actually here to talk to Matty. Is he home?'

Mr Bates frowned. 'Of course, he's home. He's upstairs. It's seven o'clock on a Monday morning. Where else would he be? Is he in trouble or summat?'

Sampson leaned forward. 'It's just a few routine questions about a party he was at on Saturday.'

'Saturday?' Mr Bates shook his head, his jowls swinging with the action, 'He wun't at no party. He were at Jake's. Never mentioned a party.'

Hearing a sound at the door, he turned and saw his daughter peeking through. 'Do you know owt about a party on Saturday night, Sarah?'

Sarah, who looked about fourteen, studied the two officers, her eyes alert and intelligent, before backing out of the room, avoiding her father's glance. A tactic Alice remembered from her own youth. Not that she'd encountered awkward questions from her parents very often. They were always too wrapped up in their own work.

'Sarah!' her dad raised her voice and the girl sidled back into the room.

'What?'

'Do you know owt about a party on Saturday night?'

Rolling her eyes in the way only a teenager can, Sarah swung one hip out and rested her hand on the opposite one, 'What you asking me for? How should I know? I'm not Matty's keeper, am I?'

'Less o' your lip, young lady. *Go* and get your brother.'

Huffing, Sarah stomped from the room, and moments later, 'Matty, the pigs are here for you', drifted downstairs.

Mr Bates' flush intensified as he leaned back on his chair. 'Don't know what to do with them. Since my wife died, I've been on my own, and they're good kids'.' He shrugged. 'At this age it's hard. They never seem to tell you the full story. Where was this party anyway?'

'It was at Simon Proctor's.'

'I thought Simon's folks were away for the weekend. That's why the three of them were staying over at Jake's.'

The sound of teenage feet stomping down the stairs greeted them before a curly haired, acned boy sidled into the room, barefoot and wearing an old pair of joggers and a sweatshirt. His sister edged in after him, her eyes agog. As she sidled past and perched on the arm of her dad's chair, Matty remained by the door, hands behind his back, head bowed. He looked like they were about to execute him.

Alice stood up with her hand extended. 'Hi, I'm DS Alice Cooper and this is DC John Sampson. You must be Matty?'

Matty offered a sweaty hand and swallowed hard. His voice cracked when he said, 'Yeah.'

'We've just got a few questions we'd like to ask you about the party on Saturday night at Simon's house.' She paused and sat down again. 'You were there, weren't you?'

Matty glanced at his dad and then, lowered his eyes. Alice could almost see a neon 'Busted' sign across his forehead.

His dad rubbed stubby fingers over his semi-bald head, pushing horn-like tufts of hair up at either side. 'Why the hell didn't you tell me you were planning a party at Simon's?'

Before he had a chance to continue, Sarah snorted. 'Duh? That's easy, Dad. He didn't say owt because you'd have stopped it, wouldn't you?'

Alice liked this girl already. Smart, sassy, no-nonsense. Just the kind of young woman she wished she saw more often in her line of work.

Mr Bates glared at his daughter and then inclined his head acknowledging the accuracy of her statement. 'Less o' your damn cheek, Sarah. Go and make a hot drink for everyone so the police can talk to your brother in peace.'

After ascertaining what everyone wanted, the girl sloped into the kitchen which adjoined the front room. Noticing that the girl had left the door open, Alice smothered a smile. *Little bugger! She'd have a promising career in the police force should she be so inclined.*

Mr Bates, face florid and voice strained, glared at Matty. 'Have you lot trashed the place or summat? Is that what this is all about? Well, you'll pay to have any damage rectified *and* you'll pay out of your own money. You hear me, Matty?'

Matty, head down, remained silent. Alice studied him for a moment, noticing the black bags under his eyes and his wan face.

'Look, Matty, why don't you come and sit down.'

Matty shrugged and padded over to the other chair where he flopped down as if his legs couldn't hold him upright for a second longer.

Alice turned to Mr Bates. 'I'm afraid it's nothing quite as trivial as damaged property, Mr Bates. Let's talk to Matty and see if we can get this all sorted out, okay?'

Mr Bates' shoulders slumped. In the five minutes they'd been in his home, Mr Bates had transformed from a dad slightly fed up with being interrupted during his normal Monday morning routine to a frazzled single parent trying to do his best for his kids, yet feeling horribly out of his depth in the presence of the police. It was a reaction Alice was all too familiar with and she knew that cracking on was the best way forward for them all.

Alice turned her attention to the boy. 'What can you tell us about the party on Saturday, Matty?'

The lad glanced at his dad, his eyes worried and when he spoke, it was in a quiet mumble. 'Simon decided to have a party whilst his parents were away. It was only supposed to be a few of us. Silly git posted it on Facebook, didn't he?'

Alice kept her voice level. She'd seen the evidence last night and thought that far from 'the few' Simon had anticipated there must have been a small army pillaging the house... and at least one of them was a murderer. 'So, how many were there, then?'

He shrugged. 'Dunno. Loads, I suppose. We didn't know half of them and they wouldn't leave when we asked, so we just chilled in the shed in the back garden for most of the night. Most of the girls were butter sket anyway.'

Since moving to Bradford, Alice had become familiar with this derogatory phrase against women and wasn't surprised when Mr Bates reprimanded his son.

'Matty! What have I told you about using that sort of language. It's not on!' He glanced at Alice. 'I don't like this, but his mates all use it.' He shrugged. 'Sometimes I think he listens to them more than me.'

Alice waved her hand 'Believe me, Mr Bates, I've heard worse... much worse. Now, Matty. You're telling me you left a whole load of strangers in Simon's house unsupervised whilst you hung out in the garden?'

Matty, biting his nails, said in a defensive tone, 'Well, it wasn't just me that hung in the garden. Simon and Jake did too.'

'For God's sake, Matty, why didn't you phone me or the police or something?'

Sampson leaned over and rested a calming hand on Mr Bates' arm. 'Please, Mr Bates, it would be better if you just let us ask the questions for now. You can discuss this with your son later, after we've gone, okay?'

He glared at his son. 'Hmph, I suppose it'll have to be.'

Alice leaned forward and looked directly at Matty. 'When was the last time you saw Simon?'

Matty looked up at her, his eyes shining with unshed tears. 'That's just it. Me and Si and Jake fell asleep in the shed and then, when we woke up, Simon was gone. We went into the house to look for him and it were a mess.'

Talk about understatements!

Tears flowed down his cheeks, his voice was thick, and now that he'd started to talk, the words rushed out of his mouth like they tasted vile and he just wanted to spit them out. 'The house was trashed... Everything broke and it stank and then we went through to the front room–' He hiccupped and suddenly he threw his head into his hands and sobbed. 'Jake said we should just get out of there, pronto, like.'

His dad looked at the police, his face drawn, and then, when Alice gestured, he moved over to perch on the arm of his son's chair, much like his daughter had done earlier. His arm went round his son and he pulled him close. Sarah appeared with a glass of water and a handful of tissues, which she handed to her dad, taking a moment to squeeze his shoulder.

What a lovely, caring family. Shame she'd had to come bursting in and upset them all. Content to allow Matty time to compose himself, Alice scribbled a few notes in her book and waited. Minutes later, Sarah returned, plonking a tray of drinks on the coffee table. She nudged her dad aside and took his place beside her brother. 'Come on now, Matty. You've got to pull yourself together. Once you've told them, you'll feel better, won't you? Now, come on.' She handed him a new tissue and waited till he'd blown his nose before saying, 'Go on, tell them what you know!'

Alice suppressed a grin. For all she was younger, Sarah had taken on the maternal role. She could empathise with that, because her own eccentric parents had often left her feeling she was the parent and they were the children. Much as she loved them, she had sometimes wished her parents were a little more conventional. It would have been nice to be nagged for *not* coming home on time or to have a home-cooked meal on the table at a proper mealtime, rather than three hours after most people had eaten.

Matty squeezed his sister's arm as if she was his lifeline. Maybe she was. 'We didn't see it at first. We were trying to pick up bits and pieces as we went, then, when we moved round the side of the couch, she were there.' Matty began to tremble and his voice shook, despite the tears flowing down his face, he continued. 'It stank of puke and she was covered in it and Jake said she were dead. He said we'd get blamed, so we just ran out.'

Matty's dad groaned and fell back in his chair. Sarah hugged her brother tightly.

Fuck, they'd found the girl and run out assuming she was dead. Alice hoped the PM would confirm that... for their sakes. Matty's complexion had taken on a green hue and Alice wanted to keep going before he crashed. Her tone warm and encouraging she said, 'You're doing really well, Matty.'

He sat staring at his hands in his lap for long seconds before he spoke again. 'We couldn't find Si. Jake and me, we couldn't find Si and we've been phoning and texting him, but no reply. What if he's dead, too?' Jerking his head up, he stared right at Alice. 'Is he? Is Si dead, like that girl? I told Jake we should phone someone but he just kept saying no. He gets so arsy. I shouldn't have listened to him.'

Alice shook her head. 'We don't know where Simon is. We haven't been able to find him. We hoped you could help.'

Matty glanced at his dad again and sniffed.

Alice lifted one of the teacups, dolloped in some sugar and handed it to Matty before doing the same for his father. 'Look, Matty, I know this is hard, however, we need to ask these questions. So drink your tea, calm down and get yourself together.'

Alice busied herself preparing drinks for Sampson and herself, then taking a sip, she sat back, smiling at Matty, who had slurped half of his tea and seemed a little calmer. 'Ready?'

Matty, face tear-streaked, eyes bloodshot, straightened.

Sensing he was focussed, Alice started to question him. 'Right, I'm going to take you back to the beginning. First of all, when did you plan the party and who did you invite?'

'Before Si's mum and dad went off, that's when he planned it. We'd only invited a few kids from our year and Simon said it would be boring, so he posted it on his wall on Facebook.'

Alice frowned. 'On his wall? Does that mean anyone who was his friend on Facebook could see the invite?'

'Well, yeah, and some of us posted it on our walls, too, and we shared it.'

Alice glanced at Sampson with raised eyebrows and turned back to Matty. 'How many friends do you have on Facebook, Matty?

'Nearly a thousand.'

'And Simon?'

He shrugged. 'Same, I suppose.'

'Okay, so at this party, did you know everyone?'

'No.'

'How many did you know?'

'Apart from Jake and Simon and a few from school and Tayyub, nobody.'

'Tayyub? Is that Tayyub Hussain?'

'Yeah.'

Alice frowned. 'So, how many *didn't* you know?'

Matty shrugged. 'Dunno, maybe thirty or forty of them.'

Bloody hell, thirty or forty? That was some bloody party and the neighbours didn't notice a thing. Talk about selective hearing!

'Did Jake or Simon know them?'

'Si knew some that we didn't, although Jake and me didn't know most of them, and then well…,' he glanced at his dad, 'We got a bit drunk.'

Folding his arms across his chest, Mr Bates cursed under his breath. Matty's shoulders hunched and he shrank away from his dad, focussing his gaze somewhere above Alice's right shoulder.

Sensing the lad was holding something back, Alice slid forward on her chair. 'What is it Matty, you've got to tell us everything!'

He glanced at his dad again. 'Well, Jake had some weed.'

Mr Bates' muttered curse was louder this time and Matty flinched 'And then… it was a bit scary in the house with the bikers and all, so we went into the garden. On the way out, someone shoved a bottle of cider at us and we took turns downing it. Don't know who gave us it. Can't remember. It was after that we fell asleep in the shed. Jake reckons it was spiked.'

'The cider?'

'Yeah.'

'You said something about bikers?'

'Yeah, they came in with two lasses. I didn't know them.' He thought for a second. 'Think Si did, though.'

'Bikers? Your age?'

Matty shook his head. 'Nah, older than us, twenty or thirty or summat.'

Interesting. What the hell were twenty-plus-year-old bikers doing at a kid's party?

'And the girls they were with?'

'One was younger, maybe fifteen like. Don't know though, not for sure. I think she was the one we found, though.'

Mr Bates closed his eyes and took a deep breath. 'How much bother is he in, then?'

Alice shook her head. This whole situation was crap. Mr Bates had enough on his plate, and if Matty was telling the truth, he was more like a cowering puppy than an arch criminal. Mind you, the law might not see it quite like that if the PM showed they'd left the girl to die. 'I don't know yet, sir. Obviously, he should have informed us as soon as he discovered the body. We'll need to check out his story with his friend and re-interview him formally at the station.' She grimaced when she saw a tear roll down Matty's cheek and land on his hand. By the door, his sister stood, her face taut, her body rigid. All trace of her earlier ebullience had vanished.

Alice knew it was important to make it clear to Matty how much trouble he was in. 'This is serious. You and your friend left an unconscious girl at a crime scene and you didn't phone for an ambulance.' Feeling like a bitch, yet knowing she had to stress the enormity of the situation, she pushed her point home. 'How would you have felt if that was your sister and two lads had just left her there?'

Matty scrubbed his hand over his face, and glanced at Sarah. He swallowed hard, 'I'm so sorry, so sorry. That poor lass. Jake told me to keep schtum. He kept saying it'd be okay if we just kept quiet.' He turned and flung himself into his father's arms as if he were a toddler. Mr Bates' arms went around his son. His eyes sparked and despite his pallor, a determined look was on his face. Alice knew Matty could depend on his dad throughout the ordeal that was to come.

'I think you should phone the school and your work. It's going to be a long day.' Alice turned to Matty. 'When you come down to the station to make an official statement, we'll take blood and urine tests to check for drugs. Now, where did you think Si had gone when you woke up?'

'We thought at first he was tidying up, you know?' 'Cause his folks were due back last night.'

'Okay, so you and Jake went through the house. Did you go upstairs at all?'

'No, never got the chance, 'cause then we found that girl and we just skedaddled.'

'So, you didn't go upstairs on Sunday morning?'

Matty shook his head.

'What about Saturday night?'

He frowned. 'Don't think so. We just pissed–' he glanced at his dad, '... er, I mean peed in the garden.'

Charming! Not quite housetrained yet!

'What about into Simon's mum and dad's room? Did you go in there?'

'Eh? No. I've never been in there.'

'Okay, so tell us about the girl. Did you recognise her?'

Matty began to shake his head then changed his mind. 'Well, I didn't *know* her. Didn't know her name or owt, think she came to the party with those biker lads I was telling you about. I told you that. Great big blokes in leather jackets.'

Alice got up. 'You've done well, Matty. You need to come down to the station and we'll need your fingerprints, too.'

Matty, wide-eyed, jumped up. 'Oh fuck, you don't think I did it, do you? I never was near her, honest!'

'Calm down, Matty, it's all procedure. Now if you can just give DC Sampson a list of all the people you knew who were at the party, along with contact details, whilst I speak to my boss, that would be great.'

Alice went outside and stamped her feet as she waited for Gus to answer his phone.

'Hi Gus, just finished the interview with Matty Bates. He's coming down to the station in an hour.'

'Did he ID either girl?' asked Gus.

'No. He knew about Jade Simmonds but couldn't ID her. Says he'd no idea about the girl upstairs. Tend to think he's telling the truth about that. Can we have somebody there to take samples for drugs, please. Also, just a thought, maybe get Compo to check all their social media accounts. Simon posted an invitation to his party on his Facebook wall. So, it was visible to nearly a thousand people and Matty said some of them then posted it on their walls, which opened it up massively. We'll never process all the information without someone who knows what he's doing.'

'Right, Alice, I'll get on to that. Can you get back here for 10:30 briefing?'

Alice glanced at her watch. 'It's already 7:45 and we've still got Jake to interview. Although by the sounds of it, he'll be a harder nut to crack.'

Chapter 19

07:15 Cricklewood Police Station, Brent

'Jerry, it's me, I need a favour.'

Jerry Johnston screwed up his face wishing he'd followed his first instincts to ignore the ringing phone and continue walking out of the office. His shift had finished and he wanted to get home. Who wouldn't, if they had the promise of a shag followed by breakfast in bed, before a good long sleep? He sighed. The voice on the other end of the phone was trouble and he thought he'd heard the last from him. 'What the fuck is it this time? I thought we were square?'

The caller's placating tone did little to reassure him. He'd heard it all before too many fucking times to count. As far as he was concerned, he'd paid his dues for being caught with his trousers round his ankles and his dick in the dried-up pussy of a prostitute informer. Hell, it had been four bloody years ago. It hadn't even been a memorable shag and now, there it hung like a fucking huge dildo on a chain round his neck just waiting for Steve Knowles to yank it whenever the bastard saw fit. The thing was, he knew he couldn't afford to ignore Knowles. Jerry's wife was sexy as hell – nonetheless, she was a damn harridan, too. She'd chew him up and spit him out if she ever got wind of *that* episode and then it'd be bye-bye to conjugal joys at shift end, never mind the fry-up afterwards.

'Look, this is the last time. I promise, Jerry. Then we're square, okay?'

Knowles tone was pleading, yet Jerry knew it was all an act. That was the thing with Knowles, you never knew *quite* where you stood. He'd have your balls in a vice if the mood struck. Jerry sighed and cupped his balls as if to protect them from whatever it was Knowles wanted now. 'Right, go on, what is it?'

'You're a mate, Jerry. Straight up, a pure mate. Name's DS Alice Cooper. Worked out of Brent. Something went tits up a while back. What was it? I want enough shit to cover my granny's roses, okay?'

Jerry turned and walked back to his desk, all hope of his morning panning out as he'd planned destroyed. 'Right, okay, give me a couple of hours?'

'An hour, Jerry. An hour and phone me back on this number, right?'

Chapter 20

07:30 Bradford Royal Infirmary, mortuary

With his usual stoicism, Gus marched along the antiseptic corridors of the post-mortem suite, hopeful that, to the casual observer anyway, he'd appear eager to reach his destination. In reality, he wished he could run in the opposite direction. After being sick in the public toilets, he'd splashed cool water on his face, confident that would disguise his nerves. *Why was he getting worse every time he had to attend a post-mortem? He'd never been this bad before.*

One glance in the cracked mirror above the wash basin told him he'd been unsuccessful. His angular face was tense and a slight pallor made him look jaundiced. Hell, even his blue eyes looked insipid, his dreads flat and mousey. He braced both hands against the sink and gave himself a good talking to. *Taffy is coming for his first ever PM and I have to show the lad some fortitude. I can't go being sick in front of him.*

Grimacing at his reflection, he acknowledged that he had nothing left to bring up. The coffee he'd drunk that morning had splashed its way down the toilet bowl, leaving his stomach churning. *This is not going to be one of my finest hours.*

Over the years, Gus had developed a technique of shallow breathing during the post-mortems. Despite this, the closer he got to his destination, the more he became aware of the gradual merging of antiseptic and rotten body smells. It may well have been his overly vivid imagination, but, to his mind, there was no mistaking the odours seeping along this corridor in the bowels of the hospital that gripped him in a stranglehold. No matter how new their ventilation system, how much they cleaned and sprayed, the stench *always* clogged up his throat, bringing a million snapshots of previous post-mortems to mind.

Reaching the door, he swallowed, took a deep preparatory breath through his mouth and pulled the prepared hankie from his pocket. *This was getting to be a damn habit – he'd need to stock up on his Vicks.* Before his nostrils completely filled with the nauseating stench, he thrust it under his nose and breathed deeply from within the hankie hoping it would serve the dual purpose of disguising the god-awful smell *and* operate as smelling salts when the grinding and sawing noises became too much for his queasy stomach.

By the time Gus had donned his scrubs and folded his greasy hankie beneath the mask, Taffy was in the room. The lad, to give him his due, didn't shy away from unpleasant things. He stood as close to the trolley as he could, and seemed determined not to miss anything. Gus, lacking Taffy's enthusiasm, positioned himself at the back of the room, leaning against the metal sink which, to date, he hadn't had to use. Still, after his earlier performance, he couldn't dismiss the possibility and he found it reassuring to have the receptacle within easy up-chucking distance.

Should the pathologist require his observation, Gus could step forward and see the horror of the autopsy table in all its glory. Otherwise he hoped to remain as ignorant of the gore as Taffy seemed keen to investigate it.

Chapter 21

07:55 Unknown Location

So fucking disorientated. Head's thumping, and every time I blink, it's like someone's stabbing my eyes with broken glass. I'm in that sort of no-man's-land, halfway between being stoned and sober; my hands shake. Mouth's dry as fuck. Must've swallowed the contents of a dregs bucket. Tastes like shit. Shadows waver and weave around me. Making me fucking dizzy. Not sure if it's all in my head.

When I strain through the grey darkness they look unfamiliar and threatening, like ghosts or demons or summat. Maybe it's like that old bugger Scrooge. Maybe I'm being haunted by the Ghost of Christmas Past. That'd be a laugh. There's a shape in the corner right in front of me. It's all spindly looking, like an old man bent over. I blink twice. It's gone and instead there's a box. If I blink again, maybe it'll go, too. There's a bundle of stuff in the other corner, can't see it at all now, maybe it's gone... disappeared... maybe a ghost's taken it. 'OOOOOOH!'

Hope not. Might need it.

Green lights still there, up on the wall. Sometimes it's red. Then it flashes green for a while, then back to red again. It's a camera. CCTV in a fucking cell! Sickos out there watching me. What sort of fucked-up idiot gets off on watching a lad trapped in a freezing dungeon? Hope they're enjoying the fucking show. Hope they're happy seeing me suffer.

'Are you fucking happy, you bastards? Fucking sick bastards!'

Shit that hurt, shouldn't have moved. Now I'm thinking about my head again... and the cold, the fucking freezing cold. Wish I was at home right now in my own bed. I need to get up. Need to see what's what. Need to focus, get my stuff together. God, I'm starvin'. Could eat a dozen Snickers bars right now. What is it Matty says? – 'could eat a scabby horse.' *Tosser!*

I need a piss. Jesus, think my bladder's going to erupt if I don't relieve myself soon. I inch myself upright, taking it real slow. Pounding head. Feel dizzy. I put out my hand. Use the wall to balance. Aw, its slimy, Yuck! Now the blanket's fallen to my waist. The air slaps me like a blizzard, my teeth chatter, my body shivering. Didn't expect this cold. Wrapping my arms round my chest, overlapping them, I rock back and forth, trying to quell the shivers. When it stops, and my mind clears a bit, I take a deep breath and swing my legs round to the side of the camp bed. It wobbles and for a second I think it's going to collapse, so I stand up.

The concrete's freezing against my bare feet, so I fall back onto the bed, making it shake even more. Need to get something on my feet and there's a pain in my groin now, too. I scrunch up onto my knees and tilt my upper body over the side of the bed and rummage around on the floor for my trainers. Hope there's no dead mice or owt. Hate mice... Shit, what if there are rats? What's that sound? That's definitely a rat... bet it's a rat. Read somewhere once that they eat you, even if you're *not* dead. Fuck's sake. What a way to go.

The sound of my own breathing's freaking me out now, so I hold my breath and listen. There's nowt, though. Nothing. Not a damn noise. Maybe I imagined it... or... maybe there's a bloody battalion of rats all holding their breath, same as me, waiting till I move before they pounce, their sharp clawed paws gouging chunks out my face and their teeth gnawing at my toes. Wouldn't even feel it, they're too damn cold.

Take a deep breath, Simon. Ground yourself.

Hoping the noise will dispel my fears, I laugh. The sound echoes around the room, bouncing back at me, mocking me, making me jump. I bite my lip and put all thoughts of rats to the back of my mind as my fingers ferret around, my knuckles screeching in pain every time they connect with the hard floor. Got to find my trainers, got to piss. My hands skim over something and I yank them back, nearly bricking it. *Thought it were one of them rats for a minute.*

I laugh again, although this time I keep it inside. I'm not brave enough to disturb the silence yet, so I grab my trainers and pull my body upright onto the bed till I can sit cross-legged. The grey seems lighter now. Must be getting used to it. The shadows are still eerie, though I can make out shapes in the corner. I inhale once, the air dries my throat even more. So damn thirsty! Needing a slash and being thirsty at the same time's not a great position to be in.

Fuck, if I'm not quick, I'm going to piss myself. Fucking tongue's glued to the top of my mouth, can't even swallow. Fuck's sake! *Come on! Damn fingers won't work. Shit, no. Can't piss myself. Not now. Not done it since I were a kid and I remember what happened then. Shit! Don't go there, Simon. Just breath. Nice... and... slow.*

That'll do. Only got the laces half undone but it'll do. I drop the shoes onto the floor and dangle my legs over the side before slipping my feet in one at a time, not caring that they're my best Nikes and I'm squashing the heel. Shuffling along, I use my fingers against the moist wall for balance until my toes connect with something solid in my path. It's cuboid and stands to just above my knee. My fingers explore the plastic and find the lid. As soon as I lift it the smell of disinfectant hits my nostrils and I release a sigh of relief. Yanking my fly open, a torrent of urine splats into the bowl in an almost never-ending flow. A flick of my dick to release the final few drops and I pack it away, uncaring that the residue soaks into my boxers. Nobody there to tell me off, now. Nobody at all. I shiver. It's like I'm the only one left in the entire universe.

Chapter 22

08:00 Bradford Royal Infirmary, Mortuary

Whilst removing Jade Simmonds' liver, Fergus McGuire was well aware of his son's preparations. It never ceased to amaze him that Angus had still not developed a thicker lining to his stomach. Fergus' hopes of Gus following in his footsteps had taken a knock when at the tender age of twelve, the laddie threw up watching a cow give birth. What was supposed to have been a magical father and son bonding experience had turned into a major trauma for Angus – one that had never left him. The glance he now threw in his son's direction was a combination of concern that Angus *would* actually faint this time, and admiration, that despite his revulsion, he still attended PMs, time after time. *Stubborn boy! Just like his mother when she's got a bee in her bonnet.* He smiled beneath his mask.

Closing his mind to his son's discomfort and aware of Taffy's interest in the proceedings, Fergus directed most of the general data to him as he weighed and dissected organs. Jade Simmonds' post-mortem was straightforward. She was normal in every respect for a girl her age, except for the fact she was dead. Dr McGuire soon pronounced cause of death to be asphyxiation on her own vomit, more than likely caused by excessive consumption of alcohol. The lab had identified traces of semen in her vomit and in swabs taken from around her mouth. Various tests would be carried out to check for the presence of drugs in her body and to ascertain her exact alcohol levels.

There were scratches on her neck. He took some skin scrapings from her nails for DNA testing. When Jade's post-mortem was complete, he cleaned up, changed his clothing, and moved into an adjoining examination room. It may not have been unheard of for him to have to perform two PMs in one day, however, it was rare he had to conduct two on such young victims in such quick succession.

What in Heaven's name was the world coming to? Fergus' chest was heavy, as if a block of cement resided there, weighing him down and making his movements sluggish. He tried to shake off the inertia as he began the PM on Victim Number Two, the unidentified girl from the bedroom. *How the hell was this slip of a girl still unidentified?* First glance told him that although slim, she wasn't undernourished and her young body showed none of the signs of homelessness. She looked free from drug or alcohol addiction and seemed healthy enough… apart from the obvious injuries to her chest and the absence of life. *Someone somewhere was missing a daughter and they didn't realise it yet. How tragic was that?*

Fergus was glad when Gus indicated that he and Taffy had to leave. One less thing to worry about. The boy's shoulders had slumped a little more with each incision and, not for the first time, he wished Gus would delegate the PMs to someone with a hardier stomach. Gus and Taffy would come back later to talk over the findings with him and, in the meantime, if he came up with anything notable, he'd text Gus. As they exited the room, Fergus saw Angus drop an arm round the younger man's shoulders and ruffle his hair. It reminded him of when Angus was a laddie and he'd done the exact same thing to him.

Chapter 23

08:05 Paradise Road, Cottingley

Alice drew up at the kerb in front of Jake Carpenter's house and looked out at the quiet road that was a sharp contrast to Matty Bates' busy Manningham Street. Jake's house was a newly built semi-detached with a postage stamp garden at the front. Two cars sat on the drive, in front of a sizeable double garage. One was an older Audi and looked well-used, the second was a five-year-old BMW that shone as if it had been recently waxed. It was clearly the owner's pride and joy. She turned to Sampson. 'The three boys have very different backgrounds. Wonder how they hooked up.'

Sampson looked at his notes. 'All three lads go to City Academy, which is more than likely where they met. School's a great leveller and City Academy takes kids from all over Bradford.'

Alice knew the school and the head teacher there, Patti Copley. It was up Manchester Road and had earned a good reputation as one of Bradford's beacon schools. As far as schools went it seemed friendly and efficient enough to Alice. Then again, schools were most definitely not her thing. She grinned. The mention of City Academy reminded her of Gus' 'big secret'. He thought she didn't know about his dalliance with Patti Copley. *Phew, Idiot! Did he really think he could keep that quiet?* If there was gossip regarding Gus' love life then *she'd* be the one to find out about it. Mind you, no way was she going to tell him about the bet she, the school secretary and Naila had about how long it would take Patti and Gus to hook up. No, she wasn't daft enough to let him realise that she knew him better than he knew himself.

The curtains in the front room were open, and inside Alice could see the shadowy figures of people getting ready to begin their working week. Such a shame she was going to set it off to such a bad start. Hey-ho... one person's annoyance was another person's pleasure, and she would get a truck load of pleasure from seeing Jake Carpenter squirm. If Matty Bates' account of Saturday night was accurate then this little scrote was a bit of a ringleader and Matty Bates was a damn sheep. Well, that was her take of the situation, anyway, after seeing the series of text messages between the lads since Sunday morning. *Idiots!* She'd keep an open mind though, just to be sure. After all, she had been wrong about people in the past. 'Come on, then, let's go and spread some joy.'

Sampson rammed his notes back in their folder and got out of the car. Halfway up the path, Alice turned to him, 'You want to lead on this one? I want to be ready to do my mean and moody act if Jake's as stubborn as Matty made out.'

Without waiting for his reply, she marched up the steps and rang the bell. Within seconds she could hear a voice from inside, getting louder as it neared the door. 'Who the hell is that at this time? They're going to make us late. Jake, get your damn bag and let's get cracking. What's got into you this morning? First you miss your bus and now you're going to make me late, too.'

The door was flung open and a woman in a business suit and a blouse that revealed too much cleavage made to push past them. 'Sorry. We're running late. Whatever it is, you're going to have to come back later or speak to my husband if you can drag him away from his damn computer.'

She turned her head and yelled back into the house. 'Come on, Jake. If you want a lift, get a wriggle on.' Then with a step towards the stairs she raised her voice again. 'Danny, there's somebody at the door.'

A young lad ran down the stairs jumping the last two and then ground to a halt. His eyes met Alice's and his face paled. Alice tilted her head to one side and with a cold smile held his gaze for a moment, before turning it to the woman and offering her warrant card. 'I presume you're Mrs. Carpenter? I'm DS Alice Cooper and this is DC John Sampson, we'd like to come in.'

Mrs Carpenter looked at the card and then at Alice. 'Look, I don't know what this is about but you've caught us at a bad time. If it's about those damn quad bikes you're going to have to come back later on, after work.'

Moving to block the woman's exit, Alice spoke in her most polite voice. 'It's Jake we're here to speak with. Perhaps if you're too busy, his father can be his appropriate adult.'

A frown crossed Mrs Carpenter's forehead and her mouth fell open. Alice stepped into the hallway, hiding the dart of satisfaction that made her heart skip a beat at having knocked the other woman off balance. Her 'May I?' was a redundant platitude.

As the three adults looked at him, Jake backed away, his eyes flitting from one to the other. He was bricking it and satisfaction bubbled in Alice's chest. *Little bugger deserved to feel uncomfortable.* After all, he and Matty had left a young innocent girl who was in trouble without even phoning an ambulance. *A little bit of squirming wouldn't do the boy any harm whatsoever.*

'Jake?' the single word went up at the end and Mrs Carpenter's lips pursed. Jake ignored his mum and kept backing into the kitchen. She turned to Alice, blinking as she watched her son's retreat. 'What's this all about?'

No doubt if Mrs Carpenter hadn't had Botox, her forehead would have wrinkled with concern. As it was, it was difficult to ascertain whether the woman's tone betrayed anxiety or annoyance. Following Jake towards the kitchen, Alice flung a bomb over her shoulder. 'It's about the party that Jake attended on Saturday night at Simon Proctor's home.' Before the other woman could ask any more, Alice added, 'Maybe you could fetch your husband and we can get started.' She waited till Jake's mum was halfway up the stairs before adding, 'Oh, and I'd call your work. Let them know you'll be late.'

Seeing Sampson suppress a smile, Alice mouthed, 'What?' at him and then winked. She revelled in getting folk on edge and, if Matty was right, Jake Carpenter might be a more difficult nut to crack. She needed to see if the two lads' stories matched and she didn't want Jake or his parents to think they could mess them about. If they were cooperative she'd dial down her sombre expression a notch.

In the kitchen, Jake slid onto a chair and rested his elbows on the table with his hands clasped before him. Head bowed as if in prayer, he remained silent. *Good, he'd need all the help he could to squirm out of this one.*

From upstairs the sound of loud voices, one female, the other male, drifted down. It seemed that Mr Carpenter was no more happy about their morning visit than his wife had been. *Good.* Alice liked to have them at a disadvantage if she could. She walked over and pulled out the chair next to Jake and motioned for Sampson to take the one opposite. *Might as well use the parents' tardiness to their advantage.* They'd effectively hemmed Jake in and, unless the parents wanted to make an issue of the seating arrangements, it could serve them well.

Humming under her breath, Alice made a quick inventory of the kitchen. Large and airy, there was a faint smell of burnt toast and coffee in the air. *Probably more of a muesli than a fry-up sort of family.* The rhythmic sound of a tumble drier drifted through from a door to the right; presumably the utility room. Magnets showing a family of four enjoying various rides at a theme park covered the fridge, holding up letters from school about parents' evenings, and a shopping list. The Carpenters were, it seemed, running low on tofu and loo roll. From the photos, Alice recognised Jake and his mum. The younger boy must be at school and if the voices from upstairs were anything to go by, Alice was about to meet dad. On the wall next to the fridge a large family organiser was turned to November, bearing the names Mum, Dad, Jake and Benny. It appeared the Carpenter family had an active social life. From where she sat, Alice could see that on Saturday Jake was supposed to be having a sleepover at Matty's. *Strike one for Jake!*

Footsteps on the stairs warned her of the Carpenter parents' arrival. Mum had slipped off her high heels and now wore a pair of old slippers.

Mr Carpenter was in jeans and a T-shirt, his hair wet as if he'd just got out of the shower. He had one of those rolling walks that made Alice think of cowboy films. 'What's all this?' He stood just inside the kitchen, arms folded over his chest, and glared, first at Jake and then at Sampson, ignoring Alice altogether.

Sexist git! Alice inclined her head, telling Sampson to take over. *All boys together, let's see how that goes!*

Sampson stood up and offered his hand to Mr Carpenter. 'We're here to talk to Jake about a party he attended on Saturday night at Simon Proctor's house.'

If she'd blinked, Alice would have missed the flare of anger in Danny Carpenter's eyes as he looked at his son. 'Jake wasn't at a party on Saturday night, were you, Jake? He was staying over at his friend's house.'

With a self-deprecating smile that made Alice proud of his acting skills, Sampson shook his head. 'I'm afraid that's not the case, sir. We know Jake was at the party.'

Sir? Alice only just managed not to roll her eyes.

Carpenter frowned and glanced at his wife. 'Pop the kettle on, Lou, bloody gasping, I am.' He pulled out a chair and sat down next to Sampson. 'What's all the fuss about anyway? The Proctors got their knickers in a twist because *their precious boy* got up to no good when they were away? What happened, one of their bloody pot plants get broken or did the lad raid their drinks cabinet and drink all their champagne? Hoity-toity bastards.'

At his father's words, Jake flinched. The vibration of his leg bouncing up and down under the table made Alice want to reach out and still it. The kid was nervous as hell. *Wonder what he's going to say for himself.*

'Simon's missing, Mr Carpenter. That's one of the reasons we're here.'

Mr Carpenter snorted. 'The lad's probably hiding. He'll be stopping at one of his mates till it all blows over.' He leaned over and prodded his son on the arm. 'You know where Si is, Jakey?'

Still looking at the table, Jake shook his head.

Accepting a mug of tea from his wife, Mr Carpenter slurped and then released a resounding belch, before standing up and gesturing to the door. 'Well, looks like you've had a wasted journey, officer. My Jake can't help you.'

'Hmm,' Sampson made no move to stand up. 'Then there's the other matter we'd like to talk to your son about.'

If she hadn't been expecting it, Alice would have jumped to her feet and shouted *bravo*! Sampson had lulled the dad into a false sense of security and was now going to pull away his safety net. With any luck, it'd emphasise the seriousness of the situation and get them to assert pressure on their son to tell them everything he knew.

Jake's leg stopped bobbing and his head jerked up. It looked like he was in suspended animation. The Carpenters frowned and Mrs Carpenter moved to stand by her husband, her arms folded under pert breasts. They exchanged a glance and then looked at their boy. Jake shook his head and licked his lips. It was only the thought of the missing boy and the two dead girls that stopped Alice from extending a hand and squeezing his shoulder.

Carpenter's eyes narrowed and the bonhomie left his voice. 'What other matter?'

Sampson laid his folder on the table and began shuffling through it. 'The matter of the two dead girls found on the Proctor property.'

Before his father had a chance to respond, Jake blurted out, *'Two?'*

His tone mild, Sampson looked at the boy and asked, 'Why? How many were you expecting, Jake?'

Before Jake could answer, his dad stepped next to his son. 'Don't say another word, Jake.' He turned to Sampson. 'We want a lawyer.'

Chapter 24

09:35 The Fort

Relieved to escape the last of the post-mortem on the unidentified girl, Gus munched on a toasted tea cake he'd procured from The Chaat Café. Perhaps it would settle his still gurgling stomach. What he'd really like to do, though, was go for a run, but he didn't have the time. He'd sent Taffy off to chase up missing persons before heading up to Cottingley Ridge to see if anything had come up overnight. You'd think by now someone would have noticed the girl was missing. Simon Proctor's friends would be at the station soon and he wanted to interview them himself, so until they arrived he'd get on with some paperwork before the briefing.

A frantic scraping accompanied by three rapid kicks to the incident room door had Taffy rushing over to open it. Gus glanced up from the pile of statements he was reading and saw a huge box held in the middle by a pair of hands. It was held so high it obscured the face of the person holding it. Sampson, a foot taller, followed, puffing heavily as he looked for somewhere to deposit the box he was carrying.

Close behind them was a short stocky man wearing a khaki cap with IT Supplies stencilled on the front and towing a trolley piled high with various monitors, screens and computer stuff. He parked his trolley, and ignoring everyone in the room, pointed to a series of empty computer tables in the top left-hand corner of the room that were surrounded by boxes of technical equipment. 'Right, it's all going over there.' At that, he turned and walked out.

The man carrying the box deposited it on Gus' desk, much to Gus' annoyance, and followed the IT man out. Gus frowned and glared at Sampson who shrugged. 'I only helped him off the lift with it. It's nowt to do with me.'

Compo jumped up from behind his PC, face glowing, and skipped over. His wide smile created a deep dimple on each of his chubby cheeks making him look like a kid as he bounced from foot to foot. 'It's arrived, Gus! It's bloody here!' He clapped his hands like an over-excited two-year-old and touched each of the boxes. 'All my new gear. State of the art, this is. State of the bloodeeey art.' He clicked his fingers together gangsta style. 'Can't wait to set it up. Wanna help?'

A snort followed by a coughing fit from Alice had Gus glaring in her direction. 'Shut it, Al!'

He turned back to Compo, and swallowed the disparaging words he'd been about to make. *Least the lad was happy. Why would he want to burst his bubble?* 'Think I'll give it a miss, Comps. Bit busy you know. Two murders and a missing boy to find.'

'Yeah, yeah... busy, busy, busy,' said Compo, hefting one of his precious boxes into his arms and heading over to the empty PC station.

Gus grunted. *Bloody nerds!* 'Comps, when will you be up and running? We need your input on this.'

A Mars Bar appeared as if by magic in the younger man's hand and he chomped down on it, chewing with his mouth open, a trail of soft toffee dangling from his lips.

Give me fucking strength! Like we've got time for Mars bloody Bars.

Two gulping swallows later, Compo said, 'Aw, I'll be up and running in fifteen. Just need to plug in and boot up... easy as sneezy.'

Avoiding meeting Alice's eyes, Gus risked a glance at Sampson who had averted his gaze. 'Eh, I'll help Compo then, shall I? Many hands, light work and all that.'

Ten minutes later, Gus looked up from his paperwork and saw that already, with Sampson's help, Compo had off-loaded his equipment and was now studying Simon Proctor's laptop.

Gus continued to sift through the neighbours' statements, his mood dipping more with every report he read. What was it about these people? Yes, they'd heard loud music. Yes, they'd suspected a party at the Proctors'. Yes, they knew Jane and James Proctor were away for the weekend. Yes, they heard motorcycles roaring round the cul-de-sac but it had been 'short-lived'. No, they didn't want to interfere; not their damn business – and as a result, two young girls had lost their lives, two families were devastated and a young lad, number one suspect or not, was missing. These were the same people, who, his notes told him, had logged thirty-five complaints about wedding fireworks going off during the summer in the Manningham area; yet they couldn't deal with stuff happening in their own back yard. *Bloody pathetic!*

He took a slurp of coffee, grimacing when he realised it was cold and stood up to make a refill. Breathing in the welcome aroma of freshly ground coffee, Gus glanced over to see how his nerd was getting on. Compo, catching his eye, waved for him to approach his newly-configured computer station. Gus looked in admiration at the range of machines and the tangle of wires and keyboards that surrounded them. Thank God, he could stick to his reliable old desktop!

Compo had a laptop open on the desk. 'This is Simon Proctor's. I got the uniforms to bring it to me. Wanted to see what I can find out about our missing teenager.'

Gus saw that the laptop was hooked up to one of Compo's machines. Compo would be running a forensic analysis, which would, if they were lucky, bear fruit.

Crowding round the laptop, Gus, Sampson and Alice looked to where Compo was pointing on the screen. 'Look, I've pinpointed the wall posting the kid made about the party. We need to identify the kids that came. One of them must have seen something, even if his best friends are saying nowt. So, what say I print you off a copy of his friends' details and their friends' details? That'll give you some names to target.'

Gus' heart sank. That list would be a mile long. Alice had told him Simon Proctor had at least a thousand friends and each of his friends probably had the same amount. No way could the team look through that lot. Swallowing his impatience at Compo's naïveté he just about managed to keep his voice level. 'Look Compo, we don't have the manpower to go through thousands of names. We need quick, succinct info.'

Compo, oblivious to Gus' impatience, pressed a button. 'Yeah, what I'll do is get rid of duplicated names, cross reference re school, geography and age and see what we come up with. Then, I can put some filters in place to prioritise the list.'

Alice glanced at Gus, her eyebrows raised and a 'duh' smirk on her face that made Gus want to question just how much of Compo's proposition *she'd* understood. Instead he focussed on the task in hand. 'What does that mean?'

Compo glanced up at him, 'Well, this programme won't duplicate the names of friends shared by Jake and Matty, for example. It'll sort them into categories like friends, family, school mates and provide ages so if you want, I can filter out kids over the age of, say... twenty.'

Alice plonked down next to Compo. 'Thirteen. Some of those girls can look older than they really are.' She thought for a minute and added, 'Can you make that age thirty for men and twenty for girls?'

Compo's fingers flew over the keys. Any groups you want left out for now? Family members, for example? I can save them in a separate file.'

Gus thought for a minute, then looked at his team. 'Help me out here, folks. I think we need the ages Alice suggested. We need school friends as a group. Maybe non-relative contacts of Si's within the age brackets who don't match with anyone else. Can you do criteria like hobbies?'

'Yeah. What hobbies you interested in?'

'Biking... of the motorcycling sort?'

'...and photography?' said Sampson.

Alice, warming to the task, butted in. 'Also, those that live within a fifty... no, make that twenty-mile perimeter?' Tapping her lip with a black varnished fingernail, she frowned. 'Oh and did any of that group "check-in" to Cottingley on Saturday night? That'll be our first port of call.'

Compo, punctuating keyboard activity with the dunking of digestives in a glass of Tango, hummed 'You Really Got Me' by the Kinks as he worked. Until, with a final flourish of fingers over keys, he slumped back in his chair. 'Okay. I've linked all your PCs to mine. Anything flashing green on your desktop needs looking at as a priority. When it's been read, it'll stop flashing. Up to you which folder it goes in, then. When the statements come through I'll put them all in a folder, okay? And as you go on, if you want me to flag up key words in the statements, I can, okay? Maybe I'll put motorcycles in for now, anyway.' He glanced at Gus for approval and then, pressed a button. 'Right, the names are on your desktop files. Uniforms will be busy. We've narrowed it down to fifty possibles.'

Gus grinned. 'Good work, Compo. Now, can you collate the kids who attend City Academy from that list.' He turned to Alice. 'Looks like a school visit might be in order.'

Alice tossed her head, 'Yeah and I wonder why that's brought a smile to your otherwise miserable face... nothing to do with a certain Patti Copley, is it?'

'Aw, piss off, Al.'

Seeing Alice's smug expression, Gus tutted and moved back to his desk. So, what if the thought of seeing Patti Copley again made his face flush? It was as much nerves as attraction. She was one amazing woman and he'd be damned if he'd discuss his private life with Alice.

Chapter 25

09:55 The Fort

Striding along the corridor, hair bouncing like Zebedee, Gus realised Alice and Sampson were almost running to keep up. He ground to a halt looking sheepish. 'Oops, charging ahead of everyone again, sorry.'

Grinning, Alice winked at Sampson. 'Doesn't matter. Sampson and I enjoyed watching your ass wiggle.'

He grabbed his stomach and rocked back and forth on his heels 'Ho, ho, ho, I can hardly contain myself.' He winked at Sampson. 'Al, which one of these two idiots will be the easiest to crack?'

Alice looked at her partner in crime. 'What do you think?'

Sampson grinned. 'That's easy.' He jerked his head towards interview room one, where he'd deposited Matty Bates half an hour earlier. 'Him. He's already shitting bricks.' He blushed and glanced at Gus. 'If you'll excuse my French.'

Gus slapped him on the back. 'No need to stand on ceremony, Sampson. Say it like it is. No room for ambiguity that way.' His eyes narrowed as he considered which of the two to take into the interview room with him. Sampson needed the experience, so he opted for him. 'Come on then, you can be my sidekick. Keep quiet, say nothing, and look deferential, okay?'

Sampson grinned, only just managing to refrain from rubbing his hands together in excitement.

Gus pulled his shoulders back, fixed a frown on his face and crashed through the door into the interview room with Sampson scurrying along behind. With huge strides he approached the table, looking like an ancient bronzed god risen victorious from the ashes, his dreads unfettered around his face, his eyes flashing.

As Matty Bates watched him approach, his face paled and he gripped the edge of the table tightly till his fingertips went white from the pressure. Gus glowered down at the boy with narrowed eyes for long seconds, and then he grabbed a chair and scraped it across the floor causing Matty to jolt backwards as if he'd been struck. Swinging the chair round, Gus straddled it, resting his arms along the back of the chair. This was his favourite interview position. He thought it made him look tough, like Clint Eastwood playing Dirty Harry. With another frown, he slapped a file on the table. 'Get the tape set up, Sampson. We need this on record.' Ignoring the father, he turned to Matty.

'Right. Spill!'

Matty glanced at his father, whose face cheeks had slackened at Gus' loud entry. Mr Bates cleared his throat and opened his mouth to speak, but was stopped by Gus' icy glare. Gus raised one hand and shook his head, before turning back to the boy.

Matty gulped and his eyes skirted the room looking for an escape that didn't exist. Gus raised an eyebrow and narrowed his eyes to a slit before slowly repeating himself.

'Spill!'

'Wh– what do you mean?'

Pursing his lips, he looked at Sampson, who shook his head as if Gus had just announced a death sentence. In a quiet, yet far too reasonable tone, he enunciated his request for the third time. 'Spill the bloody beans. That's what I bloody mean. What *really* happened Saturday night?'

The lad cast his eyes downwards, shoulders slumped. One hand raised to his cheek and he began worrying at an inflamed spot. The pimple burst and a blob of pus spurted out and landed on the table.

For fuck's sake! Bloody teenagers!

Mr Bates, hands shaking, wiped the offending slurry off the table with a near decimated tissue and then rummaged in his pocket, before producing another one for his son. With a cautious glance towards Gus, he put his arm round the boy.

All of a sudden Gus' enthusiasm for playing bad cop dissipated. These two were in awe of him, not like some of the little scrotes that he came across. These were law-abiding folk who'd got caught up in something too awful to think about; the sort of thing they read about in the papers or saw on the news yet never imagined themselves being involved in. He had a job to do; however, he didn't have to enjoy doing it.

Mr Bates pulled his son's hand away from his face. 'Look, Matty, if you know more than you've said already, you've got to tell the…' he glanced at Gus and winced 'er… policeman everything. Simon may be in real trouble. Now, blow your nose and smarten up.'

Matty blew loudly into the hankie, looked at the product of his efforts and crumpled the tissue into a ball in his hand. Despite his shaking voice, the lad managed to hold Gus' stare. 'Look, I don't know what happened to Si, honest. All I know is we smoked some bud and we were spaced out. Chilled, you know?'

Gus rolled one hand a few times in a circular motion to indicate that he wanted more.

'Si was talking to some blokes. Those bikers I told you about earlier.' He turned to Sampson for confirmation. 'Then we grabbed some cider and wandered down to the shed to sit and smoke.' He bit his lip and glanced at his dad. Then he glanced back at Gus, before looking down at the table and mumbling, 'Well, Si had some blues, so we took a few of them and then...' He shrugged. 'Well, we spaced out and went to sleep. When we woke up Si was gone, just like I told you.'

Aware of Mr Bate's gasp at his son's revelation, Gus swallowed his sympathy. 'So, nobody spiked your drink?'

Matty shrugged. 'Well... maybe. Never reacted like that to the blues before, like. Jake reckons someone spiked them.'

'You took the pills voluntarily?'

Again, a nod. The kid was shaking, his hands kept creeping back to his acned face and his dad had lost all colour. His hair was dishevelled from all the times he'd run his fingers through it. Gus hated how the system favoured the middle classes. Poor Matty's dad had probably never been in a police station before and was prepared to trust his son to the system. He could have lawyered up, but he didn't realise that. He wasn't a regular offender who knew how to screw the system, nor was he of the same class as Jake Carpenter's family. *They'd* known their rights and had been quick to get legal advice. Gus thought the lad was telling the truth. He just needed to be sure. Hating having to do it, he leaned forward, slamming both hands on the table and speaking loudly. '*It doesn't add up!*'

Matty jumped, wide-eyed and dropped his used tissue on the floor. Hands, empty now, he began to knead his thighs as Gus continued. 'You see, I think you're lying. I think *you* bought those pills. I think *you* gave them to your friends and I think *you* know what happened to Simon. You know that's supplying and it carries a custodial sentence, don't you?'

Mr Bates' face paled and Gus thought the older man might vomit. He didn't really believe that Matty had bought the drugs, although he wanted to judge the boy's reaction nonetheless.

Uncommon Cruelty

Matty gulped and shook his head from side to side, 'No, *no*! Si bought them. Me and Jake just shared them. I don't have money for that sort of stuff.'

'Rubbish, *you* took the pills, you, or you and your mates, killed the two girls and that's what really happened.'

Matty looked at him. '*Two* girls?'

Gus stared at him for a full minute. 'Okay, maybe you only killed the one downstairs, so who killed the other one?'

Matty's face paled. 'I think I'm gonna be sick.'

Sampson stood up and helpfully offered him the empty metal bin. He took it and held it in his lap his hands wrapped round it like it was his favourite cuddly toy. Then he leaned over and dry retched a few times.

'Get him some water, detective.'

When Sampson returned with the water for Matty and a cup of tea for his dad, Gus leaned across the table and looked straight at the boy. 'Look Matty, Simon's missing. There's a mum and dad who had a daughter yesterday and now they don't. We don't yet know yet if her death is an accident or not. On top of that, we found another dead girl. Now, *her* parents don't know she's dead yet. However, in a little while, me and Sampson here are going to have to go and tell them. That's not the worst of it, Matty.' He shook his head morosely. 'No, the worst of it is that I'm going to have to tell them she was *stabbed* to death. Do you understand, Matty? That girl upstairs was *murdered* on Saturday night.'

Matty's voice quivered. 'I *swear*, I didn't know. Jake and me didn't go upstairs on Sunday. We only saw that first girl and we should have told you. I know that, but we were so scared and then Si was gone. We didn't know what to do.' Tears spilled down the lad's face and Gus gestured for his dad to give him a tissue.

Sighing, Gus leaned towards the boy and when he spoke his voice was calmer and kinder. 'Look, Matty, you've done some stupid things; however, I don't think you're a killer. We need to speak to Si, so if you know where he is, tell us.'

'Honest, I don't. I really don't!'

The lad knew nothing further about the two girls' deaths or his friend's disappearance. 'Okay. Here's what we'll do. You tell the truth, and, believe me, I'll know if you don't, and we'll look at the minor charge of possession of drugs instead of kidnapping and possible manslaughter, okay?'

Matty swallowed and looked gratefully at Gus. 'Yes. Okay, whatever you want. I'll tell you the truth.'

'Who bought the weed and who supplied you?'

'Si's got a number of some Pakistani dude. He rings it and then we go up to Heaton village and hang around near the church. A young lad rides up on a bike. We give him the money and he gives us the bud.'

'Who's the lad?'

'Dunno, sometimes an Asian kid, sometimes a Polish kid.'

'Name of the dealer?'

'Dunno. Honest, it's Si gets it, we don't usually have the money, me and Jake.'

'What about the vallies, the blues?'

'Honest, Si got them.'

'Where from?'

Matty frowned. 'Someone at the party, I'm not sure who. Wait, hold on, I reckon it might have been them biker dudes, cos I saw him high-fiving them. Or there was some Asians out the back at one point – didn't know them either. Maybe they sell it.'

'Okay, so who were the bikers, then?'

'Dunno. Never seen them before. There were two of them, a bit older than us – in their twenties maybe – with them two girls.' He frowned again. 'Didn't know the girls, either. They were younger, I think.'

'Right, so you went to the shed to smoke your spliffs, drink your booze, pop your pills and fall asleep. When did you waken up?'

'Dunno, might have gone to the shed about two or three, then we got up early. We were starving... always get the munchies after smoking.'

Gus and Sampson left the room with Mr Bates tearing a strip off his son. If it hadn't been for the seriousness of the situation, Gus might have felt sorry for the lad.

'Well, what do you make of that, Sampson?'

Sampson put on a gormless expression that looked just like Matty's. 'Dunno.'

Gus laughed. 'We'll pass the entire weed information onto drugs, not that they'll be interested in that. Also, see what information they can give us on blues and, in particular, the suppliers of.'

Alice had watched the interview. 'Bloody weird, this whole thing, isn't it, Gus? One murder, one possible accidental death and a missing boy. Doesn't make sense, really.'

The exact same thought had crossed Gus' mind whilst he was interviewing Matty. If the girls hadn't been found in the same house, any link between their deaths would be tenuous at best. 'No, it doesn't. There's something we're missing at the moment. It's too coincidental that the girls died at the same party, yet their deaths are so dissimilar. I'm of the opinion that they're unrelated. The nature of their deaths, to me, hints at two different killers. God knows what to make of Simon Proctor's disappearance. Is he running scared or is he complicit or even responsible?' He took a slug from the Wee Bru he'd found on the desk, and grimaced when he noticed it was flat.

'Listen, Al, you head in and set up the interview with the other kid. I want to catch Mr Bates to reassure him we won't be pressing charges on the drugs this time. Just wanted to give the kid a fright.'

Alice laughed. 'You certainly did that, poor kid nearly pissed himself.'

'I like playing bad cop. It's a good stress buster. Anyway, when I've done that, I'm off to see Simon's parents again, see if they've got anything to add and also to share the news about the drug use. Bet they won't take too kindly to that. Simon isn't *quite* the golden boy they'd like us to believe. DCS Macclesfield has arranged for a televised plea for Si's safe return, so I'll brief them on that. Also, Al, set Matty up to look through some piccies of bikers whilst you're interviewing Jake, yeah?'

Chapter 26

09:30 Unknown Location

Must've dozed off. Lost all track of time in the silence. Cold's nipping my nose. What if it falls off? What if I get hypothermia, frost bite? Seen a documentary about that, with some explorers in the Antarctica on fucking sledges. Fuck, hope I don't get that. Half my nose will be mangled – it'll look like mince. Yuck, I'd look like fucking Quasimodo. Who the hell would lay me then? One of them got their arm stuck in a rock – stupid bastard! Least that's not gonna happen to me. Most I could get my arm stuck in would be the fuckin chemi loo. *Death by shit! Ha ha, that's funny, death by shit!*

Glad I found the lamp, though. I keep it on low. Got to save the gas. Don't know how long I'll be here.

Least it's not too dark. Not like before. Can't be bothered moving. Exhausted. Fucking camera's still going off and on. Wonder who the fuck's watching it? Wish I had my phone, or my laptop. Wonder what's happening on Facebook. Bet they're all talking about me. Maybe some of the girls will be crying. Wishing they'd been nicer to me before. Bet they'll be eating out of my hand when I come home. I'll be spoilt for choice. Matty and Jake'll be dead jealous.

What the fuck's that smell? I lift the blanket and waves of stale body odour waft out. God, I stink. How long have I been here? Can't remember. A panic flutter bubbles up from nowhere. How long did I zone out for? Hours? Days? Shit, surely not days.

What am I going to do? What am I going to do?

Fuck, where's my phone… need to check the date? A bubble of panic explodes like a popped balloon in my chest. Where's it gone? Shit, I remember! The party! Music blaring, more and more people squeezing in, dancing. Fuck, it was hot. House like a damn Tardis. Needed some air. Down to the shed with Matty and Jake… *Breathe. Breathe slow… Nice and slow.*

Idiot. Check your watch, Si.

Monday. It's only Monday morning. Everything's fine. I'm fine. There's no windows, that's the problem. No daylight. Nothing to keep my body clock synchronised. I read about that. About folk who go crazy because they can't see the day change to night. People trapped in places like this… confined spaces, in the dark, with no company and no daylight. Fuck, it's happening again. I need to breathe. Need to calm down. What did it say in the books? What did it say? *That's me… I'm going stir, fucking, CRAZY!*

'I'm fucking craaazy. Can't sleep, Can't see… Oh fucking craaaazy…la di da di la.'

I throw my head back and laugh. This time it doesn't upset me to hear my voice ricocheting around the cellar. I welcome it. It's a friend I can talk to, have a conversation with. I jump up and start doing star jumps. Need to get my head right. That's it… move about. Sing. Talk to myself.

Need to piss again. That's all I seem to do. Piss, sleep, snack… repeat! Piss, sleep, snack… repeat!

Aw shit, fucking toilet lid's caught my finger. Is it bleeding? Jamming my finger into my mouth, I suck the blood away like a baby on its dodi. Aw… fuck, that's gross. Tastes of filth and stale piss. *Yeuch!* I spit, then again. Bloody taste won't go. Where's the water? Two glugs, a gargle, spit… ah, that's better. Feel a bit light-headed after the star jumps so I sit down to piss, pushing my dick between my legs, like I'm a toddler.

Don't want to go there... not a fucking toddler! Don't think about when I were a toddler. Think positive. Forget that shit. It's in the past. *Breathe... slow... breathe.*

Least it won't splash onto my Nikes. Shit, I stink. BO and summat else. Urine... like the lads' toilets at school. Vile. I dangle my penis for a minute more before standing up, I pull my boxers and jeans up, don't bother fastening them... let it all hang loose, baby!

Wonder what's happening outside? Mum and Dad will be home now. They'll have seen the state of the house. She'll be furious about the damage. She always keeps it so damn clean. Never a thing out of place, couldn't breathe there, sometimes, it was stifling... not any fucking more.

They'll have phoned the police. She'd have been hysterical, and Dad would have taken charge. Wonder where they are right now? Somewhere warmer and more comfortable than here, for sure.

They wouldn't be at home, though. Coppers will have cordoned it off, like on those stupid CSI programmes mum always watches. Crime scene tape, police, tents... everyone looking for me... there will probably be a TV interview and I'll be in all the papers. Maybe a search party?

Wish I knew how close they were. Fucking freezing here.

Chapter 27

09:35 The Fort

'That you, Jerry?' Knowles had answered on the first ring. About bloody time too. What didn't the tosser get about 'urgent'?

Knowles heard a toilet flushing through the line and when Jerry spoke he had to strain to hear him.

'Yeah, I got what you want. Mind you, I'm not sure how much shit it is.'

Knowles glanced round, making sure that he was still alone in the office. Last thing he needed was anyone overhearing him getting the dirt on DS Alice 'butter-wouldn't-melt-in-my-mouth' Cooper. 'Never mind. I'll be the shit judge, if you don't mind.'

'Okay, okay, keep your hair on and I'll tell you what I got.'

Knowles' lips tightened. Johnston better watch his tone. Didn't the idiot realise that his balls were in a noose and he, Steven Knowles held the end of the rope. Easy enough to tighten. Little by little, he could make Jerry Johnston wish he'd never met him. Knowles was more than happy to tighten it, should the need arise. Clearing his head of his annoyance, he tuned in to what the other man was saying.

'This DS Alice Cooper seems pretty clean, to me. She was on the fast track. Selected for one of these new units they've set up to streamline us. Anyway, seems like she'd been part of a sting on this drug group. Only thing is, stupid cunt didn't realise her DI was dirty. So, they go into the sting and she's just about to put the finger on the head of the drug ring, bloke called Big H, when something bad goes down. This is where it's all a bit hazy. Anyway, the official line is that she senses something behind her and turns, instead of turning straight round she does some dodgy martial arts type spin to the side and ducks, just in time to see her DI, firing a dirty gun right at the spot where she'd been standing. Seems she reacted quickly and managed to grab the gun and clout him on the head. By the time the armed response lot get there, the DI's bleeding and unconscious on the floor and the druggie's cuffed to a pipe.'

This hadn't been what Knowles had wanted to hear. He didn't want to know that Alice Cooper was a damn hero. No, he wanted dirt on the bitch. 'Fuck! There must have been an enquiry or something?'

On the other end of the phone, Jerry laughed. 'Yeah, there was. There had to be because the DI, bastard by the name of Kennedy, ended up in a coma – still is, apparently, and with no signs of coming out of it either.'

'That right, Jerry?' That was interesting. Had Cooper used unnecessary force? 'So, what's the gen on the enquiry?'

'Well, seems Big H, in order to shave a few years off his sentence, gave evidence against Kennedy. Swore Cooper acted in self-defence and that he supplied the DI with the dirty gun. Cooper was following leads that would implicate her DI. Big H said the plan was to kill Cooper, he'd escape, leave the country and Kennedy would be the hero who managed to wrestle the gun away from an armed man, unfortunately too late to prevent the death of his colleague. Big H said he thought Cooper was getting a bit too close to the truth.'

'So, she's the fucking heroine in all this. Not what I wanted you to dig up, Jerry!'

Jerry snorted. 'I've left the best bit for last.'

'Ah, knew I could rely on you. Let's have it.'

'Well, DI Kennedy was apparently diddling his DS.'

Knowles mouth curved into a smile and he punched the air. This was more bloody like it. 'Go on, I'm all ears.'

'That's right. DS Cooper and DI Kennedy were an item. So, stupid cunt was not only betrayed by her boss but by her lover too. Cooper, after the enquiry, which by the way, was hushed up, disappeared for a good three or four months.'

'Where did she go?'

'This bit's not a shovel o' shit I'm telling you, it's a bloody great tractor full of the stuff.'

'Okay, okay, I'm listening.'

'Rumour has it she nearly resigned; then, instead, some smart-ass higher up forced her to have compulsory, intensive, psychiatric treatment because she lost her marbles after it all. Just fell to pieces, by all accounts.'

'Oh, so maybe DS Alice Cooper isn't quite the whizz kid she thinks she is. Looks like she's got a crack in her stiletto after all, hmm? Any chance of getting access to her psychiatric report, Jerry?'

'Oh shit, come on. I can't be doing that. I'm not cleared for that sort of stuff.'

'Come on, Jerry, try the back door. You can do it, can't you?'

Chapter 28

10:30 The Fort

To say Gus was disappointed would be a mega understatement. He was fuming. Alice and Sampson had reported back that he interview with Jake Carpenter had turned out to be a series of monosyllabic 'no comments' delivered in a dour, truculent voice, overseen by a disinterested solicitor. At the end, the solicitor had pulled a statement from his briefcase and read it to the officers. The upshot was that his client, Jake Carpenter, had been drugged on the Saturday night at the party and when he woke up he'd left the property. He had no knowledge of any dead girls nor did he know of his friend Simon Proctor's whereabouts.

Gus was thankful, yet aware of the underlying inequality, that meant that, whilst Jake Carpenter's family had the wherewithal to lawyer up, Matty Bate's family had not. At least he'd been able to reason with Matty without being hindered by the bureaucracy of the legal system. Often, he wondered who exactly it was designed to protect, for sometimes, so it seemed to him, it was *not* for the benefit of the damn victims.

Wishing he could take a run round Heaton Woods to rid himself of the tension knot in his neck, Gus walked into the interview room. *Ah, well coffee was the next best thing,* and with a smile he accepted a steaming mug from Alice before pulling his chair to the front of the room and sprawling on it, legs on Sampson's desk.

Savouring the aroma and allowing the warmth from the mug to soothe his frazzled nerves, he lifted the mug to his mouth. Before he could take a sip, though, Compo raised his head and grinned. 'Have you let those young lads go yet?'

Sensing the boy had got something for him, Gus jumped to his feet, and carried his mug over to Compo's workstation. Wondering whether it was worth mentioning the smear of mayo on Compo's cheek and deciding against it, Gus said, 'You mean Simon's friends?'

'Yip, them are the ones.'

'Well yes, didn't think we'd get much more out of them.' Then seeing the twinkle in Compo's eye, he grinned. 'Unless of course you've got something worth bringing them back in for.'

Compo swivelled his computer chair round, extended his arms to chest height and rolled his hands over one and other like he was leading a class of five-year olds in a rendition of 'Wind the Bobbin Up'. His actions were accompanied by a tuneless rap, with every line punctuated by one hand raising, index finger pointing upwards, before recommencing their rolling. '...Who's got the dirt? Compo's got the dirt! I say who's got the dirt...'

Deadpan, Gus mimicked his actions and joined, 'Compo, Compo, Compo, Compo, Compo's got the dirt... aaah!'

Alice, Taffy and Sampson ambled over, as the pair were high-fiving. *That felt good.* Gus realised it was the first time in a long time that he'd done something impromptu like that...and enjoyed it. *The new meds must be working.*

Compo, still giggling, swung his chair back to his screen. 'Uh, huh. I sure do got some dirt.'

Trying not to cringe at his American accent and hoping Compo hadn't picked up the habit from Taffy, Gus, folded his arms over his chest and leaned his thighs against the table behind. 'Go on then, Compo, spill the beans. What you got?'

Taking a swig of coke, Compo began to explain.

Gus looked at his colleague, amazed at the complicated, technical explanation being thrown at him and shook his head. 'Cut the techno babble, Comps. Just give me the end result. I don't really care how you got it.' Seeing Compo's eyes light up at his last statement, he amended it. 'Within the constraints of legality that is.' Then, in a much lower voice he added with a wink, 'Unless of course it's completely undetectable or unprovable.'

Compo's crestfallen face broke into one of his childlike grins and he raised his arms palms upwards towards Gus. 'Okay, boss, straight lingo. I accessed the three lads' private Facebook conversations.' He stopped and pursed his lips in concentration, 'Well actually, I've accessed *all* their conversations. The only ones I've had time to look at so far, are the ones between Matty, Jake and Simon. Maybe one of the uniformed officers could go through the others, I've linked them up to the group computers so everyone has a copy.'

Gus gestured for him to continue.

Crossing one leg over the other, Compo began to tap on the table with one finger. 'Simon and Jake had a conversation three months ago regarding the purchase of blues, otherwise known as vallies or diazepam.' He handed a printed transcript to Gus.

'The long and short is that Simon wanted Jake to put up some money to buy blues to sell on around the school and at gigs, et cetera. Jake wasn't into that and told Simon not to be so daft.

'It seems young Simon had an unnamed supplier and they could make one hundred per cent. There's a few convos between them: it's all there.' He pointed at the sheets Gus was perusing. 'Jake, good lad, held his ground. Seems that Matty was too much of a wimp to be included in this convo. Simon told Jake he knew Matty "defo" wouldn't do it, so he kept him out the loop.'

Gus clicked his fingers. Fucking brilliant. If the mayo on Compo's cheek wasn't an issue, Gus would have kissed the lad, there and then. Compo bounced up and down on his chair. 'That's not all, boss. That's not all.'

Gus raised an eyebrow and took a second lot of transcripts from Compo.

'Separate conversations going on a few months. Start date March 27, 2017. Still with Jake but also including Matty too this time. The summary is that Simon saw a MILF in school one day and–'

'MILF?' Gus frowned whilst Alice, Taffy and Sampson groaned.

'Duh? What planet you living on, Gus?' Alice, jabbed him with a pointed fingernail, one for each word she uttered, 'Mums. I'd. Like. To. Fuck! MILF. Get it? All the horny teenage lads use it these days. Girls use DILF.'

Gus screwed up his face in disgust, 'Don't tell me – Dads I'd like to fuck. God, what happened to the innocence of youth?'

'The internet and social networking.' Compo's voice was matter of fact.

Gus sighed. 'Anyway, go on.'

'Well, turns out the daughter of the MILF is called A. No full name *or* surname. You'll have to get that info from Jake or Matty. So, the guys have a bet about Simon and the mother and daughter.'

Gus stopped thumbing through the transcripts. '*Really*? Ugh. Horrible little bastards, aren't they?' His thoughts flicked to Patti Copley, who was head teacher to all three boys. *Wonder what she thinks about all this. God, on second thoughts I wonder what acronym they'd use for her. HILF or TILF no doubt, as in head teachers or teachers–* He had the grace to feel a tad embarrassed that the thought of adolescent males lusting after Patti irked him. He hadn't told Alice that he and Patti had been on a couple of dates and, now that her school was on the sidelines of yet another investigation his team was involved in, he was even more reluctant to confide in his colleague. It was none of her business anyway. It was early days and the last thing he needed, with his track record, was for it to reach his parents' ears. Pulling his thoughts away from his 'almost' girlfriend, he tuned back into what Compo was saying.

'Yeah, you got it. Simon bet that he could have sex with them... the MILF, that is, *and* the daughter.'

What the fuck? The more Gus was hearing about Simon Proctor the less he liked him. Maybe he was just old-fashioned. Maybe all lads were like that these days. Hell, he remembered Mo, Greg and himself poring over Playboy magazine when they were still at school. His cheeks reddened when he remembered the crush he'd had on his French teacher, Mrs Claire. She'd been hot, they'd all agreed. He supposed she'd been his MILF. Perhaps the world hasn't changed so much after all.

Compo continued. 'Over the last few months, he's basically befriended the daughter, got himself included in their family life and managed to get a blow job and a fuck out of it. Dirty little bastard. Apparently, he got proof on his mobile phone of the blow job and recorded them fucking in her house. From the convos, it seems that the other two boys both saw the evidence and paid up.'

Gus exhaled and rubbed his hands together. 'Good job, Compo. We needed a break. Seems that Simon wasn't the little angel his teachers and parents thought. We'll get the boys in and get an ID on which girl and her mum he's referring to.' He spun on his heel and then continued the movement, so he'd completed a full circle, 'Wait a minute. You got the date he recorded the sexual activity?'

'Early July this year, judging by their texts, why?'

'Simon Proctor was a minor then. His birthday isn't until the end of August. Was the sexual activity with the mum or the daughter?'

'Unclear. Again, those lads will be able to clarify, you'd think.'

'Taffy, I want you and Sampson chasing that lead down. We may have another offence on our hands.' He dragged his fingers through his hair. 'Like we don't have enough to be going on with.'

Striding over to get a caffeine fix, he was once more halted in his tracks by Compo.

'Oh, one more thing. The lads mentioned some unspecified group and talked about Simon infiltrating it to get to the mum. Maybe worth asking them what group it was, too.'

'Well done.'

Blushing, Compo shrugged, his cheeks flooding with colour. 'Right then, I'll trawl through the rest of Simon's convos, see what I can come up with.'

'While you're at it, get a warrant to access their phone records. See what's been going on there.' Gus turned to Sampson. 'After briefing, pull the lads back in again. I'm done soft soaping them. They need to start co-operating. Right, let's get this show on the road. Alice, will you do the honours.' Gus grinned and tossed her a whiteboard marker.

Groaning, Alice made a pretence of reluctance as she caught the marker, moaning under her breath just loud enough to raise a laugh from the team. 'The perils of being the only one with a legible hand in this damn set-up.'

Gus ignored her and continued. 'Victim One, no ID so far. Still waiting for full PM results from Doc McGuire.

Here's a picture of the crime scene. You'll see our killer left a calling card. Anyone got anything to add?'

He glanced round the room, before continuing. 'Okay, actions as follows: Sampson, contact missing persons, provide a copy of photos taken after she's been cleaned up a bit and see if any reports came in over the weekend.'

Just then the door opened and Sergeant Singh, the duty officer, popped his head round.

'Sorry to interrupt, Gus. Just got this from missing persons, thought it sounded like your girl.' He waved a sheet of paper in the air. Taffy, who was closest, jumped up to retrieve it and handed it to Gus, who glanced at the photo and grimaced.

'Thanks, Hardeep, looks like you're right. It's our girl.' He handed the sheet to Alice who stuck the picture next to the existing one. 'Right. Her name is Sue Downs, age fifteen. Sampson, you'll come with me to notify the parents, though before we do I want to find out what the rest of the post-mortems threw up. You'll come with me to the mortuary, Taff. Afterwards, Sampson and I will do the notification. Let's crack on with this, though.'

Walking over to the enlarged crime scene photos, Gus pointed at the red writing. 'This is in lipstick. Sid's seeing if it matches any of Mrs Proctor's lipsticks. "Redeemed". Mean anything to anybody?'

Alice crossed her legs and mused. 'Well, I suppose it could be some religious fanatic on the loose…?'

Sampson glanced up. 'Or the boyfriend… Maybe they had sex, and then had an argument. He flipped and stabbed her, leaving the writing to put us off track? Maybe Simon Proctor is the boyfriend?'

'Could be anyone at this stage. We need to get her photo to the uniforms who're interviewing friends at the school and see if we can come up with any sightings of the girl on

Saturday night, and a name for the boyfriend. Those damn boys need to tell us who was at the damn party.'

Chewing on an overflowing sandwich, Compo waved his hand in the air. 'My programme's showing that a sizeable chunk of those saying they were coming to the party were from City Academy. Not to say they all rolled up on the night, but good enough reason to check out the school, I reckon. I'll print off their names and addresses.'

'Okay, Sampson and Taffy, you can follow up on that at the school later.'

Whiteboard pen in hand, Alice sucked in one cheek. 'Sure *you* don't want to go to the school, Gus?'

Gus glared at her. 'Focus, Al. Less of your damn cheek.' This was exactly the sort of crap he'd wanted to avoid and here he was on the receiving end of it anyway. God knows what she'd be like when she found out.

She grinned and kept writing up the actions.

He waited till she'd had finished and then pointed to the second board. 'Meet Jade Simmonds, age 15, possibly asphyxiated on her own vomit. The pathologist isn't ready to sign off on her yet, as he found some skin under her nails, bruises to her wrists, and a few scratches and a pressure mark on her neck. Oh, and traces of semen in the vomit around her mouth. Taffy and I notified parents last night. Alice, I want you to go back and see what else you can find out about her. Particularly about those bikers you mentioned. There can't be that many biker groups in Yorkshire, can there? Compo, you check that out.'

Gus sat on his chair, rolling a pencil over his fingers and studied the boards. 'For the time being, we'll consider that Jade Simmonds' death may be separate from that of Sue Downs. Those damn bikers bother me. Comps, check with child sex and grooming crimes. See if they've got owt on bikers.'

He moved along to the third board. 'Lastly, this is Simon Proctor, sixteen years old, missing since Saturday night or the early hours of Sunday morning. He hosted the party, so he may just have split to avoid the trouble. We need him back, to rule out any funny stuff and to get his statement. The uniforms also have photos of him and his parents will do a TV appeal later on today.'

Gus glanced over at Compo. 'See if you can work out how Simon's interlinked with both victims. Friends in common and that sort of stuff. Any cross-over between the three of them – just in case their deaths are linked. Bloody minefield, this.'

He looked round again. 'Have I missed anything?'

Alice, biting the tip of her tongue as she wrote, said, 'Yeah, someone needs to interview this Tayyub bloke with the camera.'

'Yeah, you and I'll do that this afternoon. You go to the school first and I'll do the death call and then re-interview the boys. We'll meet here when you're done. Alice, you hound the labs for the tests on the kids' drug usage and find out what the CSI got from the garden and shed.'

Chapter 29

10:35 The Fort

James Proctor realised that his wife was too keyed-up to remain at The Mansions Hotel for any longer. She'd not slept and as a result, neither had he. She'd refused to eat breakfast and spent her time phoning Simon and his friends on rotation, all the while pacing like a caged animal. The room was stuffy with three of them in it and James wished the FLO would just leave them on their own. Instead, she plonked herself down on the only comfortable chair and babbled a lot of annoying rubbish. He knew it was probably designed to distract them, but it had the unfortunate effect of making him want to tell her to 'shut the fuck up' – words he'd never uttered in his entire life. Aside from that, the woman's perfume was so strong it made his eyes sting and his nose itch.

At last, he'd had enough and insisted they leave the hotel and walk along North Park Road to Lilycroft Police Station. Perhaps the fresh air would do them all good. Even then, he'd had to battle with the FLO who wanted to drive them to the station. Seeing a chance to escape their keeper for a short time, James suggested they walk and she take the car. However, that was not to be, so the three of them had bundled themselves into warm coats and left the hotel. Was it only twelve hours ago that he and Jane had been laughing as they shagged in the car?

For the entire walk, the FLO had dawdled behind, moaning about the cold, reckless drivers and the 'vermin' squirrels that frolicked in the trees in Lister Park. James' nerves were becoming more and more frazzled. He wanted to throttle the woman.

He'd hoped when she got them ensconced in a quiet waiting room, with functional, cushioned chairs and then departed, that they'd have time to recoup. Time to relax, just the two of them, and let their guard down. He was trying to work how he could broach the subject of what they should tell the police about Simon with Jane, when the FLO reappeared. Her cheerful smile irritated the hell out of him and he wanted to open the window and scream out the tension that was building through his body.

Fussing and wittering, she deposited a mismatched duo of mugs on the small coffee table between them, retaining her own mug between her fat fingers. Anticipating that she was about to sit down on one of the empty chairs, James stood up, took her by the elbow and guided her towards the door. 'My wife and I would appreciate some privacy until DI McGuire is ready for us.'

Her face fell as if she'd suffered an enormous slight. 'Oh, I'm supposed to stay with you.' And she settled her enormous backside in the chair right between them.

James looked at Jane who was slumped, her gaze blank, her pallor worrying. Every muscle in his body tensed. Each and every emotion that he'd subdued since the previous evening, began to bubble just beneath the surface of his chest, causing a tightness that threatened to explode in a tirade of uncontrollable grief, anger and frustration. He closed his eyes and attempted to count to ten, knowing that if he let go, *just* for a second, no, even a *nanosecond*, all hell would be deposited on this irritating woman's head.

His skin crawled with nervous energy, an excess of caffeine and lack of sleep. From the depths of his fuzzy eyes, he glowered as she flicked through a magazine. *As if she's at the bloody dentist's.* Each rustling page clawed at his head like chalk on a blackboard, but, oblivious, she continued. Holding his head, he made a dart for the door, still, she managed to get there first, wedging her ample proportions between him and his sanity. A feral cry left his lips and he visualised himself stretching his fingers to breaking point round her flabby throat and throttling her. When the door opened, and DI McGuire walked in, he sagged against the wall, breathing in fast pants, his chest tight, his heart racing.

* * *

As soon as he entered the room, Gus saw three things. The first was that James Proctor was having a panic attack. The second was that, apart from fear, on the man's face, there was an almost feral expression that was directed towards the FLO. The third was that Jane Proctor was disassociated from the former two. Gus wished he'd paid more attention to his misgivings the previous evening. This FLO was a mismatch for the Proctor parents. Instead of soothing the proceedings, making things easier, she had alienated her wards and that was no good.

'I've got it. Just leave.' Gus directed his words to the FLO and held the door open for her to leave, his lips tight, and his eyes boring into her. Her cheeks flushed as she stood and, without looking at either of her charges, left the room.

Gus shut the door and went to direct James to a chair. No stranger to panic attacks himself, he spoke in calm tones and began to breathe, slow and easy, synchronising his own breaths with James', conscious all the time that Jane hadn't reacted at all. Once James' breathing had normalised, Gus moved to the seat opposite the couple. 'Feeling a bit stir-crazy? Can't say I blame you.' He jerked his head toward the door. 'She's a bit too cheery for my liking, too. I'll call her off, if you like.'

James gave a single barking laugh. 'God, please do, before I strangle her. We don't need minding. We just need to do *something*. It's the sitting around doing nothing that's killing us.' He leaned across and took his wife's lifeless hand in his and squeezed.

At last Jane re-engaged. She blinked a few times, looked down at their entwined hands and then placed her other hand on top of her husband's. 'That awful woman gone now, James?'

Gus released a silent sigh. *Thank God. Thought I'd have to call a doctor in.*

With a slight smile, her husband concurred. 'Yes, she's gone. We need to talk to Detective McGuire now, Jane. Can you focus for a bit?'

Jane looked at Gus and then straightened. Despite her bloodshot eyes there was an alertness about her. She leaned over and picked up a bag that lay at her feet. From it she took out a carrier bag and unwrapped an A4 sized picture frame. For a moment she held it in both hands and looked at it before raising two fingers to her lips, kissing them once and then pressing them to the glass. Without uttering a word, she handed the photograph to Gus.

Gus took it. The glass was broken and the frame was sticky to touch. Jane Proctor must have taken it from the bombsite on Sunday night. He couldn't blame her. Gus had already seen pictures of Simon Proctor, however this one seemed special to her. It was also recent and would be excellent for media usage. In it, Simon was standing with his dad, a football under one arm. He was laughing right into the camera, head thrown back, even teeth glinting in the sunlight. He looked happy and carefree. His dad was also grinning and had his arm round his Simon's shoulder. Presumably, Jane Proctor had taken the photo. Simon stood, just an inch or two shorter than James. A faint fuzz of designer stubble stood out on the boy's chin. His hair, the colour of mahogany, was short at the sides and a bit longer on top. The acne that so plagued his friend Matty was absent from Simon's skin. He was a good looking young man. Gus hoped he wasn't also a dead one.

'Tell me a little bit about Simon. We know he was friends with Jake and Matty, but what about his interests?'

A slight smile on her lips, Jane brushed her hair back from her face. It looked like she hadn't brushed it this morning and she seemed oblivious to the stain on the front of her shirt. Gus made a mental note to get an officer to get them some basic supplies. They only had the contents of their weekend bags and they wouldn't go far.

'Simon's a good lad. He enjoys his football. He was on the school team for a while. He plays rugby too, although that's only recent. He had a growth spurt when he hit puberty, until then he'd been small for his age. Afterwards he played the odd game of rugby; football was his passion, though. Other than that, more often than not he had his head stuck in front of that computer of his or mixing tracks on his laptop. Fancied himself a bit of a "Naughty Boy".'

Gus frowned and Jane laughed. 'Naughty Boy's a DJ and record producer. He's quite famous. Simon wants to do IT at uni. Sees himself as the next Mark Zuckerberg or, failing that, Simon Cowell.'

Gus had seen the computer set up in the lad's room, yet until he saw Compo's face light up when it was delivered to the incident room, he hadn't realised just how sophisticated it was. Maybe the lad would see his dream come true if Gus could find him in time.

'DCI Chalmers has arranged for you to do a television appeal, if you're up to it? You can either write your own statement or we can do it together. It's just a simple straightforward appeal for Simon to come home and for anyone who's seen him to contact us. I'll get someone to come in when we're done here.'

Gus noticed that the prospect of being proactive had removed some of the tension from their faces. He wished he didn't have to venture into the area he was about to. However, time was of the essence and he needed as much information as he could get. For the time being he'd decided to hold back the MILF information. After he had a grip of the overall picture, he'd venture down that avenue, for now though, he was content to explore other areas. 'I've just finished talking to Matty and Jake and some information has come up.'

James Proctor frowned. 'What sort of information?'

'It appears that Simon smokes marijuana on occasion. Did you know that?'

Jane looked at her husband, the anxiety lines reappearing across her forehead. Mr Proctor replied. 'Not for certain, no. I thought a couple of times I could smell it. He denied it.' He shrugged. 'All the young lads seem to do it these days. Long as it didn't affect his studies, I was happy to turn a blind eye.'

'Hmm, it seems that, on Saturday night, he also had possession of some blues, or vallies as they're called.'

Jane Proctor looked puzzled. 'No, no I don't believe it! Simon wouldn't take drugs. Not hard stuff. Where would he even get them?'

As his wife spoke, James Proctor bowed his head. He remained silent, although the hand that wasn't holding his wife's clenched on his thigh until the knuckles whitened.

Gus directed his gaze to him, 'Does it surprise you that Simon may have had possession of drugs, Mr Proctor?'

Mr Proctor glanced at his wife and then shook his head, 'Simon's a good lad. He wouldn't do that sort of thing. I think you've been misinformed.'

Gus continued to observe the other man. The colour on his face darkened and a sheen appeared on his top lip. Gus decided to push a bit more. 'Well, we were hoping maybe you'd have some idea. As yet it's unclear if this was a one-off on Saturday or not.'

Jane sat forward, her new-found animation a stark contrast to her earlier demeanour. 'I'm certain it was a one-off. Simon's a good boy. He'd *never* do anything like this. Are you sure it wasn't Jake or Matty? Matty in particular, he's not as... well... similar to us as Jake is.'

Gus' previous sympathy for the woman faded. He'd no time for snobbery and truth be told, Matty seemed more petrified than guilty. 'According to the other two, Simon was the one who bought the marijuana and the pills. Matty doesn't have access to that sort of money, apparently.' A white lie here and there was sometimes called for and Gus had no qualms if it got results. He was sure Jake would confirm Matty's story in the end.

Jane screwed up her face, 'Who knows where that sort of lad could get money from, DI McGuire. I'm quite sure he could, if he wanted to.'

Mr Proctor laid a hand on his wife's knee, 'Jane, come on now, that's really not fair. Matty's always been very polite and his dad is on his own bringing him and his sister up.'

Jane snorted, 'Well, I'm convinced those two are a bad influence on Simon.'

Gus stood up. 'We'll bear that in mind, Mrs Proctor. Now, are you alright at The Mansions for now? I'm not sure when you'll be free to return home.'

She shuddered, and a tear rolled down her cheek. 'We'll never go back there. I couldn't ever live there again. It's tainted. Our beautiful home is *spoilt* for us now.'

Biting his lip, Gus resisted the temptation to say that the lives of the families of two young innocent girls were forever tainted, not just bloody bricks and mortar and a designer Jacuzzi bath.

'We're moving out of the hotel today,' said James. 'Fortunately, a friend's mother died recently.' he paused and wafted his hand in the air. 'Not fortunate at all. I don't know what I'm saying. Anyway, we'll move into her house this afternoon on a temporary basis. It's on Quarry Street, near the allotments.' He handed Gus a paper with the address and phone number. 'You will let us now if you hear anything, won't you.'

Chapter 30

11:30 Outside The Fort

Fighting with a brolly, torrents of rain trickling down the inside of her loosely fastened coat in the middle of a gale, was not Alice's idea of a relaxing break. Hair sticking to her scalp, fingers slipping on the metal handle and droplets of water trickling down her cleavage, all conspired to make her want to throw a tantrum and flounce back inside the police station.

Adding insult to injury, the sudden appearance of a much sturdier brolly, held aloft by a hand she was all too familiar with, had her cursing under her breath. This was the last person she wanted to set eyes on and certainly *not* when she wasn't at her best. The urge to kick the umbrella's owner in the shin was almost too much for her. *One bloody shag in a weak moment and he thinks he can pounce on me, holding bloody brollies up and no doubt expecting a repeat performance. He'd be damn lucky!*

With remarkable self-control, Alice ignored the momentary relief from the pounding rain and persevered with her own inferior telescopic umbrella. When it finally complied with her frantic button-pressing, it was, by sheer chance, aimed at her unwanted saviour's grinning face. Feeling the recoil of a discharged weapon hitting its target, she made no attempt to hide her smirk.

Alice side-stepped the reporter Jez Hopkins, who, eyes watering, was pressing his nose with gentle fingers. 'Haven't you learned, bigger isn't always better?' Ridiculously pleased with herself, she pulled her coat round her, all annoyance with the rain and her wet condition dissipating. Almost as an afterthought, she turned back, one hand resting lightly on her hip. 'Mind you, in your case I suppose *that* analogy doesn't apply. That's probably why you feel the need to indulge your macho egotism in oversized toys and gadgets.' She turned and continued across the road to The Chaat Café.

However, seconds later, umbrella discarded and jacket streaming with rain, Jez ran past her, spun on his heel and began walking backwards in front of her, hands out in front of him. 'Oh, come on, Alice, give us a chance, will you? I'm not the enemy and I have never used anything you've told me in print. I swear.'

Alice glared at him. 'What the hell are you on about? I've never told you a damn thing, now get out of the way, you idiot. It's pouring down and I want to get indoors.'

She made to dodge round him, but he was too quick and anticipated her move. She tried to side-step him and again he jumped in front of her. Lips set in a thin line, Alice raised her head and glared at him. Then, seeing his usually perfect hair matted to his skull and his pleading expression, she stopped and laughed. He was persistent, she'd give him that. He'd been pursuing her for weeks, now. Ever since in a moment of sheer stupidity, after the thing with Gus' mum, when she'd let her guard, as well as her knickers, down and indulged in an adrenalin releasing shag, he'd hounded her. Not enough to call it stalking… just enough to flatter a girl. He seemed different. Maybe a near-miss with a serial killer had made him grow up a bit. Not that she was prepared to find out. If Gus ever got wind of her 'indiscretion', he'd be less than impressed and her job was worth more to her, than a dalliance with Jez Hopkins, no matter how satisfying said dalliance had been.

Jez frowned and then looked down at himself. 'Okay, okay, I look a mess,' he looked up at her, lips twitching,

'I did get rid of my over-inflated macho ego *and* I ditched my rather large tool.'

She laughed and then sighed. 'One drink, Jez, okay? Just one drink and that's all, so don't be getting any ideas.'

Linking his arm through hers, he dodged under her brolly. Alice hoped nobody was watching her and tilted her brolly in a vain attempt to hide from any prying eyes in the station. Just then a large red Vectra passed close to the kerb and a tsunami of mucky water washed over them.

'Fuck... that car's been parked up the entire time I waited for you and *now* he decides to drive off! What was his rush that he couldn't have slowed down through the damn puddle?'

Alice laughed. 'Come on, stop moaning or you'll put a dampener on my lunch break. We need to go somewhere I won't bump into anyone from work.'

'Anybody would think you're ashamed of me.'

Alice looked at him. Was that genuine hurt in his tone or was he just playing her? She'd be careful to make sure she didn't let anything slip about the case.

Chapter 31

11:45 Quarry Street

The house was cramped compared to what they were used to, yet James Proctor found himself appreciating the feeling of being enclosed. It felt safe. When Jane was in the kitchen, he could see her through the arched door separating it from the living room and there was only one double bedroom and a box room upstairs, just big enough for Simon when he came home. James ran his hands through his hair – *if* he came home. What if whoever killed those girls had their boy? What would he be doing to Simon? Was Simon already dead? It was a damn mess and it wasn't as if Simon had had an easy life.

Listening to Jane, pottering in the kitchen, making more tea that either of them would drink, he stood by the living room window and looked out over Heaton Hill. On many occasions when Simon had first joined their family, he'd brought the lad here. He'd taught him how to kick a football, how to hold a cricket bat… and, he hoped, how to trust. Now, in one huge catastrophe, Simon was in jeopardy once more.

It hadn't been easy for them, since the adoption. At first, Simon had been introverted and lacked trust. Not surprising, considering what he'd been through. First abandoned by his birth mother, then shunted through the foster system, never staying in any one placement for long and then all the other stuff too. Too much for one young kid to have to deal with. He and Jane understood he was 'difficult' when they'd taken him on. They'd been told about his history and they'd been prepared to take a chance on the boy. It had been hard. Sometimes near impossible, yet they'd done it.

Simon had been the victim of abuse in two separate foster homes. Then, just as he was about to be taken to safety from the foster parents who had abused him last, tragedy had struck. Poor kid had been hospitalised for weeks and undergone intensive psychiatric treatment for trauma. No wonder he found it hard to connect, to trust.

Over the five years they'd had him, Simon had changed. He loved them. Showed them affection. On occasion he was distant, needing his own space. He and Jane had worked round that – they gave him his space. James turned as his wife walked in carrying an old-fashioned tray with a picture of Salts Mill on it. It was a little strange, using a dead person's things, even though they had no choice. They were homeless and this small contained house was preferable to the anonymity of Lister Mansions. He took the tray from her and guided her to the sofa. She sat resting her hand on the yellowing antimacassars that covered the sofa arms.

'How much should we tell the police about Simon's past, Jane?'

Her startled blue eyes looked up at James and her lips tightened. 'We tell them nothing, James. Not a damn thing.' Her fingers picked the fringe of the antimacassar. 'You know how judgemental people can be. That McGuire thinks he killed those girls and if we tell them about Simon's past, his anger management therapy, he'll be an easy target.'

James agreed with Jane, still, his stomach clenched. The last thing Simon needed was to be blamed for that. He was damned if he'd allow Simon to be held to account for something he was incapable of. James picked up his phone. He'd call DI McGuire three times a day until he brought his son home to him. No way would he let him forget they had a missing lad to find.

Chapter 32

12:05 Bradford Royal Infirmary Mortuary

According to his dad the second PM had been more complicated than the first, although cause of death was finally ascertained to be severe stabbing to the abdomen.

Gus and Taffy were perched on uncomfortable seats in Dr McGuire's cramped office. They'd declined his offer of a wee dram in favour of coffee and Gus was relieved that, in here at least, the mortuary smells were non-existent. Piles of paperwork balanced at an acute angle on his dad's desk among discarded cups and pens. Pride of place, though, was a photo of Gus, Katie and their mum in their garden. His parents' dogs lay at their feet. Katie's long legs were stretched over their mum's knees and Gus hung over her shoulder. All three had stuck their tongues out. He remembered the day well. He'd been around sixteen, around the same age as the Proctor boy... and the two girls whose autopsies his dad was about to tell them about.

Cup of black coffee in his hand, Gus was ready to hear a summary of his dad's findings. 'Go on then, Dad, let's hear it in English. Tell me about Sue Downs' death.'

Fergus cleared his throat. 'I measured the depth and length of the wounds and looked for any unique markings that would offer a clue to the weapon. I also sent off the nail scrapings and so on for testing, to ascertain which, if any, drugs were in the wee lassie's system. I'm still awaiting results from the lab. The most surprising finding was that she was around four months pregnant at the time of her death.'

That was a turn-up for the books. Perhaps her being pregnant was a contributing factor in her death? Maybe one of the lads at the party was the dad. That would be the first thing they'd check out. Not that he was looking forward to telling her parents their dead fifteen-year-old daughter had been pregnant.

'She was a healthy teenager between fourteen and eighteen years of age. Cause of death was repeated stab wounds to the abdomen as she was lying on the bed. Lividity shows she was killed more or less *in situ*, although someone, presumably the killer, positioned her body in a star shape. We already knew she'd had sex prior tae her death, as evidenced by the presence of lubricant consistent with condom usage in and around the vaginal area.'

He paused and patted his jacket pockets absently. Gus continued to sip his coffee, savouring the warm deep flavours. He knew that his dad would give a detailed summary, so he had no desire to rush him. Experience had proven that rushing him only slowed everything down.

Fergus, finally finding what he was looking for, shoved a cigar in his mouth, although in adherence to the smoking laws refrained from lighting it. He sat back and crossed his legs. 'I think the sex was consensual. Nothing to say otherwise, anyway. We'll send both a sample of foetal tissue and the hankie found at the crime scene off for DNA testing. That's no' tae say that the man who she had sex with killed her, or for that matter that he's the father of the bairn.' He frowned. 'Disnae even mean that the father of the bairn was the killer.' he puffed out his cheeks and shook his head like a fat chicken disappointed to find she's flattened her eggs.

'Might be an idea tae get a swab from the father of the house... Proctor, was it? Might have been his tissue stuffed down the back of the bed, post coital with his wife, I suppose. Some of those posh folks can have right mucky habits.

Didnae look that old though, I have to say, but best cross our T's.' He tilted his large head to one side and scrunched his mouth, making the cigar bob up and down as he did so, 'Unlikely, really, I suspect, bearing in mind how tidy the bedroom was. You never ken, do ye?'

He sighed and shook his head sadly before continuing, 'The knife was a common kitchen knife. No unusual striations. No shorter than four inches long and an inch and a half wide. The cuts themselves were purposeful with nae hesitation marks, although I would say *not* frenzied. "Frenzied" implies out of control and, though there were twelve cuts, each appeared quite purposefully administered. Not a queasy person, I'd guess. They weren't particularly angled at any major body organ from what I could tell – just the abdomen – maybe the womb?' He shrugged. 'Who knows?'

'Might it have been a woman, Dr McGuire?' Taffy sat on the edge of his seat like he was determined to be top of the class. Gus tutted and shook his head. If he didn't like the lad so much he'd be well pissed off with his being a bloody Goody Twoshoes.

'Aye, laddie. It could've been. Or a teenager – male or female. I'm not really narrowing the suspect pool for you.'

In full swing now, Taffy jotted a note in his book, 'Not an amateur then; perhaps not their first crime?'

'Well, I don't know about that. Does purposeful, with no hesitation, indicate experience or just a cool head, Taffy? You're the detectives. You work it out.'

Taffy scribbled again.

What the hell? Does the lad have the memory of a slug or something? Can't he remember a few bits and bobs? Gus wanted to crack on and he knew his dad would happily answer inconsequential question after inconsequential question. He cleared his throat and sent a warning look in Taffy's direction.

Taffy bit his lip sank back in his chair as Dr McGuire continued.

'The other victim, the lass we identified on sight as Jade Simmonds, was sixteen years old. She died of asphyxiation after choking on her own vomit. Again, a healthy lassie, who's now deid.'

Gus crushed his plastic coffee cup in his hands. 'Would you say it was an accident, then?'

Doc McGuire tilted his head to the side, and then shook his head. 'I can't say for certain yet, Angus. I'd like to get the DNA results back on her nail scrapings. Feels a bit off to me, particularly with those few scratches at her neck and the bruising I found on her wrists. I can't sign off on her yet. Parents can come to ID any time after one. Now, I better get cracking on.'

He stood and plonked a reassuring hand on his son's shoulder. 'I have faith in you super-sleuths to find out what's gone on, meanwhile, I must say cheerio and get on tae my next PM; homeless bloke, drunk on Shipley Glen. Fell into the rocks below. Poor soul! No' a pretty sight.'

Back in the car heading towards The Fort, Taffy tapped his fingers on the steering wheel and frowned. 'Okay, looks like two isolated incidents to me. Jade, I reckon, will end up being accidental death; the other girl was clearly murdered. Mind you, the missing boy's a bit of a worry. Is he another victim or maybe he's responsible for stabbing the girl?'

Whilst pleased to see the young lad using his deductive skills, Gus couldn't help wonder why it had taken him so long to come to the same conclusion he and Alice had drawn even before they'd left the crime scene. Experience, perhaps. At least the lad was analysing and that was a damn good start for a fledgling detective.

Chapter 33

13:30 Nab Wood

'This is the part of this job that I like least.' Gus sat in the car beside Sampson. The rain that bludgeoned the windscreen matched his mood. 'It doesn't get easier. No matter how many you do... So let's just get in there and get it over with.'

He pushed open the car door and waved a hand in greeting to the family liaison officer, notably *not* she of excessive cheeriness and ample proportions, who had pulled up behind them seconds before. At this rate they'd be running out of FLOs. Together, they walked up the path of the ex-council house and knocked on the door. This was a well-tended street, just up from the Cornerstone Project and a nice row of shops, with a play park for kids adjacent. Right now, the park was empty and Gus could see it hadn't fallen foul to graffiti or vandalism like some of the parks he'd seen.

The man who answered was as tall as Gus and double his width. His arms were muscled and the grease under his nails hinted at him being a mechanic or something similar. His face seemed pinched around the lips and his nod was tense when he acknowledged that, indeed, he was Mr Downs.

As soon as he read Gus' warrant card, a muscle started to thrum at his temple and his eyes darted towards the front room, where a woman's voice rang out followed by quick footsteps. 'That you, Sue? You've had us,' The woman stopped when she saw the trio at the door, her hand lifted to her mouth and her face paled.

Gus saw this reaction time and time again; that moment when a hopeful parent became aware that hope had forsaken them. It never got any easier. Mr Downs swallowed hard and then stepped back from the door, waving them through the carpeted hallway into a small, tidy living room. The Downs followed and Gus took the chair opposite the sofa, gesturing for them to sit down together. The FLO made her way into the kitchen with a 'I'll get the kettle on' and Sampson took the other chair, notepad at the ready.

The telly was on mute, a series of disjointed images flitting across the screen. As if irritated by it, Mr Downs grabbed the TV controls from the sofa and flicked it off. Looking round the room, Gus saw photos of the couple before him, and the girl in the morgue. It seemed that Sue Downs was an only child. This always made it seem worse to Gus. Not that he believed that a living child could somehow make up for a dead one; but he wondered if, maybe, the comfort they gained from being a family rather than just a couple could make them stronger. Most couples seemed to fall apart after the death of their only child.

He leaned towards them, but before he had a chance to break the news, Mrs Downs was in tears as if her mother's intuition had prepared her for this moment. Mr Downs wrapped her in his wide capable arms. 'She's gone, hasn't she?'

For a minute Gus was unsure whether he meant gone as in disappeared or gone as in dead, so he hesitated.

'Tell me straight, what happened to my girl? We need to know what happened.'

Wishing he was anywhere else but here, Gus lowered his eyes. It was the only way he could afford them a modicum of privacy in their grief. 'I'm so sorry, Mr and Mrs Downs, Sue was found last night in a house in Cottingley. She'd been stabbed to death.' Experience had told Gus that a direct approach was often the best. Nonetheless, he prepared himself for any of a number of responses, each as tragic and heart-breaking as the rest.

Mrs Downs' crying increased in pitch. Her husband buried his face in her hair and rocked her back and forth wordlessly. After what seemed like hours, but could only have been a minute or so, their sobs subsided. Mr Downs wiped his face with the back of his hand and looked at Gus. 'You got the bastard that done this, then?'

Gus shook his head. 'Not yet, Mr Downs, but we will.'

The big man looked diminished. He appeared to have shrunk, as, with gentle fingers, he wiped his wife's tears away. 'What was she doing in Cottingley? She told us she was staying at Maggie's on Saturday night, and when she wasn't back by nine last night, we phoned Maggie and she said she'd not seen her all weekend.'

He wiped his nose again. Mrs Downs clasped and unclasped her hands in front of her. When she spoke her voice shook. 'Why would she lie to us?'

Gus shook his head before clearing his throat. 'I have to ask this, Mr and Mrs Downs, and I appreciate it's hard, though I really need to know. Did Sue have a boyfriend?'

It was Mrs Downs who answered. 'No, she didn't. She was too busy with her sports to be bothered with boys.' She frowned and lifted her gaze. 'Are you telling us our baby was molested?'

Gus bit his lip. 'Look, Mrs Downs, there's no easy way to hear this. Sue had, what we believe to be, consensual sex just prior to her death.'

Mrs Downs shook her head violently from side to side. 'Consensual? No, never, she's only fifteen, she must have been raped.'

'That's not all, Mrs. Downs. The pathologist discovered that Sue was around fourteen weeks pregnant.'

Mr Downs paled. 'No, no, you're mistaken, she was only a girl.'

Wishing he was anywhere other than right in that room with this poor couple, Gus shook his head, 'I'm sorry, so very, very sorry.'

Chapter 34

14:35 The Fort

Gus got Sampson to drop him off at the top of Scotchman Road, saying he'd catch up with him at The Fort in thirty minutes. So far, the day had been pretty full-on, and after devastating his second set of parents in as many days, he'd been wired and on edge. Experience told him that if he didn't work off some of the excess adrenalin surging through him, then he'd be functioning below par for the rest of the day. He couldn't afford to be less that one hundred percent, not in the middle of a big case. His leg had stiffened up too, again the result of too much forced inactivity. A brisk jog down Scotchman Road, in lieu of a warm-up, followed by two laps of Lister Park and a swift run up to The Fort would do the trick. Slipping into a pair of joggers and his old trainers, Gus got out of the car and waved Sampson off.

The rain felt cool on his face as he jogged past the Scotchman Road allotments. They were deserted apart from one old man in a raincoat, pottering about near one of the sheds. It seemed the owners were battening down for winter. Cars lined the streets and crowds of adults surging towards each of the two primary schools, told Gus it was nearly home-time. It seemed to Gus that schools were starting earlier and earlier in the morning and finishing earlier in the afternoon, too. Patti had told him it was so they could fit in more of the administration side of the things required by the government.

The Polish shop at the end of the road catered to the changing community in this part of Bradford and, as Gus ran past, he waved to the smokers who hung about in the makeshift centre opposite the gym. It never failed to amuse him that half the shelter's occupants wore Lycra and trainers.

By the time he got to the ornate gates that marked the side entrance to Lister Park, Gus was beginning to regret his decision to run. Rain now pounded like hailstones against his face and by the looks of the dark clouds that hung low in the sky, it wasn't about to stop anytime soon. Increasing his speed, he ran around the park, feeling his leg muscles straining as he did so. He may well suffer for it later, but right then it felt good to be exercising.

Cutting short his planned two laps and foregoing his stretching routine, he exited the park at Oak Lane, nipped over to Mo's to grab a bag of samosas for the team and then pelted up the road. By the time he arrived at The Fort, he looked like his dad's proverbial 'drookit craw'. Rain streamed from his dreads into his eyes and his clothes were sodden as he ran up the steps, waved a greeting to Hardeep and headed for a quick shower. *Boy, that was just what I needed!*

Showered, changed and warm, with his batteries recharged, Gus savoured the quiet of the incident room. Alice and Taffy were en route to deliver an appeal to the pupils of City Academy. He hoped Patti wouldn't land him in it with Alice... no, that was stupid. Of course, she wouldn't. Patti was far too discreet to talk about personal things with his sergeant. Alice, however, was not always as circumspect and it was *that* thought that concerned him. He didn't want Al with her size fives marching in and wrecking what was only just beginning to bloom. He grimaced. *What the hell.* If what he had with Patti was worth pursuing, then even Alice's interference wouldn't deter them.

A yelp from Compo's side of the room didn't worry Gus as he was well used to Compo's erratic noises. However, when it was followed almost straight away with, 'Fucking hell, Gus, you gotta see this!' he was on his feet in an instant and striding across the room to peer over Compo's shoulder.

'Set my PC to notify me of any activity around Simon Proctor… and fuck me, look what's just come up!'

The screen was fuzzy, yet Compo's unusual lapse into profanity told him there was something of value on the screen.

'What is it Comps? I can't–'

As he spoke, Compo worked his magic and, the screen became clearer. There was an image of a young lad, huddled under a blanket on what appeared to be a camp bed. Compo pressed some more keys and the image enlarged on the central screen they used to share footage.

Gus stepped away from Compo and arms crossed over his chest looked at the big screen. 'It's Simon Proctor, isn't it? It is him.'

'Yep, looks like him and the site it's come up on is a YouTube channel entitled Simon Proctor. I discovered the channel earlier but there was nothing on it. This just pinged, five minutes ago.'

'So, what are you telling me? Someone's set up a YouTube channel under Simon Proctor's name and is screening this video… Is it live?'

Compo shrugged. 'The time frame says this footage was taken at around eight this morning. Of course, it could be doctored, whoever took it could've manipulated the time. It's not live. It's been uploaded in the last few minutes, but that can be done remotely or even automatically. In terms of the channel, anyone can set up a YouTube channel and give it any name they want. I've got one dedicated to my dance moves. It's got 500 followers.'

Less distracted by the thought that Compo showed off his erratic dancing on a public platform than by the fact that 500 people were foolish enough to want to view it, Gus paused to collect his thoughts.

'Shit, this is in the public domain. Can we pull it before anyone else sees it?'

'Too late, Gus. It's got over 1,000 views already and rising. Whoever posted it tweeted the link from a Twitter account under the name of 'Where's Simon?' The image is a photo of Simon with a 'Where's Wally?' bobble hat and jumper superimposed.'

'Fuck!' Gus' fingers racked his still damp dreads. 'Can you do owt about it, Comps? Link it back to the sicko who's posted this stuff? I'll need to let the Proctors know what's going on. Not that this is any bloody indication of Simon's current state of health. Fuck, Fuck, Fuck.'

'It'll take time. I'll see what I can do. Can't say how much computer knowledge this joker will need till I start unravelling the layers. I'm on it.'

Gus grabbed his coat and headed out for what he expected to be a very uncomfortable chat with the Proctors. They'd just done their TV appeal and it had gone out on the local news channels and radio. Now, he had to tell them their son was incarcerated in what looked like a dank and dark cellar and was alive early this morning – but they had no indication that he was still alive now. Whoever had come up with this sick idea wanted to torment the Proctors, which opened up an entirely different suspect pool. From being a kids' party gone wrong, this had become something far more complicated and infinitely more sinister.

Maybe the party had been coincidental. Maybe kidnapping Simon Proctor was always going to happen with or without the party. Gus snorted. He didn't believe in coincidence. His gut feeling was that two dead girls and a missing lad, regardless of the spanner they'd just been thrown via social media, were linked. Time would tell. Meantime, he was getting heartily sick of talking to desperate parents. At least this time he wasn't making a death call.

Chapter 35

14:45 City Academy

It was as if she was about to be fed to the lions. Alice stood at the podium, heart thudding like an erratic basketball player pounding up the court, and tried to ignore the 600-plus faces that looked up at her. The hall was hot and smelled of boiled cabbage and lemons. Behind her, Taffy, legs crossed and relaxed, sat next to Patti Copley, with a further two uniformed police officers sitting behind them. She didn't think her usual technique of imagining her audience naked was at all appropriate under the circumstances, so she just had to grit her teeth and get on with it.

'You all know why we're here, don't you?'

A whisper of acquiescence breezed through the crowd before they settled into dutiful attention again. Alice smiled in what she hoped was a confident, yet reassuring manner. 'I know this must be very hard for you, some more than others, however, we desperately need your help. Simon Proctor was in Year Eleven at this school and he's missing after the house party on Saturday night. We don't know if he's safe and well or not. We need *your* help to find him.

'Another student, Sue Downs, was murdered at that same party and we need to find out as much as we can about her in order to discover who did this. Sue was in Year Ten. For the rest of today and all day tomorrow these two police officers, PCs Bryant and Bashir, will be here.'

Both officers' smiles were much friendlier than the one Alice had mustered. Looking completely at ease, they raised their hands and waved into the crowd of teenagers. *Why couldn't she have done it like that?*

'You have all been given leave to approach these officers. You can tell them *anything* you know, whether it's a big detail or a small one about whatever happened on Saturday evening.

'If you were at the party and haven't already been interviewed, please come forward. If you've already been interviewed and have something else to contribute, please do so. Thanks for your patience.'

As the pupils slouched out in lines, Alice turned to Patti Copley. 'Really appreciate you letting us do that. You never know, some of them may have some critical info for us.'

With a slight wave of her hand, Patti's lips tightened. 'One of my pupils was murdered and another is missing, it's the least I can do. I only hope you catch whoever has done this soon.'

Alice and Taffy left the hall, smiling at students as they went. She was pleased to see the two uniformed officers interacting with the students. Maybe they'd be lucky and pick up a clue. Meanwhile, much as she longed to quiz Patti about Gus, even she realised that would be inappropriate, so she settled for a firm hand shake and a 'Hope to see you again soon,' before she left.

Chapter 36

16:10 Manningham

The chat with the Proctors had gone about as well as Gus had expected. Jane had dissolved into floods of tears and no matter how much he attempted to make it clear that this in no way indicated that Simon was still alive, she refused to believe it. She insisted on making references to 'when Simon comes home' and 'the future' which alarmed Gus. The more she invested in Simon's safe return and dismissed all other possibilities, the more she wound herself up for a cataclysmic fall, should he be harmed.

Mr Proctor, on the other hand, was full of bluster and admonitions about the lack of progress on the investigation and by the time Gus exited the house his stomach felt like it had been through the wringer.

Now, he headed along Heaton Road to meet Alice at Chatsworth Place. Slipping into the passenger side of her distinctive Mini, he groaned. His muscles ached as he struggled to fit his legs into the confined space. *That'll teach me not to do a proper warm-up and stretch afterwards. Might need to find time to nip down to Sports Direct in Foster Square for a pair of new trainers. Shame, really. I've had those ones for years and they're comfortable.* He shrugged. That was a lie. They were well past it, he just didn't want to take out a second mortgage to get a pair of good ones. A faint whiff of grease told him that Alice had stopped off at McDonald's en route. *God, that girl packed the food away. She is getting as bad as Compo!*

Rolling his shoulders to ease the crick in his neck, Gus filled her in on the YouTube channel and the Proctors' reaction to it.

'Fucking hell, Gus. This is getting more screwed up by the minute.'

Looking out at a young child in bright red wellies being pulled away from a puddle by an older woman. 'Shame things can't be simple, like that.' Gus pointed at the child.

Alice followed his gaze and grinned. 'Used to love jumping in puddles when I was a kid.'

Gus raised a sceptical eyebrow. 'Yeah, when you were a kid? Sure, I saw you doing just that last time it rained when you had those grotesque purple wellies on.'

Alice laughed. 'You're only young once, Gus. You could do with being a bit more light-hearted. Bet Patti Copley would love jumping in puddles.'

Gus shook his head and snorted, getting out of the car. *Not going to reply, it'll only egg her on.*

The perpetual muggy drizzle had darkened the recently blasted sandstone row of terraces, where Tayyub Hussain lived with his half-sister, to a mucky brown. The front back-to-back house stood in a quiet cul-de-sac, secluded from the noisiness of Oak Lane by a side road, a ginnel and a row of trees ready to shake off their autumn browns for the winter. A well-trimmed hedge gave privacy to a tiny square lawn, a small shed, a few shrubs in ceramic plant pots and a menagerie of softly swaying light catchers and wind chimes, which tinkled in welcome as Alice and Gus walked up to the front door. Alice took off her glove, rapped on the door and then gave the letterbox a small clatter for good measure. She grinned at Gus as footsteps approached from inside. Seconds later the door opened a few inches and a petite woman with her hair tied back in a pony tail stared accusingly at them. Gus introduced himself and Alice as they held out their IDs.

'We just want to have a little chat with Tayyub, if he's at home.'

The woman looked first at Gus, then turned her attention to Alice.

'He's not in trouble, is he? Is it something to do with that Simon Proctor's party? Never did trust that lad, but Tayyub thought he was great.'

Gus shook his head. 'Tracey, isn't it? Can we call you Tracey?'

At the girl's nod, Gus continued. 'We just want to chat about the party. We're talking to everyone who was there. Did you know Simon Proctor has gone missing and we found two dead girls in the house?'

Tracey paled. 'I'd heard he was missing. Can't say I'm bothered about him: he wasn't very kind to Tayyub. I didn't know about the girls. Were they murdered?'

Gus shrugged. 'We're not giving out details yet, Tracey. Could you get Tayyub for us?'

'Yes, yes, of course. He's upstairs, but before I call him down, I'd like to have a word with you. Come inside, so I can talk to you about Tayyub.' She led them through to a small living room, with a couch, a chair and a telly in it. A couple of paintings hung on the wall and a vase of fresh flowers was the only ornament on the dresser that stood along the back wall.

'Tayyub's got Asperger's syndrome.'

Gus frowned. 'What's that?'

Tracey sighed. When she spoke, it was almost by rote, as if she'd lost count of the number of times she had to give the same spiel. 'People with Asperger's syndrome are on the autism spectrum. For Tayyub it's fairly mild, however under stress it becomes worse. He sometimes has difficulty in social situations and stuff. He doesn't always understand jokes and can take them quite literally and this can lead to confusion. He's easily frightened and can get distracted by a lot of background noise.

'In fact, when he was younger, he used to curl up in a ball at school and rock back and forth. We eventually worked out that the normal noise of the classroom was distracting him and he couldn't concentrate. Ear defenders made it easier for him to focus on specific things and helped him tune out the background noise.

'He's a really talented photographer and knows anything there is to know about it. I suppose you could say he's compulsive about that – and his PC. He's recently started a small business doing photography and editing and everything. It's slowly picking up. He's got his bedroom all kitted out with his computers and printers and stuff and he's even converted the little cupboard under the stairs into a darkroom – hence my hoover sitting by the front door.'

Alice looked at Gus, who shrugged. 'So, he'll probably be nervous of us, yeah?'

'Definitely.'

'Okay, thanks for telling us. It's useful to know that. Sit in with us: it will make him more comfortable.'

Exhaling, Tracey relaxed visibly. 'I told him it was dodgy to take photos of his friends pissed and stoned but he said he was getting paid for the images and a video and it was all going to be kept confidential anyway.'

Gus and Alice exchanged glances.

'He got paid to take photos on Saturday night?'

'Look, I'll go and get him: it'll take a while because he'll have to shut down all his stuff.'

Five minutes later, Tracey appeared at the bottom of the stairs accompanied by thudding footsteps as a tall boy followed her. She walked into the kitchen and he followed, loping in the unbalanced manner typical of teenagers who've not quite grown to fit their new lanky frame. Tayyub stopped just inside the door, head down, casting nervous glances at the two visitors.

'Come on, Tayyub, sit down. You're not in any trouble but these police officers need to talk to you.'

Tayyub shuffled into the room and grunted an incomprehensible greeting whilst Gus smiled in a friendly manner. 'We need to ask you a few questions about the party at Simon Proctor's house on Saturday night, Tayyub. That okay?'

Tayyub avoided meeting his gaze. Gus took it as acquiescence.

'Okay, for starters, did you invite anyone to the party?'

Tayyub looked puzzled and glanced at Tracey. 'Nope.'

'Did you post any details about the party on your wall on Facebook or mention it to anyone?'

Tayyub shrugged. 'Never posted it on my wall, I spoke about it to Si and Jake and Matty, though.'

He leaned back and took a sip of the tea Tracey had given him, then, with a splash, dunked a biscuit in it. When the sodden biscuit was fully deposited in his mouth he frowned again. This time when he spoke a shower of moist brown cookie crumbs sprayed across the table and his words were indistinct. 'Oh, and The Young Jihadists.'

Gus glanced at Tracey and Alice, before speaking. 'The Young Jihadists?'

Tayyub grabbed another biscuit before replying. 'Yeah, they paid me to film bits of the party for their youth forum.'

Gus struggled to keep the surprise from his face.

'They what?'

'They paid me to film the party for their youth forum. Fifty quid, cash in hand.'

'So, you're telling me that this group wanted you to film Simon Proctor's house party?'

Tayyub glanced up now and frowned. 'Yeah and edit it afterwards, too. Why, have I done something wrong? They said it were only for the youth group. You know educational, like.' Tayyub squirmed on his chair and his eyes darted nervously round the room.

'No, no, you've not done anything wrong. Tell me, Tayyub, who are The Young Jihadists?'

Tayyub sniffed, stopped squirming and took another slurp of his tea. 'Just a youth group from that new mosque off Oak Lane. All gold it is, and green. You know the one with the huge minarets and the loudspeaker that chants all that prayer stuff out.' He laughed. 'Not that it makes any bloody sense with all the static that comes with it. Sometimes it sounds like Darth Vader.' He grinned at Tracey, 'Or, on a really bad day, like our Tracey singing in the bath.'

He ducked as Tracey laughed and cuffed him lightly on the shoulder. 'Cheeky bugger!'

Gus laughed too and winked at Tayyub. 'Do you go to The Young Jihadists group, Tayyub?'

He grinned. 'Nah, they're too bloody mental. Jihad this and jihad that.'

'Mental?'

'Yeah, that's all they go on about, 'our jihad as young Muslims'. Especially that Shamila.' He thought for a minute and then lowered his voice to a whisper, 'And bloody Tariq. Between you and me that's only 'cos he fancies her. Shamila, I mean. Anyway, I ain't really Muslim, am I, Trace?'

Tracey smiled. 'You can be what you want to be, Tayyub. It's up to you. No, you're not really Muslim. You don't go to the mosque or owt.'

'Can't sit still for long enough, can I, Trace?'

'No Tayyub, you can't.' And as she spoke Gus noticed the lads leg bounce up and down and realised that he'd continually fidgeted on his chair the entire time they'd chatted.

He grinned. 'Tell me, Tayyub, did you film a lot of the party?'

He shrugged. 'Most of it, I guess.'

'You reckon you've caught most of the people who were there on film, then?'

Tayyub beamed, his face lighting up. He was clearly at ease speaking about his hobby. 'Probably. Party was boring and I didn't know half the folk there so I just wandered round recording. Kept myself to myself.'

'Do you have all the footage, still?'

'Course I do. I always back up and keep copies. I'm professional.' Stuffing another biscuit in his mouth he pointed upstairs. 'I'll show you, if you like.'

'I would like that, Tayyub. I would like that very much.'

Tayyub grinned and began to disentangle his long limbs from the kitchen table. Gus rested his hand on his arm. 'Hold up, Tayyub. Tell me a bit more about The Young Jihadists.'

Tayyub fell back into his chair and screwed up his face. 'What do you mean?'

'Well, can you give us names and stuff?'

'Oh yeah, I've got all their numbers and that.'

He opened his phone and jotted down a series of names and numbers which he handed to Gus. 'They're the ones I know. Come up and I'll show you my stuff, if you like.'

Walking into Tayyub's bedroom was mind-blowing. In the course of his career Gus had access to many teenagers' bedrooms, however, Tayyub's was like no other. For a start, it was neat and orderly with a single bed in the far corner and computer workstations taking up the remaining wall space. The carpet was criss-crossed with a series of wires, some of which were taped down, which must have made it a devil to hoover. On the workstations themselves was a range of computer equipment and accessories similar to the ones Compo had brought into the incident room

Tayyub, clearly in his element, sat in his computer chair, whilst Tracey brought two folding chairs. 'What do you want to see? The beginning of the party or what? Or maybe the edited version I prepared for the group?'

Gus looked at the monitors and printers in awe before answering. 'Well, Tayyub, let's just start at the beginning and take it from there.'

Tayyub flicked a few switches and pressed play. It soon became clear that Tayyub was extremely skilled at his job. There was no discernible camera shake and he slewed smoothly between scenes to give a comprehensive overview of the area he was recording.

The screen showed the recording to have taken place at 21:00 on Saturday. Tayyub had focussed in on Simon, Jake and Matty, who were engaged in some sort of three-arm linked cheers. In the background the thrum of music could be heard, with frequent bursts of laughter interspersed with shouting. The three boys were flushed and had obviously had a few drinks.

Then, Si posed for Tayyub and began to roll a joint, commentating in a slightly drunken way as he did so. 'First you get the Rizla and then you carefully position the baccy along the centre.' He looked conspiratorially at the camera, 'you get the smoothest smoke that way.'

He then carefully took a small clear cellophane bag from his jeans and carefully dispersed some weed along the baccy. He winked at the camera. 'Now the rolling is the most important part of the joint. It's all in the wrist action.'

A series of guffaws accompanied his words to which he responded, 'Dirty fuckers.'

He then licked the Rizla and sealed the joint before popping one end into his mouth and lighting the other. He inhaled deeply with his eyes closed and then slowly breathed the smoke out.

'Aaah, that hit the spot.'

He passed it onto Jake who repeated the process. Suddenly the music increased in volume and the recording moved through into the dining room where a crowd of young lads watched a girl in stilettos gyrating on top of a shiny dining table. Tayyub focussed in on her feet moving, clearly showing the scratches she was inflicting on the table.

Tayyub pointed at the monitor, 'Mrs Proctor will be mad when she sees that.'

The recording then moved up to the girl's face. She had long blonde hair cascading down her back, and as she danced with her eyes closed, her arms snaked up and tousled her hair in a parody of a porn movie. Miniscule braless breasts jiggled provocatively beneath her thin T-shirt. Her hips encased in skintight jeans swayed sensuously in time to the rhythm.

Then a voice rose above the music. 'Come on, get them off.'

Suddenly, with that one shout, the atmosphere changed from harmless giggling stupidity to testosterone-fuelled demands. Soon, all the boys were cheering, egging her on, jostling with each other for a better view.

'Come on, show us your tits.'

'Let's see your cunt!'

'Fucking whore. Give us a shag.'

Then, as one, the drooling red faced boys began clapping and stamping their feet on the floor and the chant became an insistent rhythmic, *'OFF, OFF, OFF!'*

The girl's dance became more explicit until she kicked her shoes into the crowd and then raising both arms up she crossed them and in a single sweep pulled her T-shirt right off.

'More, More, More!'

She stepped to the edge of the table and raising her arms into a dive position she fell forward onto the eagerly mauling hands of the teenage boys. Suddenly, as if from nowhere, a figure in a dark hoodie pushed a path through the boys and angrily thrust them aside. A glimpse of long dark hair and the unmistakeable swell of breasts were the only indication of the rescuer's sex. She finally reached the giggling, supine girl. Snarling and shoving at the lads who fought half-heartedly through a drink- and drug-fuelled stupor, she hoisted the girl to her feet, covered her with a coat and dragged her unceremoniously from the crowd of drunk jeering boys.

Gus glanced at Alice who glared at the screen speechless with horror.

'Okay, Tayyub, pause it there for now.'

Tayyub obliged, leaving a sea of contorted male faces on the screen.

'Uggh. That was awful. Fucking little turds.'

Gus glanced at Tayyub who had kept his eyes averted the whole time. 'What do you think of that, Tayyub?'

He shrugged. 'Pissed, weren't they? And Mrs Proctor's table's fucked, innit?'

'Who were they, Tayyub? The blonde girl?'

Tayyub frowned. 'Goes to our school. Don't know her name. She's younger than us.'

'What about the other girl, who was she?'

Tayyub shook his head and then shrugged. 'Don't know all the boys, either. I'll write down the names of the few I know.'

'You do that Tayyub. Em, how much more footage have you got of the party?'

'Couple of hours. Maybe a bit more, maybe three. I just wandered round taking it as and when, some of Si and the lads pissing around like, and some other stuff.'

'Any footage of the two biker guys?'

'Yeah, loads of them. They were playing a game with the girls they had with them.' He screwed up his face. 'Doing blow jobs on Mrs Proctor's couch and stuff. I didn't like them.' He shook his head. 'She'll kill Si, when he gets back.'

'Alright, Tayyub.' I think we've seen enough for now. Any chance you can give us all your footage so we can study it at the station. We'll need you to sit down with our computer expert to ID as many people as we can from this.'

Tayyub looked vaguely surprised. 'Well, okay, I suppose so. Does this mean Mrs Proctor is really, really mad about her scratched table?'

Gus opened his mouth to reply and then shut it again. 'Look, Tayyub, the reason we need all this stuff is that two bodies were found at the Proctor's house on Sunday night and Simon has gone missing.'

Tayyub looked at them, his face worried. 'Bodies? You mean dead bodies?'

Gus inclined his head in silent agreement.

'I didn't see no dead bodies, DI McGuire. I'd have told Tracey if I had.'

Gus saw the boy was worried. 'No, no, we know you didn't see any dead bodies, however, maybe you taped some people who might have done it.'

Tayyub relaxed. 'Oh yeah, you're right, I might have. There were some well dodgy gits there on Saturday.'

'Look Tayyub, here's what we'll do. I'll get a police car to pick you and any equipment you need in an hour. It'll take you and Tracey to the station and you can help Compo, our expert, to identify and maybe create mug shots of each person there on Saturday, okay?'

Tayyub began pressing buttons and taking discs out of sleeves.

Chapter 37

16:50 Unknown Location

Must have dozed off again. Nowt else to do in here. Still no sounds from outside. Sometimes I think I can hear traffic. Might be my imagination. Hear those fucking rats though... think they're real. Scampering about. Bet there's spiders too. Big fuckers. Hairy too. Hate spiders, hate rats, hate this fucking smelly dungeon.

'Incy wincy spider... up the fucking spout.'

'AAAAAAAhhhhh! Anybody hear me? Can you fucking hear me? I'm here in a bloody freezing old, smelly old pit!'

Don't know why I bother. No-one's there. The walls are too thick. Brick all the way round. I started to count them earlier. Got to 552, then I lost count. I started at the door, fucking big wooden thing, hinges the size of a tree trunk. At first, I touched each brick as I counted. They were wet – not just a little bit. They were sodden. So, then I stopped touching them and tried to just use my eyes. Made me dizzy though; moving them up and down. If I hadn't found the bottles of water I'd have been tempted to lick them like I've seen on Bear Grylls... then again, maybe not. Maybe it's the rats' piss pouring down the walls. They can give you diseases, can rats. Started the plague... or was that the fleas?

Fucking fleas again. Shut up thinking about fleas.

They're all over the blanket... I'll die of the plague and when the coppers find me they'll have to wear them big bird beak masks. They'll all come in like tossers, flapping their arms. *'... da da da da. La la la la, Fuck la fuck la, fuck la fuck da.'*

Get a grip, Si, get a fucking grip. You're losing it, man!

Must be dark outside by now. I press the light on my watch and it lights up the dial. Nearly five o'clock. Monday night's fish 'n' chips night. *'First day of the week, Simon, we deserve a treat, don't we?'* Would kill for fish and chips. Mushy peas! Curry sauce! Lister Fisheries or Heaton Chip Shop... don't care – either'd do. Bigger portions from Heaton. Heaton it is then.

'Vinegar?'

'Oh, yes, please, don't mind if I do. And ketchup, five sachets please.'

I can smell it. Fish and chips and vinegar. It's right there. If I open my eyes I'll be at the kitchen table– *Oh no, stop it, Si!* Not the table... the girl... the dancing girl, *'Off, off, off off!'* The scratch. Fuck, she'll be angry, will my mum. Loved that fucking table, didn't she? Now it's ruined, scratched!

What time's it now? Ten past. I shake my watch. Maybe it's stopped. Maybe the cold's fucked up the battery. No, the second hand's moving. Wish it were nine o'clock. Why does it have to pass so slow?

'A little bit of da da da da. A little bit of la la la ladi da di dah.'

Chapter 38

17:45 St Anne's Road Mosque, Heaton

Gus drove into the mosque car park on Iqrah Drive, just off Oak Lane, with Alice. It was one of the newer more ornate mosques in Bradford with a golden dome and graceful minarets. The sandstone brick wall that encapsulated the grounds was a creamy yellow, which contrasted with the dingy sandstone of the surrounding terraced houses. It provided a secure parking area and in one corner there was even a small fenced-off playground with swings and a slide. As well as being a place of worship, Iqrah Mosque had community rooms for youth meetings, wedding celebrations and religious festivals – only Muslim festivals. Although forward-thinking, the mosque had yet to open its doors to Bradford's other faith communities.

Prayer time had just ended, so the car park was filled with men of all generations in white kameez and prayer hats. Although some of the older generation sported beards, a few dyed streaky red with henna, the younger generation, in the main, were clean shaven. The upper part of the mosque prayer room was dedicated to women and children and so from the side door flowed a steady stream of women, wearing hijabs or burkas or just loose head scarves, which some removed from their heads on exiting the mosque.

This area of Bradford had mainly Pakistanis from the Mirpur District in Pakistan, meaning that most of the chatter in the car park was in Punjabi, with the occasional flurry of English spoken here and there or the odd word interspersed amid the conversations.

Gus got out of the car, wondering how many of the crowd would recognise him as a police officer, and how many of those would do so because of their own criminal activities. As he glanced around he heard a familiar voice call his name and within seconds he was engulfed in an embrace.

'You've missed prayer time, Gus.'

Laughing, Gus hugged his friend back. 'Ah well, you know me, Mo. Not the most religious of folk. I'd probably be struck down in a ball of fire if I attempted to pray in any one of the many religious establishments Bradford has to offer.'

Mo slapped him on the back, smiling widely and shook his head in overstated disapproval. 'We'll make a believer of you, yet.'

'You've had twenty-odd years to convince me and you've not managed, yet. Can't you just give me up as a bad job?' Before his friend could respond, Gus changed the subject. 'How are Naila and the kids?'

A serene smile spread across Mo's face making him look like a teenager. 'They're great. Girls are wondering when Uncle Gus is due a visit.'

'Tell them, soon. Tell them I miss them and give them each a huge kiss from me.'

Turning to Alice, Mo grinned. 'Good to see you, Alice. He been behaving himself?' Mo waved his hand in Gus' direction, laughing when Alice snorted. 'Humph, him? Behave? Well I'll leave you to work that one out.'

Glancing round the emptying car park, Mo looked at his friend and lowered his voice. 'You here on official business, Gus? Hope there's nothing iffy going on at this mosque. It's been a huge asset to the community and it would be a shame to see its good name tarnished.'

Gus lowered his voice to match. 'It is official business. We're meeting the leaders of a youth group that meet here, The Young Jihadists.'

Mo exhaled a relieved breath. 'That's okay then, they're good kids.'

Gus frowned. 'The name's a bit inflammatory though, isn't it?'

'Yeah, in this climate, it is a bit. Their angle is that they've reclaimed the term 'jihadist'. Speak to them. I'm sure whatever this is about is nothing to do with them. Zarqa sometimes meets with them. As I say, they're nice kids.'

'Look Mo, strictly between us, it's about those two deaths and the missing teenager up in the village. There was a religious message beside one of the bodies and then we found out this jihadist group paid to have the house party recorded.'

Mo frowned and shook his head. 'Recorded? You mean videoed? Well, that's not right good, is it? Wonder why they'd do that?' His brows knitted together as he continued. 'Let me know if we need to be worried, Gus. I could have sworn those kids were okay; but in this climate, it's always hard to be sure.'

'I'll give you the heads-up, Mo, I promise. In fact, I'll pop by yours after to collect a mixed batch of samosas for the briefing. It always pays to keep the troops nourished.'

'The ones you bought earlier finished already.'

'Compo! Scoffed them all before anyone else got a look in.'

'Keeps me in business, does your man Compo. How many do you want?'

Gus shrugged. 'You better make it thirty. They always demolish them like they're going out of business.'

Mo laughed and strode off to his car with a wave.

Gus and Alice walked round the side of the building to the community rooms and after being cleared in by the security guard they were directed along a corridor.

Furnished in the muted pastel colours of most community centres, a faint smell of kebabs and sweet rice lingered in the air. The huge kitchens to the back were presumably catering for a function of some sort; perhaps a wedding or party. Gus' stomach growled. He wished he'd grabbed a samosa before handing the bag to Compo earlier.

As they neared the end of the hallway, a teenage boy and girl popped their heads out of the last door. The boy, dark skinned, with an easy smile and stocky stature, showed a set of even teeth as he extended his hand. 'You must be DI McGuire. I'm Tariq, the chairperson of The Young Jihadists and this is Shamila, the vice-chair, or as we like to say, "the chair of vice".' He wiggled his eyebrows comically, whilst Shamila rolled her eyes and, ignoring his joke, extended her hand. She was a slender girl in jeans and jumper, whose ornate hijab was a work of art. Her handshake was firm and she looked Gus in the eyes as she spoke. 'Ignore Tariq, he's an idiot.'

The security guard had clearly let the kids know they were on their way. Gus introduced Alice before the teenagers led them into a comfortable meeting room with red covered comfy chairs, a small library in the corner and a few computer workstations.

Looking round Gus said, 'Nice space.'

Shamila gestured to a group of chairs round a large table. 'It's great, we're lucky to have such wonderful facilities. Do sit down.'

As Gus and Alice made themselves comfortable, Tariq spoke. 'We've an idea what this is about. It's all over school about Simon Proctor's party and the two bodies and him being missing.' He shook his head. 'It's a terrible business, it really is, and we'll do anything we can to help.'

'That's good to know, Tariq,' said Gus. 'First off, can you tell us a bit about your group and its purpose? The word "jihadist" is quite hot in the current political climate, so we need to clear up just what your group is about.'

Tariq and Shamila exchanged glances, and as if an unspoken agreement had been reached, Shamila spoke. 'DI McGuire, we are British. We were born here and some of our parents were too. We visit Pakistan or Bangladesh, but our *home* is Britain.'

She looked between the two detectives before continuing, her voice serious, her eyes never wavering from their faces. 'Sometimes being Muslim *and* British throws up choices that are difficult to make.' She placed a slender hand on the table, 'For instance, do we stay true to our religious and cultural views or do we blend in with white British society? Do we live in two worlds; one at home and one outside the home, *and* if we do, how do we reconcile the two? These are hard questions for any teenager, but for us it's doubly hard; hence the existence of the group. It's to help young Muslims, like us, to find a path through life as a British Pakistani or Bangladeshi or Indian Muslim and to help *us* make choices based on our *own* experiences, not those of a culture that is sometimes dated and often has no basis on religion.' She thought for a moment and added, 'The experiences of our elders were so different from ours.'

Gus could see what she was talking about. When he and Mo had grown up together, things had been very different. 9/11 hadn't happened until they were in their late teens, and on the whole, although he and Mo were from very different backgrounds, they had rubbed along nicely together. Things were very different for these kids and he sympathised with them. It was great to see such mature and responsible teenagers. He hoped they were what they seemed on the face of it. It wouldn't be the first time teenagers presented as normal, law-abiding citizens, only to perpetrate some awful act at a later date.

Shamila stopped for a breath and Gus took advantage of the gap to ask a question. 'Why jihadists? A term usually associated with Muslim terrorism.'

Tariq leaned forward then, his face intense. 'That's just it. *They* – Daesh, Boko Haram, Al-Qaeda and the rest have no right to call themselves jihadists. In Islam, the jihad is a *personal* struggle to overcome and surmount your own doubts or weaknesses. It is *not* carte blanche to annihilate people who do not share your religious beliefs. *We* chose the name because *we* are jihadists in the purest form of the word. We are young Muslims trying to live Islamically in a non-Islamic country. Daily, we face challenges from within our faith in the form of ignorance and outdated cultural practices as well as from the temptations of Western society in the form of drugs, alcohol and free sex, et cetera.'

Shamila pushed a loose strand of dark hair under her hijab and took over. 'We are educated and we are well aware of the problems within our own community that most of us want to turn a blind eye to. We don't. We want to address the fact that much of the weed that circulates in Bradford is supplied from within this community. We want to prevent our generation of Muslim boys from using prostitutes, like some of our elders do, and from looking down on the choices that Western non-Muslims make and disrespecting people on the basis of their individual choices. We want to find a balance. That's what *our* jihad is.'

Gus crossed his legs and thought for a minute. He could think of a few politicians who could benefit from this analytical approach. 'Okay, so your jihad as young British Muslims is to weave a path through life in a cosmopolitan country. Am I right?'

Both Shamila and Tariq bobbed their heads up and down like those annoying dashboard dogs.

Alice shifted in her chair and leaned across the table. 'You've got all the right rhetoric and no doubt you think that you've got God on your side, however, it could all be a big cover-up, couldn't it?'

Gus repressed a smile. Alice was nothing if not direct. She wanted to get to the bottom of this and her tenacity would ensure she did. Besides, if Zarqa was involved with this group, Gus needed to make sure they were legit.

The slight smile faded from Shamila's face, and Tariq, eyes wide, stared at Alice. Shamila glanced at Gus, as he leaned back in his chair, folded his arms and waited. Alice narrowed her eyes. 'Thing is, we're living in a world where the word "jihad" has an altogether more threatening meaning than what you've just outlined. We'd be foolish to take you at your word. Why should we? Radicalisation is a real problem among teenagers and we've got a job to do. Not only are we keen to or find out what you know about Simon Proctor's party, we also need to discount your involvement – and that's before we even look at the possible radicalisation issue. This is all about politics, isn't it?'

Shamila pushed back her chair and glared at Alice. 'No, it's not about politics! Not directly anyway. It's about identity and modesty and personal choices and living fruitful lives in *our* country.'

Alice tapped her long fingers impatiently on the table. 'Yeah, is that right? Then, why did you pay Tayyub Hussain to video the party at Simon Proctor's?'

Shamila sat down and shifted uncomfortably in her seat.

Glancing between the two women, Tariq, pushed his hair back from his forehead before he spoke. Gus noticed that he'd softened his voice which lessened the tension in the room. 'That was her idea.' He gestured towards Shamila and grinned. 'Told you she was the chair of vice.' When he got no response from either woman, he continued, 'She had this bright idea that in order to work our way through some of the issues we face, we should have first-hand experience of it... well as near to first-hand as we could get. We knew Si was having his party, and although we were invited, it didn't seem like a good idea. So, Shamila asked Tayyub to record the party and edit it to illustrate how people behave when they're drunk or stoned and out of control. We were going to use it at Friday's meeting as an educational discussion point.'

Alice scowled. 'Didn't you think people might object to you showing them drunk or stoned in a video? Isn't it an infringement of their civil liberties?'

Shamila looked down at the table and Tariq looked abashed. 'We asked Tayyub to fuzz out the faces.'

'Hmm, well. You won't be getting your tape for your discussion group. A word of advice: next time you want to do that, use the telly as a resource. All the soaps have examples of free sex, booze, drugs, dealing drugs and the rest. Now, you'll have to come down to that station to make a statement.'

Gus stood up and leaned over them forcing them to look up at him. 'We *will* be keeping an eye on your group and we *will* consult with other departments to ensure your status as a youth group remains as innocent as you claim.'

Shamila looked up, wide eyed. 'Are we in real trouble? Will I get a record? I want to go to uni and I won't get in if I have a record.'

Alice grimaced. 'No, you won't get a record if you're telling the truth, but do yourself a favour and think stuff through before you act.'

Gus, feeling they'd made their point *and* frightened the hell out of the kids in the process, decided to bring the tension levels back down. 'Look, your group sounds like a good idea. Kicking ideas around with your peers is a productive thing to do. Truth is, if circumstances had been different and Simon Proctor's party had gone off as planned, we wouldn't be here. You're not in trouble... yet, although we'll need your statement and we *will* be investigating your group. So if there's anything any of your members need to tell us, it would be better for them to come to us rather than let us find out ourselves.'

Shamila and Tariq began to get up. Gus shook his head and rummaged through a folder. 'Before we go, look at these photos. Do you recognise any of them?'

The teenagers leaned over and studied the photos. 'Are those the dead girls?'

'Yeah, do you know them?'

Shamila, face pale, shook her head and looked away. Gus looked at Tariq. Tariq met his eyes, glanced down at the photos again and shook his head.

Gus frowned at the boy.

'You sure?'

Tariq's smile was forced as he gave a single nod.

Gus moved away from the table. 'Okay, a full list of your members and a statement before the end of today, okay? Now Tariq, come and show us out of this maze, please.'

Tariq guided them back through the corridors to the car park. When they were outside, Gus turned to the lad. 'Right then, young Tariq, who's the girl in the photo and why were you so reluctant to ID her in front of Shamila? Is she a girlfriend or something?'

Tariq shoved his hands in his pockets and looked at the floor. 'Course she's not.'

'You did recognise her?'

A shrug.

Gus sighed. 'Look, she's dead, Tariq. Tell us what you know, for God's sake.'

Tariq shuffled his feet and shrugged again. 'Don't know her name, okay? I've seen her around though.'

'Around where? Who with?'

He sighed and thrust his fingers through his hair. 'Fuck's sake, this is shit.' He kicked the wall, then turned to Gus. 'I've seen her with Adnan, okay? She was his girlfriend!'

'Who's Adnan and where will we find him?'

Tariq kicked the wall again. 'Adnan is Shamila's brother, in't he? You'll find him at her address, okay? Now, have you got enough?'

Gus patted him on the shoulder briefly before following Alice to the car. When they got in he turned in his seat to face her. 'What do you reckon, Al?'

'They're just kids trying to make a difference. Tariq fancies his chances with Shamila. Shamila likes him but needs to loosen up a bit... oh, and we need to get anti-terrorism to check the group out, just in case. Not that I think they'll throw anything up.'

That was almost word-for-word what Gus' thoughts were. A bunch of kids trying to figure out who they were. Put his, Mo's and Greg's teenage efforts to shame. They'd been more interested in girls and smoking behind the bike sheds than trying to better their lives. How times change!

Chapter 39

20:45 Marriners Drive

Gus leaned back and took a long swig of lager straight from the bottle. Alice took a more desultory sip of Zinfandel. They were sitting in his living room, having been exiled from the incident room by Compo, who was getting fed up with them asking if he'd got any further in narrowing down the source of the YouTube video. Whilst Taffy and Sampson had opted for a pint in The King's Arms, Gus wanted to get back home for Bingo and Alice was happy to accompany him. He'd lit the stove as soon as they got in and the room was toasty. The arresting painting of Bob Marley with serpent dreads, that his dead friend Greg had painted, was illuminated by strategic lighting and hung in centre stage on the chimney breast. Gus had positioned the couch so it had the best view of the painting, and now he and Bingo were flopped on it, with Alice curled up in a chair opposite. 'One hell of a day, huh, Alice?'

'Well...' Alice counted off on her fingers. 'You survived not one but two PMs, and also notified both sets of parents of their children's deaths. Had two 'chats' with the Proctors, one of which was to inform them that their son's abductor had posted footage of the lad in a dank cell. However, look on the bright side. We've witnessed the two extremes of teenagers "playing out" with the vile footage Tayyub took, which contrasts with The Young Jihadists trying to make sense of their world. Basically, today has been a steep learning curve.'

Gus absent-mindedly stroked Bingo, who was burrowed against his left, nose resting on his knee. 'Yeah, though we're not a lot further forward with finding the missing boy, the bikers or Sue Downs' killer. Not sure we should have held off for the foetal DNA, you know. Maybe we should have grabbed Adnan tonight.'

'We'll get more from the lad if we have the full picture. He's not got a criminal history, is well behaved and, like his sister, won a bursary for Bradford Grammar School. He's a low-flight risk. Besides, you've got uniforms keeping an eye on him for now.'

'You're right, Al. We need to make sure we've got everything lined up. Not sure a night in a cell for a fifteen-year-old lad is a great idea. We've only got one witness who has identified Adnan as going out with the dead girl, after all. Don't want to be too heavy-handed at this stage. You'd think if there was substance to Tariq's claims, that other kids would have come forward with the same info.' Scratching Bingo's ears, he grinned when the dog stuck out his tongue and licked his wrist before succumbing to more scratching with a wag of his tail. 'Knowing our luck, the press will be all over us like fucking maggots on a dead donkey, now the second girl has been identified. That Jez Hopkins is the biggest maggot of all and he'd better steer well clear of me. Still not forgiven him for sneaking into the hospital to get an interview with my mum when she'd barely recovered from her ordeal. Insensitive little toe-rag!'

Alice choked and with tears streaming down her face, placed her glass on the table. Bingo jumped up and ran whimpering to the coughing girl. Gus leaned over and walloped her twice on the back, making her gasp for air. 'You alright, Al?'

Despite her paroxysm, she glared at him. 'Ouch, that bloody hurt, Gus!'

Sitting back down, Gus took another swallow of lager to empty the bottle and placed it on the coffee table.

'Was only trying to help. Thought you were going to choke to death and I can't lose a member of my team. Not on this damn case.'

Wiping her eyes, Alice, her voice all mock innocence, said, 'Patti was asking after you today.'

Gus's cheeks grew warm and he feigned confusion. 'Patti?'

Alice burst out laughing. 'Don't *'Patti?'* me, Angus McGuire. You know damn well who I mean. Hell, even your ears have gone all red. Gus and Patti up a tree K.I.S.S.I.N.G.'

'What are you? Ten? Grow the fuck up!' and he walked through to the kitchen to grab another beer from the fridge with her laughter ringing in his ears.

Chapter 40

21:25 Marriners Drive

Knowles threw his still lit cigarette end out the car window and watched it sail down to land in a puddle where a quiet hiss extinguished it. The steamy whirls from his coffee were more a testament to how cold it was in his car than to how warm the coffee was. Nonetheless, he drank it. After all he'd bugger all else to do whilst he waited for Alice to come out. He wasn't entirely sure why he was following Cooper. He wasn't stalking her – just wanted to keep an eye on her. She'd humiliated him and he wasn't going to take that lying down. He needed to find something incriminating to bring her down and if Jerry couldn't come up with anything, then he'd have to do it himself. He was determined to bring that little whore to the ground with a huge, well-orchestrated bang. No more than she deserved! He rubbed his fingers over his still tender cheek.

A vibration near his thigh made him smile. *Probably Jerry-old-mate with more ammunition for me to use.* 'Yeah.'

There was a second's delay before Jerry spoke. 'It's me. Couldn't get the actual report; however, I managed to find a loose-lipped DC in the same unit. Apparently, there were doubts about her suitability to be employed in tense or stressful situations where her life or that of a fellow officer could be at stake. In other words, she should be pen-pushing not taking up a DS position in a special unit.'

'She must have got the all-clear in the end, though?'

'The DC I spoke to hinted that they'd got rid of her 'cause she was a wreck. Couldn't trust her judgement. Felt she wasn't reliable. Were happy to send her up to the "Northern Powerhouse".'

'So, it was Brent's choice to get rid of her, not her choice to move to Bradford?'

'Seems like it.'

'Okay, mate, thanks.'

Humming tunelessly, he pushed the phone back into his pocket. Bloody bitch was full of it right now. Wonder if any of her colleagues know just how much of a liability she was? He reckoned not. Well, he'd be happy to spread the word. In fact, he'd get on with that first thing in the morning. He knew a few loose-lipped coppers that'd soon get things moving. Cooper wouldn't know what had hit her when the rumour mill got working.

He grinned, seeing her earlier on with Jez Hopkins had been a stroke of luck. He'd made sure to capitalise on her indiscretion by giving Hopkins some inside gen on the dead girls and the missing lad – anonymous of course. He was no damn fool!

TUESDAY

Chapter 41

03:25 Unknown Location

Been dreaming! Dreaming about being found... Detectives slamming their way through the metal doors, guns drawn, flashlights piercing the darkness, bobbing round my cell, clearing the room, like the FBI. Christ, my heart's hammering, can feel where my nails have dug right into my palms. Images of the parents weeping, faces contorted reaching out to me. Can almost smell mum's floral perfume and the faint tang of dad's sweat, like when he first comes home from work, before he's had his shower. I like those odd wafts when he hugs me... got used to it over the years. Different from before when all I got were a thick ear... or worse! Wonder if I'll see them again?

What the fuck's that noise, though? Feel groggy as hell. What the fuck is it? I force my eyes open and strain my ears. Where's it coming from? Not the rats. No, definitely not the rats. Fully awake now, I shrug the cover off, and struggle into a sitting position on the camp bed. Feel woozy again, must be the mildew... either that or the drugs. Noise is louder now. Can't quite place it.

I reach down, fingers stretched wide and pat around on the floor for the torch. I find my trainers, first one then the other. Picking them up, I pull them onto my knee and keep feeling for the torch. Must've put the lamp off last night, 'cos it's really dark. Can hardly see owt. Just them creepy shadows again... and the camera light. It's gone green again. I look right at it and glare. Wonder if it caught my dream. Bet I looked like a right pillock. Hope I wasn't too much like a fucking pussy.

Don't want my fans see me being a wuss. Gone off again now, anyway. Nowt I can do about it. I feel calm now. Not like before. When I were bricking it. Maybe it *is* the drugs.

Fucking racket, though. Wish it'd stop. Giving me a damn headache on top of the one I've already got. It's like a whimpering child punctuated by the occasional dull thud. At last, the torch! I put my hand in front of the lens to dull the light, switch it on and point it towards the noise. At once it goes silent.

I study the bundle in the shadow on the floor in the middle of the room… a girl, half covered by an old blanket, lying on her stomach. *How long has she been here?*

She's blindfolded and gagged. As if sensing me looking at her, she turns her head and tries to lift it from the floor. Her cracked lips carry a bluish tinge. Blood soaks the dirty rag that strains between her teeth, stretching her mouth open in a gargoyle's grimace, face bruised, one cheek swollen. From beneath the blindfold a single tear rolls, making the dirt on her face streak.

At first, I don't know what to do. At least she's not dead… not like the others. She's one lucky cow!

I shimmy over her and grip the edge of the blanket. It's damp against my fingers. In one swift movement, I yank it off, recoiling as a pissy whiff hits my nose. *What the fuck? Has she pissed herself?*

She's grunting and groaning and trying to struggle. *Probably scared shitless!* Not that she can move much because she's hog tied. I reach out one hand and rest it on her forehead. It's clammy despite the penetrating cold and she struggles more, shivering and moaning. I'm scared to speak, so I focus on trying to untie her ankles. Stupid, fat, frozen fingers won't move. I'm fumbling, drawing more blood as she struggles against me. *Fucking stay still, will you? Can't untie you if you're moving about like a jellyfish on speed.*

Chapter 42

07:25 The Fort

Alice glanced at her watch as she scurried over the road, thankful for the red light that had stopped the traffic. The Chaat Café wasn't officially open so early in the morning, but Ken, the chef, always made an exception for Alice. Waiting for her usual pain au chocolat and steamy full fat cappuccino to go, she nabbed Ken's newspaper and flicked it open at the front page.

'Oh fuck!' Her eyes skimmed the page – although the headlines had told her everything she needed to know.

Ken glanced over from the frothing machine. 'Alright there, Alice, love?'

She glowered and shook her head, 'Actually, not so good, Ken. There's a shitload of trouble waiting to fall and I've got a horrible feeling, some, if not all of it, is going to land on my head.' Ken studied her woebegone face, popped an extra pain au chocolat into the paper bag and said, 'There you go, that'll cheer you up.'

Wishing wholeheartedly that he was right, Alice, balancing her bag and coffee in front of her, retraced her steps and made her way across Lilycroft Road to The Fort. This was *not* how she'd anticipated her day panning out. She'd wakened that morning feeling positive that things would move forward on the case.

Now she was cursing her meeting with Jez Hopkins the previous day. *Why had she let her guard down with him yesterday? Just because he'd looked cute with rain pouring down his face and his hair plastered to his forehead? She'd been taken in.*

Not that they'd spoken about the case – she'd made certain he knew not to go there, yet it seemed someone had been talking and now it would look like it was her. She could only hope no-one had seen them together.

Dragging her feet, Alice took the stairs for once, barely ignoring Hardeep's cheery greeting as she entered the station. Pushing the door to the incident room open, she sighed. Thank God, Gus wasn't there yet. Keeping her head down, she ignored Sampson and Compo's greetings and hurried over to her desk, hoping that when the shit fell, it would offer her a modicum of protection from Gus' wrath.

She'd barely settled herself when Gus strode purposefully through the door, hair bouncing like a mane round his head. Without breaking stride, he walked to the middle of the room and flung a pile of newspapers onto the table with a resounding thud.

A prickle raced up Alice's back. It was horrible when Gus was in a bad mood and she couldn't shake the guilt that clenched like a febrile crab in her stomach. She really had to get a grip. It wasn't as if she'd done anything wrong. It wasn't her who'd leaked the stuff to Jez Hopkins. She only hoped Gus would believe her.

'What the fuck is this?' He picked up the top paper and threw it to Sampson. The next one landed unceremoniously on Alice's desk, while another one flew over her head to land on the floor beside Compo. A further paper landed just short of Taffy's desk and finally Gus stood holding *The Chronicle* up in front of him so they could all read the headlines. His finger stabbed accusingly at the by-line.

'See this? It says *Jez Hopkins*.'

He shook the paper and then stabbed his finger at a piece of writing halfway down the first paragraph. 'And see this? It fucking well says, and I quote, "A source close to the investigation admits they are no further forward in solving either the murder of Sue Downs, Jade Simmonds or the disappearance of Simon Proctor."' He glared round at them, blue eyes clouded dark, a ferocious lion berating his pride.

He flung the paper down, marched over to his own desk and flung himself onto his chair. A heavy nervousness hung over the room as Gus flicked rapidly through some notes on his desk. Pausing at one, he ripped it from the pile, thrust it in his pocket and stalked back to the front of the room. Everyone kept their heads down, supposedly reading the papers he'd thrown at them. His entire body tense, Gus prowled back and forth across the front of the room, waiting till they'd finished reading. When the last person had placed their newspaper down in front of him, and all eyes were directed at him, he scowled round at them.

'Right, anyone got anything they need to tell me? Any burning confessions? Any admissions of indiscretion?' He slammed a fist on the table. 'If there is... *now* is the time to speak, for if I discover later that somebody on this team held back on me, then they're out on their arse. Clear?'

There was a moment's silence as Gus' words sunk in, followed by an exchange of surreptitious glances. A crippling viscosity hung in the air and then Alice scraped back her chair and stood up. This was horrible, nevertheless there was no way she was going to let a cloud hang over the entire team. She hadn't leaked one thing to Jez, yet she knew she had to let Gus know she could be implicated. She knew all too well how efficiently the gossip mills at The Fort turned.

Gus glared at her in silence.

Swallowing hard, Alice cleared her throat and with her fingers resting lightly on her desk she looked directly at her boss, ignoring everyone else in the room. 'I think you should know from me, before someone else tells you, that I went for lunch with Jez Hopkins yesterday.'

Waves of heat flushed her face. She bit her lips and then continued, 'I promise you, Gus, that we never spoke about the case. He didn't ask and even if he did, I wouldn't have given him anything. I'm not stupid. Whoever the leak is, I swear it's not me.'

She fell, more than sat, back onto her chair.

Gus glared at her, his face betraying nothing and Alice knew there was worse to come. She was right.

From his pocket Gus took out the piece of paper he'd crumpled and put in there earlier. 'Well, would anyone like to explain this, then?' He waved the paper in the air and glanced round. Nobody responded. Gus placed it on the desk and ran the side of his hand over it to flatten it before lifting it up again. 'Let me read it to you. "*For your information, and in light of today's headlines, DS Alice Cooper was seen yesterday afternoon sharing an intimate lunch with Jez Hopkins in the Ling Bob, Wilsden.*"'

Gus' eyes, sparking, glared round at them. Alice, her face scarlet now, avoided eye contact.

'Well, which of you felt the need to stoop to tittle-tattling to me via an anonymous note?'

Gus sighed and sat on the table, his feet resting on a chair. He ran his fingers through his hair, making each lock project at a different angle. 'First of all, I don't expect to have to warn my team off of sharing delicate information with the press. Whoever told them about "REDEEMED" being written above the body has A: caused untold upset to Sue's family; and B: given away valuable info that we could have used to nail the killer; and C: probably encouraged every religious nutter in the district to phone in to confess.'

He glared round at them, and then focussed his gaze on Alice who bravely tried to meet it. 'Secondly, this anonymous note is shite. It's unworthy of any detective on my team so, I sincerely hope none of you wrote it.

'Thirdly, Alice, you did right to fess up about having lunch with Jez and I do believe you. I don't think for a minute you gave those details to him. We are detectives, but we're also human. I don't expect to police your relationships outside the office. Just make sure those relationships don't bring disrepute on us.'

The tension in the room abated as everyone shuffled back to their work stations. Gus held Alice's gaze until she looked away. She hated to be on the wrong side of him. Much as he gave them a lot of leeway, he would not be happy that she'd met with Jez Hopkins. Shit, pissing Gus off was the last thing she wanted.

Gus shook his head. 'I'm not going to waste any more energy on this. What's done is done. I know we get a fair amount of passing traffic through here, so from now on, we leave nothing sensitive around. Compo, can you get somebody to put one of those code locks on the door? Let's get on with the briefing.'

Compo looked distracted. 'Eh, Gus…'

Gus sighed: sometimes he wished people would just spit it damn well out. No time for preliminaries. 'Yep?'

Compo hit a button on his PC and the large white screen at the front of the room was filled with an image of Simon Proctor on the narrow cot flailing his arms, limbs tangled in his sleeping bag. The time and date flashing at the bottom of the screen said 03:25. Proctor had been alive and traumatised only an hour ago. He looked at Compo, but the other man's head shake told him that they were no closer to working out where Proctor was being kept or who was uploading the video footage.

Chapter 43

09:30 Oak Lane

The insistent rapping on the closed door had Mo hurrying to answer. Popping his head out and seeing his friend standing there, he opened the door wide.

'It's a bit early in the day for samosas, even for you, Gus.'

Gus followed him into the shop and plonked himself down on one of the tall bar stools that stood along a marble top. 'Not too early for sweet spicy chai, though, is it?'

Mo shook his head and walked to the back of the shop which lead into a large kitchen. He called for tea, got no response and then called again, this time in Punjabi, and much louder to make himself heard above the babble of women's voices.

Mo came back and sat next to Gus. 'Those bloody women do my head in, you know?'

He screwed his face into what he clearly believed to be an old woman expression, raised one hand and rapidly pressed his fingers and thumb together. 'Nyah, nyah, nyah, all day long.' In a typical Pakistani gesture of impatience, he wafted the fingers of one hand near his head and expelled a short puff of air. 'What do they find to talk about, huh? They see each other every bloody day.' Two mugs of chai appeared at the hatch between the counter and kitchen and Mo brought them over.

One look at Gus' expression had Mo laughing aloud. Gus was right: he was behaving like an old grouch and the sooner he knocked that on the head the better. Grouchiness wasn't his style. He knew it was because of the stress Zarqa was causing at home. He and Naila just couldn't seem to agree on a strategy. This hurt Mo. He and Naila were normally on the same page, but perhaps on this one he was too emotional. Far too emotional. He'd have to rein it in and spend time working something out with his wife before it got too bad.

Forcing a smile to his lips he walked back over to the counter. 'Right, what brought you here this early? It wasn't chai, and it wasn't to laugh at my expense, so what was it?'

'You know that girl from The Young Jihadists, Shamila?'

'Yeah, what about her? She's a good girl.'

'It's not her I'm asking about, it's her brother, Adnan. What's he like?'

Mo moved to the sink and washed his hands, before sitting down behind the counter where he filled his samosas. 'It's quite a sad family, really. Dad's a bastard. In prison for gun running and pimping. He throttled one of his prostitutes, apparently. The mother has only got her aunt and uncle, who are her husband's parents – cousin-to-cousin marriage. He used to beat her about a bit, too, and now the poor woman rarely comes out of the house. Shamila seems to be the decision-maker and I think it was her that got them out of the grandparents' house and into their own little back-to-back. What's the lad done?'

Gus played with his empty cup as he spoke. 'Well, you know Shamila's friend, Tariq?'

Mo grinned. 'Tariq, who has a crush on Shamila and looks set to follow her to Bradford University rather than spread his wings a bit, because she won't leave her family? That Tariq?'

Gus grinned. 'Young love, huh? Yes, that's the one, right enough. He grudgingly, very grudgingly in fact, told me that the dead girl, Sue Downs, was seeing Shamila's brother.'

Mo grimaced. 'Ooh, not good.'

'Exactly, and this bit is between us only, Mo, okay?'

Mo nodded as he stuffed minced lamb into a samosa triangle.

'She'd had sex just before she died and although they used a condom, we may have DNA from a semen stained tissue at the scene.'

Mo raised his eyebrows, 'Shit, I hope the boy wasn't involved.'

'After what you've told me, so do I, but so far that's the only lead we've got.'

'Well, you have to follow it, mate, you have to follow it.'

Gus headed to the door and then turned. 'Is the kid overly religious do you think?'

Mo laughed. 'Everybody's "overly religious" to you, Gus.'

Gus scowled. 'You know what I mean.'

'No, I don't think so. I'm fairly sure he doesn't even pray the requisite five times a day, and I bet he's missed a few fasts at Ramadan. A lot of the young ones do. He's not a zealot, Gus. He wouldn't be going around shagging underage girls if he was, would he?'

Chapter 44

10:15 Unknown Location

Had that dream again. The one with the detectives breaking down the door and my parents reaching out to me. This time though their faces were all shrivelled and aged, like years had passed. *What if it takes them years to find me? Can I hang on that long?*

They won't be angry with me. Not about the party, anyway. No, in the midst of everything else, the party will have faded into nothingness. Wonder what they're doing. Mum'll be beside herself and Dad'll be trying to keep her calm. That's what they're like. A united front against the world. Solid in their togetherness, with me just a fucking afterthought. What's that stupid old saying? 'Two's company, three's a crowd.'

Sometimes they make me feel like that... like I'm in the way, second best. Always fucking second best. Missed my fucking football match twice in Year Ten and got bumped from the team. All because he had a stupid works trip and we'd all got to go. Could've stayed with Matty... *'Oh, no, don't want you spending time in Manningham.'* Snobby bastards! Should see some of the places I lived in before. In comparison, Matty's house is a fucking palace! Maybe now they'll regret that. Now that I'm missing... now that it's too fucking late!

Need to calm down. Time to focus on my safe place. Need to get through this. The enforced inactivity's getting on my tits. Need to pull myself together. If I fall apart I'll never survive. Need to get a grip. Can't focus. My leg muscles keep twitching and I stink. Really stink now. Wish I could shower. Nice long shower...

'Da da da fucking shower, shower, shower la la la...'

Feels like hours since I'd been wakened by the girl on the floor, whimpering and writhing against the ropes. Her struggles had been futile. Ropes were so tight, I'd had trouble undoing them. Stupid cow kept squirming, making it worse. By the time I'd got her ankle ties off, the ropes were saturated in blood and my frigging nails were mashed. Her wrist ties came off much easier, thank God! She just laid there like a sack of potatoes, sobbing. *How was I supposed to think with that fucking racket going on?*

Now, I'm on my own again. She's gone... *The girl has left the building!* And I'm stuck here without Elvis in the damn jail! Her snivelling whimpers don't seem so bad after all. At least it had been company... while it lasted anyway. Wonder where she is. Dead? In a hospital? Lying in the gutter?

Camera light's on again. Feel like flashing to my audience. Won't though – too many pervs out there who'd get off on that sort of shit. I'll just lie here, try to keep warm and ignore it. I feel itchy. Can't stop itching, driving me mad. Fucking fleas! That's all I need. Can't even scratch my arms properly. Not with my scraggy nails.

Chapter 45

10:30 Manningham

The littered alley leading to Adnan Mustafar's house was filled with pre-school children standing about, wellies covered in filth from the potholes, sucking mucky thumbs and staring wide-eyed at Gus. As he passed them, he was aware of them stepping into line behind him, following him down the ginnel. He turned and scowled at them in his best 'sod off and leave me alone' look. 'You shouldn't follow strangers, you know. They might be bad men.'

They stared blinking up at him like he was a petting animal at a farm, until he turned away. Still they continued to follow him. 'Paedophile's wet fucking dream,' he murmured, opening the gate, slipping through and closing it quickly behind him, so they couldn't follow him through. *Just call me the Pied-effing-Piper!*

Blue paint curled and bubbled off the door, although the uneven slabs in the garden were weed-free. An old, hard-bristled brush leaned beside the door and, judging by the absence of debris on the floor, it was used often. A miniscule shed stood in one corner. It was secured by a heavy-duty padlock and its small window was boarded up with damp plywood.

The heavy net curtains in the window at the front of the house twitched, so Gus rapped with his knuckles on the peeling door. From behind, he heard the unmistakeable sounds of a safety chain being applied before the door was opened and a small woman, her hair covered by a head scarf, peeped out.

Gus showed his ID. She shut the door, unhooked the chain and then reopened it fully. With a small hand movement, she invited Gus to sit down on one of the two sofas in the room, which were covered by bright geometric patterned sheets. He glanced round, throat clagging with the almost overpowering scent of incense which lingered in the air. A framed picture of Mecca, the only wall decoration in the room, hung above a small gas fire. The carpet was worn and every surface shone. A cramped cellar head kitchen was squeezed into one corner of the living area. A single pan bubbled on the gas stove and Gus recognised the aroma of spicy chai cutting through the incense. Opposite the other sofa was a door that led upstairs.

The woman stood near the kitchen area wringing her hands, her gaze intent on Gus. She still hadn't uttered a word, so Gus didn't know if she spoke English. As her face was expressionless, he couldn't judge what she thought about a police officer appearing on her doorstep. He smiled. 'Is Adnan here? It's him I've come to see.'

Her eyes studied him for almost a minute before she answered in almost accent-free English. 'Is he in trouble of some sort?'

Gus stretched his lips wider, his cheeks straining and hoped it didn't look too much like a grimace. He hated having to comply with the social niceties. However, he saw no need to upset anyone. The woman before him was clearly Adnan and Shamila's mother and, from what Mo had told him, she'd had plenty of interactions with the police in the past. He had no desire to distress her any more than was necessary. 'I really need to talk to him, Mrs Mustafar.'

She side-stepped into the kitchen, flicked off the gas and moved the pan, just as the boiling spicy milk rolled to the top. 'That means he is. I knew something was up.

He's not been himself the past few days. Can't you tell me what's happened?'

'I'm really sorry Mrs Mustafar, I really need–'

The door at the bottom of the stairs opened and a skinny boy looked through. He glanced at his mother and then at Gus. Gus saw the fear in his eyes and the way his grip tightened on the door handle when he realised who it was.

Gus stood up and walked towards him, hand outstretched. As he introduced himself the boy flinched. Mrs Mustafar inserted herself between the two men and addressed her son. 'Adnan, this policeman wants to speak with you. Are you in trouble?'

Adnan refused to meet his mother's eye. 'I've done nowt wrong, Mum, honest.'

She shrugged and sighed. 'Then you should go with the policeman and get it sorted out. I'll wait here by the phone in case you need anything, okay?'

Adnan turned then and looked at his mum. He hesitated briefly and then went over and hugged her. 'I've not done nowt wrong,' he repeated and without another word he walked past Gus and out into the garden.

Feeling like a cad, Gus followed Adnan from the house. 'You've not even asked what this is about and I would have been happy to talk with you in your home in the first instance, Adnan.'

Walking beside Gus, hands shoved deep in his pockets and jeans hanging off his skinny arse, Adnan sniffed. 'I know what it's about and if I hadn't been such a fucking coward I'd have come to see you yesterday. Besides, my mum doesn't deserve any more grief. It's best I come to the station.'

When they reached the unmarked car, Gus opened the passenger door for Adnan to get in.

Clicking his seat belt in place, Adnan waved at the children who'd grouped round the car. 'Thought there'd be two of you, and maybe even handcuffs and definitely a police car... not this.'

Gus got in the other side and switched on the engine. 'Yeah well, I looked at your police record–'

Adnan swung his head towards him. 'I don't have a record.'

'My point precisely. You're seventeen, with no police record, working in an apprenticeship and the school had only good things to say about you. Didn't think I'd need the heavies.'

Adnan nodded and slumped down in the car seat.

'Mind you, doesn't mean I'm a pushover or that I think you're innocent. I'll reserve my opinion till I've interviewed you.'

A silent nod was the only communication between them for the rest of the journey.

Chapter 46

11:20 The Fort

Having deposited Adnan in interview room one, Gus arrived at the incident room and tried to open the door. It wouldn't budge. He leaned his shoulder on it and shoogled the handle before finally noticing the flashing red light on a keypad just below his eye line. He pressed the button and waited. After a bit of static and a brief skirmish, a disembodied voice demanded to know his business.

'I'm leading the fucking investigation, does that give me entry?'

He laughed as he heard a muffled 'Oh shit, it's the boss,' swiftly followed by footsteps approaching. Compo, Diet Coke in one hand and KitKat in the other, opened the door and took a quick step back as if expecting a rollicking.

Gus ambled in. 'Good work with the door, Compo, just need to make sure we've all got the code to get in.'

'Oh yeah, forgot about that.' He scrabbled in his pocket coming up with a small card with a chocolate stain in one corner and six numbers written on it. 'Best memorise that, boss.'

Gus took the card, looked at the numbers and shoved it in his pocket. No way was he going to admit to Compo that he couldn't even memorise his bank card PIN with four digits, never mind these six digits. It was then he noticed that everyone was crowded round Compo's computer. 'Got something, Compo?'

Compo's face lit up and he led Gus over to his table.

'I've finished rationalising the Facebook contacts lists and so I started going over the stuff young Tayyub recorded and I found a few things. The first thing is that I've IDed the girl dancing on the table. Jenny Gregg, fifteen, from Cottingley, attends City Academy.'

'Right, Taffy and Alice, you interview her, ASAP.' Then as Comp coughed he added, 'After we've seen what else Compo's got for us.'

Gus grinned his approval, and Compo continued. 'I got something else, too. I was just about to show the team this. I'll run it through the projector so we can see better.' He frowned. 'To be honest, though, I don't really think any of us want to see it.'

Gus looked at him sharply. 'You okay, Compo?'

'Yeah, you'll see what I mean when you see it.' And with that Compo switched off the lights and started the recording.

Tayyub appeared to be sitting in the Proctor's living room idly recording passers-by, focussing here and there. At 22:35 there seemed to be some commotion off camera. Tayyub pointed the camera out of the living room towards the front door where two massive blokes in leather jackets stood, each with their arm round a skinny girl. Gus recognised the one on the left as Jade Simmonds. They came in and kicked over the small table at the bottom of the stairs and stared pugnaciously at a couple of lads who quickly lowered their heads and sidled past and out the front door. The two bikers' fists bumped. One of them grabbed a can from a lad who was coming down the stairs and pushed his way past Tayyub with the camera.

'Play it again, Comps.' Gus again watched the bikers entering the premises. With any luck they'd be able to get a better image from this footage. They were thugs, through and through. From picking up two young girls to vandalising the Proctors' property to leaving Jade Simmonds to die alone and uncared for. He'd have those bastards, if it was the last thing he did. Such a waste. If the next hour had played out differently, Jade would have been alive on Sunday morning. Maybe nursing a stinker of a hangover, but alive none the less. Bloody animals!

Compo fast forwarded to 22:55. The bikers and their girls were over by the window with Simon Proctor. Although Simon's back was to the camera his body language indicated he was neither frightened nor worried. As they watched, Simon high-fived the two bikers and flung his head back, as if laughing. One of the bikers placed an arm round Simon's shoulders and pulled the boy in for a hug. Whatever was being said was drowned out by the bass beat and localised laughter and chatter. Compo stopped the recording. 'There,' he said, excitement making his voice wobble, 'Do you see it? There?'

Sure enough, one of the bikers took a clear bag out of his pocket. In it were little blue pills. Simon took the bag, hid it in a plant pot behind the curtain and rummaged in his back pocket. He handed over a wad of money. The biker flicked through the cash, kissing it, before putting it away in an inner pocket with a laugh. He thumped Simon on the back and walked away, Jade and the other girl obediently following behind.

Again, Compo fast forwarded, but this time before pressing play, he said, 'This is bad, okay? Believe me it's bad.'

Tayyub had zoomed in on the bikers as they walked from the dining room to the living room. Anything, or anyone who happened to be in their way was swatted away like an annoying midge. They approached the couch and one of them yanked a boy, who was snogging his girlfriend, up by the collar. The couple didn't argue as the two bikers wedged their arses into the middle of the couch and pulled Jade and the other girl down into either corner. Although Jade looked pale and sleepy, the other girl seemed alert.

A few minutes were taken up by the bikers belching and drinking beer, with the girls laughing encouragingly. The background noise diminished as the teenagers became aware of the bikers in the living room and edged away. Deep voices, talking insultingly about everything and anything, drifted through the room. They referred to the girls as their 'bitches' or sometimes their 'hos' and the girls giggled like the kids they were. Pills and bottles of beer were shared, until Jade grabbed the arm of her biker. 'Feel sick, help me up.'

He laughed and jeered at her, moving his hands in and out close to her face to make her dizzy. Jade paled visibly and then suddenly lurched to the side and vomited over the arm of the sofa onto the carpet beneath.

'Fuckin' mingin' cow!' The biker pulled her upright by the hair and slapped her on the face.

Jade's eyes shot open and she lifted a hand to her face. 'Ouch, that was sore.'

He laughed. 'Well, it were meant to be.'

Jade looked miserable. 'Can't I go home now? I'll get a taxi?'

'You'll fuckin' stay here till I say you can go, right!'

The other biker grinned. 'You tell the bitch.'

There were a few more minutes of loud obnoxious behaviour and then the other biker said, 'I know, let's have a race.'

'What sort of fucking race?'

He flung his head back and laughed.

Gus, stepping closer to the screen, imagined he could smell the BO and alcohol wafting from the man. His skin tightened as if a million pins were being pressed simultaneously into his body. Sensing that the scene was going to play out in an even more despicable way, Gus wanted to look away... yet he knew he couldn't.

The biker nodded at the two girls, his tone full of glee when he spoke. 'A blow job race. First to swallow the lot wins.'

The first biker waved his arm in a circular movement above his head and whooped. 'You hear that, Jade? We're having a blow job race. First to swallow wins, okay?'

Jade looked up at him, her voice was barely audible. 'I'm going to be sick again. Just wanna go home.'

The two men got onto their knees on the couch and straddled the girls. Two large jean-clad backsides filled the screen and the girls' faces were obscured. A few moments of wobbling as the men found their balance by reaching out and gripping the back of the couch with one hand. The unidentified girl's giggle, was punctuated by Jade's slurred pleas, 'No, stop it, I'm gonna be sick, please. Don't feel well.'

A slap rent the air and then it seemed that the two men were fumbling at their flies before, for an agonising couple of minutes, all that could be seen was their thrusting butts. Gus had an urge to push his fingers in his ears to drown out Jade's fading moans. It continued till Jade lay in a heap on the couch and the other three left the party. The time was 23:28.

The team were silent. Dry mouthed, Gus realised he'd clenched his hands into tight fists. He wanted to slam one into the wall. Perhaps that would release the tension across his shoulders. On the other hand, it might just break his hand, shatter it into clouds of dust motes. The tightness in his chest wasn't panic, although it felt similar. No, this time it was fury; huge and all-consuming. It threatened to swallow him whole, so he opened his hands, forced his fingers wide and pumped them open and shut for a few moments before he spoke. 'Compo, get stills of those men and get them out to every bloody police officer in the county. Get them into every damn database we have. I want them found.'

Before Gus had finished speaking, Compo handed him a printed photo. 'I've sent them out already – knew we should be quick on this one.'

Alice stood up and stretched. Her face was pale yet determined. 'Do you think that constitutes murder, Gus?'

He shook his head, his face red with anger. 'Probably not. Probably can't prove she actually asphyxiated during the act. I'll speak to my dad. We'll get the bastards for drugs, for sexual and physical abuse of a minor, lewd behaviour, assault on any of those kids they touched that night. We'll fucking get them, good and proper.'

'I swear I saw that fucking bastard held her nose to force her to swallow.' Compo's expression was one of disbelief. 'How could he do that? Give me ten minutes with either of those two and it'll be their own dicks they're swallowing.'

'Hear, hear,' echoed Alice.

Gus looked at his team. Sampson and Taffy had remained silent throughout. Taffy, wide-eyed, looked ready to cry, and Sampson, folding a piece of paper again and again into a square with precise, measured movements, was breathing heavily. He knew how they felt. There were some things you just could not un-see and this was one of them. Gus knew he wouldn't be the only one having nightmares that night. He made a mental note to refer them for counselling when this was all over. You couldn't let these things fester… he knew that only too well. 'Look, you lot, everybody go out, have a walk in the park or something for half an hour, clear your heads and then come back and we'll get on with nailing the bastards, okay.'

Chapter 47

11:55 The Fort

Whilst his team took the half hour to process what they'd seen on the tape, Gus sat at his desk and studied the crime boards. They were no further forward accessing where the footage of Simon Proctor had come from. Although Compo was working like a man possessed, every lead had, so far, turned up a dead end. Hits were coming in from the images Compo had taken of the bikers but nothing conclusive. Gus wanted to rattle something loose, yet he could see no way of doing that right now. Despite telling himself that he wasn't doing his body any favours, he'd drunk another cup of coffee, ignoring the swishing gurgle in the depths of his stomach. If they could locate Simon Proctor they might get a lead on the bikers. On the other hand, Simon Proctor may well be dead.

Compo's computer pinged just as the man himself returned to the room. Rosy-cheeked and carrying a plastic bag, no doubt filled with provisions, Compo bustled over to his PC.

'Another video on Facebook, Gus.' And, without waiting to be asked, he filtered it onto the screen.

Within seconds, Gus was looking at Simon Proctor lying in the same position on the bed. The date stamp said the footage had been taken at 10:15. The footage was shadowy and Gus could just about make out a small lamp illuminating the scene. At least the lad's not in complete darkness. 'Why the delay posting the video, Compo?'

Munching a packet of crisps, Compo shrugged. 'No idea. It's as easy to schedule it as it would be to upload it real time. Seems like whoever is doing this is playing with us.' Compo wiped his greasy hands down his trousers and flexed his fingers before rattling them across his keyboard. 'However, every time he posts something, he's giving me more to play with. I'll get this toe-rag, don't you worry.'

Drumming his fingers on the table top, Gus bit his lip. What the hell was Simon's abductor playing at? Why abduct Simon Proctor? The more he learned about the lad, the more he disliked him. Who would be in a position to abduct him, keep him incarcerated and post footage online? This was a puzzle. He wasn't even sure whether Sue Downs' death was linked to the disappearance or not. The coincidence of poor Jade Simmonds' death was one thing but abduction as well… that just seemed one step too far. However, he knew that if anyone could break the code or whatever it was, it would be Compo. Right now, though, that didn't help him.

As Alice walked through the door, colour back in her face and her step a little lighter, Gus stood up. *Thank God.* Maybe Adnan would set them in the right direction. 'Al, you're with me. I've got Sue Downs' boyfriend in interview room one. He has a social worker and a duty solicitor with him. Hardeep took his prints when he came in, and I don't want to keep him hanging about for too long.'

Alice grabbed a notebook and pen and followed Gus along the corridor.

Once in the room with the recording equipment set up, Gus introduced everyone for the benefit of the tape, before reading the lad his rights. 'Look, Adnan, I'm not going to lie to you, it looks bad that we had to come and get you. That you didn't come forward yourself. It looks suspicious, so, if I were you, I'd think very carefully about what I'm saying. You need to tell us the truth, okay?'

Adnan nodded, his hands clasped tightly on the table before him.

'Right, Adnan, do you know Sue Downs?'

Adnan bobbed his head once and Alice leaned forward. 'You've got to speak, Adnan, for the tape, okay?'

Gus repeated the question.

Adnan swallowed. He looked like he'd burst into tears at any moment. 'Yes, I knew Sue.'

'Was she your girlfriend?'

Adnan shrugged, then glanced at Alice. 'Sort of, she was sort of my girlfriend. You know? We went out sometimes.'

'Were you with her on Saturday night at Simon Proctor's house party?'

'Yes, yes, I was, she were fine when I left. I didn't hurt her, honest.'

'Were you in Mr and Mrs Proctor's bedroom with Sue?'

'Yeah.'

'Did you have sex with Sue?'

Adnan paled and he looked down at the table. 'No.'

'Sorry, I'll repeat the question. Did you have sex with Sue Downs on Saturday night?'

Adnan twisted his fingers. 'No, I said no, didn't I?'

'Would you volunteer to a DNA test to eliminate you from our enquiries?'

Adnan considered this for a minute. 'Yeah, yeah, suppose so.'

'When were you with Sue in the Proctors' bedroom, Adnan?'

He shrugged. 'Don't know, probably got there after those fat biker blokes arrived. I popped my head into the living room and they were being dicks so we went upstairs.'

'What time was that, roughly?'

'Probably around half-eleven or so, maybe a bit later.'

'Were you and Sue alone in the room?'

Adnan blushed. 'Well, yeah. I locked the door.'

'Why did you lock the door? Was it because you planned to have sex with Sue?'

'No, no, just in case those bloody bikers came up, that's all.'

'So, what were you doing in the bedroom with the door locked?'

Adnan started to weep. 'Nothing… we weren't doing nothing… just snogging and that, that's all.'

'What's *and that*, Adnan?'

'Don't know what you mean, I didn't do owt to Sue. I liked her… I'd never hurt her.'

'When did you leave the room, Adnan?'

He wiped his nose with his sleeve. 'Don't know… maybe half-twelve, one-ish, I didn't check the time.'

'Why didn't Sue leave with you?'

'Dunno, she wanted to stay.'

'Did you have an argument?'

'No, no, we didn't.'

'So why did you leave without her? You see what I mean? If you didn't have an argument, why do you leave without her?'

Adnan shrugged.

'Did you argue about the pregnancy?'

Adnan's head shot up and he fired a frightened glance at Gus. 'What pregnancy?'

'Sue was fourteen weeks pregnant when she died. Whoever killed her also killed her baby.'

Adnan laid his head down on the table and wept again. The social worker put his hand out and touched the boy on the shoulder. 'Maybe Adnan could have a break?'

Gus turned to Alice. 'Get him some water, will you, and I'll have a coffee.'

Alice left the room and Gus looked at Adnan. 'You need to pull yourself together and start talking to us. Start telling us the truth.'

The social worker passed the lad a tissue whilst the duty solicitor looked at his watch as if he had somewhere more pressing to be. As Adnan wiped his face, Gus said, his tone caustic, 'You in a rush or something?'

The solicitor had the grace to flush as he shook his head. Gus scowled at him and waited, arms crossed, till Alice returned with drinks for everyone.

'Right Adnan, let's go back to the beginning. You were in the bedroom with Sue for about an hour. You locked the door. Did you have sex with her?'

Adnan began to shake his head, but Gus raised his hand. 'Don't deny it, Adnan, we've got DNA to prove it was you.'

Adnan thought for a minute. 'No, no, you don't. I didn't.'

Gus opened the box file he'd brought in with him and took out a clear bag with a soiled tissue in it. 'We found this tucked down the back of the bed, Adnan. You used a condom and when you took it off you wiped yourself with a tissue and it ended up down the back of the bed, didn't it?'

Adnan stared at the bag and swallowed hard before replying. 'Yeah, I did have sex with her on Saturday night and that is the tissue I used. I ain't the father of that baby. That's the first time I ever had sex with her… or anyone else.'

Gus looked at him and bit his lip. 'Did you know she was pregnant, Adnan?

'No, she didn't say.'

'So why did you leave her behind?

'Well after, you know… after…' he pointed at the tissue, 'after that, she started to cry and got all upset and all and she started shouting at me and told me to go. In the end she was hysterical so I just went. I just left her there, honest to God, I never killed her.'

Gus clipped the tape off. 'We'll leave it there for now, Adnan, but we're going to have to keep you in.'

Walking back to the investigation room, Alice glanced at Gus. 'I'm not sure I want the answer to this, what exactly *was* on that tissue you showed Adnan?'

Gus laughed. 'Ah well, Compo has many uses. I snatched the only non-chocolate smeared hankie from his bin before we left.'

'Gross, but good idea, tripped him up nicely.'

Gus looked at her. 'What do you think?'

Alice gave a half-hearted laugh. 'I think that poor lad will never have sex again.'

'You believe him, then?'

She sighed. 'Yeah. Do you?'

'Yeah, I think I do, which means someone went into that room after he left and took a knife to her – maybe the real father of the baby?'

'I'll see if we can get any more from her friends on that issue.'

Chapter 48

13:05 The Fort

Gus, with Alice and Taffy, watched and listened to Jake and his father through the one-way mirror. Despite his obvious attempt at nonchalance by sprawling in the plastic chair and folding his arms across his chest, Jake's right leg bobbed up and down under the table.

His father sat next to him, a small frown between his brows, as he spoke quietly to his son. 'Look Jake, why have they brought you back in? They must think you have some more information.'

Jake refused to meet his dad's eye. 'Well, I don't.' His voice was high with indignation and he quickly cleared his throat and repeated in a lower tone. 'I don't, okay? I don't.'

Mr Carpenter looked round the room and sighed. 'Well, they obviously think you do, Jake, so, if I were you, I'd start racking your bloody brains to come up with something. God, Simon's parents are in a right old state, so if you know something you're not saying out of some misguided loyalty, let me tell you lad: This. Is. Not. The. Time. Okay?'

Jake frowned and lowered his head.

'I said, okay?'

Jake gave an exaggerated sigh.

'Okay, Okay. Stop going on at me, alright.'

'No, Jake. It's not bloody alright. Your best mate's gone missing and two young girls have been murdered at a party that you were at without your mum and me knowing. It's far from bloody alright.' He ran a hand through greying hair.

Gus grinned and jerked his head towards the door. Mr Carpenter seemed a bit more on edge than he had earlier. Perhaps the seriousness of the situation had sunk in now. 'I think that's our cue, Alice.' Then he turned to Taffy. 'Watch and learn. Take notes. Think if you'd do something differently from us. There's no set code for this. You need to develop your own technique – work out what works best for you. Oh, and look for tells that Alice and I might miss in there, like that leg of his bobbing up and down like a duck in a mud puddle. That's a sure tell that we've got him on edge. It might get faster if we hit a raw note – and be ready to report back when we come out.'

Taffy sat down with a pad of paper in front of the mirror, looking determined to miss nothing that would come in handy.

Gus marched briskly through the door, his dreads bouncing as much as the lad's leg. Frowning at Jake, he marched over to the table and with a sigh, pulled the chair out and sat down. Alice bustled in behind him and at Gus' gesture she silently set up the recorder, then dragged a chair to the table and sat down with her arms folded, mirroring Jake.

'Nice of you to come back down again, Mr Carpenter. I know you're a busy man and this is a bloody waste of your time. If Jake here had told us everything last time, we wouldn't have needed to pull you in again.'

Mr Carpenter frowned at Jake and then looked at Gus, all trace of resentment gone from his face. Instead, he resembled every other worried father Gus had encountered within these four walls; pinch lipped, and anxious. 'I'm sure Jake will tell you all you need to know this time. Won't you, Jake?'

Jake's head fell further to his chest. His dad prodded him with his finger. 'Did you hear me, Jake?' His tone was threatening. 'Sit up and at least look like you're a bloody thinking being.'

Glowering, Jake reluctantly pulled himself upright in his chair and laid his arms on the table.

Gus narrowed his eyes and glared. 'This is a murder enquiry as well as a missing person enquiry. Do you think I've got time for idiots like you withholding evidence?'

Jake bit his lip and stared at him.

Raising an eyebrow, Gus leaned forward with his hands linked on the table nearly touching Jake's. His tone was quiet but his anger was clear in his flashing eyes. 'Well?'

Jake shook his head and leaned back in his chair.

'Right then, now we've got that clear, perhaps you'll tell me about the drugs – and I'm not talking weed, okay?'

Jake's dad turned abruptly in his chair, his lips tightened and his face was red. 'For fuck's sake, Jake!'

Jake glanced at Gus, then at his dad, then back to Gus again. 'I don't take owt, Dad. Honest, I don't.'

Gus raised an eyebrow again and pursed his lips. He pushed some stapled sheets of paper across to Mr Carpenter. 'Have a read of that, sir. Jake, can you just tell us what you know.'

Jake leaned over as his dad lifted the paper, trying to read the typing. His dad glowered at him and leaned back. 'Answer the DCI, Jake. *NOW!*'

Jake swallowed and looked back at Gus. 'Honest, I didn't have owt to do with it. It was Si.' He shook his head in emphasis. Gus merely returned his gaze.

Jake looked away. 'Si wanted me to buy some blues with him. I said no. I didn't want to get involved in that stuff. I'm off to uni next year, don't want a criminal record and that.' He risked a glance at Gus who remained expressionless. 'I think Si bought some anyway. He had a few at the party but I think he got those that night. Sometimes though, he pissed off at gigs – dunno where he went, like, or what he done. Recently, though, he had a bit more money than usual. Maybe he was selling them at Tequilas.' He shrugged. 'I don't know for sure. When I got really angry at him for pestering me to buy them, he stopped talking about them.'

Gus frowned. 'And you never asked?'

Jake shook his head.

'For the tape.'

Jake glanced at the tape. 'No, I never asked about them. I didn't want to know.'

'You must have asked him who his source was?'

Again, Jake looked at the tape. 'No, I never asked. It was bound to be some dodgy cunt.'

Mr Carpenter broke off from reading the transcripts. 'Jake!'

'Sorry. Some dodgy guy.'

'He must have given you a clue?'

'Nah – maybe somebody off the internet. Si was a bit of an idiot at times. Wanted to be a big shot.'

'Look, this drug thing is serious. It may be that they've got something to do with his disappearance. If you know or even suspect anything at all – you better let us know. It's seventeen years for dealing blues you know.'

'I didn't deal any blues. It was Si.'

'You knew about it, didn't you?'

Jake took a deep breath. 'Maybe those biker guys. Si didn't seem too bothered that they were at the party, but me and Matty were scared shitless. They looked like right mean fuckers.'

'Would you recognise them again?'

Jake bit his lip and thought for a minute. 'Yeah, I reckon I might.'

'Okay then, after this interview you can go through some of our biker photos and see if you can ID them.'

Jake stood up.

Gus scraped his chair back with unnecessary noise and leaned towards Jake. 'Where do you think you're going?'

Glancing at his dad, Jake slumped back into his seat. 'I thought I had to look at photos?'

'Yes. When the interviews over... It's *not* over yet. So, sit yourself back down and get comfy.' Gus opened his file and slipped another copy of transcripts over to Jake's dad, who took them with a heavy sigh. Jake didn't even attempt to sneak a peek this time. Instead he looked pale-faced at Gus, waiting for the inevitable.

Gus rubbed his hands together. 'What do you think is in there, then, Jake?' He gestured towards the papers in his dad's hands.

Jake shrugged and sniffed, his eyes filling up with tears. 'I don't know.'

'It's more transcripts of your FB convos with Simon.' Gus scratched his chin. 'Any ideas what's on them?'

A single tear rolled down Jakes cheek and his voice wobbled when he spoke.

'No.'

Gus grinned. 'I'll give you a clue: MILF.'

Jake's dad broke off from his reading and glared at Gus. 'What does that mean?'

Gus smiled at Jake. 'I think Jake can tell us, can't you?'

Jake glanced at Alice as if looking for a way out, before lowered his chin to his chest again. When he spoke it was in an almost indiscernible mumble. 'Mothers I'd like to fuck.'

'What?' His dad looked puzzled.

'It's like a code or something some of the lads use when they see one of their mate's mums that's good looking. Don't worry, none of them say that about mum.'

Mr Carpenter raised his eyebrows and with a slight smile looked at Gus. Despite the severity of the situation, Gus' lips twitched as his eyes met Mr Carpenter's.

'Not sure quite how to take that... Best we don't tell your mum in case she takes it the wrong way,' said Mr Carpenter. Then, smile gone, he turned back to his son. 'You telling me that you boys use those sorts of terms about women? I thought we'd brought you up better than that?'

Jake ran his hand over his cheek to brush away the tear. 'It's not just us, Dad. The girls use it too, except they say DILF.'

Slowly, his dad shook his head and raised his eyes to the ceiling. 'Don't tell me, the D stands for "dad"?'

Jake opened his mouth. Mr Carpenter held up his hand. 'No, don't say it. I already know it's not used about me!'

Jake threw a quick glance between his dad and Gus, his brows pulled together. Then he shrugged as if to say 'what the hell'.

Gus, despite enjoying the conversation between father and son, intervened.

'Let's keep this simple, Jake. We know all about Simon and the bet, okay? The only thing we *don't* know is the identity of the mother and daughter involved – who was it?'

Jake shrugged 'I'm not sure. The photo was a bit indistinct with her.' He glanced at his dad. 'Well, what I mean is, you couldn't really see her face.'

'So, Simon did have photographic evidence that oral sex took place between him and somebody's mother.'

Jake frowned and thought. 'Well, now you mention it, it was definitely Si, but, well, it could have been anybody doing it, I suppose. That's what Matty and I thought afterwards. We tried to get our money back, but he wouldn't give it.'

'How did you know it was Simon and not something he'd got off the internet?'

'Well, it was his boxer shorts. I can't, like, ID his – well, you know what.'

Alice coughed and Gus glared at her. 'Sorry, tickle in my throat.' Her choice of words sunk in and she bit her lip as Gus mumbled, 'Nice turn of phrase.' He turned back to Jake, 'Of course not.'

'And it was his mum's cushions.'

Gus glanced at Alice. 'You mean it happened at Simon's house.'

Jake nodded. 'Yeah, in the front room. I recognised the couch and cushions.'

'Was there a recorded version of them having sex?'

'Yes,' Jake said, 'It happened in the woman's house and it was pretty steamy, I can tell you.' He looked at his dad and winced. Ducking his head, he mumbled, 'Sorry.'

'Right. Did he use a name for the woman?'

'No, but she kept using his name, you know, when he was like, em… you know…' He glanced at his dad again. 'Pussy petting.'

Mr Carpenter exhaled. 'For Christ's sake.'

Gus ignored him and continued questioning Jake. 'You mean you could hear the woman calling his name as he performed oral sex on her.'

Jake exhaled and his shoulders relaxed. He was evidently relieved not to have to spell it out in front of his dad. 'Yeah, that's it.'

'Did the recording demonstrate whether full intercourse took place?'

'Yes, yes it did. I heard – well, em… Yes, it did.'

Gus took pity on him. 'Perhaps you can give a full transcript of what you can remember from the tape, at the end of the interview, without your dad present.'

Jake heaved a sigh of relief. 'Yeah, thanks.'

Gus tapped his finger on the table and frowned. 'Jake, what doesn't add up to me is that you don't know who either the mum or daughter are. The daughter was referred to as A in your conversations via FB, I can't believe you don't know who it is.'

'Si wouldn't say. He could be really secretive. All I know is she's in Year Ten 'cause it was Year Ten parents' evening when he saw her. We were doing the refreshments.'

'If he established a relationship with the daughter in order to get to the mother, surely you knew who it was? You must have seen him with her. According to our computer expert he only has male friends listed under A in his Facebook account and on his phone.'

'Don't know. Honest, Si was really secretive about stuff. Got the impression she was a bit of a geek, though. He said he joined some club with her but he wouldn't say which one, just that it was weird. Maybe he told Matty, though I doubt it.'

'Hmm. Don't suppose there's any copies of either the photo or the video?'

Jake fidgeted on his chair. 'Well, Si, like, sent it to my phone.'

'So, it's on your phone now?'

'Yeah.'

'Will you give permission for us to access the photo from your phone and save it?'

Jake fumbled in his pocket and handed his phone to Gus.'

'The recording?'

Jake sighed. 'It's on there, too.'

'We'll delete both from your phone after we've copied them. Now, you stay here with DS Cooper and give your version of the transcript for the tape.'

He turned to Jake's dad. 'If you'll come this way there's a chair in the corridor where you can wait, or if you're happy to leave him here till he's looked at the photos, you can get back to work and I'll have someone drop him home later.'

After saying goodbye to Mr Carpenter, Gus went back to Taffy. 'Right, Taff, drop his phone with Compo and tell him to go through the lot whilst he's got the chance and have him see what he can do with the photo to enhance it. When you've done that, I want you to sit in with Alice to interview Matty. You will take the lead on that, okay?'

Taffy looked startled. 'Me?'

Gus slapped him on the back. 'Yeah you. Use what you've just seen as a template and improvise to find your own techniques. You need to practise to get it right. Alice will make sure you've covered everything.'

'Great! Thanks boss, appreciate the chance.'

'Right, I'm off to interview a head teacher.'

Chapter 49

13:45 Unknown Location

Can't stand much more of this. Freezing and hungry, but what's worse is the not knowing. Anything could be happening out there and I just don't frigging know.

I pace the room – six giant steps this way and eight giant steps that way. How many baby steps? Fucked if I know. I'm not playing *What's The Time, Mr Wolf?* on my own. No chance. Bad enough when we used to do it at primary school. Me? I preferred *Kiss, Cuddle or Torture?* Wonder what psycho thought that one up? I loved it though. Loved the torture... until the teacher told me off for being too rough with the girls. They asked for it, though. They chose torture... I just carried it out. Remember Jessie Graham? Little fucking bitch said torture, so I pinched her nipples. That's torture, right? You'd think I'd done summat wrong the way her mum moaned on and on – fuck's sake it was only a game. Waved bye-bye to another fucking foster family with that one, didn't I?

That's the thing. They give you a label and then you're stuck with it. I was the kid nobody wanted. The kid who picked on girls. The smelly weirdo with no mum. Soon as they make you a non-child – a monster – then it's easy for them to do what they like with you. Too fucking easy. Well, some of them found out the hard way, didn't they?

Wish I was at home though, in my own bed. Should've brought my duvet – wasn't the plan though. Could've brought something else. Feel like I've got scabies again.

Scratch, scratch, scratch, every two seconds. Got them once when I was little – itchy as fuck!

Shut up, Simon!

It had to be the blanket. Had to make sure. Had to stick to the plan. Wouldn't even moan about that girly damn fabric conditioner smell on my duvet. Fuck, it's cold! Blanket's useless and I think it's got fleas. Nicked it from the bitch's garage, so it might have. Maybe her old man used it for the horses or something. Just my luck.

Now, I've thought about it, it's worse than when I had a pot on my ankle. Nearly got caught that time. Shouldn't have jumped off the roof. Only just got away before they arrived, I could hear the sirens getting louder as I skirted round the back and down towards the viaduct where I'd left the van. Surprised the parents didn't smell it on me when I got home. The pair of them are stupid though. Unless it's about *them*, they don't notice owt – too busy shagging and pawing each other. You'd think by their age they'd have got over that shit, wouldn't you? What a fucking adrenalin rush it was, though. Perfect timing, perfect execution… until I fell, that is. *Ha ha!* It was great.

I bang my fist to my forehead. What a plonker! What am I thinking. Didn't I pack some clothes in my rucksack? Where is it? Under the bed. I pull it out and unzip it, shoving my hands down to the plastic bag at the bottom. Like it's a huge Christmas present

'La la la X-mas trees, X-mas gifts, da da da, X-mas snow, X-mas bells, X-Men! La la la, da da da, dum, dum, dum… Christmas.'

Pulling the bag past my money and tins and stuff, I open it, just a little at first. I press my nose to the opening. Bliss! Fabric conditioner! Poofy, but who the fuck cares? I'll get changed and then I'll have a sandwich. Don't really need the freezer box. At least it'll stop mice from eating my supplies.

Aw no... not again.

'Stop it, Simon. Focus on something else... not the rats. The clothes. Put your joggers on, they'll be comfy. And your big sweatshirt. The brown one.'

I bundle my dirty clothes together and drop them on top of the clothes I'd worn at the party. Won't be needing them again. Got plenty money to buy more, anyway. Stupid cow never noticed odd bits of jewellery going missing. If they notice now, they'll put it down to the party. Pure fucking genius!

Brilliant – socks. Thick ones. Aw, nice. Soft and clean... fucking crotch is itchy though. Fleas? Nah, sweat. I dip my hand down, scratch and sniff. Fucking cheesy or what? Joggers on, sweatshirt on. Tuna sandwich, here I come!

Chapter 50

14:05 The Fort

'Gus, you've got a visitor.' Hardeep had somehow managed to get the code for the incident room and stood in the entrance, his fingers gripping the door, only the upper half of his body visible.

About to put his coat on and leave for City Academy, Gus groaned and stopped, one hand in the jacket. 'Hmm, who?'

'Tommy Ache.'

Compo popped his head up from behind his barricade of PCs holding a half-eaten Branston Pickle and cheddar roll in his hands. 'I've got some antacid, Gus.'

Gus blinked, what the hell was Compo on about now? 'Yeah, you'll probably need it, the amount of Branston you've got on that sandwich.'

Compo looked at his roll, took another bite and shook his head. His voice was muffled when he spoke. 'For *you*, not for me.'

'Eh? I haven't got a sore stomach, Comps.'

Hardeep, the duty officer, cast his eyes upwards and sighed. 'Bloody hell, if we're relying on you lot to solve serious crime, we're up to our ears in dog poo and not a pooper-scooper in sight.' He looked at Compo. 'I said *Tommy* Ache not *tummy ache*. He's a friend of Gus.' Then he looked at Gus who, with a pencil stick through his dreads, looked particularly gormless. 'He thought I said *tummy* ache so he offered you antacid tablets. I've explained it to him, so are we all clear on this?' He eyeballed the pair of them, as if daring them to question his assertion.

'Now, do you want Tommy Ache or not?'

Gus shuddered and threw the folder he was looking at back on his desk. 'No, I don't want Tommy Ache. Can you pass him on to… someone else… anyone else?'

Hardeep smirked. 'If you're sure… You don't mind him going over your head to his best mate, the boss?'

Compo grimaced. 'Oh, he's a friend of DCI Chalmers too, is he?'

Hardeep laughed, his large belly wobbling in the process. 'Good God, no, I were talking about Gus' mum. Tommy and her get on like a house on fire, don't they, Gus.'

It was hard to believe that Hardeep could find any more smirk, but he managed it somehow.

Gus rolled his chair away from his desk and over to the coffee machine. 'Yes, "house on fire" is a good way of describing their friendship. Tommy Ache's his nickname – from his time at her Majesty's Pleasure. My mum's got him embroiled in her latest artistic hobby.' Shuddering at the memory of his mum's life drawing of Tommy Ache that had been re-located from its original position at the top of the stairs to the dining room, Gus sighed. The last thing he needed was to spend time right now with Tommy Ache. Unfortunately, he knew it would all pass much less painfully if he just bit the bullet and got it over with.

Hardeep winked at Compo, who was now licking Branston from his fingertips.

'Bloody life drawing, Comps. Can you believe it?'

'You mean in the scuddy, like?'

Gus slurped his coffee, agitation sending his hair bouncing erratically over his head. 'Exactly.'

Compo looked puzzled. 'What's that got to do with Tommy Ache, though?'

Gus sighed and laid a hand over his eyes. 'Oh Compo, if you only knew.'

'Well go on then lad, tell us,' urged Hardeep from the door.

Gus scowled at him as Compo clicked his fingers.

Then in a lightbulb moment, Compo grinned. 'Oh yeah. I were there the day she showed us that painting. Right good Yorkshire puds your mum makes, Gus.' Compo's eyes glazed over and Gus shook his head. How anyone could rate his mum's cooking was beyond him, but her Yorkshire puddings? Seriously? And how could Compo remember more about those Yorkshire puds than the damn monstrosity he had to look at every time they sat down to eat? Mind-blowing, truly mind-blowing.

Alice joined him by the coffee machine, giggling. 'So why's it still bothering you so much? I thought you and your dad convinced her to put it at the top of the stairs?'

Gus jumped to his feet, his eyes wide open and his hands gesticulating widely. 'Why is it bothering me? I'll bloody tell you. She's gone and moved the bloody thing and mounted it in the bloody dining room, in pride of place right above the fireplace. Right opposite where I sit for Sunday dinner.'

Gus turned to Compo. 'So, now, not only do I have to contend with my mother's god-awful cooking, I also have to chomp my way through her meat and two veg whilst trying to avoid seeing Tommy Ache's meat and two veg. Could bloody Sunday lunch at home get any worse?'

Catching Hardeep's eye, Gus groaned. 'Okay, okay. Send him up, then, might as well get it over with.'

Tommy strode over, stretched up and embraced Gus in a hug with a two-cheeked kiss.' 'Gus, my lad, look at you. You get more handsome every day. Just like your mother.'

Gus cringed, but managed to smile and offered him a coffee. Tommy undid his jacket and carefully hung it across the back of the chair before sitting down on the chair and tugging it till it was as far under the desk as it would go. Gus, feeling Tommy's knees brush his, pushed his chair slightly away. 'Right then, Tommy, what can I do for you?'

Tommy raised a hand that was missing the top half of his three fingers and used what was left of his index finger to tap the side of his nose. 'It's more what I can do for you. I've already given my statement, but I didn't like the look of that constable. Too bloody uninterested for my peace of mind. Knowles was his name. Anyway, I couldn't settle, feeling sure he was going to fuck up any investigation, so here I am.'

Gus hearing the name Knowles could sympathise with Tommy's misgivings; however, that wasn't enough for him to take on someone else's investigation, even if he had the time, which he did not. On the other hand, Tommy was insistent and if he didn't do something, he'd appear every five minutes, thus taking up even more time. Resigned to the lesser of two evils, Gus sat back and switched on his recorder. 'Okay, Tommy, tell me what you witnessed.'

Tommy sat up straight and leaned in slightly to the microphone and began. 'Well, it was about 6.25 am when I left The Turf. I'd had a wee bit too much last night and Jeffy gave me a blanket and let me sleep in the snug. Anyway, I proceeded down Emm Lane and then turned into Wilmer Road where at just before 6:30 am, I saw it.'

'Saw what, Tommy?'

'Well, that's just it. I saw nothing, 'cause it wasn't there yet.'

Gus opened his mouth to speak, reconsidered and closed it again, as Tommy continued. 'As I opened my front door it was precisely 6:30 because my clock boinged once. It does that you know, one boing for the quarter hour and the full amount on the hour.' He waited for Gus to nod before continuing.

'Well, I was desperate for a wee you know, so I nipped to the kitchen, popped the kettle on, then had a wee, then I went to the living room to open the curtains. That's when I saw it.'

'Saw what exactly, Tommy?'

'Right where I put the bins. It was right there, like a tangle of summat. So I got me specs out and that's when I saw it was a girl. I ran out the door, grabbing my coat, and down the steps to the kerb. She was naked. Covered in bruises and unconscious. I could feel a pulse so I covered her with my coat. Didn't want the neighbours next door ogling her. Then I phoned the police.'

'Right, so you already told all this to the other officer?'

'Yeah, well, all except this next bit, 'cause I forgot in all the excitement, when I got to the kerb I looked along the street both ways and there at the Emm Lane junction was a van-type thing, light coloured, with its indicator on to turn right, only it didn't, it turned left.'

'Right, Tommy, well, I'll certainly put in a follow-on call to the officer and see what's come of the investigation.'

Tommy clapped his hands like an over-excited performing seal. 'Yes, you do that, son.' He scratched his pate. 'You know, son, I've seen that van before, just can't think where.'

'Well, let us know if you remember.' Gus edged Tommy towards the door as he spoke.

'Well, I'll see you on Sunday, anyway, Gus. Might have remembered by then.'

Gus frowned 'Sunday, you mean–'

'Yes, Sunday lunch. Your mum's invited me.' Tommy, oblivious of Compo's sudden need to stuff his fingers in his mouth, waved ta-ta with his deformed hand and left, just as Sampson came in.

'Sampson, just the man. Need you to find out a bit more about a mugging/dumping which that pillock Knowles dealt with this morning. Tommy's got his knickers in a twist about it and I'll never hear the end of it if I don't cast a glance over it to make sure Knowles is doing his job. Follow up on it, see what you can find out and report back to me.'

Seeing Sampson's scowl, Gus patted him on the back. 'I know we're up to our ears. It shouldn't take too long. Just get on with it. You'll be done by the time I'm back from City Academy.'

'Say hi to Ms Copley,' said Compo. Gus, eyes narrowed, glanced at the lad, but Compo was busy with his PC. *Need to stop being so damn paranoid!*

Chapter 51

15:45 City Academy

It had been a major operation to get through the security at the front gate of the school, past the receptionist and into the ultra-modern office in which he now sat. Gus was relieved he'd had an excuse to leave Alice behind. No way did he want her knowing glances plaguing him for the drive through town; and he certainly didn't want her smart-ass comments.

This was the first time he'd had to consult with Patti on the job since she'd allowed him to interview two of her students whose father had been brutally murdered earlier in the year. The thought of seeing her always tied his stomach in knots, however, this was a little different. Instead of anticipation, his palms sweated with an emotion he could only describe as dread. This was new territory for them to traverse in their fledgling relationship and, after Gabriella's eventual hatred of his job, he was reluctant to expose Patti to it quite so soon. Not that Patti was anything like his ex-wife. On the contrary, Patti was strong, independent and above all, seemed to understand Gus' sense of duty. After all, she shared a similar work ethic in her own job.

Bright, clean and very organised though the office was, Gus had an overwhelming nostalgia for the head teacher's office in his old high school, Belle Vue Boys. True, there had been a faint smell of cigs in the air and a decidedly strong smell of ammonia as you passed the boys' toilets en route for the office, still, it had character. Well-worn chairs with springs that pinged unexpectedly, bruising your bum, stood facing the enormous desk. From behind a scattering of stationery, papers and books, Mrs Matthews used to peer over her glasses at you. Unless you were there to be punished, she always seemed to have the time to listen to you.

Ah, how times had changed. Now, sitting outside Patti's office, with a smartly coiffed woman in a navy business suit clacking away on her PC opposite him, it was like waiting to discuss a large unauthorised overdraft with his bank manager. A discreet buzz warned him he was about to be allowed into the inner sanctum of Patti's office. The secretary grinned and motioned for him to go in. *What the hell is she grinning like that for?* Gus shrugged. He was probably imagining things. Alice had wound him up so much he'd become paranoid.

The door closed behind him and Gus found himself facing a grinning Patti. Heat washed across his face and he grinned back, all of his carefully rehearsed words fleeing his mind.

She gestured for him to take one of the soft chairs next to a coffee table. 'This is awkward, isn't it?' She laughed, warm and low. 'Seems your work and mine are inextricably linked once more. I presume this is about the murders and Simon?'

'Yes, I'm afraid so.' Stretching out his legs, Gus took a moment to look at Patti. Sometimes he still had to pinch himself. How he'd ever worked up the courage to ask her out was beyond him. According to her, she'd all but forced the words from him, however he chose to remember it differently. Truth was, he knew he was punching well above his weight. Tall, intelligent and drop-dead gorgeous, Patti was also down to earth and undemanding. Like him, she was of dual heritage with a deep tawny skin tone and green eyes. Today, her hair was in neat tight corn rows and she wore a knee-length skirt with a simple blouse. The matching jacket hung on a coat stand near the door with a heavier jacket to the side. Underneath were a pair of wellies and an umbrella. He grinned. *Looks like Alice was right about Patti and puddles.*

He turned his attention back to Patti. 'Additional information has come our way, and although I'm not at liberty to divulge much, I hope you can help. It will certainly push the investigation forward.'

'Well, I'll see what I can do, of course. We're all in absolute shock about the whole thing. What is it you need?'

'Well, what I need is a list of any girls in Year Ten whose first name begins with an A.'

Patti raised a perfectly shaped eyebrow. 'Surely you don't suspect one of our Year Ten girls?'

'No, no, of course not. We just think this particular girl will be able to give us some crucial information.'

Without another word, she walked over to her computer and typed. Within a few minutes she had a list of all the girls in Year Ten and with a further few deft strokes of her keyboard, she had ordered the list alphabetically by first name. She turned the screen so Gus could share the view.

'As you can see, we don't have any Year Ten girls whose first name begins with A. Are you sure it was Year Ten?'

'Well, that's what I'm told.'

'Hmm.' She looked at the computer screen with a frown and then wiggled her mouse, pressed a button and the list re-configured before Gus' eyes.

'Aha, That's better. I've ordered it alphabetically by middle name and we've got three now. Sidrah Ali Mukhtar, Jane Alicia Bright and Claire Ann Brown.'

'Great.' Gus was impressed. 'Fancy taking over my job?'

Patti laughed. 'Not a cat in hell's chance of that, Gus. I think we can discount Sidrah Ali Mukhtar. She's always known as Sidrah – Not many Muslim girls would use the name Ali as a nickname.'

'Can you tell me anything about the other two girls including what sort of clubs they're in?'

Mrs Copley tapped her fingers on the table, then leaned over and lifted her phone. 'Can you get Haleema to come here ASAP, please?' She turned back to Gus, 'This is a big school and much as I'd love to know all the pupils individually, I have to admit that I don't. I've called for the Year Ten head, Haleema Arshad – she'll be able to give you more information.'

As she finished speaking, there was a knock at the door and a tall woman with straight black hair tied back in a ponytail entered. 'You wanted to see me, Ms Copley?'

The head teacher shook her head and waved her hand towards Gus who'd stood up and now offered his hand to the woman. 'This is DI McGuire, he'd like to ask you a few questions about two of your girls in relation to the unfortunate events at the weekend.'

Haleema Arshad's smile faded, as she shook his hand before sitting down next to him. 'So sad. Those poor parents. Sue was a lovely girl. Never in trouble. One of our best students. Such a loss. And as for the Proctors, they must be devastated. I pray Simon is found safe and well.'

Gus smiled and gestured for Haleema to sit down opposite him on one of the comfy chairs.

Patti strode round from her desk and slid onto a third seat. 'You don't mind if I stay, do you? It's incumbent on me to be here, when it concerns our students.' She tilted her head at Gus, her eyebrows raised as if asking a question.

A slight smile played at the corner of Gus' mouth. He was quite sure that short of grappling her to the floor and man-handling her out of the room, Patti would be a difficult subject to oust. As the thought crossed his mind, Gus was aware of a slow blush warming his cheeks. *What the hell was he thinking? Damn, he should have left this for Alice to deal with.*

Gus shook his head, 'No problem at all.' He turned to Haleema. 'Can you tell me a bit about Jane Bright and Claire Brown?'

She frowned, 'Jane Bright? Oh, you mean, Ali Button?'

Gus glanced at Patti. 'Do I?'

'Well you might. Ali or Alicia is *legally* still called Jane Alicia Bright, however, because she's in the final stages of being adopted by her foster parents, we agreed, when she started here, to use their surname on the class register.' She turned to Patti who was nodding. 'You remember, don't you?'

'Of course, I just forgot it was that name. On the central files she's listed as Jane Bright, although on the class registers she's called Alicia Button. The adoption will be finalised before Christmas. I had a letter about it the other day.'

'So, she uses the name Ali? All the other students and teachers call her Ali?' When Haleema nodded, Gus continued. 'What about Claire Ann Brown?'

'Oh, Claire's another lovely girl. Tries her best, not as academically gifted as Ali.'

Patti cleared her throat. 'I think the inspector's asking if Claire uses her middle name or her first name.'

'Oh, yes, of course.' Haleema turned to Gus. 'No, Claire's called Claire.'

'Okay. You said Ali was new to the school, is that right?'

'Yes. She came in January, transferred from a school in Leeds. When the adoption was finalised, her parents wanted to move her to a school near their home so she could make friendship groups in the area.'

'And has she made friends in the area?'

Haleema folded her arms and sat back in the chair. 'Well, to be honest, I don't think she's extended her circle of friends beyond what it was before. You see, the Buttons are part of a church called The Family Church of Christ. We have quite a few families in the same church and Ali seems mainly to have been friends with those pupils.'

'What about Simon Proctor? Did she know him?'

'Well, she may have known him, I suppose. He's in Year Eleven so there's a bit of an age gap there, still, it is possible.'

'What's she like?'

Haleema glanced at Mrs Copley.

'Ali's a bit – oh I don't know – eccentric, I suppose?'

'In what way?'

'She finds it difficult to make friends. She's very quiet and she's always scribbling in a book. The Individual Needs Department have tried to involve her in groups. However, she's not interested. Academically she's very bright although she doesn't contribute in class.' She hesitated and again looked to her head teacher for permission.

'It's not really that surprising. From the limited information the adoptive parents have given, her biological parents were overly controlling and restricted contact with her peers. They hinted at some sort of abuse, but were reluctant to divulge very much as the move here was supposed to be a new start for Ali. The theory being, to leave her baggage behind with the adoption.'

'So, she must have a social worker? Is she on the "at-risk" register?'

Patti answered. 'We can't give you details of Ali's social worker. I know she will have been removed from the at-risk register when she was deemed she was no longer at risk and the adoption process began. You would need to approach social services... perhaps even the family.'

'Well, what are the parents like – the adoptive ones?'

'Very involved in her learning, very supportive. Mum doesn't work, Dad's a vet. Does a lot of the work at York race course, I believe.'

'How old are they?'

'Hmm, Hard to say. I think she's probably mid-thirties and he's possibly a few years older. She's quite pretty, dresses fashionably, and tries to get Ali to dress nicely too. I've seen them arm in arm in Top Shop looking at clothes, Ali refused to buy anything.' She laughed. 'Her mum was really disappointed, but Ali said she was comfortable in her jeans. Dad's a bit quieter than mum, greying slightly at the temples. All in all, a nice family.'

'Any other children?'

'No, Ali's the only one.'

Chapter 52

15:50 Bradford Royal Infirmary

Sampson was pissed off. Why did he have to take the girl's statement, just because Knowles was an arse? It wasn't as if he'd nowt else to do. After all, he was investigating two murders and a missing person. He shrugged and took a deep breath. Nowt he could do about it, after all. Gus said it would be good experience for him and he wanted to keep on his good side.

A&E wasn't as busy as he'd seen it. Too early for pub brawls and not late enough for the after-school rush. Still, a fair amount of blood, nausea and moaning as he walked up to the reception area to enquire after his witness. He was directed along beige corridors randomly dotted with bright paintings at eye level, into an asthmatic lift and finally to a ward where a pretty, yet no-nonsense, sister scrutinised his ID, before escorting him to a side room at the far end of the corridor. She knocked perfunctorily and entered, smiling widely at the girl's visitors, her parents presumably. She introduced him in a far friendlier tone than the one she'd spoken to him in.

Sampson looked at the girl and saw tears rise in eyes that were sunk beneath high cheekbones, coloured in varying shades of purple. He paused and frowned, wondered if he'd seen the girl before. He looked around for a chair to give the girl time to compose herself, and when he sat down next to her, he smiled at her and then at her parents. 'I know this is difficult for you. I'm here to take your statement, love.'

Her father ran great rough hands over his face and pinched the bridge of his nose. 'God, can't it wait? She's been through enough. Look at her. Just let her rest.'

His wife put out her hand and gripped her husband's arm tightly. 'Gordon, they've got to act quickly. You know that. We want them to catch the bastards that did this, so they have to question her.' She raised worried eyes to Sampson, before turning back to her husband. 'Look, you head out and get us all some coffee, I'll stay here with Jenny, okay?'

As he looked at his daughter, his eyes filled up. Clumsily, he crossed to her bed to kiss her, then hesitated, seemingly when he realised there was barely an area of unbruised skin. With a sigh, he blew her a kiss. 'I'll be back soon, honey.'

Jenny's mum watched her husband leave and then held out her hand. 'I'm Sally Gregg, Jenny's mum.'

Sampson shook her hand. 'Thanks for your help there. It's a difficult time, you're right. However, we do want to catch these buggers.'

He turned and studied Jenny, who lay with her eyes closed. 'Can you hear me, Jenny?'

Her eyes flicked open and looking straight at him, she swallowed with difficulty before speaking. 'Do you know what they've done to me?'

Sampson shook his head.

Tears rolled slowly down her cheeks. 'Neither do I. All I know is that every inch of my body hurts. I've got concussion, three broken ribs, numerous fractures, two in my skull, four broken fingers, a broken wrist, a dislocated knee, a fractured cheekbone and I still don't even know if I've been raped.'

Sampson glanced at her mother who held a glass of water and angled a plastic straw to her daughter's mouth. Jenny sipped and attempted a lopsided smile at her mum.

However, the pain was clearly too much and she soon let her head fall back onto her pillow.

'I'll tell you what I remember, though it's not much. I got in from school, dumped my stuff, grabbed my bag and left.'

'This was when?'

'Around 4.15 Monday night. I walked up to Ali's house and we had our tea.'

'Ali?'

'Oh, Ali Button. She's a friend of mine. I was having tea at hers and sleeping over after we'd been to The Prayer Chair Meeting.'

'The what?'

Jenny's mum offered her daughter another drink and explained, 'The Prayer Chair is an activity organised by the Youth Brigade of our church. They take The Prayer Chair into shopping centres and towns on a Saturday and encourage people to use the chair to seek redemption from their sins.'

Jenny looked at him. 'We were meeting to discuss where we would go on Saturday.'

'Who else was at the meeting?'

Mrs Gregg handed him a piece of paper with names, addresses and contact numbers of all the group members. 'I anticipated you'd need this.'

Sampson folded it and put it in his pocket. 'So, you got to the meeting at...?'

'7 pm.' Jenny frowned. 'It finished about 7:45 and I felt a bit tired, so I told Ali I was too tired for a sleepover and I'd just go home and really, that's about all I remember.'

Sampson read his notes. 'Did you leave the meeting with your friends?'

Jenny frowned and shook her head, 'Don't know. I suppose so. We usually walked together and split up at Ashwell Road near the top of Emm Lane to go our separate ways.'

'You can't remember?'

A small sniff, 'No.'

'They've taken her bloods to see if she's been given anything. You know drugs or something.'

As Jenny began to weep, her mother moved over and took the girl's hand in hers, talking all the while in low soothing tones.

Realising he wasn't going to get much more from the girl, Sampson stood up. Something niggled at the back of his mind, just out of reach. He took a step towards the door before it clicked. He knew why Jenny Gregg looked familiar. Although, covered in bruises as she was now, he could have been forgiven for not making the connection. 'Jenny, were you at Simon Proctor's party on Saturday night?'

Jenny's body stiffened and she pulled her hand from her mother's. 'Yes, yes, I was. How did you know?'

Mrs Greg stared at her daughter, her mouth an O-shape. 'You were supposed to be at Ali's on Saturday, Jen. Why would you go to a party instead?'

Sampson wanted to roll his eyes, but refrained. When would parents realise that their kids only told them the half of what they got up to?

Jenny's mum, brow gathered even tighter, her eyes dull and a single circle of colour on each cheek, turned to Sampson. 'Has she done something wrong? Why are you asking about that party?'

'Look, Mrs Gregg, we need to speak with everyone who was at the party. Simon's still missing and two girls lost their lives that night. Have you any idea where Simon is, Jenny?'

Tears, coursed down Jenny's cheeks. Like a toddler about to throw a tantrum, her head moved from side to side in denial. 'No, No. I don't know anything about Simon. I can't remember owt, okay?'

Despite the girl's obvious distress, Sampson had the impression she wasn't telling him everything. Memories of the footage Tayyub had taken showed another girl pulling Jenny off the table. He wondered if that was her friend, Ali.

Deciding to report back to Gus before asking any more questions, Sampson said his goodbyes and left the room. Jenny Gregg wasn't going anywhere in the near future and, perhaps, Gus could convince her mum to let her talk to them with another adult present. That would be the best solution.

Chapter 53

17:15 The Fort

'Eureka!'

Compo appeared from the depths of his computer station like a bear from hibernation, clutching a sandwich of indefinable origin and wearing a haggard, yet satisfied, look. He moonwalked across the room, twirled and, realising he had an audience, glanced down at the floor, his ears pink. 'Got a hit on the bikers!'

Gus contained his smile. Compo's enthusiasm was just the tonic he needed right now. Things didn't seem to be going anywhere very fast but at least Compo seemed to have come up with something. 'The floor's all yours.'

Compo looked at Gus, his ears becoming even pinker. 'You mean, you want me to tell *everybody*?'

By everybody, Gus took it that Compo meant, himself, Alice, Sampson, who'd just returned from Bradford Royal Infirmary, and Taffy. Not exactly an intimidating audience, still Compo hated reporting from anywhere other than behind his computer. It would do him good to venture out from his comfort zone every so often and this was a safe environment to test the waters. Gus leaned back on his desk, arms crossed over his chest. 'Seems the quickest way to disseminate info, Compo. On you go.'

Compo glanced round the room and then moved to the front, pulling at the bottom of his Beatles 'Eleanor Rigby' T-shirt and dragging his feet like a recalcitrant toddler. He cleared his throat and concentrated his gaze on an area far above their heads. 'Used Tayyub's video to narrow in on the tatts for the Blow Job Guy.' As if realising how bad his words sounded Compo made an eek expression with his mouth and shuffled his feet.

Gus had to admit the expression 'Blow Job Guy', wasn't the most sensitive of descriptors, but what the hell? It was only amongst the team and it was clear which guy Compo referred to. As Compo hesitated, biting his lip, Gus rolled his hand in a get-on-with-it gesture.

Standing a little straighter, Compo continued, rephrasing his description this time. 'The guy with the skeleton dressed in leather and riding on a motorbike tattooed on one arm and on the other a skull-wearing a helmet with the letters FB interlaced across the forehead. I thought the letters might mean summat, so I cross-referenced in the dark web and found a bikers' organisation called the Fugitive Bandits. It seems to be a less organised, more self-serving unit than the Hells Angels and has no links with them. It deals in drugs of all categories, has financed meth labs and imports heroin for distribution. Recent reports from vice show leanings towards grooming girls via the internet and possible child prostitution. Also, they have links to the bikers who rampaged in Kirkstall Road in Leeds in 2016. I'll keep trawling to see if I can find a location in Yorkshire for these guys.'

Taking a deep breath before wiping his forearm across his brow, Compo continued. 'I also cross-referenced Jade Simmonds' social media activity and came up with an internet name for our dude. Appears he's called Hard Rock. Jade had been PMing him for weeks and from the printout, which I've sent to your individual PCs, she arranged to meet him on Saturday. She also mentioned Simon Proctor's party.'

'Any real name yet for the guy?'

Compo shook his head. 'Not yet. I've set up a cross reference with known biker dudes, circulated the tatts images to tattoo parlours and contacted vice. Shouldn't be long till we get the bastard.'

Looking embarrassed and uncertain, Compo began to make his way back behind his screen until Gus stopped him. 'Hey, Compo.'

He turned and Gus smiled. 'Brilliant work.'

Compo's ears went pink again and a shy smile hovered round his lips before he disappeared behind his PC. Soon a tell-tale rustle told the rest of the team that Compo was comforting himself with food.

Just as Gus was about to share what he'd learned at the school, Sampson cleared his throat and moved to the front of the room. 'I think I've got something, too, Gus.'

Gus inclined his head and repositioned himself on the edge of his table and gave Sampson his full attention.

'I went to BRI like you asked and interviewed the girl. Her name is Jenny Gregg.'

Much as Gus was happy for Sampson to have his minute in the spotlight he wished the lad would just get on with it. They'd loads to do and he didn't have time for all this pussyfooting about. They should all just get to the damn point. He took a deep breath and released it, slow and long. He had the sense to realise that his impatience was a symptom of stress and, having no intention of going back to how he'd been earlier in the year, he took another breath and focussed on what Sampson was saying.

'Seems she was at Simon Proctor's party on Saturday. I think she was the girl dancing on the table, you know. The one that the other person in the hoodie pulled off.'

Gus frowned. 'You think? Didn't you ask her?'

Sampson flushed. 'Yeah, I did... well, I asked her if she was at the party and she said she was. Her mother was in a right tizz about that and the girl's well beat-up, so I thought maybe we could try and interview her with a non-related adult present. I reckon we'd get more that way.'

Exhaling, Gus gave a reluctant nod. Much as he wanted the information yesterday, Sampson had made the right call.

'Poor kid's been beaten up and is doped up on morphine. The results of the rape kit have been inconclusive so she doesn't even know if she'd been raped and she was near-hysterical when I was there. I decided we could tick that box tomorrow and just work on the assumption that she was the girl. I'm fairly certain she is.'

Much as it would have been ideal to have positive confirmation that it was Jenny Gregg on the table, Gus agreed that there was no point on upsetting the girl when she'd just been through a vicious attack that could have left her dead. 'You did right, Sampson. Now how does this tie in with Simon Proctor's party, the two dead girls and Proctor's disappearance? Connected, do you think?' He turned and glanced round the room at each of his detectives in turn.

Alice slurped some coffee and shoved a digestive biscuit in her mouth before replying. 'Course it's related. Too much of a coincidence for it not to be. Well, that's what you're always banging on about, anyway, Gus, isn't it?'

Gus shook his head in mock despair. 'Banging on about? I think you mean I make the valid point that there is no such thing as coincidence in our line of work.' He turned to Sampson. 'What else did you get from her?'

'Only that she was supposed to sleep over with her friend Ali on Monday night, but didn't. I sensed they may have fallen out and that's how they got separated.'

'Aaah,' Gus clicked his fingers. 'That's the name that I got from the school this afternoon. Ali Button's family are involved with a church called The Family Church of Christ.'

Lips turned down, Sampson continued. 'Seems that she'd been at a youth meeting at some weird church or other to discuss Prayer Chair sessions in town.'

Gus sensing that he was going to like Sampson's reply as little as Sampson did, said, 'And those are?'

Before Sampson could reply, Alice jumped to her feet, eyes flashing, 'It's a fucking exercise in public humiliation in the name of religion, that's what it is.'

The room went silent. All eyes turned to Alice who stood clenching and unclenching her fists, her small chin raised, her eyes darker than Gus had ever seen them.

He lowered his voice, his tone calm, 'Okay, Al. You want to share what you know about it with us?'

Alice gave an abrupt nod, gulped in some air and paced back and forth for a minute. Gus sensing she needed the time to collect her thoughts, moved over to grab a coffee. By the time he'd perched himself, yet again, on the edge of his table and was blowing into his mug, Alice was ready to begin.

'When I was fourteen we lived in Southampton for a while. My gran was ill and she wanted me to take her to a church that had sent a leaflet to her claiming it could cure her of her cancer. Both my parents tried to convince her it was futile and that her cancer had gone too far. She insisted, but my mum refused to take her. So, I did. Every week I took her to the public Prayer Chair sessions; still she continued to deteriorate. The church, which wasn't an official church, in fact, then asked her to attend three times a week. Against my parents' wishes, I continued to take her.' Alice wiped a tear from her eye. 'I'd have done anything for my gran, you know?'

Gus understood exactly what she meant. He'd never met his own grandparents but he knew he'd do anything for his mum. And never more so than after what had almost happened to her in February.

'It became clear that she was getting even more ill and that's when they started to do The Prayer Chair in private. Concentrated praying they called it. What I didn't realise was that what they were really doing was convincing her to leave her money to *them* when she died. They were so skilful. Whilst I waited outside, they worked on an old sick lady until she signed everything away to them. Then, not content with that, they started to blame me for the fact that she wasn't recovering. I was just a kid. I didn't know any better and we were keeping it secret from my mum. They started to accuse me of having impure thoughts and doing impure deeds and it was those that were poisoning my gran and making her ill.'

Gus' chest tightened at the thought of what his friend had gone through. Not only was she trying to help her gran but she was witnessing her deterioration and being blamed her for it, into the bargain.

'They told me the only way I could rid my gran of the toxins was to do a public denouncement of all my sins. They gave me a document with a list of questions about which boys I liked in school or if I liked girls. If I ever thought about touching myself or those boys. If I'd ever touched them, or kissed them. All sorts of private stuff that I gave them because I believed in them.'

Sensing that the worst was yet to come, Gus moved over and put his arm round her shoulder. Alice shrugged it off and glared at him. 'I'm not a fucking kid, Gus. I can do this. I don't need you to hold my damn hand, okay?'

Glad that Alice was still displaying some of her legendary independence, he held his hands up, palms facing her. 'Whoa! Okay, I'll just back off.'

Alice snorted, 'Yeah, right.' She sniffed, 'The weekend after that they took me to the city centre and they got their Prayer Chair out. The minister and his disciples went round drumming up support to see a "major cleansing" and when they'd gathered quite a crowd they made me sit on the chair.'

She sighed, 'That's when the second biggest humiliation of my life happened.' She glanced at Gus, '*You* already know the biggest one.'

Gus inclined his head and she continued, 'The bastards tore into me. Using all the ammunition I'd given them. They named the boys I liked and revealed my "dirty" thoughts in front of a crowd of people in Southampton high street. They ridiculed me and demeaned me and made me feel like the biggest Jezebel there ever was, that wasn't the worst of it. Oh no. What was worse was that in the crowd, unseen by me at the time, were some kids from my school. You can imagine what happened on the Monday morning, can't you?'

Gus could imagine only too well. No-one was crueller than teenage kids. Alice must have gone through hell.

'What happened to your gran, Alice?'

'She died, Compo, and all her money went to that despicable minister. The thing is, there are all sorts of fake churches from all faiths setting up and appealing to the vulnerable. No self-respecting church would condone or initiate such self-serving nonsense. After my gran died, I went back every week for a while and watched them do similar tricks on vulnerable members of the public until one day, the police came and arrested them and took them away. Turns out someone a bit more savvy than my folks had challenged their methods and the minister was imprisoned. I think it was right at that point I decided I wanted to be a copper. Never again did I want to be in a position where someone could abuse their position over me… and I've only ever been in that position one other time.'

As Compo opened his mouth to ask about that, Gus frowned at him and shook his head. Compo, taking the hint for once, shut his mouth and started working his magic on the PC.

'Looks like this group isn't the same as you encountered, Alice,' said Compo. 'Looks like there are new groups setting up every five minutes and the Church of England has its work keeping an eye on it. Seems the minister has come over from the states with the aim of recruiting families. Don't get what's wrong with the Church of England myself; my granny says they do a lovely funeral.'

Compo clicked a switch and a video of a middle-aged man standing in the midst of a group of teens with an ornate wooden chair before them explained with an American twang that The Prayer Chair Project was a way of taking Christianity into city centre streets and to show that there was a place in church for the youth. Although it all seemed innocuous enough, Gus had never been a fan of missionary religious practices. As far as he was concerned, faith was best left for people to come to themselves and, where possible, he avoided the leaflet giving, prayer-spouting, religious folks that seemed to dot every city centre street.

Things were becoming more and more intriguing. He'd make sure they interviewed the Buttons, the Greggs and the church leader.

'Sampson, you and Taffy check out this vicar and his band of merry teens tomorrow. We need to find out more about them especially as Jenny Gregg was taken after attending a meeting with them. Compo, see if you can access CCTV from the church in Frizinghall all the way up to Ashwell Road, for Monday night between seven and eight-thirty.'

Chapter 54

18:15 Tetley Street

Steven Knowles had just about had enough for one day. McGuire was strutting around like a fucking peacock, issuing orders left right and bloody centre. Although Knowles had been relegated to data crunching shit for the vice team, he was still in earshot of DI Perfect's comings and goings. It made his blood boil, so he'd decided to work to the clock for once. Actually, he generally *did* work to the clock. The only difference was, he usually didn't let on to anyone that he was sloping off early. Today though, he'd made a point of looking at his watch bang on six o'clock, scraping his chair back and logging off his computer, before grabbing his coat and leaving. 'No overtime for the likes of us,' he'd said over his shoulder to the goodie Twoshoes who were rattling off files like there was no tomorrow.

Now, under cover of darkness, he'd driven via the back roads to Tetley Street. *Bound to be a skanky bit of skirt willing to service a copper for nowt at this time of night. Trade would be slow this early, so I'll not be keeping them away from their proper clients.* He smirked. *Do them good to keep in practice.* Limber up them jaw muscles before the onslaught of dirty old men descended for a quick one on their way home from work. Just as well he'd got there early. Last thing he wanted was somebody else's sloppy seconds. He drove down the road that separated Sunbridge Road from Thornton Road and dipped into the wasteland area to the left as he drove down. There were no cameras here, and although the road was potholed, it was clearly well-used. The girls hung out round the back, off the main street, which decreased their chances of getting caught by the police. He knew from experience that unless they were flaunting themselves on Thornton Road before dark, they were usually left alone.

As he'd expected, there were three girls huddled together, their heads bowed and the glow of cigarettes shone through the dark illuminating their faces. He didn't recognise any of them and, to be honest, he wasn't really fussed which of them got in his car. He allowed the car to slide to a gentle stop and waited. All three girls' heads had raised when he'd stopped the car. He saw them exchange words and then the shortest of the three broke from the group and, hips undulating in what she, no doubt, considered to be a sexy appealing manner, she approached. Knowles snorted and lowered his window before flicking his cig butt into a pile of gravel. *Looks like a fucking pregnant duck with haemorrhoids – good job I'm not planning on giving it to her up the arse.*

She leaned one arm on the open driver's window, ensconcing him in a bubble of cheap perfume and damp air as she fluttered her eyelashes.

Stupid cow will wish she'd left it for one of the other mingers! With a grin, he flashed his warrant card at her, relishing the way her face fell, when she realised she'd been nabbed. She glanced at her friends with an open-handed 'What the fuck?' gesture and sighed. 'Okay. How can I make this go away?'

Knowles smirked. *That* was the sort of business acumen he admired in these girls. They knew when it was best to just count their losses and give a bloke a BJ. *Sound business practice, if you ask me.* He jerked his head to the passenger side. 'Get in, then. Let's you and me have some fun.' He pretended not to see the scowl on her face as she wobbled round to the passenger side, with a lot less swagger than she'd had a minute ago.

Once she was in, he slid the car into gear and drove further into the derelict land mass before doing a wide spin and pointing the car back towards the entrance. Behind them the lights from the NCP carpark gave off a dull glow when he put the headlights out. He rummaged in the side compartment of his door and brought out a towel which he laid over his thighs, tucking it up and round under his buttocks. 'Just in case there's a spillage. Come on then, darling, let's get those luscious lips juiced up, shall we?'

Five minutes later, job done, Knowles pulled the ends of the towel from under his bum and wiped his shaft down. The girl was wiping her mouth, spitting into a tissue as she did so. In the confined space of the car, the air was musky, so Knowles cracked the window open an inch as she looked up at him a coy smile on her lips. 'Was that good for you, Mr Knowles?'

Knowles started to grin, pleased that the bitch knew her place. Then, he frowned. How did she know his name? He certainly hadn't given it and she would have to have been some ace speed reader if she'd managed to catch it when he flashed his warrant card. He opened his mouth to speak, but she reached over and placed a vice-like hand on his knee. Her long fingernails almost piercing the skin. He grabbed her wrist and twisted her arm. 'What the fuck do you think you're playing at?'

She pouted up at him, all wide-eyed innocence, 'Don't you recognise me, Mr Knowles?' This time, when she said his name she placed a special emphasis on it.

His grip loosened on her wrist and she pulled it away, rubbing it where his fingers had left a red mark. He must have visited her before, yet he hadn't recognised her when she'd first approached. Reaching up, he flicked the inner light on and turned sideways to get a better look at her. Her emaciated frame belied the teenage chub that softened her cheeks and made her dark eyes look huge. His eyes were drawn to the love heart tattoo on the swell of her breast. She looked almost pre-pubescent. For a moment his heart skittered in his chest as he pondered the likelihood of him engaging in a sex act with an under-sixteen-year-old. *Fuck! Surely not.* Trouble was it was so hard to tell nowadays and he wasn't one for asking to see their birth certificates before letting them suck his dick. Who the hell would?

His eyes lifted back up to her face. Her expression was earnest as she studied him. Shaking her head, her eyes narrowed and her lips stretched wide revealing a row of white, straight teeth, 'I'm your Stacey's mate, Mr Knowles. Remember me now, do you?' Last time I saw you was when you took me and Stacey skating at the ice rink. I'm Julie. Remember me now, do you?'

A cold sweat erupted on Knowles' upper lip. Shit. His daughter Stacey wasn't even fifteen yet. How the hell could this be her friend? He recognised the name, though. Peering at the girl who'd just had her lips round his knob, the blood drained from his face, leaving him shaking. He could see her now. She'd lost some of her innocence along the way.

He recalled Stacey telling him Julie's mother had got blind drunk one night and dropped her keys. They'd found her the next morning, dead under a nearby bush. The irony of that story was that the door hadn't even been locked. If she hadn't been so drunk, she'd have tried the lock and got in. Knowles remembered feeling sorry for the kid, then when she'd moved schools, Stacey had lost touch with her friend.

Julie was grinning at him, her eyes alight with a calculated gaze that Knowles recognised from his dealings with other desperate human beings. 'Looks like I've got myself a meal ticket, doesn't it, Mr Knowles?' She laughed, a piercing sound that splintered the night air into a trillion fragments. 'Unless, of course, you want me to tell them back at The Fort about how you forced me, a fourteen-year-old, to go down on your old man dick?'

He reached over and gripped her arms and shook her once. 'You won't fucking do that, Julie. You know you won't.'

She flung her head back revealing a slender neck and laughed again. 'You sure about that? Try me and see?' With a childlike giggle she pursed her lips before saying in a sing-song voice, 'Oh, I forgot. You already did try me, didn't you?'

Anger flashed through Knowles and he shook her... harder this time. Her increased near-hysterical laughter taunted him. He flung her back against the door and slammed his fist into her face before sliding both hands round her delicate throat and pressing. Adrenalin made him savour her bulging eyes as her frantic fingers scrabbled for traction against his strong hands.

'You don't ever mess with me, bitch. Got it?'

* * *

Two hours later, headache pulsing at his temple, Knowles parked up in front of his house. All the lights were on and nobody had thought to close the curtains. Stacey and his younger daughter were dancing in front of the TV. Must be on the damn Wii again. They were always on it.

He lifted a shaking hand to his face and pulled his fingers from his cheeks down to his chin. What the hell had he done? How could he go in there and face them, knowing what he'd done? He closed his eyes and braced both hands on the steering wheel as if to ground himself. There was nothing for it. He just needed to get in there and put all of this behind him. There was nowt else for it.

He'd just opened the car door and was preparing to drag his exhausted body from the car when his phone pinged. Using any excuse to delay the inevitable he pulled his phone from his pocket and saw that it was from Jerry. Wondering what had prompted the other man to contact him out of hours, he flicked the text open. As he read, his lips lifted up and he took a deep breath. What was it they said about every cloud?

Feeling lighter by far, he got out of the car and moved over to his front door, a smile on his lips. Things weren't so bad after all… well, not for him anyway. Maybe DS Alice Cooper would have a different slant on things. He fucking hoped so. He really did.

Chapter 55

18:55 St Anne's Road Mosque, Heaton

Tariq didn't know what to do. On the one hand he wanted to wrap his arms round Shamila and hold her tight. On the other, he was all too aware that he was in the mosque and that, progressive though this particular mosque was, he might be pushing the boundaries a bit too far if he was caught hugging a girl who was *not* his sister in one of the meeting rooms. He sighed and took a step closer to the crying girl.

This was exactly the sort of dichotomy he and Shamila had set up The Young Jihadists to discuss. Their non-Muslim peers hugged each other freely as a matter of routine; in greeting, to offer comfort, hell – just because they damn well felt like it. Yet, some among their culture considered even the most innocent of physical contact between the opposite sexes *haram*. Tariq had uncles who refused to shake hands with women, even in a professional setting, and he couldn't get his head round that. Especially when he knew that one of them wasn't *quite* so circumspect on his weekly trips to Thornton Road. It wasn't just the men, either. Some of the women refused to shake hands, too. What was so wrong in shaking someone's hand in a professional capacity? These extremes of opinion within the faith elders made it difficult for the youth to ground themselves. To find their own way. To live within both their faith and the norms of their country.

He edged closer to Shamila, whose tears had streaked her face with mascara. What the hell? He couldn't just let her cry her heart out like this and not do something. He reached over and pulled her to his chest, wrapping his arms round her heaving shoulders and mumbled words of comfort. Her body stiffened for a nanosecond and she pulled her head away from his chest and looked at him through tear-filled eyes. His lips lifted in an embarrassed smile. He returned her smile and she rested her head on his chest once more. Tariq hoped she couldn't feel his arm shaking.

Despite enjoying the heady smell of her citrusy perfume and the lurch of emotion in his chest, guilt hung heavy in his heart. He was to blame for Shamila's brother's arrest. It was he who had told the police about Adnan's relationship with Sue Downs. Shamila would be *so* angry if she knew what he'd done.

She was speaking now, her voice muffled, and Tariq strained to hear her words, 'He didn't do it, you know? Adnan would never have hurt her. He's not like that. I don't even understand what he was doing at the party and why he was upstairs with her.'

Tariq hesitated. How could he respond to this? *Adnan's been seeing her for weeks. I knew about it, but he swore me to secrecy?* Or *your brother kept secrets from you and Sue was just one of them. He probably didn't tell you about the weed or the coke either, did he?* In the end he couldn't trust himself to say anything, so he continued holding her until a cough from the doorway made them spring apart.

A hot flame of colour flushed his cheeks. Thank Allah, it was only Shiraz. Thrusting his hands in his pockets, whilst Shamila turned away and tried to rectify the damage to her make-up with a tissue and a small mirror, Tariq said, 'You okay?'

Shiraz snorted and, his gaze flitting round the room, focussing on anything except Shamila, said, 'You okay, Sham? Heard about Adnan. Sucks, dun't it?'

Shamila straightened her back, walked over to the table, pulled out a chair and sat down, her hands sifting through a sheaf of papers she'd put there earlier. When she spoke, her voice was resolute, making it clear she did not want to discuss her brother. 'Yeah, it does. He didn't do it and they'll soon prove that, so let's just get on with this meeting. Where is everybody?'

She'd no sooner asked the question, when the door opened again and a line of teenagers drifted in. Tariq hoped Shamila hadn't noticed the nervous glances each of them sent her way. It was clear they'd all heard about Adnan. They'd more than likely have been talking about it ad infinitum since the news broke. Each of them would have their own perspective on it, although most, he hoped, would realise that, Adnan, despite being an idiot some of the time, was at heart a good lad. He wouldn't have killed Sue. Tariq knew he'd been besotted by her, trailing after her like a lovesick puppy. He tried to still the insistent thought that The Crossbow Cannibal hadn't been on the police's radar either... until he had.

As they sat down, some slouching over the table, hoodies up over their head, some with prayer hats on ready to pray after the meeting, he smiled. He was proud of the group he and Shamila had created. It encompassed a range of kids from the area all with different views of Islam and how they could keep their faith and yet live within the wider communities. There had been, from the start, a tacit agreement that they wanted to be part of a wider society. Not just this little neck of the woods here in Bradford Nine. The discussions had been heated at times, yet Shamila's quiet persistence had made them confront and discuss things they hadn't been able to before. That was why they'd asked Tayyub to record Simon's party. They wanted to experience the sort of parties the white kids had. See what they did, how they behaved when they were drunk.

Mind you, glancing round at some of the lads, Tariq knew fine and well that some of them had experienced a lot of those things for themselves. His gaze rested on their youngest member, fourteen-year old Zarqa. Her dad ran Mo's Sa'MOsas on Oak Lane.

Zarqa had been quiet for a few weeks now and today she looked pale and distracted, as if she wasn't really with them. He hoped things were okay with her. He'd make a point of asking her at the end of the meeting.

'So, we can't see Tayyub's recording as the police have confiscated it. Beside which, when we've got two girls dead and with Simon still missing, it would be in bad taste to talk about it tonight, anyway,' said Shamila.

Shiraz snorted, 'Yeah, especially since your brother's the number one suspect for one of the murders. Maybe Adnan's bumped off Simon, too?'

The rest of the room gasped as Shamila turned to Shiraz, but before she could answer, Zarqa, lifted from her reverie, swung in her chair towards Shiraz. 'That's not funny, Shiraz, and you know it. You're a dick!'

'Who you calling a dick, Zarqa? Butter wouldn't melt in your mouth, huh? What about your mother? We've all heard about her, haven't we, lads?'

'Aw, shut up Shiraz, you're well out of line,' said Liaqat, casting a nervous glance towards Zarqa as she jumped to her feet, and shouldered her way past Shiraz.

Wrenching the door open, she turned. 'You know summat, Shiraz? You're an idiot.'

As the door slammed behind her, Tariq thought that the thud signalled the beginning of the end of their group and he wanted to run after Zarqa and replay the entire conversation without Shiraz's taunting words.

For a moment there was silence and then Shamila stood up, rested her knuckles on the table and, glaring at Shiraz, she addressed the entire group. 'Anyone else got any wisecracks like that one?'

Chapter 56

20:05 The Fort

Throwing the incident room door open so forcefully that it banged against the wall, ricocheting and almost hitting her in the face as she marched through, Nancy Chalmers yelled, 'Gus!'

Jolting upright, Gus jerked his neck and cursing under his breath, he scowled at Nancy. Couldn't she have entered like a normal person? There was no need for her to storm in like a whirlwind, making everyone jump. A quick glance round the room told him that, in fact, he'd been the only one affected by Nancy's entrance. Everyone else was intent on their jobs and hadn't even glanced up. Gus, on the other hand, had been so focussed on the crime board that her entrance had surprised him. He told himself that it was nothing to do with him being on edge, yet he had the grace to admit to himself that the opposite was true.

He'd been staring at the crime board, fully immersed in trying to work out what the connection was between Simon Proctor's disappearance, Sue Downs' murder and Jenny Gregg's abduction, torture and subsequent release. None of it made sense. They'd more or less cut Jade Simmonds out of the equation on the grounds that she was a victim of the bikers they were still tracking down. Tayyub's video footage showed that the bikers had left the premises not long after they'd forced Jade and the other girl to perform oral sex on them. Gus' fists clenched. He hated misogynists and these ones took the fucking biscuit.

He could still see the footage. Hell, he wished he could un-see it. The biker with the skeleton on the motorbike tattoo had grabbed Jade's hair to try to rouse her, yanked her head right up and shook it hard before pushing it back to her chest when she didn't respond. Not content with that, the bastard had aimed a kick at her legs which made Jade's entire body lurch forward, before landing back into the position in which they'd found her. Had she been dead then? If that bastard had just checked, maybe she'd still be alive. He'd be glad when Compo had ascertained their whereabouts. Gus, for one, was ready to blow apart their perverted little faction. He looked forward to getting justice for Jade Simmonds' family and, if one of them resisted arrest, well so be it, they'd have to use a little bit of force to bring them back in line.

He looked over at Compo, willing him to have located their headquarters, and saw that Compo, head bobbing in time to The Boss' *Born To Run*, from the strains drifting from his head phones was engrossed.

He wondered if he should have gone to see Ali Button and her parents tonight, but he wanted to be sure he had all the details of her adoption at his fingertips before he went. When he'd contacted social services on his return to The Fort, he'd been told that Naila, Mo's wife, was Ali's named social worker. As luck would have it, Naila was in meetings all afternoon, however a hurried text had told him she'd make time to drop into The Fort in the morning to speak to him. Good old Naila. She was very perceptive and he looked forward to getting her perspective on Ali Button. He wondered if Ali might have been the figure who pulled Jenny Gregg off the table in the Proctor's kitchen. Haleema Tariq had described her as a bit of a tomboy and Jenny had confirmed her attendance at the party and that Ali was the friend she'd gone to the church meeting with on Monday night.

Yes, he was looking forward to seeing what light Ali could shed on things.

Recovering his equilibrium, Gus glared at Nancy, 'You gave me a damn fright. Can't you be a quieter?'

Nancy harrumphed, 'Man-up, Gus. We can't all scoot about like bloody ghosts, can we?' She looked round the room until her gaze rested on Alice. 'Cooper. You and Gus, my office, now!'

Alice pushed her chair back and grimaced in Gus' direction. Gus shrugged and shook his head. He'd known Nancy for years, yet he still didn't think he'd ever get used to her erratic personality. Twisting the crick out of his neck, he sighed and gestured for Alice to lead the way through the fug of Chanel that Nancy had left in her wake.

'Wonder what you've done wrong now,' he said to Alice, in a voice that was only half teasing. Despite her brusqueness, there had been a tell-tale tautness to Nancy's frame as she'd marched back out of the room. Summat was up, of that he was very sure.

Chapter 57

20:25 Unknown Location

Jumping up, I pace the room. Can't focus on my safe place. I'm going stir crazy. I stop where the girl had lain. There are droplets of blood on the floor. They were just visible in the dimmed lamp light.

I start jogging on the spot, building up a sweat. Knackered. No energy... too weak. I walk round the circumference of my cell until I see where the ropes wound up. I'd thrown them in the corner and forgotten about them. I grab them. They're stained. Curious, I lift them to my nose and inhale the metallic scent of her blood. My crotch twitches.

Shaking them out, I hold one end in each hand, testing their length. It's ages since I've done this. I start skipping... stumble... rope tangles round my leg, try again. Then, I'm doing it and the slap, slap, slap of the bloody rope on the concrete makes me smile. It's like the echo... like a long-lost friend... like Matty or Jake, I suppose. A new feeling of resolve swamps me. I speed up... faster... faster... faster. I can do this. Everything will work out.

Sweat drips from my brow, salt nipping my eyes as I flop onto the bed. It wobbles, thank God, I'm used to it now. Know it'll withstand my weight. Do owt for some weed right now. Anything to pass the time. The exercise has left me shaky. Sweat's turning cold and I shiver. In the distance, the church bells ring.

Diiiiiing, Doooooong!
'Ding dong dell, pussy's in the well.'

Fucking pussy! Pussy must be wet if it's in the well!
'Ding dong dell! Wet pussy in the well.'

Must be about half-eight or so. Used to hate them before... the bells. Me, Matty and Jake couldn't see the point of having a practice for ringing church bells. Now though, it's comforting. We called them all saddos and weirdos before. Mrs Clements, my maths teacher is one of them. Wonder if she's there tonight?

'Hi Mrs Clements, don't yank too hard... Wet pussy's in the well.'

She told me once that bell ringing had a special name. Fucked if I can remember it, though. Bloody waste of time, yanking on a cord for an hour. I giggle. Can think of better things to yank on. I hold the bloody rope near my nose with one hand, I close my eyes and slip my hand inside my boxers. Who cares if the fucking green light's on – give some perv a treat.

Chapter 58

20:45 The Fort

Gus and Alice, walking side by side, followed Nancy along the corridor to her room. It was like being a kid in school again, being transported to the head teacher's for some damn nonsense or other that Mo had gotten Greg and him into.

Gus grinned. It had always been Mo that got them into trouble. Not that they'd ever done owt too serious. On one occasion, Mo had convinced them it'd be a good idea to hide their teacher's specs. Mrs Parkside had been livid; and when she'd found them in Mo's lunch box covered in raita she'd been even more livid. Mo had been one of those kids who, when they were told off for anything, couldn't help laughing. The more Mrs Parkside had yelled, the more Mo's skinny little shoulders had shuddered with nervous laughter, which enraged the teacher more.

What had gotten him and Greg involved in the punishment was that they'd stuck up for Mo when she'd grabbed him by the shoulder and dragged him from his desk. Gus could remember it as if it had happened yesterday. He and Greg had jumped to their feet at the same time and yelled, 'Leave him alone. He doesn't mean to laugh, miss. He's sorry. Tell her you're sorry, Mo.'

Mo had been too caught up in the nerves of the situation and couldn't stop his nervous giggling. Mrs Parkside had marched the three of them down to the head teacher's office and left them there. Three seven-year-old boys who'd do anything for each other, silently sat on the wooden bench outside the office determined to take their punishment together as one. The memory gave Gus a warmth in his heart and he realised that, for maybe the first time since Greg's death, he was able to remember him with affection that wasn't over-ridden by guilt.

Coming back to the present, Gus was aware that a couple of the officers they passed were looking at Nancy and grinning. Gus looked at her and saw what was making them so amused. Nancy was marching along the corridor in high dudgeon… in a pair of pink fluffy slippers. Gus caught Alice's eye and the two of them smothered smiles as Nancy flung open her office door and waited for them to enter.

Sure enough, the first thing Gus saw when he went in were her discarded shoes, kicked into a corner of the room. This was a clear indication that whatever had prompted her to leave her room and storm along the corridor to get them, without slipping her shoes on again, was something very serious indeed. He tried to remember if he'd done anything he shouldn't but the only thing that came to mind was Alice slapping Steve Knowles. Well, he'd got her back on that one. No way was Alice going to pay the price for Knowles' stupidity.

Tucking her skirt under her bottom, Nancy slid into her chair and gestured for Gus and Alice to take the two chairs opposite her desk. Again, the feeling of being back at school prevailed, as he snuck a conspiratorial glance at Alice. *I've got your back*, it said.

Nancy sucked in one cheek and chewed on it. Gus heart sank further. This was yet another of Nancy's tells. She was really freaked out by something and no amount of fresh flower fragrance or soothing windswept Yorkshire Moors scenery on her walls was going to calm him till he knew what was up.

'Spill.' The word shot out more clipped than he'd intended, thankfully, Nancy seemed not to notice. *Shit it must be bad! Had Knowles gone to the papers or internal affairs or what?*

Nancy jumped up and began pacing the room, the incongruous slippers no longer a source of amusement for Gus. He found he was clenching either side of his chair and made a conscious effort to relax his fists. Alice had one leg crossed over the other and despite her calm expression, the way the supporting leg jiggled up and down betrayed her nerves.

Nancy, thrust her fingers through her hair and walked to the front of her desk. Placing herself equidistant between the two of them, she hefted herself up onto the desk and focussed her gaze on Alice. Gus's fingers re-clenched. *That bastard better not have made trouble for Al. He just better not have!* However, when Nancy spoke, Gus realised that his fears had been unfounded for the reality was worse... much worse than he'd anticipated.

Seemingly unhappy with her position on the desk, Nancy eased herself to the floor and got down on her knees beside Alice, grasping one of the younger woman's hands in her own. Alice's leg increased its jogging tempo.

'I've had a call from DCS Machalski from Brent.'

With an abruptness that surprised Gus, Alice's leg stilled and her face paled. For a second he thought she was going to faint, instead she took a deep breath and moved her other hand to Nancy's where she held her two-handed grip like a limpet.

Nancy's voice as low and calm, 'God, Alice. I never dreamed I'd have to tell you this. Never in a million years did I think this would happen.'

Alice swallowed and bit her top lip before giving a single nod for Nancy to continue.

'The bastard's woken up, Al. He's fucking woken up.'

Time stood still for a moment and then, Gus saw a single tear roll down Alice's cheek. In an instant, he was off his seat and round the other side of the chair, his arms wrapped round her, holding tight. Alice shrugged him off and held Nancy's gaze. 'There's more, isn't there?'

More? What fucking more could there be? Wasn't this bad enough?

Nancy flicked a glance at him and then patted Alice's hand. When she spoke next, it was in a rush as if she was desperate to get the words out. As if they were scalding her mouth by remaining unspoken. 'He's blaming *you*, Alice. The bastard's blaming you and they're reopening the investigation. Seems Big H is changing his statement to implicate you. Says you threatened him if he didn't back you up as opposed to Kennedy, and with Kennedy being in a coma, he decided to back you.'

Chapter 59

21:50 Alice's House, Titus Street, Saltaire

Alice was in that cellar again.

She could smell the sewers and the rat piss. She could hear the rodents scampering across the rafters and it took everything she had to stop herself from shuddering. She preferred to take the lead. It had always been her position of choice on entering buildings where there was a possible threat.

Sean was behind her. His quiet footsteps keeping time with her own and the sound of his breathing, which again seemed to be synchronised to hers, was reassuring. Their intelligence was that Big H and two of his thugs were waiting to meet their snitch in the back of the cellar. The cellar ran along the bottom of four disused warehouses and was massive. A few dull lamps punctuated the dark with yellowing circles of light. Alice could see just enough to dodge the packing crates and detritus that dotted the floor. Sean had the easy job this time, because their team was outside scoping the place and would let them know if anyone else showed interest in entering the premises.

Heart thumping in her chest, Alice was aware of the familiar pooling of sweat under her armpits as she moved, arms outstretched before her, scoping the corners as she moved, gun finger ready at the trigger should she need to use it. Up ahead she heard voices, deep and low. She paused trying to work out how many different voices she could hear, but they were too quiet. Risking a quick glance behind her, she winked at Sean and then continued. A huge wooden crate barred her view of the space beyond, so with slow deliberate steps she eased her way to the side and when she had visuals on the trio of men, she stepped forward, her double-handed grip firm on the gun and her eyes focussed on Big H. His fat belly rolled over the top of his jeans, obscuring his crotch area. It was a wonder the crate he sat on withstood his weight.

'Police, hands up.' Alice's voice was firm.

Big H's two thugs began to run in the opposite direction from where Alice and Sean had entered. Alice let them go. They had a team at the far entrance, too, and they'd pick them up. On the floor in front of Big H was an unzipped sports bag. Inside were glistening bundles of heroin. Caught in the fucking act!

Alice opened her mouth to repeat her earlier order to Big H when she saw his eyes move from her and a slight smile flicker at the corner of his mouth. Adrenalin pulsed through Alice's body and a warning frisson shot up her spine. In a nanosecond she had spun round and dodged to one side. At the same moment a shot rang out and Alice registered that the trajectory of Sean's aim was right at the spot where she had stood.

Without pausing to think, she raised her leg and kicked out in one of her oft practised ju-jitsu moves. Her foot connected with Sean's waist. He stumbled, yet maintained his hold of the gun which he pointed at Alice. In that brief second, Alice realised that his service gun was kicked behind him and the one he was holding wasn't an official gun. She did a double kick to his waist which landed him on his bottom with the gun still pointing her way. Allowing her weight to propel her forward at speed, she flipped her gun in her hand so she was holding the barrel and then brought the handle down on his head with as much strength as she could muster.

Seeing Sean was unconscious, Alice spun round and saw Big H, wheezing like Darth Vader on a bad day, trying to zip up his bag. She cocked her head at him. 'Really?'

He looked at her and then plonked himself down on the crate so hard that it flattened, leaving him flat on his back like a fish out of water. Alice slipped her cuffs on him, hooked him to a water pipe and radioed for assistance.

In the time it took for help to arrive, Big H spilled all to Alice, who from somewhere, found the sense to caution him and switch her phone to record. Sean had planned it all. He'd wanted her with him so he could kill her whilst pretending to be the tragic hero who tried so hard to save her and yet failed. There was another exit that Big H and his stooges had built, leading up to the top warehouses and off to a labyrinth of back alleys. True to his word, his stooges didn't exit at the expected point and later a makeshift ladder with a hole leading to the upstairs warehouse was found behind some pallets in the corner of the middle warehouse. Alice's account, substantiated by Big H's, was enough to keep her in the clear. She, however, had lost it big-time.

Although she had no recollection of doing so, Alice must have driven home, for her Mini was parked outside in the street. A vague impression of Gus' shocked face and his outstretched arms as he tried to stop her from leaving Nancy's office lingered in her head. She hadn't wanted to stay. Hadn't wanted to hear their platitudes. She knew how devious Sean Kennedy could be. After all, she'd lived with him for two years and never once suspected he was a dirty copper. When she'd got inside her dinky little two-bedroom terrace, she'd locked her doors and drawn the curtains shut. The very thought that Sean had come out of his coma petrified her. He'd tried to kill her and he'd have succeeded if something, perhaps a sixth sense, hadn't alerted her to the danger. She'd trusted him. He'd been her lover and her boss and she'd trusted him with her life, trusted him to have her back.

How fucking naive had she been? She hadn't seen it coming. Hell, only that morning they'd made love and he'd told her he loved her, suggested maybe it was time to make their arrangement more permanent and, like a fool, she'd believed him. The memory of how happy she'd been that morning made her feel sick. She rushed into the kitchen and dry-heaved over the sink until her stomach muscles spasmed. Closing her eyes, she slid to the floor and with her back leaning against the kitchen units, she rested her forearms across her knees and, dropping her head onto them, she broke down and sobbed in the darkness.

When she was spent, she realised just how cold she was and, feeling like a woman three times her age, she pulled herself to her feet, ignoring the pins and needles that shot up her legs and into her numbed bottom. Heaving her leaden body, she climbed the stairs and, flinging off her clothes as she moved, she went into the bathroom and put the shower on as hot as it would go. As steam rose in the bathroom, she lifted a hand and swiped it across the mirror. Two dark, kohl smudged eyes stared at her from the depths of a pallid face. She lifted her fist and smashed it into the mirror and enjoyed the strange feeling of peace that descended on her when she saw the glass break like cracking ice on a pond, fracturing her reflection into a million pieces.

Taking a deep breath, she turned to climb over the bath and into her shower, only then noticing the rivulets of blood that meandered down her fingers. She clenched her fist and, as if from a distance, studied the myriad of scratches that opened along her knuckles as she flexed. For a fleeting second, she remembered the girl Neha from their previous case. Neha had self-harmed and Alice had asked her how it felt. Neha had tried to explain the release and peace that each cut delivered for her. At the time, Alice had struggled to understand, now, however, she felt a sudden rush of sympathy for Neha, who struggled with this impulse on a daily basis. Standing, head bowed, under the shower, she savoured the warmth as it soothed her.

When, at last, she stepped out and turned the shower off, her mood had lifted. Last time, she'd been a victim. This time, she was no longer a victim. She would do everything in her power to make Sean Kennedy pay for what he'd done. If he was no longer in a coma then he should be behind bars and she would do whatever it took to make sure that's where he ended up. Big H was quite clearly hedging his bets. Maybe Sean had something more on the gangster and was playing that card. Whatever his game was, *she* wasn't going to sit back and let him win.

She was snuggling into oversized pyjamas and a fleece dressing gown when the doorbell rang. Alice grinned. *Gus! He is so damn predictable… and such a worrier.*

Wednesday

Chapter 60

06:30 The Fort

Gus, hair bouncing like a mane as he stormed into the room, came to an abrupt halt. His eyes flashed at his team members, who had almost jumped to attention at his brusque entry. 'What the fuck is this?' He threw a copy of the morning's *Sun* on one table and a copy of *The Bradford Chronicle* on another.

Sampson, who was nearest, picked up *The Chronicle* and read the headlines aloud:

> Two dead, one missing and now a fourth teenager beaten and hospitalised.
> When will Bradford Police stop twiddling their thumbs?

As Sampson and Taffy moaned about the headlines, with Compo nodding his agreement from behind a bacon butty, Gus glanced round the room. No Alice. He had told her to make a late start and, after yesterday's events, he doubted she'd have surfaced yet. Between them they'd demolished a substantial portion of the Glenmorangie he'd brought round. Fortunately, he'd had the foresight to jog to Alice's house, knowing he'd need to take a taxi home later, even so, *she'd* downed more of the amber nectar than he had.

She'd spoken at great length about her feelings for Sean Kennedy and his betrayal of her, yet was determined not to succumb to the depression that had plagued her just after the event. She'd been grieving not only the loss of her lover but also the loss of what she had believed their relationship to be. Gus knew exactly how that felt. Gabriella hadn't tried to kill him, she'd just left him for his own sister. What Kennedy had done to Alice was much worse and now the bastard had the audacity to try to turn the tables on her. At one point she'd yelled, 'I should have killed the bastard when I had the chance. Now, he's bloody resurrected he'll think he's God and will do everything in his power to make me pay.'

With her words still ringing in his ears, Gus lifted the copy of *The Sun* newspaper and cleared his throat. Now that they'd seen the local headlines, Gus wanted to let the team know about the national ones, before they saw them for themselves. With everyone's attention on him, Gus spent ten minutes explaining the situation with Alice and Sean Kennedy in detail to his team. Reassuring them that Alice was still on the team and had not been suspended, he cautioned them that this may not be the position for too long. He held out the newspaper at arms' length with the headlines visible to his team.

'Hero officer accused of attempted murder by maligned coma cop!'

So far, they'd not printed her name, but as soon as the tabloids did, the powers that be would suspend her, pending an investigation. She was lucky, Nancy had argued the case for her continued employment until a preliminary investigation had been completed, citing the fact that a court ruling had previously declared Sean Kennedy culpable. Nancy had lined up a lawyer for Alice to see later on that day.

Compo sprung to his feet, the indignation on his face diminished a little by the dollop of ketchup at the corner of his mouth. 'That's not fair, Gus. Not bloody fair. Poor Alice.'

Gus raised one hand and, his expression betraying none of the doubt that had plagued him since Nancy broke the news, said, 'This *will* be sorted out. Alice is not the villain here and I'm sure she'll be exonerated before long. Meantime, for us, it's business as usual.'

He turned to Taffy and Sampson, 'You two need to take a statement from Jenny Gregg. The Proctors have come in, so I'll chat to them and, when Alice comes in, she and I will interview Ali Button and her parents. I want to catch them before they head off to school and work. We'll also check out the The Prayer Chair minister. Compo, any word on that biker gang, or identifying those bikers?'

Compo growled, shaking his head. 'Not so far. Every time I think I've got something it's encrypted. Vice have limited intel, too. They're as keen to apprehend them as we are. They reckon they are the major suppliers of MDMA in the district and want a handle on them. I'll keep on it. The thing is, in almost every biker photo we've got, their number plates are obscured and their faces are covered by bandanas. Don't worry, though, I'm on it, like an Easter...' looking round the room, his moon face broke into a massive grin. 'Bonnet! You get it. Instead of car bonnet I've used Easter.'

Gus rolled his eyes. *What the fuck? Was everyone insane?*

A buzz from Compo's PC had everyone's eyes moving to the screen at the front. Since the last time, Compo had set up an automated notification to alert them of any new footage of Simon Proctor. As Gus had come to expect, the camera was directed at Simon's bed. Although Simon wasn't actually on the bed right then. *Hope to God he's okay*, thought Gus wondering if this was the captor's way of announcing Simon's death... an empty bed in the corner of an unidentifiable bloody cellar.

'Look, there's some movement in the periphery – shadows... as if someone's moving about just outside the camera's scope.' Compo pointed and Gus saw that he was right. As they watched, Compo's fingers flew over his keyboard and he muttered under his breath.

'Anything?' Gus grimaced, suspecting that Compo's expression held the answer to that query.

'Nothing. Not a damn thing. Can't break this. All we know for sure is that the footage was taken at around half-eight last night. This bastard's playing with us.'

The fact that Compo swore told Gus just how frustrated he was. Compo rarely swore and when he did, he never, ever used that word. Gus continued to watch the screen, Sampson and Taffy standing beside him.

Simon entered the frame and shimmied into the bed. His lips were moving and he laughed a couple of times. *Cracking up or talking to someone else?* Gus suspected the former. Whoever held Simon Proctor in these conditions wasn't someone the lad would be sharing a joke with, he suspected. When the lad's hand disappeared under the blanket and moments later his head was flung back, eyes closed as his hands moved rhythmically just out of sight, Gus felt like the worst sort of voyeur. His instincts to turn the footage off were narrowly outweighed by the knowledge that it wasn't only the people on his team that were privy to this most intimate of moments. He only hoped Mrs Proctor had somehow missed it.

As the screen faded, signalling the end of the recording, Sampson moved over to Gus, an evidence slip in his hand. 'I wanted to tell you this last night, but it was after ten before Mrs Gregg called me and I thought it could wait till this morning.'

Gus took the evidence sheet that indicated that Sampson had sent something off to the lab. 'What is it?'

'Jenny Gregg's mum was going through her daughter's bag last night after I'd gone and found a folded piece of paper. When she opened it, she saw this.' Sampson offered his phone to Gus. On it was a photo of a sheet of plain white paper with a crease across the middle showing where it had been folded. Scrawled over it in red was the word, 'REDEEMED'.

'She contacted me and I bagged it and sent it for analysis. Should get the handwriting results back soonish. The other lab tests by lunch time. Seems like there's a definite link between Sue Downs' death and Jenny Gregg's abduction.'

Gus could have kissed Sampson. This was real progress. Both girls had been at Simon Proctor's party. There was no way the three incidents could be coincidence. It was all the more imperative that they speak again with Jenny Gregg and with Ali Button and her mum. Things were finally moving.

Chapter 61

06:55 The Chaat Café

The café was almost empty at this time of the morning and Knowles liked it like this. No hustle, no bustle and no trivial conversations about shite. He sat on one of the comfy seats, a croissant and a coffee on the table in front of him, *The Sun* folded next to his drink. His stomach rolled at the sight of the croissant, yet he knew he should try to eat it. Maybe it would avert the sickliness, calm it down. He grimaced and lifted it to his lips, but even the texture of the greasy pastry provoked a watering sensation at the back of his throat. If he ate it, he'd throw up. Instead, he lifted the coffee and took a large mouthful, ignoring its heat as it travelled down and landed with a slosh in his stomach. His stomach gurgled and his wife's often articulated premonitions of ulcers and stomach cancer flitted through his mind.

As he lifted the newspaper up and unfolded it, he noticed his hands shook. He laid the newspaper out on top of the table and read the headlines. So, Jerry had been right. Alice Cooper was in big bother, it seemed. Although the thought lifted his spirits a little, he was all too aware of the thunder cloud hovering above his head, waiting to unload its torrent. The thing was, he wasn't sure if he could swim to safety this time. Wasn't sure at all and with a sigh, he flung the newspaper on the seat, drained his mug and walked over to The Fort.

Sergeant Singh was on duty and called out a greeting as Knowles walked past the front desk and used the biometric fingerpad to sign in. Knowles scowled and ignored the man. No time for inconsequential chat, today of all days. No, he needed to get upstairs and see what new incidents had been reported overnight.

Chapter 62

06:55 The Fort

Gus bustled into the room, hand outstretched to greet the Proctors. 'Thanks so much for coming in so early in the day.' As he spoke, he noted Mrs Proctor's gaunt expression and the fact that she didn't move when he entered the room.

Mr Proctor, on the other hand, paced the room as if trying to burn off some surplus energy. On Gus' entry he spun round and reached Gus before he'd taken two steps into the room. Up close, Gus saw the strain around the other man's eyes and a very faint smell of BO told him that personal hygiene had taken a secondary place for now. Mr Proctor's clothes were dishevelled and Gus got the impression the man may well have slept in them. Mrs Proctor's eyes followed them, filled with a vacant, almost deathlike look that suggested to Gus she'd been medicated.

Gus shook Mr Proctor's hand and guided him over to sit down next to his wife. As he sank into the soft cushioned couch, he looked at Gus. 'Have you any news of Simon? Is it linked to this girl who was found in the road yesterday? We saw the headlines this morning and we've seen the footage.'

Gus sat down opposite the couple. He hated these couches, so he perched on the very edge, hoping that he wouldn't have to sit there for too long. 'The girl who was found yesterday was called Jenny Gregg. I believe she knew Simon and, of course, we are investigating to see if there's any sort of link between Simon's disappearance and her being found. We're working on the footage but so far we can't break the encryption. As soon as we do, we'll act on it.' He knew as he spoke that his words sounded weak.

Mr Proctor looked like he was about to say something, then he collapsed back on the couch as if he'd caved in on himself. Gus had seen these types of reactions many times before and knew that if they didn't find Simon Proctor soon, his parents would break under the strain.

'What about the footage of Simon that was posted online? Is there any more? Have you managed to discover who posted it?' He ran his fingers through his hair and glanced at his wife, 'Jane's been watching it on repeat, again and again. You need to find my son. You just do!'

Keeping his voice low, Gus outlined the things they were doing to locate the origin of the video before moving onto the real purpose of the meeting. He regretted that he had to ask the questions, however there was no alternative. It was imperative that these questions were answered, no matter how difficult it might be for the parents. Clasping his hands together, Gus made eye contact with both parents, eyes moving from one parent to the other in turn. 'I need to ask you some very difficult questions and I know they will distress you.' He hesitated as Mr Proctor took his wife's hand in his and squeezed. 'If I could avoid doing this, I would. Are you ready?'

At last Mrs Proctor seemed to register his presence. She sat up straighter and her eyes met Gus'. Gus dived in. 'It's come to our attention that Simon may have been in a physical relationship. Do you know anything about this?'

James Proctor frowned, and shook his head. Jane bit her lip and then in a slow drawl that confirmed Gus' earlier supposition that she'd been medicated, said, 'I wondered if he had a girlfriend. Over the last few weeks he's been a bit secretive. Applying more deodorant and using the shower more, that sort of thing.' She smiled as if that was a fond memory and then the smile faded from her face and her eyes shot up to meet Gus'. 'Do you think one of those poor girls was Simon's girlfriend?'

At his wife's words, James jumped to his feet and began pacing again. 'Oh, I get it. Don't say another word to him, Jane. He's trying to blame Simon for what happened to those girls. Trying to say they had a lovers' tiff and Si killed them. Well, it's not going to bloody work, do you hear me?'

Gus allowed the man to rant until he'd vented all his energy and collapsed on the seat again, before responding, his tone quiet and sincere. 'The information we have isn't regarding either of those two girls, Mr Proctor. The information we have relates to two different women. Can either of you give me any information on who they might be?'

James looked at his wife. With a slight shake of the head, Mrs Proctor gave him her answer and he articulated it. 'We've no idea who Simon was interested in, or even if he had a girlfriend. Jane just thought that, perhaps, he liked someone, that's all.'

Gus waited to see if James would add anything. He didn't and Mrs Proctor's face betrayed no emotion whatsoever. 'The thing is, two people have independently corroborated that Simon was acting in a predatory manner towards a mother and her daughter. Two of Simon's friends have told us that Simon deliberately set out to engage in relations with both a mother and her teenage daughter. Simon sent footage that he recorded on his phone of him performing oral sex on a woman, whom we believe to be the mother.'

Gus took his phone from his trouser pocket and turned it to the Proctors. Earlier he'd snatched an image that showed Simon's head and enough of their living room for them to confirm the location. 'Can you confirm that this is Simon and that this is your living room?'

Jane Proctor raised a shaking hand to her mouth and gulped, she reached out with the other hand, one finger extended to touch her son's head on the screen and then as if realising what her son was doing, she jerked her hand back and closed her eyes. Gus looked at James Proctor, whose face had flushed tomato red.

'What the hell does this prove? What's this got to do with finding my son?' Mr Proctor glared at Gus, his eyes sparking, his fists clenched on his thighs.

Gus slipped the phone back into his pocket and shrugged. 'According to our sources, Simon placed a bet with them saying he would have sex with *both* mother and daughter and from this recording and another we are in possession of, it appears that he did. Does this seem like the sort of thing your son would do?'

James exhaled and rubbed his hand over his face, whilst Mrs Proctor sat, slack-jawed, staring straight ahead. Neither of them said anything, so Gus continued. 'The thing is, the tone of his text and Facebook messages with his friends is predatory in nature. We need to get to the bottom of whether that was truly in Simon's nature or if it was just bravado. We need you to help us with this. Anything you can tell us will perhaps shed some light on things.'

Gus poured them each a glass of chilled water and, succumbing to the lure of the enveloping chair he leaned back and waited. James Proctor took a long swallow of water, his throat muscles gulping the liquid down at speed. He emptied the glass, refilled it and repeated the process. 'Simon has been quite a challenge for us over the years. We adopted him when he was ten and he'd already had a very troubled childhood. He'd been abandoned by his birth mother and had done the rounds of various foster parents. His last set of foster parents sexually and physically abused him.'

He paused and refilled his glass for the third time before taking a small sip. 'He nearly died in a house fire at his foster parents' home. His social worker died in the fire. It was suspected that the foster parents, realising their time was up, locked all the children and the social worker inside and set fire to the house. It was tragic. So you understand the trauma that Simon endured before he came to us. He was lucky to be rescued.'

Gus thought for a moment. 'Was this fire in Leeds?'

James Proctor closed his eyes for a second, before speaking. 'It was in all the papers, so when we adopted him, we changed his name. Gave him a complete new start.'

Gus remembered the case. He'd been there when they'd pulled Simon Proctor from the blazing house. He remembered that poor mite. Didn't even look half his age. He also remembered Amina Rose's body being pulled from the house too, and her husband's grief. It had been a terrible incident and nobody had won that night. Did it have anything to do with Simon Proctor's disappearance now? Perhaps his childhood experiences had made him a predatory teen? On the other hand, was it even relevant? Gus reckoned that many testosterone-fuelled teens acted in a similar way to Simon Proctor. It might only have a bearing on the case if his behaviour got him into bother. Is his disappearance linked to his sexual activities?

Gus, seeing that the Proctors had had just about enough for one day, knew he had to broach one other thing with them before he left. 'I know you have a lot on your plate right now, however, I'm duty-bound to bring something to your attention.'

Jane Proctor pushed her shoulders back as if bracing herself for whatever Gus was going to throw at them next. 'The dates of these recordings show that Simon was fifteen when they were taken.'

The Proctors blinked, clearly not understanding Gus' inference. Gus would rather have left it for another time, a time when they were a little stronger, maybe even after Simon was found. However, he knew he had to tell them now. 'Simon was a minor when these recordings were made. That means that if the woman he was having sex with was sixteen or over, she has committed a crime and will be subject to prosecution by law. You need to prepare yourselves for that.'

Chapter 63

07:55 The Fort

Gus was glad to escape from the Proctors' oppressive presence. He'd felt for them. Here they were not knowing where their son was and in the same breath being given information that was probably just too much to deal with right now.

He found James Proctor difficult to empathise with, and looking at the desperation on Jane Proctor's face drove a knife into his gut every time. She was unravelling and the only thing they could do to help was to find Simon. Where the bloody hell was the boy? There'd been no sightings of note, which made Gus think he'd been abducted. If he'd just skipped off to avoid the biggest grounding of his life, wouldn't he have returned by now or at least contacted his parents? Gus wasn't sure, although what he most wanted to do right now was confront the Button family.

A text from Alice had told him she was waiting for him downstairs. He sighed. She'd no doubt seen *The Sun*'s headlines and was keeping a low profile. *Bloody Kennedy! Why couldn't he have stayed comatose? What the hell was he playing at?* Gus passed the lifts and was halfway down one flight of steps when his phone buzzed. It was Compo demanding his presence back up in the incident room telling him the 'doo doo had hit the fan'.

Gus swivelled and texting Alice made his way back upstairs to wait for her at the lifts. At least she wouldn't have to brave the corridor on her own.

Before he'd even shrugged his coat off, Sampson, Taffy and Compo crowded round Gus and Alice. Gus waited till they'd each given her a hug before demanding to know what was so urgent.

Compo, grabbed a piece of paper which had his juvenile scrawl in red biro all over it. 'A girl's body has been found near Cottingley Ridge.'

'And?' said Gus, 'Don't they think we've got enough on our plate?'

Compo glanced at his sheet again, 'They say she's young, similar age to Jenny Gregg and Sue Downs… and she's been stabbed. Maybe it's the same bloke.'

Gus sighed. Compo was right: another young girl found with stab wounds couldn't be ignored. 'Right, I'm on my way, come on, Alice. Looks like the Buttons will have to wait.'

'Eh, Gus,' said Compo. 'Initial report indicates that she's been doused all over with bleach. Reporting officer said you could smell it a mile off.'

Well that was a turn-up. If it was the same killer, his forensic measures were becoming more sophisticated by the minute. Either way, Gus could have done without the thought of another bereaved family hanging over his head. All too often, the weight of a violent death of a child was too much to bear.

Chapter 64

08:15 Unknown Location

Cold's seeping right into my bones. Bet they'd snap like an icicle if I fell over... maybe they'd melt and I'd end up a big watery puddle on the floor. I stretch over and grab the lamp from the floor and strike a match. It takes three goes before it catches. Don't know if the box is damp or if it's because my fingers are numb. Not like I don't know how to strike a match, is it? *That's funny... damn funny...*

'Burn... burn... la la la fire fire, fire, Bradford's burning, Bradford's burning Fuck no water, fuck no water!'

Wish I had my phone. It gives off more light than this poxy thing. Mind you, the battery would be dead by now and I couldn't use it anyway. Last thing I need is the coppers tracing it.

'*Da da da – fire engines, fire engines la, la, la, set the fire, set the fire.*'

They must have found it by now. They can't be totally stupid, can they? This'll do though, as long as the gas lasts.

'*Fiii... re, Fiii...re, Fiii...re, la di la di la di dah!*'

I grab a bottle of water, uncaring that it spills down my front as I glug. Brain freeze! Drank too much, too quick! Throat's sore. Must be the cold. Not many cereal bars left. I'll have one now and another later on.

'*Pyre, fire, liar, fire, mire, la di la di la la la. Tyre fire byre, la da la da la di dah di la di dah.*'

A drip had started during the night. At first it pissed me off, it was like Chinese water torture, drip... drip... drip.

I got scared the rats would come so I tried not to go to sleep. Must've fucking dozed off, though. Now the drips are louder and faster. Must be pissing it down outside. I laugh. Maybe I'll build a boat just in case the dripping becomes a stream and then a torrent. Oh, not a boat, maybe an ark. No point in building an ark if I'm the only one on it...

'*The animals went in two by two hurrah, hurrah.*
'*The Simon and the Simaroo, hurrah, hurrah.*'

What the fuck's the line about the elephant? Fucking drips! I cover my ears with my hands.

'*Shut the fuck up!*'

I'd checked months ago to make sure that no matter how loud I yell or how hard I bang on the pipes or the door, no-one can hear. It's a strange feeling. Especially when I can hear the bells and the god-awful dripping and sometimes an occasional firework or car back-firing. Fucking cars back-firing – yeah right. Bloody drug dealers letting their runners know the goods have arrived. Shit, the coppers are thick. You'd think they'd have sussed that by now, wouldn't you?

Wednesday morning now. How much longer can I put up with this cold and the incessant dripping?

Provisions are getting low too. Only three cereal bars left. The other problem is the chemi loo. It was half-full when I swiped it and it stinks! Not sure what stinks worst – me or the loo. Huddling in the sleeping bag for long periods of time concentrates the smells... should've brought a toothbrush and deodorant. Can't fucking think of everything, though, can I? I got the main things, didn't I? The important things. It's all over there under the tarp.

Can't decide whether I should do the last recording or not? Would help if I knew what's going on. Should've brought a radio. Could've listened to local radio. They'd have been going on about it all, wouldn't they? Maybe I'm famous? Well, I will be when I'm done, that's for sure.

Wish Matty or Jake were here. We'd have a laugh. Mind you they wouldn't get what I'm doing. Wouldn't understand. How could they? Everything was hunky-fucking-dory for them. Okay, so what? Matty had lost his mum – fuck's sake, it's only his mum, not like *he* was in pain or owt. Wonder what the parents are doing to find me? – Maybe they've gone off for another dirty weekend. Nah, knowing them, they'll not give up on me. They'll keep looking. Just wish I knew how long it's going to take. I've had enough, now. Not sure how much longer I can go on. Maybe time to end things!

Chapter 65

08:55 Cottingley Ridge

There was always something heart-breaking about seeing a young girl discarded like a piece of rubbish. Without fail, it made Gus want to find the killer and strangle them. Seeing the body of dead girl at the bottom of a ditch, a stone's throw from Cottingley, was no exception. She'd been rolled over the top of the ridge and would have ended up right at the bottom, if it hadn't been for a gnarled old tree limb that had halted her descent fifty yards from the top. The indignity of this young girl lying head down, legs spread and wearing no underwear, made Gus want to punch the nearest solid object. The slashes across her abdomen intensified this feeling.

Unfortunately, the nearest solid object was his father and no matter how infuriating his dad was, Gus couldn't vent his anger on him. So, instead, now that Hissing Sid and his cronies had laid out plates for them to walk on, he helped his old man climb down to the body. The bank where the girl lay was quite shallow and meant that Dr McGuire and Gus could just about balance despite the rain-slicked grass. After a quick check of the body to declare life extinct, Gus followed his dad back up the incline, hoping that the older man wouldn't fall backwards or they'd both end up at the bottom.

When he'd hefted his substantial frame back up to level ground, where Alice waited, Dr McGuire explained his initial findings. 'Ah'd say she's been there overnight. Her hair and what little clothes she's wearing are sodden. Och, and the poor bairn's been stabbed, as we all saw, although, subject to confirmation at the PM, I'd venture that the stabbing was done post mortem.' Dr McGuire frowned. 'She's also been strangled. The bruising round her neck is extensive. However, the cause of death is unconfirmed. The stink of bleach indicates possible forensic counter measures. Other than that, you'll have to wait till the PM which won't be till late this afternoon. I've got a wee old lady and a presumed suicide this afternoon first.' He turned to Gus. 'Did ye see the wee love heart tattoo above her breast? That might be a good way to ID her if no-one's reported her missing.'

Swallowing down the retort that sprung to his lips about not telling him how to do his job, Gus bit his tongue. 'Thanks, Dad.' Turning away from his dad, he hesitated and swung back, 'How's Mum?' He asked, his voice low.

Dr McGuire raised his eyebrows. 'Oh, so *now* we're allowed to talk about personal things on the job, are we?'

Gus groaned. 'Don't be awkward, Dad. Just want to know that she's okay. I've been busy, so I've not had a chance to drop in.'

Dr McGuire leaned in and squeezed his son's arm. 'She's fine, Angus. Nightmares are getting less frequent.' He moved to take a step past Gus, towards his car, then stopped. He glanced over at Alice who was talking with Sid, her notebook drawn as she wrote. 'I saw that article in the paper this morning. Am I right in thinking it's her case?'

Gus gave an abrupt nod. 'Yeah. We're keeping it as quiet as we can. If her name stays out of the papers, they won't suspend her and hopefully she'll get proven innocent before they have to.'

His dad squeezed Gus' arm. 'You look after that wee lassie, Angus. She looks done-in today.'

Gus turned and studied Alice. He had to admit his dad was right. She was pale and looked to have shrunk overnight. Her winter coat seemed to dwarf her already small frame, yet it was the hollows beneath her eyes and the haunted look that really worried him. He really hoped this wouldn't prove to be too much for her. Time would tell. With a shrug he yelled over to Sid to attract his attention. When the other man approached, Gus asked, 'You been through her possessions?'

'Yep, no ID. Whoever rolled her down the hill chucked her bag on top of her.'

'It's not so much ID I'm looking for. Was there a note? Was her bag sealed?'

'Yeah, zipped up. It were only a small one with a purse and some money in it. Nowt else.'

Gus looked down the ravine and sighed when he saw the amount of rubbish that had accumulated at the bottom. 'Get your lot to bag everything up and to be on the lookout for a note of some description.'

If this was the work of the same killer, chances were he'd left a note behind and Gus didn't want to risk not finding it. In this climate it'd disintegrate before too long. If it was there, he wanted it found soon. With a final glance round, he walked back to his car, Alice in tow. When her phone rang, he stopped and waited for her to answer, she looked at him as she spoke into the phone, 'Right Compo, thanks, we'll look now.'

Gus was already pulling his phone from his pocket, 'Another video?'

'Yep. Compo is not a happy bunny.'

They got the footage up on their phones and watched in silence as Simon Proctor cocooned on his bed seemed to be losing it big-time. The time stamp told them it had been taken less than an hour previously. This was getting more and more frustrating.

Chapter 66

09:25 Redburn Drive, Frizinghall

Gus was glad of the short drive to the Buttons' house. He'd got Sampson to phone them to tell them to hang on at home because he wanted to interview them about Jenny Gregg's abduction. It wasn't ideal. He'd much prefer to take them by surprise, but he hadn't had any other option than to visit the scene of the unknown girl's death. According to Sampson, Mr Button had played pop at first, until Sampson had told him that it was either a home visit or a visit to the station, he'd changed his mind and capitulated, agreeing to work from home till lunch time. Ali and his wife would remain at home until after their visit.

Gus had offered to drive, but Alice had insisted, saying it kept her focussed and stopped her mind from wandering. The previous night they hadn't spoken about the probable consequences of Sean Kennedy's allegations, and although he suspected Alice would have already worked out the implications for herself, he needed to be sure of that, yet he dreaded the conversation.

Alice had chosen to back-track from Cottingley Ridge and into Heaton to avoid the inevitable traffic through Shipley to Frizinghall. She'd taken a left down Shay and Gus couldn't prevent himself from glancing out the window as they passed his parent's old farmhouse. With a jolt he saw that his mum was in the drive with the dogs, throwing a ball and laughing. As the car drew level with the newly erected metal gate, her head turned to the sound of the car and her small frame went rigid as she backed towards the house. Gus put out his hand and squeezed Alice's arm. 'Pull in for a minute. Just want a word with my mum.'

Alice indicated and pulled in. She glanced beyond Gus and then turned to him. 'Go on, I'll wait here.'

Gus got out of the car and marched to the gate. It was around five feet tall and had a state of the art keypad to the side. *Bit like bolting the door after the proverbial horse*, he thought, but he understood that it made his mum feel secure, and his dad too. Having been told, and forgotten the entry digits, Gus took a few steps back, ran at the gate and scrabbled over it, landing on the other side with a bump.

It wasn't the most secure barrier although, it did afford a modicum of reassurance for his parents without completely obliterating their view of the road. It meant Corrine could see out. Sometimes the monsters you couldn't see were scarier than those you could and Gus had advised his dad accordingly.

Smiling, all trace of her previous apprehension chased from her face, Corrine bustled towards him, all three dogs, his own Bingo included, jumping up at her side as she walked. Seeing his master, Bingo yelped and headed straight for Gus, tail wagging and his wet nose burrowing into Gus' lowered hand. Gus petted the dog, yet kept his gaze fixed on his mum as he approached her.

'You know you don't need to do that,' he said.

Corrine shrugged. 'Well, who else is going to exercise them if I don't?'

Gus shook his head. She was so infuriating. She knew exactly what he meant, and she was trying to deflect him. Scowling, he moved forward and engulfed her in a huge hug. 'You know perfectly well I'm not talking about taking the dogs out. I'm talking about playing with them here, in the drive.'

She thrust out her lower lip and pouted. 'Look, it's safe now. Your dad fitted the gates with the remote so nobody can come in unless they're admitted.' She glared at Gus. 'Other than those who blatantly ignore the "No Entry, CCTV in Operation" signs and just vault the fence.'

It was good to hear his mum joking like this. For a while, after what she'd endured earlier in the year, he'd thought his little mum would never smile again. He should have known her resilience would bounce back. After all, she had never allowed adversity to keep her down for long before.

He bent down and kissed her cheek. 'Just wanted to say hi as we were passing. Need to get a move on though, Mum.'

Corrine followed him down to the end of the path and watched with a tut as he climbed the gate again and landed awkwardly in a puddle.

Alice whirred down the passenger window. 'For God's sake, Gus, we're not having a repeat of you ruining your shoes, are we?'

Gus grinned – this was a reference to the two pairs of shoes he'd had to bin during their last case.

Before he could respond, Alice was shouting thorough the gate to his mum, 'You alright, Mrs M?'

His mother's face lit up as she saw Alice and she waved. 'I'm great, love. All the better for seeing you two. Come for lunch on Sunday.'

Gus groaned. The way this case was shaping up, he didn't think he'd be having Sunday lunch for weeks – which, on reflection, could be a good thing as his mother's cooking was always on the overdone side. Climbing back into the car he was pleased to see Alice smiling, until he remembered he still had to broach the subject of possible consequences of Sean Kennedy's accusations. As Alice negotiated the winding drive past Heaton Woods, he watched the reflection of sun shimmering through the last of the autumn leaves.

When she hit the main road, he angled his body so he was half facing her. 'Al, I know you've more than likely considered this, but I just wanted to be sure. You do realise the implications of that bastard's accusations, don't you?'

In the unladylike way Gus was well familiar with, Alice snorted. Her knuckles whitened for a mere second as she gripped the wheel tighter before returning to their former pinkish tinge. Hearing her swallow and then clear her throat, Gus waited.

Braking, to let some of the St Bede's children cross the road, Alice looked at him and winked. 'You mean that, if I can't find a way to refute what he and Big H say, I could end up locked up for a good few years?'

Gus sighed. 'It won't come to that. Nobody will believe those two over you. However, Nancy has been told that if your name hits the tabloids then you *will* be suspended until further notice. At the minute, they're doing an initial investigation, but you may be asked to hand over your badge anyway in the next few days.'

Alice gave a single nod. 'Well then, we better get this shit cleared up pronto then, hadn't we?' She negotiated her way round a cyclist and drove on till they reached the Buttons' house.

The old Victorian semis were spaced well apart and in the Buttons' drive stood two newish Audis. *Not short of a bob or two then,* was Gus' immediate thought. Walking up the short path to the front door, he saw the blinds move a little and wondered who was so nervous about their visit they'd positioned themselves near the window. He reckoned it wouldn't be Mr Button, at any rate.

Alice pressed the door bell and a faint tune drifted through the double-glazed door to them. Seconds later it opened, revealing a teenage girl in a City Academy school uniform. Her hair fell in long curling strands down either side of her face, making her already long face seem even longer. Over the top of her uniform she wore a hoodie. Each of the sleeves were pulled down over her palms and were nipped in place by her curled-up fingers. Without a word, she stepped back and, as Gus stepped forward, he saw a woman lurking by what must be the living room door. He passed the girl and stretched out his hand holding this warrant card to the woman. 'Hi, Mrs Button. I'm DI Gus McGuire, we'd like to talk to you and your daughter about Jenny Gregg's abduction.' He turned and studied the girl who, having closed the door, now stood behind Alice. The girl's gaze landed on Gus and then flitted to her mother's face before moving back to Gus again.

'Is your husband in? Detective Sampson, whom you spoke to earlier, indicated that he wanted to be present during the interview.'

Wringing her hands together, Mrs Button moved towards them. 'Yes, hold on, I'll call him. Why don't you both go into the living room and sit down.'

The room was over-warm and Gus shrugged off his fisherman's jacket as he took in his surroundings. The cream carpet was plush. The throw, draped casually over the suite, and the cushions dotted around the room, matched the foliage on the curtains. Four canvases depicting a vase of flowers cut in four, were positioned with mathematical precision on the main wall. The absence of a TV was the first thing that struck Gus. Then he remembered, from his research, that the use of TV was frowned upon by the Button's church. A bible was laid open on a stand next to the couch, as if someone had just been studying it. On the other walls, photographs of Mrs Button and Ali with a bald man who must be Mr Button were displayed. All of them were recent and ranged from a trip to what, judging by the large cross in the background and the *Family Church of Christ* slogan on their T-shirts, was a Christian convention, to a zoo and to a theme park. All quite normal family snaps, if you ignored the fact they were all dated no more than a year previously.

As Mr Button entered, Gus turned round and introduced himself and Alice again. Where his wife was slender and dressed in casual clothes, Mr Button was tall and broad, in a suit and shirt that stretched over his protruding beer belly. He had the bluff manner of a busy man, 'Sit down, sit down,' and he waved his arms, ushering them to sit. He slapped an arm round his daughter's shoulders and Gus saw her jump and then smile as her father guided her over to sit on the couch beside him. Ali, despite seeming to be a little cowed in the over-exuberant presence of her adoptive father, seemed happy to sit beside him. Gus remembered that his own father's large frame had often been a sanctuary... a protection from everything. A place of safety. He wondered if Ali felt the same way.

Seeing that Mrs Button still stood by the door, Gus spoke to her. 'Please join us, Mrs Button. The sooner we start, the sooner we'll be out of your hair.'

When she sat on the other side of her husband, Gus laid his coat over the back of one of the comfy chairs opposite the Buttons and sat down. Alice, who had shrugged her coat off so it draped down onto the carpet, sat on the matching chair like a little elf, with her feet barely touching the floor. Leaning forward, resting both arms across his knees, Gus began to speak. 'As you know, your friend Jenny was abducted on Monday night, kept overnight and then was found in the early hours of Tuesday morning. We need to know everything there is to know about what happened before she went missing. So, we need to ask you some questions, Ali. Is that okay?'

Ali glanced at her dad and he put his arm round her shoulder and squeezed. All the time his eyes never left Gus' face. Taking it as a silent warning not to upset his daughter, Gus inclined his head in acknowledgement.

'So, on Monday night Jenny and you came home from school and had tea at your house, is that right?'

'Yeah.'

'Then what?' asked Gus, 'What did you do after tea?'

Ali looked once more to her dad for reassurance and then began to speak, her gaze never once leaving Gus' face as she replied. 'It was The Prayer Chair Meeting on Monday night. That's why Jenny came to ours. After tea we did a bit of homework and then my dad dropped us off up at the church for the meeting.'

Gus handed Ali a piece of paper with a list of names on. 'Were there any other people at The Prayer Chair Meeting or is this list accurate?'

Ali read the names, thought for a minute and then shook her head. 'That's everyone. The only one missing was–' she stopped and her gaze fell to her knees.

'The only one missing was... who?' asked Gus his voice soft.

Ali, took a deep breath and glanced up at her dad. Then, looking down at her knees, she said, 'Simon. Simon was the only one absent on Monday.'

Interesting! 'Okay, so what did you guys talk about at the meeting?'

Ali looked at her dad. 'We're not supposed to say, Dad.'

Mr Button ruffled her hair. 'I think you need to tell the police, love. They're not going to go telling anybody.'

Gus glanced over at Alice and saw that she had tensed. No doubt she was remembering her own experiences of The Prayer Chair. He turned back to Ali. 'I think it'll be okay to tell us.'

Sighing, Ali started to pick at the sleeve of her hoodie with the index finger and thumb of her other hand, 'We were just planning what we'd do on Saturday. We were taking The Prayer Chair to City Park on Saturday and we wanted to do it good. Minister Evans says there's plenty of sinners in Bradford that need to be redeemed.'

Gus cast a glance at Alice to see if she too had noted Ali's choice of words. A tightening of her lips told him she had.

'We decided that I would be the sinner on Saturday and Alex and Jenny would be the folk fishers.'

'Folk fishers?'

Ali grinned. 'It's a play on the fishers of men – get it "folk fishers" not as sexist, 'cos we don't just fish men.'

'Okay, so what did you have to do if you were a sinner?'

'I'd mingle in the crowd whilst Reverend Evans preached and then when he started asking for volunteers, I'd be "fished". I'd go sit on the chair and recite my sins and everyone would pray for me and then I'd stand up and say how I felt lighter now I was sin free.'

'What sins would you recite?'

Ali shrugged. 'Oh, it was all pretend. Reverend Evans gives us a script and we memorise it. We all take turns doing it every week.'

From her chair, Alice piped up, 'Don't you believe in the Ten Commandments at your church – you know the bit about not lying... or was that Proverbs?'

Gus' heart fell. He knew where she was going with this. He'd had the same thought himself just seconds before, but he didn't want her to upset the equilibrium. He glared at her, and realised she was looking not at Ali but at the parents, both of whom had the grace to look a little embarrassed by the question. Gus cleared his throat and continued, 'Was everything normal on Monday night?'

Ali continued picking at her sleeve, her head bowed as she mumbled a few words that Gus didn't quite hear.

'Sorry, Ali, could you repeat that?'

'Said, yeah, everything was fine.'

Gus pursed his lips, 'Okay then. If everything was fine, why did Jenny go off on her own and not go back to yours, like she was supposed to?'

Ali's head jerked up, her eyes wide. 'Don't know. She said she wanted to go home on her own. That's all I know.'

Mrs Button jumped to her feet and moved round to kneel before her daughter. 'There, there, Ali, calm down. Don't be getting upset. Jenny's fine now. Isn't she, Inspector McGuire?'

'Physically, she's fine. As for the other, well, time will tell.' He waited till Mrs Button had squashed in on the other side of Ali, before continuing, 'Was there anybody hanging about on Monday night? Anyone who might have taken Jenny?'

Ali shook her head.

'Do you know anyone she'd fallen out with?'

If Gus hadn't been watching her closely, he may have missed the flicker of her eyelids and the quick intake of breath. It was time to ask one of his big questions. Keeping his tone neutral, he brushed a bit of fluff of his sleeve. 'So, you know Simon Proctor well, do you Ali?'

Ali's head fell forward again, her hair falling over her face making it difficult to see her expression. Next to her, Mrs Button tensed and stopped stroking her daughter's hair for a mere second, before recommencing the soothing motion.

'Yes, Simon was in The Prayer Chair team.'

'...and you, Mrs Button, did you know Simon?'

Mrs Button shook her head, 'No, no, I don't...'

'Grace, isn't that the boy who's disappeared? Didn't he come to tea one night?'

Ali's head jerked up and Mrs Button's mouth trembled. 'I... I can't remember. Can you, Ali? If he did, it must have been a long time ago.'

Ali swallowed hard. 'Yeah, long time ago.'

Gus stood up and retrieved his coat from the chair back and waited for Alice to get her coat back on. 'I think we're about done here.' He smiled at the parents and stepped towards the door. All three Buttons jumped to their feet, eager, it seemed, to see him off the premises. He moved into the hallway before turning towards them. 'Were you at Simon Proctor's party on Saturday night, Ali?'

Before the girl had a chance to respond, Mr Button released a guttural guffaw. 'Course she wasn't. She was at a sleepover. My girl would never attend one of those sorts of dos.'

Gus had seen Ali's expression and it belied her father's words. He trained his eyes on her until she met his gaze and then he gave a slight nod. Ali brushed past them mumbling something about catching a bus to school. Mr Button peeled off into the kitchen, leaving Mrs Button to lead them to the door. Gus stepped through the door and turned to face her. In a low voice, he said, 'You and I both know you haven't been entirely truthful about Simon Proctor. I suggest you head down to the station with Ali after school. It'll be better for both of you, if you come in voluntarily.'

Mrs Button, with a glance behind her, gave a single nod. 'Okay, we'll come then.' And she shut the door in their faces.

Once they were back in the car, Alice poked Gus in the arm 'What's with the bloody Colombo moves in there?'

Gus laughed, pleased that although she may be down, Alice still had a sense of humour. 'That hurt, Al.'

'Wuss.'

'Tell me about it,' he said rubbing his arm. 'What you reckon to the Buttons, then?'

'Well, the only one who was telling us the whole truth was Mr Button. Both the female Buttons have secrets and they know we're onto them.'

'What I found interesting, though, was that I sensed Ali Button was holding something back about Monday night as well as about Simon Proctor. Did you see the way she grew upset and couldn't meet my eye? That girl knows something about Monday night and Jenny Gregg's disappearance. When they come in this afternoon, she better be prepared to tell us everything.'

Alice engaged the clutch and swung onto the road. 'As for that fucking Prayer Chair nonsense – seems bloody duplicitous to me getting young girls to confess to sins publicly to win people into their flock. Very dubious indeed.'

Chapter 67

10:15 The Fort

Knowles was pacing up and down outside The Fort, cigarette in one hand. Every so often he raised it to his lips and took a couple of frantic puffs. He couldn't believe his luck. The bastards had found the girl already. He thought he'd managed to roll her right down to the bottom of Cottingley Ridge where, by rights, she shouldn't have been found till next summer. Just his fucking luck.

He slipped another cigarette from his packet and used the butt of his old cig to light the new one. Good job he'd had the presence of mind to fuck up the forensics. He'd be in a right pickle if he hadn't – at the last minute – thought to be doubly careful. He'd thought it was a sure bet that she'd lie undiscovered till the spring at the earliest. His chest was heavy. Like he was about to go down with a chest infection or something. Even the smoke burned as he inhaled it. Fuck, if that bottle of bleach hadn't escaped from the shopping bags last week and been rolling about in his car since then, he'd be in a real mess. There was no way they could link the bleach to him. How the hell could they? How many thousands of bottles of bleach get sold in Bradford alone in a month? No, there was nothing to link him to the bleach.

His breathing slowed, but the pain across his shoulders that had started the previous night didn't. He rolled his shoulders, trying to loosen them. Fuck, this was sore. Bitch must have been heavier than he'd thought. Gone and pulled a damn muscle now. He pressed his upper back against the rough wall and sighed with relief as the pain subsided under the pressure. Now he could concentrate. Puffing on his cigarette, he went over the steps he'd taken to dispose of Julie the previous night. The car he'd used was a pool car, so it was unlikely they'd link the car to her. He'd made sure he muddied the plates before he picked her up and didn't clean them till he'd got rid of her. CCTV up by Cottingley Ridge was non-existent, as was street lighting. Bradford city preferred to focus on the inner-city areas, despite the fact that a fair amount of drug-dealing and dogging went on up there. He'd edged the car up to the grass bank and when he'd been sure no-one was about, he'd gone around to his boot, taken out a tyre jack to make it look like he was replacing a tyre and double-checked the area. When he was sure he was alone, he opened the passenger door and dragged the little bitch out of the car and dropped her on the grass before pouring the entire bottle of bleach over her. Soon as it was empty, he rolled her over the edge and chucked the bottle after her. He'd worn gloves, so he should be okay. If he hadn't heard the sound of that stupid dog barking and the owner calling it, he'd have double-checked she'd gone to the bottom. As it was, he'd had to hotfoot it back to the car and drive off. When he'd got back to The Fort he'd signed the car in for a deep clean, like you do when someone's puked up or pissed in a pool car. He grinned; no, he'd covered his tracks. Now all he had to do was bide his time and hope they'd lump Julie's death in with the other girls and that lad's abduction.

Fuck though, that little bitch could have scuppered things for him. Trust her to get caught on a tree branch. *Bloody hooker hooked on a fucking twig. Typical.* He flicked his fag butt into the road and spun on his heels to get back to work. It was then he realised he'd missed the one very large obstacle that stood in the way of his continued freedom. His chest shrivelled as a dart of cold pierced it, the throb across his shoulders intensified and started to travel down his arm. Fuck, crap, fucking crap! How the hell could he overcome this? Instead of heading up the steps, he turned and ignoring the blaring of car horns as he ran across the road without looking. He went into The Kings Arms and ordered a double whisky. He needed to get this sorted out. A quick glance at his watch told him he'd have to wait for a few hours at least. He only hoped the press wouldn't get wind of it *before* he'd had time to act. Also, that DI Fuck McGuire wasn't on the ball.

Chapter 68

10:30 The Fort

Compo was jumping up and down like a Jack-in-the-box when Gus and Alice walked through the doors. Gus didn't have time to hang up his coat and grab a coffee before the computer nerd spoke. 'We've found the bikers!'

Gus poured his coffee, took a long sip and waited for Compo to continue. The look on Compo's face told him he'd got something good. He was bouncing on the balls of his feet and for once his hands were absent of food. 'The vice lot came up trumps. I inputted my stuff into the dark web and came up with a–'

Gus waved a hand in the air. 'Comps, I have spent a horrid hour with the parents of a missing boy, seen a dead teenager *in situ* at the dump site and interviewed another teenager who may have key information for us and all of that I've done without benefit of caffeine. Do you think you could cut the techie stuff and just share the highlights?'

Compo dunked a biscuit into the mug of coffee he'd helped himself to when Gus made his and Alice's. Gus' eyes narrowed. There was a definite overdone darkness to the biscuit in question. 'That one of my mum's biscuits?'

Compo, in his haste to reply, sprinkled some crumbs over the carpet tiles. 'Yeah, she popped in earlier. Said she'd just made them because she thought you looked peaky.'

Gus was pleased to hear that. If his mother had taken up her atrocious baking hobby again, that was a sure sign she was on the mend.

Perhaps realising that he'd overstepped the mark by helping himself to the biscuits, Compo pointed at a large container near his computer station. 'There's plenty left.' He held out his half-eaten one to Gus. 'Here, have this.'

Alice laughed as Gus grimaced. 'You're alright there, Comps. You just eat them.' Not needing telling twice, Compo stuffed the rest of the biscuit in his mouth and helped himself to another, before continuing.

'Long story short. I IDed a minor member of the chapter. That's what they call the regional groups – chapters – like in a book, you know?' Heading back to his beloved computers, Compo continued. 'Turned out he was under vice's radar for summat else. Used to be a member of a rival gang and one of the undercover team reached out to him and "extracted information".' Compo made air quotes with his fingers, 'Anyway, he gave us the chapter clubhouse details. It's in the middle of Ilkley Moor down a track you can hardly see. Look.' He got a satellite image up on his screen and pointed to a rectangular shape in the middle of the moor. Using his laser light, he traced the path from the main Moor Road up to the building. 'It's easily accessible by motorbike, not so easy any other way.' Compo did a swivelly little dance that made his bottom swing from side to side.

Hope I don't have to witness that again. Gus looked at Compo. 'So what's the plan?'

Compo marched over to his table and began rummaging through his paperwork, muttering under his breath as he did so. At last, he gave a yelp and pounced on a sheet of paper which he handed to his boss.

Gus took the paper between his index finger and thumb to avoid the unidentifiable smear that covered most of it. Peering through the grease he made out a name, Mickey Swanson, and a number.

'You've to phone Mickey. They're planning on taking them down tonight.' And Compo flicked his wrist so that his fingers made a loud snapping sound. 'Yipppeee!'

Reluctant to burst Compo's bubble, Gus felt obliged to ask, 'Any word…?'

Compo's face crumpled, 'Nope, can't get through the encryption. Getting closer, mind. We've managed to break through a few layers, but it's just taking time… too much time.'

Gus squeezed Compo's shoulder, 'You'll get there, Comps. I know you will.'

Chapter 69

11:30 The Chaat House

Gus hadn't been able to concentrate in the incident room. It wasn't that it was noisy, it was just that it was claustrophobic in there – like a lift whose sides keep closing in until you are suffocated. He'd have liked to have gone for a jog, but he couldn't afford the time. So, after he'd made an appointment to meet up with Mickey Swanson at one o'clock, he grabbed some files and left The Fort. Now, here he was, gazing at the files and not registering a damn thing. His mind kept wandering back to his interview with Simon Proctor's parents that morning. He couldn't get it out of his mind.

He could remember that little bundle being carried from the blazing building as if it had happened yesterday. He remembered the adrenalin rush he'd experienced when they'd realised the child was alive. He'd been tiny. Small for his age. Gus' mind rolled on and he saw the firefighter staggering out of the building, this time carrying a bigger bundle. He could hear Amina Rose's fiancé scream, when he realised she was dead. It had been the biggest tragedy of his early career. Social services had come under scrutiny for not identifying the foster parents as paedophiles sooner, as had educational establishments. From what he could remember, Amina's fiancé had tried to take out a civil case against social services, blaming them for the death of his wife, but Gus had moved to Bradford soon after and lost track of the developments of the case.

At the time he'd been working with DI Sandy Panesar and he was aware that she'd visited the boy whilst he was recovering in hospital. Perhaps it would be worthwhile getting in touch with Sandy. They'd lost touch after he moved over to Major Crimes in Bradford.

Picking up his phone, he flicked through the contacts. There she was. Without knowing quite why he wanted to contact Sandy, he dialled and was pleased when she answered, her voice as cheery as he'd remembered it. After he'd identified himself and they'd exchanged pleasantries, Gus told her about his case. Sandy had read the highlights in the paper and was amazed when Gus revealed that Simon Proctor was the little boy from the fire.

'What can you tell me about him, Sandy? Anything, you know, we're clutching at straws here.'

Over the phone he heard her sigh, 'You know, Gus, I visited that little boy for months, every other day. Nobody was entirely sure what he'd gone through at the hands of his foster parents and then when you add the trauma of the fire on top… I was heart-sorry for him.' She sighed again and Gus could hear her taking a drink. 'He was hard work, though. At first, he wouldn't or couldn't speak. Then, when he did start to speak, it was as if he'd just blocked it all out. He wouldn't talk about anything that happened before the fire. It was as if he'd decided the fire had erased his past and he was born from the flames… a bit like one of them what-chama-call-thems.'

'Phoenix?'

'Yeah, one of them. When I heard he was getting adopted, his social worker suggested it would be better for him if I stopped visiting. Didn't want him forming too strong a bond with me when he had a new mum to bond with. Don't know what happened to him after that.'

'Well, now you do.' said Gus.

'Hmm, poor little blighter. You'd think he'd have been through enough in his short life. You'd think the fates would just let him be.'

Gus nodded, then realising she couldn't see him said, 'What did they say about the fire in the end? Before I was transferred they were unsure of hotspots and suchlike.'

'Oh yeah. There was a bit of confusion about where the fire started and where the bodies were found, but in the end, they reckoned the kid and the social worker had tried to escape and that's why they were found away from the other kids and the foster parents.'

As Gus hung up, he felt that he hadn't learned anything new. Simon Proctor had had a shit life to date and now, with his disappearance, Gus reckoned it was a whole lot shittier for the kid. Where the fuck was he?

Chapter 70

12:15 Unknown Location

Lights on again. I peel the blanket down and pull my jumper up so the camera can see my torso. My ribs are sticking right out. They're going to break through my skin and spill my guts all over the joint. That'd look great on camera, wouldn't it? Like some sort of zombie film or summat. Not had a hot meal since I waved my mum and dad off nearly a week ago. They'd been full of... *'Behave now, won't you Simon?', 'We can trust you, can't we?'*... and like the dutiful son I pretended to be, I nodded and smiled and.... lied through my teeth.

Thinking of my teeth – yuck, my gob stinks. My teeth are all furry and when I scrape my nail down them, yellow gunge comes off. Smells fucking foul. Need a toothbrush. First thing I'll do when I get out is brush my teeth. Maybe have a bath... that all depends on everything going to plan... no reason why it shouldn't, though.

As soon as they'd mentioned the trip – dirty weekend more like – I knew this was my big chance. For almost a year, I've been working towards it, quietly, little by little. Setting things in place... and this just gave me the opportunity.

Didn't really care about Sue Downs. She'd been a bitch. Laughed in my face when I asked her out. Who'd she think she is? – fucking Beyoncé? Made her pay in the end. Just like I did before. Now, though, I've got the chance to finish off what I'd started... let all the bastards have it.

I'm starving. Can't face another cereal bar. My gut's gurgling like fuck. Hope I don't have the shits again.

Chemi loo won't hack it and then there's the issue of wiping. Fucking gross. Had to use bloody empty crisp and snack bar wrappers. Not the most soothing for an already stinging arse and not the most hygienic either. Fingers smell of crap. Have to pull my sleeve over my hands when I'm eating. Fucking grosses me out!

Wednesday today. Double PE, English and History. That's what a Wednesday looks like in real time. Not today though. Today is D-Day. Or rather tonight will be. This is the most crucial part of his entire plan. If everything's in place like I've planned then I'll be home and dry before the weekend. If not… well… I've always got plan B.

Chapter 71

13:00 Alibi Bar, Sunbridge Wells

Mickey Swanson wasn't immediately recognisable when Gus entered the Alibi bar and Lounge. The dimmed lighting and charismatic nooks and crannies packed with comfy chairs and seductive lighting made it an unlikely place for a rendezvous with a member of the vice team. He went up to the bar and was dazzled by the too bright smile of the enthusiastic bar tender, a lad who looked about twelve, but carried the boyish confidence and looks of a younger Cliff Richard. Ordering a non-alcoholic beer, Gus turned and surveyed the room. There was nobody who looked remotely like the image of Mickey Swanson that he'd formed in his own mind. With a nod to the lad, he dropped a fiver on the bar, lifted his pint, and on the pretence of searching for a quiet corner, he wandered round the room. Nope, no sign of Swanson, so Gus settled into a low chair near the open fire, stretched his legs out in front of him, and began checking his emails on his phone.

A gentle cough made him glance up and, assuming that the middle-aged woman standing in front of him wanted to take the chair opposite, he pulled his legs in and sat up straight with a smile. 'Sorry, I'm waiting for someone.'

The woman frowned as if she didn't quite believe him and then put her hand on the back of the chair, pulling it closer to the fire and sat down. Gus sighed. Life was too short to argue about the smaller things in life, so he began to heft himself back onto his feet, when she spoke. 'I take it you're the golden boy, Gus McGuire, everyone's talking about.'

Gus stopped and turned so he could see the woman more clearly. She wore, what Gus thought of as an FBI suit; Fitted, Black, Indistinctive. If she hadn't known his name, he'd have assumed that she worked in one of the offices round the corner, or a bank. She sat back and crossed one leg over the other, resting her calf over her opposite knee in what was normally a male stance. Gus' mouth quirked. He got it now. This woman was playing with him, challenging him for assuming that Mickey Swanson was a male. His grin widened and he pointed to the bar. 'I'd offer to buy you a drink, but I don't want to be shot down in flames.'

Mickey giggled in an unexpectedly girlish way and shook her head. 'Hell, I think we can dispense with the formalities, I'll have a whisky.'

Gus stopped himself from raising an eyebrow. They'd really clamped down on officers drinking on duty and he'd assumed that, like him, she'd opt for a soft drink. Her grin widened as she seemed to catch what he was thinking. 'I've worked three days straight with only a couple of hours rest in all that time. If the bastards want to discipline me for having a dram, they can stuff their job right up their collective arses.'

Gus laughed and went to get her drink. By the time he returned to the table, Mickey Swanson had settled herself with her head leaning on the headrest, her eyes closed and her mouth slightly ajar. A gentle snuffling sound drifted to his ears as he plonked her glass on the table beside her. She opened her eyes and with remarkable presence of mind reoriented herself, before grabbing the glass and taking a small sip.

'Right, here's what we're going to do about the Fugitive Bandits. Our source has given us the location and I think we need to hammer them quick. Last thing we want is your two blokes heading off into the deep blue yonder on their Harleys; and we want to get our hands on them for the MDMA as well as the firearms distribution. Our snitch says they're storing the stuff in a shed at the back of the clubhouse. However, we know that as well as dealing in guns, they carry them and we know they're not afraid to use them, as they've taken out members of rival gangs before now. Usually because they thought their masculinity was being doubted.' Mickey rolled her eyes, making her opinion quite clear. 'So, do any of your team want in on the raid? I hear you're arms trained, as is your DS Cooper – that's if she's still with us?' She tilted her head to one side and winked. 'It's your call. We can draft some over from another team; however I thought you might like to get in on the action...' she paused for a beat before adding, 'for a change.'

Gus bit back a smile. If she realised just how close to the action he'd been over the past few years, she wouldn't be saying that. He was about to tell her so, when he caught the twinkle in her eye It was becoming clear that Mickey Swanson knew a lot more than she let on. She must have her finger on the pulse if she'd heard about Alice, for that was on a need-to-know basis for now. Not giving anything away, Gus said. 'I'll speak to DS Cooper, but I'm definitely in. I saw the recording of what those bastards did to that girl and I want to be there when they go down.'

Mickey pressed her lips together and then grimaced. 'See, I wanted more of a definite commitment about your DS Cooper, Gus. You don't mind if I call you Gus, do you?'

Gus waved her question away. He wasn't one for formalities at the best of times and he was curious about why she was so keen to have Alice on board. 'Go on, I'm listening.'

Mickey uncrossed her legs and leaned forward taking another sip of her whisky. She clapped her lips together looking rather like a goldfish unexpectedly escaped from its bowl.

'Bait!'

Gus blinked. 'What?'

'Want to use Cooper as bait. She's young and looks a good few years younger than she is. Bet we could easily get her tarted up to appeal to those sick fuckers.'

Gus' stomach clenched. When he'd said he'd ask Alice, he thought he'd be asking her to sit in a police car as backup with a firearm and a bullet proof vest on. No way did he want her to be used as bait. Especially not right now, when she had so much on her mind.'

He opened his mouth to respond, but before he could speak, Mickey interrupted him. 'I know the dynamics between you and your DS. I also know she was injured last year and I'm well aware of her current circumstances. DCI Chalmers was consulted on this and referred me to you. Ordinarily, I'd have gone straight to Cooper herself, but in deference to your position as her superior officer, I was prepared, at Nancy's request, to extend you the courtesy of consulting you first.'

As Gus again started to speak, she raised a finger to stop him. 'However, before you say something that might come back and bite you on the arse, should your DS ever find out about it, I want you to consider this.' She drained her glass and returned it to the table. 'Cooper has been through a lot, as I've said. If you make this decision for her, you will, in effect be denying her a choice and, if my take on Alice Cooper is right, she will be feeling frustrated at the diminishing choices ahead of her, as Sean Kennedy continues to spread his poison, effectively shutting her options down, little by little. *This* could be the thing to give her purpose, to give her the oomph to face the challenges ahead of her. Don't deny her that, Gus. Don't limit her choices even more than they already are.'

Wishing he'd opted for a whisky too, instead of the tasteless fizz that was churning in his stomach right now, Gus sighed and leaned back. Mickey's words were powerful and he knew she was right. However, he also knew Alice. *She* would damn well jump at the chance and he would be powerless to protect her. In a rush, the feelings he'd had when he thought she'd been killed last time, threatened to engulf him. His chest tightened and a searing pain spasmed in his temple. Breathing in and out, he focussed on the drop of condensation that was trickling down Mickey's empty glass and watched as it pooled on the table top, catching the reflection from the flickering flames. Mickey was right. It was Alice's choice. 'Okay, what's the plan then?'

Mickey grinned and reached over and tapped him on the knee. 'That wasn't easy for you. I think you did the right thing. Alice will be grateful to you.'

Gus rolled his eyes. Alice had never been grateful to him for anything. Alice was Alice; a powerful force of nature and if this went balls up, he'd regret letting Mickey convince him. Putting the thought out of his head, he straightened. 'This is all off if I'm not happy with the risk to Alice's safety, and I want an option to pull her out, if it all gets out of hand, understood?'

Mickey rolled her eyes, but gave a single nod. Then, she filled Gus in on all the details. Half an hour later, with a pool of acid in his stomach, Gus stood up to leave.

'Oh, shit. I forgot to mention the fucking dogs.'

Gus halted in his tracks and did a slow turnaround. Somehow he didn't think that the dogs she was referring to were Labradors. 'Dogs?'

'Yeah, bastards have bloody Rottweilers roaming round the perimeter of the property. Fenced in, according to our source, but that won't help us when we breach the damn fence. I'd wear thick trousers and a couple of extra jumpers if I was you… just to be on the safe side.'

Fucking extra jumpers. Lot of damn good that would do when your arm's wedged between the pincer-like jaws of a damn Rottweiler. Nothing like playing things down. He hated big dogs and Rottweilers were his particular pet hate. Who the hell would want to have a dog that could kill you with one bite? Well, the answer to that was simple enough – sick fuckers who ply young girls with drugs, force them to perform oral sex on them and then leave them to die – that's fucking who!

Chapter 72

15:15 The Fort

Of course, Alice had jumped at the chance of doing a bit of undercover work. She'd agreed so quickly, Gus was sure she hadn't considered the implications. All she seemed to want was a distraction from all the Sean Kennedy stuff. He got that. Course he did. That's why he'd been so eager to get back to work after the whole thing with Greg. None of that stopped him worrying about her though. She wasn't as fragile as she looked – not by a long chalk – still she wasn't as bloody tough as *she* thought, either. This was her way of pretending she was Lara bloody Croft, but it just wasn't on. In this mood she could be unpredictable; cut corners and take chances. He was not happy about this and the only thing he could do was make sure that on the ground *he* had her back.

Irritable, pissed off and thoroughly out of sorts, Gus tried, without success, to ignore Alice's good humoured, if tuneless, whistle as they walked along the corridor to interview room one where the Button women waited. He was almost certain that it was the theme from Rocky that she was whistling, and he was well aware that she was doing it to annoy him, so he refused to rise to the bait. The thought of 'bait' made him think of the raid that evening, which in turn made him think of the free roaming dogs. *Bloody bait everywhere today!*

As if Alice's effervescent good humour wasn't enough to contend with, he'd had reproachful glances from Compo, Sampson and Taffy for the last hour. All three were pissed off at being excluded from the planned raid and had, judging by their huffy school boy looks, apportioned the blame for their exclusion on his doorstep. *What the hell!* Did they seriously think he'd suggested Alice as bait? There was that damn word again – shit, he really needed to get a hold off himself. He'd at least one murderer at large and a teenager to find. He needed to focus now on whatever information he could extract from the Buttons.

He thrust open the door and ushered Alice in, pasting a smile on his face as he did so. The effort made his face feel tight as if it might splinter if he relaxed his enforced smile. Millimetre by millimetre he relaxed his mouth, until the tension was relieved a little. He pulled out a seat and sat down opposite Mrs Button and her daughter. Under pretence of sifting through a folder —it contained blank papers – he observed the women. Mrs Button held herself rigid, elbows on the table top and her fingers clasped tight, her thumbs pressing against each other. Gus realised this was to stop her hands shaking. Her face was taut, and in the few hours since their last meeting, dark bags had accumulated under each eye. This was a woman in distress.

He looked at her daughter and saw that in contrast to her mother's erect rigidity, Ali was trying to diminish her presence by caving in on herself. Her shoulders were rounded and her arms pulled in to her body. She slumped down in the chair and sprawled her lower body under the table as if trying to hide. Gus had seen it many times before. It was the typical posture of someone with something to hide. In fact, both the mother and the daughter presented as people with big secrets and Gus was sure it was to do with Simon Proctor and his objectionable dare.

Although he felt a modicum of sympathy for Ali, he had his reservations about her mother. If she was the one engaging in a sex act with Simon Proctor, she could look forward to a criminal record and a possible custodial sentence. Although, at this precise moment, he was more concerned with the lad's whereabouts and establishing if these two had anything to do with his disappearance.

When Alice had set up the recording equipment and pushed a glass of water over the table to each of them, Gus said, 'Just start at the beginning and tell me everything there is to know about your contact with Simon Proctor over the past few months.'

Ali glanced at her mother who looked straight ahead, her throat swallowing convulsively.

Gus had no intention of belittling the mother in front of her daughter: they'd have enough to contend with any way. 'Look, Mrs Button. I'm going to ask Ali a few questions in your presence as her parent. Then, you, DS Cooper and I can have a further chat in private, okay?'

Mrs Button's posture relaxed a fraction. Her thumbs sprung apart and as Gus had surmised earlier, her hand started to shake as she lifted it to brush her hair from her forehead. She met Gus' eyes and exhaled.

Gus shuffled his chair round so it was angled towards Ali. The girl kept her head bowed and moved her body closer to her mother. Mrs Button put out her hand and gripped Ali's hand.

'So, Ali. When did Simon Proctor first start to show an interest in you?'

Ali shrugged.

Gus maintained his patient tone, 'Look Ali. You're going to have to speak. For the tape, you know?'

Ali glanced at the recording equipment as if it was going to jump up and bite her on the nose.

'So, when did Simon start showing an interest in you?'

Ali pulled her hand away from her mother's grip. 'Dunno. Few months back maybe.'

'In what way did he show an interest, Ali?'

Again, the shrug, 'Kept bumping into me near my house or outside school. That sort of thing. Then he joined the church and started coming along every week.'

'Your dad said earlier that he came to your house for tea, is that right?'

'Yeah,' her tone was sullen, almost angry now.

'Was it you who invited him for tea?'

'No!'

The ferocity of that single word made Gus wince. She continued, her tone sneering and accusatory, 'It were her.' She jerked her thumb at her mother. 'It were her *stupid* idea. Thought I didn't have any *friends*. Thought I should have a *boy*friend. Thought *Simon* would be perfect for me... until–' she stopped and clamped her lips together, staring straight ahead, her eyes blazing.

Gus glanced at Alice. Alice leaned forward and put her hand on Ali's hand, 'Until what, Ali?'

Ali shook her head. 'Until nothing, okay?'

Alice, her voice calm, yet persistent, continued, 'I think you were going to say something very important just then, Ali. Something that would help us understand Simon a bit better. Perhaps even something that could help us find him. You do want him found, don't you?'

Ali rubbed her heel of her hand up her nose and sniffed. 'Yeah, course I do.'

Her voice wavered and Gus wasn't sure if that was the truth. 'Did you like Simon, Ali?'

Without hesitation Ali snorted out her answer, 'No! I hated him!'

Mrs Button sighed and again ran her hand through her hair. 'Can you tell me why you hated him, Ali?'

Shaking her head, Ali began to pluck at her sleeve, like she'd done earlier. 'He was a knob, okay? Wouldn't leave me alone. Thought I'd be interested in him.' She glared at Gus, her lips curled, her eyes flashing venom.

Behind the venom, though, Gus could see a young girl in pain. It was as if she wanted to tell him something more but couldn't get it out. Perhaps having her mother here had been unwise. Maybe he should have opted for an impartial observer.

Giving her space, Gus leaned back in his chair and waited. Mrs Button had bitten her lip so hard it was bleeding, yet still she gnawed at it, as if the discomfort was a distraction from the questions her daughter was being asked. It was a strange dynamic between these two and he couldn't quite work it out. 'Why *did* you hate Simon?'

Ali gulped and folded her arms over her chest. 'You should ask her.' She glared at her mother. '*She* can tell you *all* about Simon, can't you… *Mum*!'

'Ali?' The word was almost a whisper stolen back by her mother's lips as soon as it was released into the room. Mrs Button raised her hand to her mouth and stared at Ali with wide eyes.

Ali glared back at her mother. 'It's alright for you to fuck young boys, is it, *Mum*?'

The word 'Mum' hung in the air. The venom behind it was scorching. Mrs Button flinched. Before they'd started the interview, Gus had wondered if Ali was aware of a connection between Simon Proctor and her mother. Well, now he had his answer and judging by the mother's response, she hadn't been aware of her daughter's knowledge.

In one word her daughter had thrown into doubt her entitlement to call herself a mother. What the hell had the woman been thinking? She'd only just welcomed Ali into her home as her daughter and for some reason had been compelled to risk everything for a cheap shag with an underage boy. He didn't know if Mrs Button realised it, but her actions had put Ali's adoption in jeopardy. There was no way the girl would be allowed to stay in her new family now – even if the family could withstand the inevitable chaos when it hit the news. Mrs Button would be on the sex offenders register and Gus didn't know many families that could withstand that. His heart went out to Ali. All the girl had needed was a stable and loving home and she'd ended up in the middle of this. *Life could be a real fucking bastard at times!*

Mrs Button reached out to her daughter but Ali shrunk away from her.

'Ali, sweetie. I'm sorry.'

Ali refused to meet her mother's eyes. Her lower lip quivering, Mrs Button tried to connect with her daughter once more. 'How long have you known?'

Turning her head, Ali glared. 'Since he sent me the recording of you and him in *our* home.'

Mrs Button's face paled and she closed her eyes. 'There was a recording?'

Ali nodded. Tears were streaming down her face now, her breath coming in quick snatches. 'I don't get it, Mum. At church Reverend Evans goes on about not committing adultery and you and dad sit there all smug, nodding and agreeing with him. You tell me that the church helps us follow God's rules… and then you do *this*?'

Mrs Button fell to her knees beside her daughter, her hands grabbing at Ali's, her cheeks awash with tears. 'I know, I know, Ali. I don't know how it happened. I just don't know. He flattered me, I suppose.'

Ali snatched her hands away. '*Dad* flattered you. Why couldn't he have been enough? You're just fucking selfish. Just like my real mum. Selfish to the core. You had your family… the one you told me you'd always dreamed of, the one you said *I* made complete.' Mouth screwed up,

Ali shook her head, her eyes narrowed, no sign now of the flashing temper in them, just a dullness that to Gus signalled defeat, 'Well you fucked that up, didn't you? They'll never let me stay with you now. Not in a million years. I hope fucking Simon Proctor was worth it. I really fucking do.' And Ali jumped to her feet and delivered a short sharp slap across her mother's cheek.

Alice and Gus both jumped to their feet at the same time. Gus stepped back, allowing Alice to go to the sobbing girl and lead her from the room as Mrs Button knelt, in supplication on the floor, cradling her cheek with one hand. Gus moved round and helped the shaking woman to her feet and sat her back in the chair. He called out for some coffee and waited till it arrived before continuing the interview.

'You realise I'll have to charge you, don't you?'

Hands once more clasped in front of her, Mrs Button swallowed hard, a single tear trickled down her cheek. 'Will I be able to see my husband? I need to try to explain it to him.'

'Yes, I'll arrange for him to visit. DS Cooper will have contacted him to come for Ali.' He raised his head. 'If you don't return home whilst awaiting your trial and have no contact with Ali, she'll be able to stay at home with her dad. Is that perhaps something you'll consider?'

With a humourless laugh, she said, 'Kyle won't have me back now anyway. I've shamed him in the eyes of our church, in the eyes of God and, perhaps more importantly, to him at any rate, in the eyes of his York racecourse clients.' She took a deep breath and raised her eyes. 'However, he dotes on Ali. He'll do everything he can to make sure she's alright.' Stirring her coffee with the plastic spoon, she continued, her tone almost conversational, 'It's both of our second marriages. Our second chance at life. Kyle lost his fiancée in tragic circumstances a while back and it took him a long time to get over it. She was pregnant at the time and so he lost her and the baby in one fell swoop.'

Recognising this was her way of building up to talking about Simon Proctor, Gus leaned back and sipped his own coffee. 'What happened to her? Car crash?'

'No. It was a house fire. She was a social worker and had gone to take some children away from their foster parents because they were under scrutiny for child abuse. The foster parents set the fire and Kyle's fiancée was trapped. Although one of the kids got out, she died.'

Gus heart skipped a beat. This was madness. It couldn't possibly be the same case he'd just been talking to Sandy Panesar about, could it? Kyle Button couldn't be Amina Rose's fiancé, could he?' Like a bucket of cold water to his face, he heard Sandy telling him that she'd met Amina's fiancé *Kyle* once. He was certain that was the name Sandy had used. He thought back. He'd only seen the fiancé once. The man had been distraught and it was dark. Gus had been transferred to Bradford soon after and didn't see the case through to the end. However, if Simon Proctor was rescued from the same fire that had killed Kyle Button's fiancée, then the coincidence was too great to be ignored. Keeping his eagerness, from his face, Gus kept his tone level. 'Was that in Leeds?'

'Yes, it was in Leeds a few years ago. Kyle moved to Bradford, got involved in the church and that's how we met.'

Gus' mind was full of the implications of this information. Knowing that right now, he had to get to the bottom of why a pretty thirty-some woman with a nice lifestyle and a newly adopted daughter would risk everything for a teenage boy, Gus filed that snippet away in his mind for later use.

'So, Simon Proctor. How did that come about?'

A couple of tears rolled down her cheek, so Gus pushed a box of tissues in her direction. Perhaps after he'd heard her story he'd be able to muster up some sympathy for her. Right now, though his sympathies lay with her daughter and to a lesser extent, her husband.

She plucked a tissue from the box and rubbed her cheek with it. 'I don't know how it started. Not really. Simon joined the church a few months back and he made friends with Ali. I was so pleased – overjoyed in fact. Ali had found it difficult to make friends apart from with a couple of the girls from church,' she nipped her lips together. 'Kyle and I didn't want to encourage any more of *those* sorts of friendships.'

Gus frowned. '*Those* friendships?'

She wafted her hand in the air, her mouth screwed up. 'You know? Those sort of "friendships".'

'I'm afraid, I don't know.' Gus was pretty sure he *did* know what she meant, but he'd no intention of letting her off the hook by allowing her to breeze over it. He'd no time for people who rolled their attitudes back a few centuries in the name of their religion and then displayed a total disregard for its dictates in their personal life.

She lowered her voice as if she thought she'd be struck down if she spoke in normal tones. 'Lesbians! Ali told us she "liked" girls, and that sort of thing is against our religion.'

Gus wanted to wipe the smug expression off her face, instead he inclined his head. *Wasn't committing adultery with an underage boy also against her religion?* He hated this sanctimonious crap, however he was too well trained to allow his personal feelings to vent when he knew he could extract some valuable information if he kept schtum.

Mrs Button continued. 'Simon was interested in Ali. I could tell. He kept watching her and making excuses to sit next to her in church. We thought if she was involved with him, she'd stop all this silly "fancying girls" stuff. We even consulted with Anthony – that's the vicar – and he agreed with our strategy. He was even going to incorporate her renouncement of those thoughts on The Prayer Chair on Saturday in City Park.'

God, the poor kid! Maybe she'd be better off with a different family after all. Trouble was, there weren't many who'd take on a fifteen-year-old.

'She pretended she wasn't interested in him, but we thought that was just a ploy. She was just attention-seeking with the other stuff. Who wouldn't want a good-looking, well-spoken lad like Simon?'

Well, Ali for one, by the sounds of it! Gus' expression didn't waver as he listened to her explain about inviting Simon over for tea, despite Ali's protestations.

'He was polite and well mannered, helped with the dishes, commented on my new hairdo and such like. Ali was obstinate. Sometimes I couldn't understand her wilfulness – not at all.' Her gaze drifted upwards and she began wringing her hands. She was getting to the crux of the story now.

'Simon started to call round when nobody else was home. He'd be polite and we'd just chat. Sometimes about things at the church. Then,' she frowned, 'I'm not sure exactly when things changed. He started to comment on my clothes or my make-up. Sometimes, he'd brush past me just a little too close. Then he began to tell me how attractive he found me. It was…' She paused and rubbed her nose with the tissue. 'Exciting. He made it seem exciting and dangerous. He'd look at me as we chatted, his eyes never leaving my face. He made me feel like a woman again. He made me feel desired.'

'You must have known it was wrong, though. You're not stupid. You knew how old he was.'

'Of course, I did. I knew he was a child but he was *so*… charismatic… *so* insistent… he made it easy to forget his age.'

Gus felt the familiar wave of nausea build in his throat. He'd heard more than his share of paedophiles saying similar things... blaming the minor for their inability to control their desires – their warped urges. It didn't matter how manipulative Simon Proctor had been, she was the adult in this. *She* should have called a halt to it all before it became physical.

He glanced at the recorder. He needed her admission on tape so he just went for it. 'Did you knowingly perform oral sex on a minor?'

She lifted her head, her eyes swimming in tears. 'Yes, I did... but you don't understand. He *made* me do it.'

'Are you saying Simon Proctor raped you?' He'd seen the tapes and to his mind there was no evidence of coercion to be seen. Maybe a jury would decide differently. You could never tell.

'No, no, it wasn't rape. It was...' She threw her hands up in the air. 'I don't know what it was. It was as if he couldn't get enough of me for a few weeks. We'd even spoken about moving up north, maybe to Scotland, when he turned sixteen and then, all of a sudden... he dropped me. Stopped returning my calls and my texts. Just nothing.'

Gus frowned. There had been no record of calls from Mrs Button's phone to Simon Proctor's. 'What number did you phone him from?'

Exhaling a loud puff of air, she grimaced. 'He gave me what he called a "burner" phone and he had one as well. It was so his parents and Kyle wouldn't find out.'

'He supplied the phones?'

'Yes.'

The fact that Simon Proctor supplied the phones was intriguing, however, no matter how manipulative he might have been, the law was the law and Mrs Button had committed a crime.

Chapter 73

17:15 The Family Church of Christ, Frizinghall

The lay preacher, who called himself the Reverend Anthony Evans, welcomed Gus and Alice into his home with a *joie de vivre* that had Gus wanting to gip. *Why couldn't folk be normal?* There was no need to display an effervescent bonhomie all the time and especially not on such a grizzly day. The minister had a faint American accent and Gus knew from his research that he'd come as a missionary from Ohio to spread the word of God in the UK.

Home, to Anthony Evans, was a converted church known as St Augustine's, which now stood on deconsecrated ground. From The Family Church of Christ's website, Gus had discovered that Anthony Evans had taken over the derelict building a decade ago and restored many of the church's original features, whilst making it into a home for himself, his wife and his family. The back of the building, where Gus and Alice had entered, was the church and the front was the family's living quarters.

Where the original church had no doubt had wooden pews and cold sandstone slabs, the restoration had created an open carpeted area with many comfortable seats dotted around. In the back corner stood a stack of foldable chairs, that Gus recognised from his research as being the ones used for Sunday services. Judging from the video clips they were Evangelical in nature and involved a lot of repentance, with stirring exhortative sermons, led by the Reverend. Nothing like the sermons he remembered from school assemblies, which were so lacklustre and constrained, he'd often been in danger of falling asleep.

The website made it clear that should you join the Family Church of Christ, your entire life would revolve around the church, its activities and its members. That worried Gus. Its lack of transparency brought the word 'cult' to mind, although there had been no such allegations levelled at the church. He knew other small churches existed in Bradford, but most of these had links and worked with the larger established churches. The Family Church of Christ, however, did not. Memories of Alice's story about her experience with another Prayer Chair organisation that had been exposed as fraudulent, rang alarm bells for Gus.

Not a church goer himself, he had no problem with faith itself. His best friend Mo was a devout Muslim and he had other friends who were equally devout Christians. It was the insularity of this church, the lack of scrutiny from the outside world, that alarmed him. There'd been too many instances of mosques in Bradford abusing their standing in the community for Gus not to be dubious about this organisation. Fundamentalism could rear its head in any community.

A stove sent out a warm glow from the far end of the room and spotlights and candles made the space seem airy and bright. What fascinated Gus, though, was the way Evans had hollowed out the area leading up to the bell tower and made a feature of the huge ropes that hung down and were fanned out and hooked along the circumference of the hollow. The pastor followed his gaze and said, 'We're not allowed to ring them on a Sunday, so we make up for it on a Tuesday night. They make a lovely sound that carries as far as Bolton Woods, I'm told.'

They must be the bells Gus often heard from Mariner's Drive, which wasn't far from here. He turned to the self-appointed minister, a middle-aged man with a receding hairline, wearing jeans and a crew-neck jumper. He looked ordinary, with his easy grin and frequent hand gestures, and Gus wondered what had driven him to set up his own church in England. 'How large is your congregation?'

With a polite smile, Evans, his voice a low drawl, said. 'We have around twenty families and another twenty or so individuals,' He gestured to a group of three well-worn Chesterfield chairs and waited till Gus and Alice had sat down before joining them. 'We're quite dynamic as a church. We organise many social events for all ages and we're like one large family unit. If one of us is in trouble, we are all in trouble.' He lifted his hands, palms pressed together and touched his lips with his fingertips, 'We've been praying for Simon and feel his disappearance most acutely.'

'What were your impressions of Simon?'

'He was keen and eager to please. He had a thirst for knowledge and understanding of God. He revelled in his communion with God and thrived in our care.'

'And his parents? They weren't church members?'

The pastor's lips tightened. 'No, they were not members and having met them since Simon's disappearance in my capacity as Simon's mentor, I better understand why Simon considered *us* his true family.'

'They didn't respond well to your visit?' asked Alice, her eyebrows raised as if in surprise. Gus knew that this was an act. Knowing Al, she sympathised with Jane and James Proctor's reaction.

'No. In fact they were quite rude. Seems they had no idea Simon was spending so much time with us and were, shall we say, unhappy with it. I extended my sympathies and told them our door was always open. Simon's dad got quite enraged and I left straight away.'

Gus took over the questions. 'We've been talking to the Button family. Seems they were close to Simon. Ali comes to your Prayer Chair group with her friend Jenny, the young girl who was abducted after attending your meeting, doesn't she?'

A fleeting frown crossed his face and was replaced almost straight away by a smile, 'I've already spoken to your officers about that night. Jenny said she had a headache and left early. She told me she had a lift, otherwise I would have insisted on getting my wife to drive her home. We have an old run-around van that we use for church business.'

'Yes, I've seen your statement about that. It's not really Jenny I want to speak with you about: it's Simon.'

'Oh? I've also given a statement about Simon to your officers.'

'We wanted to check that nothing further had come to mind regarding Simon or his demeanour or the relationships he had with other members of the church.'

'Simon was well liked in the church. He was friendly, social and outgoing. He got on well with everyone. I think Ali had taken a particular shine to him.'

Gus pressed his lips together. 'Mmm, about that, you do know Ali is gay, don't you?'

The pastor again clasped his hands together and touched his lips once more with his fingertips. 'She's a child. She doesn't know her own mind.'

Evans' sanctimonious tone irritated Gus. It was easy to brush away teen concerns under the auspices of the 'he or she is a child' label. As if being a young adult meant your issues, concerns or problems were somehow less important or worthy of addressing than an adult's. If he ever had kids, he would do his utmost to make sure he listened to them. In an effort to maintain a neutral tone, Gus forced a smile to his lips. 'I'm aware of the advice you gave to her parents regarding her sexuality. Very *Oranges Are Not The Only Fruit*, wasn't it?'

The preacher hesitated, his gaze never leaving Gus' face, as if he were sizing him up before responding. 'The advice I offer my flock is private and I can't discuss it with you.'

'Oh, that's okay, Ali and her mum told us that you advised that Ali denounce her sexuality as a sin on Saturday as part of your Prayer Chair recruitment in City Park. I'm here to tell you that, should that go ahead with Ali still under the protection of the adoption services, I would be compelled to investigate the matter as possible abuse. Do I make myself clear?'

Anthony Evans eyes narrowed. 'Abuse? The girl has been traumatised and is "acting out". I'm saving her from committing an abomination in the eyes of God.'

'That may be your personal opinion, however, the laws of this country override that. Ali has a right to her sexuality and if you continue on this course of action, I will intervene. By the way do you have a permit to take your chair into City Park? I'd suggest you make sure your paperwork is in order.'

They left the church premises a few minutes later and stood in the drive between Alice's Mini and the vehicle the minister had mentioned earlier.

'Bit trusting of them,' said Alice, nodding towards the battered old Ford transit van.

'Eh?' said Gus attempting to squash his legs into the passenger side footwell of Alice's car.

Alice slid into the driver's side and smirked, clearly enjoying Gus' muffled curses, 'They've left the keys in the ignition... very trusting of them?'

As Alice started up the Mini, a tall lad with long dank hair and enough spots to warrant a dose of Acne-Clear strode down the steps from the church, yanked open the van's door and jumped in. Without glancing to either side, he drove off, tyres shrieking in protest. Gus tutted and then when the lad braked momentarily at the gate, indicated left and then turned right, Gus tutted once more. 'I'll have him for that. Can't they tell their rights from their bloody lefts these days? Go after him, Al.'

Alice, mumbling something that sounded like 'mardy-arse', followed the mucky old van. As they reached the traffic lights at the top of Frizinghall next to the grammar school and opposite Lister Park, the lad once more indicated left but got into the right-hand lane.

Alice drew up parallel to the lad. Rolling down his window, Gus tried to catch the lad's eye. However, he was too busy bouncing his head like an Iron Maiden fan to notice Gus. Gus flung open the Mini's door and, with effort, extricated himself, pulled his warrant card from his pocket and rapped on the driver's window. The lad started and looked up, his face paling when he read the card that Gus had pressed against the window.

Ignoring the paaps from the driver's behind them, Gus waited till the lad rolled down the window and directed him to move through the traffic lights onto Emm Lane and into The Turf car park.

When he got back in, Alice said, 'We really have time for this, Gus?'

Having the grace to admit to himself at least that he was reacting to Evans' superciliousness as much as anything, he shrugged. 'It'll only take a minute. I'm not going to book him, but he does need a reminder to indicate; besides, I'll need to check his licence. Looks barely fourteen to me.'

'Hmm, that's what the traffic officers are for.'

Alice followed the van, which was now being driven with overzealous care. She pulled in and parked up beside it. 'You're on your own, Gus. I'm reserving my strength for later.'

Scowling at the reminder of the operation later that evening, Gus got out of the car and approached the lad, who was shivering by the side of the van. The boy handed Gus his driving licence, which named him as Paul and showed he was, in actual fact, almost nineteen. *They all look so young these days. Must be getting old.* Not sure if the lad's shaking was a reaction to his scowl or the fact that the lad wore only a thin T-shirt, Gus made an effort to smile. Before he had a chance to say anything, the boy spoke.

'Reverend Evans lets us use the van. It's a communal one. I in't stole it or owt. He's got it insured for some of us. Helps us get our licences and all.'

Bloody hell, of all the stupid irresponsible things to do! 'You're telling me that the van's left there for any of you lot to help yourselves to?'

Rubbing his arms, which Gus saw were now covered in goose bumps, the boy managed to spit out between his chattering teeth, 'Yes, that's right.'

Idiot! 'The keys are always in the ignition, doors open?'

Again, the lad agreed. Gus shook his head. Who in their right mind would leave a vehicle unattended for the use of a bunch of teenage drivers? It was ludicrous. He was sure that, if he wanted to, he'd find a number of things to book him on, but his earlier bad mood had dissipated. It wasn't the lad's fault that Anthony Evans was a jackass. 'Look, Paul. You indicated left, but turned right when leaving the church premises and again on approaching the traffic lights at Keighley Road.'

Paul grimaced. 'Indicator's fu– Eh broken!'

Gus scowled. 'What do you mean "broken"?'

'It's swapped over. I keep forgetting that I should indicate left if I want to go right and right if I want to go left. Wires are crossed or summat.'

God's sakes. Can it get any worse? 'Does the Mr Evans know about this electrical fault?

'Yeah, been like this for weeks. He says he'll get it fixed when he's got time, but he's a busy man, you know.'

Too damn busy to ensure the safety of these kids? It's like giving them a loaded gun that was always going to back-fire. Irresponsible git. 'Look, give me the keys. The vehicle's unsafe to drive. I suggest you go into the pub and get someone to pick you up.'

As Paul walked off to the pub, phone to his ear, Gus slid back in beside Alice. 'Negligence. Sheer bloody negligence. I'll have the pious pastor for that. Needs teaching a lesson, that one. Endangering kids' lives like that. As if Bradford doesn't have a bad enough reputation for youth traffic violations and accidents.'

Taking out his mobile, Gus phoned into Hardeep at The Fort and explained the situation. 'I want traffic to look the car over and then pay a visit to the delightful Reverend Anthony Evans. Far as I'm concerned, they can throw the damn book at him.'

Chapter 74

18:15 Paprika Lounge Heaton

Gus was trying hard not to think of the delicious meal they were having as 'The Last Supper'. They'd had more footage of Simon Proctor, but no breakthrough. Poor kid seemed to be losing it. He'd displayed his belly to the camera, clearly aware that someone was watching him. Who knows what must be going through his mind.

Gus had thought getting out of The Fort would take his mind off Operation Biker Chick that was due to commence at 21:30, but Alice's incessant talking about it made that impossible. Fed up listening to her, he changed the subject. 'What did you think about the Buttons?'

They hadn't had the chance to discuss the interview in detail, because Nancy had wanted to be briefed about the raid this evening. And then they'd wanted to put the wind up the Reverend Anthony Evans. Now, he wanted to get Alice's take on things. They'd left it up to Mrs Button to tell her husband about her infidelities, and when asked what she wanted to do, Ali had elected to return home with her dad. Poor kid, no sooner does she get adopted than her new parents and her church question her sexuality and ridicule her in public and, to top it all, she finds out her mum is having sex with a school friend.

Alice put a piece of poppadum in her mouth and chewed. 'Think the link between Mr Button and Simon Proctor is too big a coincidence to ignore?'

Grabbing the last piece of roti before Al had it, Gus took a bite. 'Definitely. Kyle Button was quite convincing when he said he hadn't realised that Simon was *that* kid. Hell, the guy nearly fainted. I thought he was going to keel over. It was a lot for him to take in all at once. First, he finds out his wife's been screwing a fifteen-year-old friend of his daughter, then he's told Ali's adoption is at risk because of said wife's behaviour. Finally, we land the double whammy on him that Simon Proctor was the child who survived the fire that killed his pregnant fiancée. He'd be forgiven for freaking out. He seemed quite genuine, I thought.'

Alice spooned a dollop of rice onto her plate and with a vigorous wrist action mixed the dahl in before stuffing a huge spoonful into her mouth. Gus watched, half amused, half frustrated with her, when bits of rice fell out of her mouth as she ate. God, she was becoming more like bloody Compo every day. Next, she'd be scoffing his mother's burnt offerings as if they were ambrosia from the gods.

Alice swallowed a mouthful, took a long slug of water and wiped her fingers on her napkin. 'Well, I'm still not sure about the dynamics between the wife and Simon. I know that *legally* she's guilty, yet that business with the burner phones is a bit off. Why would a fifteen-year-old kid looking for his jollies buy two burner phones? And why would he record the sex tapes, and then, to crown it all, send it to Ali? He seems like a bit of a sick fuck to me.'

Gus grinned. 'Glad to see you've not allowed your analysis to ruin your appetite or your ability to present a cogent and technically-phrased argument for the prosecution. Hell, a lawyer could just take that statement straight to court.'

'Ha bloody ha! Very damn funny.' She glanced at her watch and jumped to her feet. 'Come on. Got to get a move on. I'm being "made over" back at The Fort.'

Frowning at her eagerness to present herself to the lions, Gus grabbed her arm. 'You sure about this? You don't need to do it, you know?'

Grinning, she pinched his cheek hard and said, 'Oh, but I do. We both know I could be out on my arse tomorrow, so I aim to go out with a bang.'

Shit, thought Gus. *Wish she wouldn't use words like 'bang'!* He peeled a couple of twenties from his wallet, waved to the waiter and followed her out.

Chapter 75

19:10 The Fort

The incident room was more crowded than usual and Gus hated it. One of the vice team had grabbed his chair *and* his coffee mug. Compo looked like he was trying to merge into the wall behind his PC, and Sampson and Taffy kept sending petulant glances his way. *Still not forgiven me for not getting them on the raid!*

Alice, on the other hand, was in her element. Dressed in a skintight crop top and leggings with heels that made her a good half foot taller, she was strutting around looking like the cat who'd got the cream, while Gus was of the opinion that 'a lamb to the slaughter' was more apt. They'd made sure she had the look of a girl trying to appear older than her years. Her make-up was heavy and somewhat inexpertly applied. The clothes they'd given her were a complete contrast to her normal gothic black attire. And, despite her added inches, she did look very young. They'd wired her up and put a GPS monitor onto the underwire of her bra.

The plan was she'd saunter into the pub their targets frequented in Keighley. According to the snitch, they were having some sort of celebration in honour of a new member joining the One Percent club. Gus had been told that One Percent was the term used to describe biker groups like the Hells Angels and referred to the fact that ninety-nine per cent of bikers were law-abiding whereas the other one percent, the one percent they were dealing with tonight, were not. This information did not reassure him.

Once in the bar, she was to attempt to attract the attention of the two bikers. Mickey had intimated that that would be easy as they were always on the lookout for young fresh meat. A description that made Gus' heart sink even more. Because of his ethnicity, he wasn't allowed in the pub, which was a watering hole for Keighley's resident bigots and racists and *that* annoyed him, too. He wanted to be as close to Alice as possible. The fact that two other officers would be inside didn't reassure him one bit. He was relegated to a parked car with Mickey Swanson, twenty yards up the road, with a view of the pub door. Alice would, if all went to plan, get herself invited to the clubhouse and would, whilst partying with them, distribute miniscule cameras and microphones around the premises so the teams outside could see what was going on and judge the time to raid the joint. Gus tried to ignore all the things that could go wrong and instead focus on the fact that Alice was capable of anything. He only hoped her nerve held.

Chapter 76

21:15 The George, Keighley

Alice had held it together in front of Gus. He was such a bloody wuss and she knew he was worried stiff about her. She wasn't scared as such, not really. It was more of a low-level, constant rush of adrenalin. As soon as she walked into the pub, she'd be fine. All her old instincts from Brent would kick in and she'd get into character, just like that.

To make it authentic, she'd got on the bus three stops away and got off outside the fish and chip shop opposite The George. As she waited to cross the road, she looked at the pub. Even from here she could hear the low-level thrum of a bass beat interspersed with deep laughter and guttural tones. The outside of the pub was tired. Paint peeled off the sign as it swayed half-heartedly in the slight breeze. Even the lighting had a sad, yellow, nicotine-stained glow to it. Seeing a gap in the traffic, she walked across the road, trying to ignore the fact that the shoes nipped her toes and the cold night air was making goose bumps appear on top of her goose bumps. She thought of her heavy winter coat with longing… and then, she was at the door. Two monster-sized Harleys stood outside. With any luck, they'd belong to her guys. If not, maybe the owners would be heading to the clubhouse later anyway. She'd be adaptable.

Pushing open the door, she swaggered in, chewing gum and with her hips swinging side to side. She marched over to the nearest empty bar stool and deposited her clutch bag on the counter before getting out her phone and texting.

She was aware that her presence had been noted and went full-on playing the part of a disgruntled friend who'd been stood up and was trying to contact someone. The bartender approached, a bar towel slung over his shoulder. Alice glanced up. 'Vodka coke, please.'

From behind her, she felt rather than heard the air displacement as someone approached her. The faint, unwashed smell of sweat mingling with leather drifted to her nostrils.

'I'll get the lady's drink,' said a gruff voice.

Alice summoned up the innocent, teen girl grin she'd been practising all day. 'Wow, really? Thank you.' And she was in, as simple as that. She hadn't expected it to be quite as easy, but sometimes in undercover work you're dealt a winning hand.

Chapter 77

22:25 Outside The George, Keighley

It was ages since Alice had entered the pub and Gus was getting more and more anxious. He hated inactivity at the best of times and the cramped confinement of Mickey Swanson's vehicle irked him. His shoulders ached and no matter how hard he tried, he couldn't seem to untense them. He and Mickey could hear everything that was happening in the pub and with every passing minute it seemed that Alice was having to come up with ever more inventive excuses not to fulfil some sort of sex act with those two jokers. It put him on edge. If they took a step too far, or if Alice said the safety phrase; 'my shoes are too tight', he'd be over there in a flash... except, he knew he wouldn't. He'd leave it to their two plants inside to initiate some sort of distraction – that was their brief, after all.

They needed to get the bikers on possession of both the drugs and firearms, and they needed as many of the Chapter members as possible in the clubhouse before they raided. This was a multi-faceted attack and getting those responsible for Jade Simmonds' death was only one aspect of it. He was lucky he'd been allowed to tag along and he knew he was there only because Nancy had pulled some strings and Mickey seemed to like him for some reason.

Inside their vehicle it ranged from freezing to boiling as Mickey alternated between having the engine on for warmth and turning it off to avoid looking conspicuous. She'd slipped her bullet proof vest off earlier and run in to get them chips, but Gus couldn't eat anything.

His stomach was too unsettled. Mickey, on the other hand, worked her way through both packets of chips with clear enjoyment.

'Love chips!'

Gus raised an eyebrow. 'Never have guessed.'

When at last the pub door swung open and the two bikers emerged, Alice between them, Gus was relieved. The three of them stood looking at the bikes for a good ten minutes, Alice alternating between running her hand over the shiny metal and running it over the taller of the two men's arm. It made Gus' skin crawl. Visions of how these men had treated Jade Simmonds were at the forefront of his mind as he watched.

'She's brilliant, isn't she?' said Mickey, gripping her steering wheel and peering out the window. 'Got them in the palm of her hand.'

Gus could only nod. Mickey had summed it up. Alice was leading them on, using a blend of playfulness and sensuality that Gus had never seen from her before. One of the bikers took off his leather jacket and Gus heard Alice cooing her thanks as she slipped it on and zipped it up before climbing onto the larger of the two bikes behind the taller biker. The jacket dwarfed her. The sleeves covered her hands and it tucked under her bottom as she sat. The guy who'd given her his jacket leaned over and extracted a helmet from the box at the back of his bike and plonked it on her head, fastening it, before kissing her noisily and tapping the visor down.

Then they were off, accelerating and roaring into the flow of traffic causing a taxi to brake and honk its horn. It wasn't Gus' job to follow. They knew where the bikers were headed and the GPS transmitters they'd planted on the bikes and on Alice would tell them if there was any deviation from the expected route.

Half an hour later, Gus and Mickey drew up in a lay-by further up the road from the track leading to the clubhouse. It was out of sight of the bikers unless they missed the track and drove past, but that was unlikely. Their source had told them these two were regular patrons of the Chapter's facilities. From the bushes to their right, one of Mickey's men appeared and confirmed that Alice and the two men had shot past them a couple of minutes before. Game on!

Chapter 78

22:25 Unknown Location

Not long now, thank God. It's getting colder. It's like someone's thrown a bucket of cold water over me. And the dripping... fuck's sake, the dripping. Bloody pouring down the walls. Puddles all over the floor now, mixing with the piss and the blood. Clothes are soaked. How am I supposed to carry them? They'll weigh a fucking tonne, but I can't leave them here. Just have to manage.

'Fi...re, fi...re, watch it burn, la, la, la, da, da, da. Fi... re, Fi...re da, da, da, la, la, la.'

Can't remember a time I've ever been warm. Hoodie and blanket do fuck all... except make me scratch. Fucking great bug welts all over my arms and thighs. That'll look good when they find me, though... authentic! Fucking fleas. Never mind, I'll get my revenge. What I'd give right now to be at the Hare and Hounds, sat in front of that big log fire of theirs, one of their cheese burgers in front of me... Ace!

'Log fiii... re. Keeps me saaa...ne. Bu...ur...ur...n, la la la.'

Warm bed. That's what I need. Wonder if they've found my stash. Could do with a score right now... you know? Take the edge off. Maybe should've hid the stash. Nah, what teenage lad doesn't have a stash these days? Hell, bet even old Jane and James smoked some wacky-baccy when they were young. What am I thinking, though? The coppers will have taken my shit. They'll have searched my room *and* the shed. They'd have told Mum and Dad too, and she'd have had that face on her. The one that says, 'I don't know where he gets it from. It must be his birth mother because it's certainly not from us.'

Wonder if they've been on telly, yet? What I'd give to see that. The pair of them, holding on to each other like a pair of Siamese twins, crying and pleading for his captor to release him. If they knew the half of it... bloody inspired. Everything planned to a T. Just need to follow through to the end and I'll be in the home straight.

At this stage, my options are limited. The most important thing is to get out of this alive. That's the main aim, however it's the variables that are the issue. Too many variables. A joint right now would clear my thinking. Relax me a bit, take my mind off the cold and hunger.

Not long now, Simon, for Christ's sake. Just hold it together. Plenty of time for joints when I get out. Right now, I need to focus on my getaway. I know what needs to be done. Just need to make sure it's timed just right. There's no room for mistakes. No margin of error.

Then... back to my old life, nobody any the wiser, loose ends tied up... Revenge complete.

Or, worst case scenario... Plan B. Either way, I'll have done what I set out to achieve.

Chapter 79

23:15 The Fugitive Bandits Clubhouse, Ilkley Moor

Alice had loved the drive from Keighley to the clubhouse. The wind, the speed, the weaving between vehicles gave her a real rush.

Then, before she knew it, she was at the track leading to the clubhouse and was being bounced around like a rag doll on the back of the bike. Her grip tightened round Biker Joe's middle and the wind whipped his laugh away as he accelerated more. He was trying to frighten her, so she refused to scream. She had faith that, although *she* was pretty low on his list of precious things, his bike *was* number one. He wouldn't risk damaging it.

He decelerated and braked just in front of a solid wooden fence that rose eight feet off the ground. Sticking up from the top were jagged shards of glass. *Very security conscious*! Balancing the weight of the bike, Joe pulled off his glove, reached over and pressed a button. A fuzz of static came over the line. He gave a mumbled response which was followed by a buzz and the gate opened, admitting both bikes into the compound.

Fifty feet away from the fence was a large stone bricked building that was only just visible in the light of the moon until a door opened and light spilled out onto the dirt track. Twenty or so Harleys were lined up around the yard. When Joe got off the bike, she followed suit and, after retrieving her clutch bag from the pocket, slipped off her borrowed biker's jacket and laid it over the saddle. Bruce Springsteen's 'Born To Run' blared from the open door and men of all shapes and sizes, the majority clad in leather, tattooed, baldheaded and heavily bearded, spilled from inside. Some of them had their arms round girls who looked barely old enough to tie their own shoelaces.

'What the fuck, Joe? Why you brought her with you? Who the fuck is she? Some fucking minger from Binger?'

Alice recognised the coarse reference to the less salubrious women of Bingley and wanted to swipe the smirk of his face. Tilting her head back, she looked into the eyes of the tallest man she'd ever met. Her gaze dropped downwards to the gun that was directed inches from her stomach. In response, her muscles clenched and the flicker of fear that flashed over her face wasn't altogether an act. The thug with the gun threw back his head and laughed, addressing the group of leather clad men ranging in age from mid-twenties to their fifties, who hovered at his shoulders. 'See that? She's bricking it.'

Alice shuffled back a little. Judging by the way the girls darted wide-eyed glances between Alice and 'Giant Man', she was in trouble. The few inches she'd gained with her backward shuffle weren't enough for her to manoeuvre into any self-defence move. Not that it would matter. She was outnumbered. It was then that she became aware of another, much more ominous sound from behind her. A quick glance told her that two Rottweilers were pacing, saliva drooling from their huge jaws. They were so close to her that she was sure she could feel their hot breath on her naked arms and she imagined them pressing their sharp teeth into her arm. *Shit, this wasn't good.*

Just as she thought she'd be shot and fed to the animals, Giant Man grinned and winked at her. A rumble of laughter left his throat and he gestured to the dogs to scat. With low whines they disappeared into the darkness and Alice released a slow breath. Flapping her hand in front of her face, for the benefit of the officers listening in, she said in a breathless voice. 'Shit, mister, you had me there. Thought you were going to shoot me with that big shotgun and feed me to your two mutts.' She winked at him and added, 'Seems you're happy to see me, though.'

The man released another burst of laughter and laid a shovel sized hand on her shoulder, nearly knocking her onto her back. 'Come on, darling, you're with me.'

'She's mine,' said Joe, his voice petulant. The big man turned and punched him in the stomach. 'Stop your fucking griping. The girl's mine, right?'

Joe doubled over, retching, and the acrid smell of beer-tinged vomit mingled with the exhaust fumes hung in the air. Before Alice could say anything, two of the other men stepped forward, hooked their arms under Joe's shoulders before hefting him to his feet and dragging him into the clubhouse.

With exaggerated politeness, Giant Man turned and held out his crooked elbow to Alice, as if he was escorting her to her school prom. Using her practised smile, Alice put her arm though his and allowed him to guide her inside. *That had been a close shave, but she couldn't afford to betray her fear. She needed to hold it together and get the cameras situated inside. Soon as they were up and running, she'd be safer.*

The first thing she noticed was the over-abundance of near life-sized photographs of Harley Davidsons pinned to the walls. Each one had a pouting, near nude woman, oozing raw sex, straddling the saddle. The second thing was the massive pool table and pin ball machine that took up one corner of the massive room and was being utilised by five men who hadn't formed part of her earlier welcoming party. Couches and chairs occupied by a handful of other men with girls on their laps created a maze through which

Giant Man guided her. A distinctive smell of male sweat pervaded her nostrils and Alice didn't have to think too hard to identify the source of its musky accompaniment.

Along the far wall was a makeshift bar stocked high with spirits optics and beer barrels and it was to this area that she was led. Breathing through her mouth, Alice followed, her eyes alert for places to stick the pin-head cameras she'd been given. Now, she was inside the clubhouse, her confidence had diminished. She counted around fifteen men and, what was more worrying, at least ten women who could become hostages. She needed to make sure her team outside had the full picture of the inner layout. Pulling out her compact mirror and lipstick, Alice concealed a camera on her finger, before applying the lipstick. Shoving the items back inside her bag, she stretched up and tapped the front of the beer barrel. 'Can I have some of this?'

'You want to try our homebrew? Reckon you got the stomach for it, do you?'

Alice doubted very much that she had the stomach for the sludge that was handed to her in a mucky glass, but at least she'd got one camera up and running. All she had to do was place the others and locate the drugs and firearms. *Easy!* Looking round the room, she realised that, apart from the gun her host carried across his chest as if it was a baby, there were no other visible weapons in the room. Not that *that* meant anything.

Each of these men would carry at least one concealed weapon. However, what was more concerning was the fact that the room seemed to take up the size of the entire clubhouse except for a walled-off area in one corner. Judging by the fact that she'd seen two men exit the small room, while pulling up their zips, this could only be a toilet. So where were they keeping the goods?

Chapter 80

23:30 Tetley Street

Shit! Which of the two whores had been with Julie Dyson? He hadn't paid much notice to the two hookers who'd been standing with Julie the other night.

Maybe they hadn't paid any attention to him either, but he couldn't be sure and *that* was the problem. He couldn't go around topping all the fucking hookers in Bradford, yet he couldn't leave anything to chance. He couldn't go down for killing a piece of street scum. Not when he'd got a family at home to look after. Fuck, his back was still hurting and he'd been sick. Bloody ulcers, that's what it was, just like his wife had warned him of. Why were his fingers tingling like that? Even inside his gloves they must be cold.

In the confines of the patrol car, he tried to stretch his shoulders. It was hard to focus with the pain and he really needed to focus right now. What the hell should he do? The way he saw it, he had two options. One, take care of the four that were there right now. Fuck that would be difficult. Two maybe, as there weren't many punters who picked up four girls at once. Or option two, sidle home with his tail between his legs and pray the prossies hadn't seen owt. The bleach would have taken care of the forensic side. It was the damn prossies that were the problem for him.

His knee jigged up and down as he tried to make his decision. It was dark in the street wasn't it? Doubt they'd have seen him. Think, Think, Think! What should he do?

If he went for any of these four, he'd risk exposing himself... and he wasn't even sure they were the ones. The pain across his shoulders intensified, so he popped another couple of Ibuprofen. All those painkillers were rotting his gut. Wished he'd thought to get some Gaviscon when he bought the tablets. He had heartburn now.

Leaning forward, he stared at the cluster of girls. Shit, it's so dark over there, they wouldn't have been able to see him... not clearly anyway. No, definitely not. With a last glance at the women, he pushed his clutch in and drove off, hoping he wasn't going to rue the decision he'd made, to let them live.

Thursday

Chapter 81

00:30 Ilkley Moor

Gus had spent an uncomfortable five minutes on the back of a specially adapted electric motorbike with all the suspension of an overused mattress, but at least he was now stalking the perimeter of the fence with Mickey, who'd arrived on the back of a similar bike.

Every so often Mickey would stop and fiddle with her tablet. To say they were anxious about the length of time it was taking Alice to set up a visual inside the clubhouse was an understatement. They had one camera up. However, it had a limited view of only a fraction of the house and made it difficult to estimate the number of bodies inside.

Nervous tension had Gus' blood wired. He was jumpy and had already snapped at Mickey twice. The fact that he could hear Alice inside was reassuring, although the filth she was having to deal with made his blood boil. They'd gathered from her whispered comments on a loo visit that she couldn't locate the goods and that was worrying. What if they weren't on site? They only had the snitch's word on that one and God knows how reliable he was. Another worry was that they'd learned that at least three of the women inside were comatose and could be vulnerable hostage risks when they raided. The other concern was that because the clubhouse appeared to be soundproofed they were reliant on the limited audio from Alice's mic and Gus wasn't happy with that.

'At last, another camera.' Mickey's voice sounded as relieved as Gus felt. He moved to her side and peered over her shoulder. They now had visuals on a group of bikers playing pool, with another two snogging some girls on a sofa nearby. All of the visuals were being streamed to other officers around the perimeter, and also to Compo, who was working his computer to get IDs and, hopefully, backgrounds on some of the men inside.

The idea was to wait till Alice had ascertained the whereabouts of the firearms and drugs before they implemented a co-ordinated explosion at intervals around the perimeter to allow them access to the grounds. After gaining entry the SWAT team would swoop in to round up as many Fugitive Bandits as they could. This had to be done at speed, before the bikers could get to their Harleys and take the chase outside the confined space of the deserted moorland. If, as was looking likely, Alice failed to locate the goods, they were to wait till either she was leaving the premises or until she signalled for help.

Mickey's split screen ran footage from both the cameras Alice had managed to place. As they watched, Alice walked past, carrying a pint glass filled with a dark brown liquid. She turned her head towards the camera and sneaked a wink. Despite his annoyance with her for taking a risk, Gus grinned. She was irrepressible.

'Looks like she's–' He didn't get to finish his sentence because all of a sudden, the top camera moved and frantic cries filtered through the tinny speakers.

Alice's voice saying, 'Let her go. She fucking said *no*,' was the last thing he heard, before an explosive shot rent the air, followed by a scuffle and the sound of a female groaning. Gus was off before Mickey had given the order to 'GO, GO, GO!' Without waiting for the smoke to clear from the nearest fence explosion, Gus threw himself through and headed for the clubhouse. Spotlights illuminated the building, leaving the approaching officers in shadow.

The clubhouse door burst open and the hulking frames of the bikers were lit up as they dove through the door one at a time. One of the officers yelled a 'Police!' warning which was ignored. Gus was desperate to get to the door. His eyes raked over the exiting figures to see if any of them were carrying Alice or dragging her behind them. He got to within twenty yards and a big fucker with biceps on top of his biceps, planted himself in front of Gus, a knife in one hand and a chain in the other. *Fuck's sake, I don't have time for this.*

Gus feinted to the right and then back to the left. The biker, weight slowing him down, followed Gus to the right but couldn't keep up with his direction change, so he swung his chain towards Gus' at knee height. Gus jumped and felt the weight of the chain skim his shin as he moved past his assailant. From the corner of his eye, he saw two armed officers point their guns at the man, who, in the spirit of 'fight till the end' started stabbing his knife in their direction. A single shot to the arm put an end to that nonsense, and Gus was pleased to see him sink to his knees, cradling his injured arm against his chest.

From his left, a wave of warm air fanned his face and a warm damp dog smell hit his nostrils, moments before he was flung onto his front, hot drool slopping onto his cheek as one of the Rottweilers snapped at his face. The weight of the animal pushed Gus' chest onto a clump of bracken making it difficult for him to catch breath. With one hand trapped under his body, he attempted to push himself forward with the other, but the animal was too strong. Raising his free arm, he covered his face just as the animal's teeth clamped round it. The pain was excruciating and he screeched. The animal tossed his arm like a ragdoll and Gus was sure it would be yanked from its socket. Every second with the dog on top of him felt like forever. He could feel something warm and sticky hit his face and trickle down towards his mouth. It was only when it reached his lips he realised it was his own blood. Using the last of his strength he jerked his hips, hoping that, by moving his lower body, he could dislodge the dog. Which was when he felt a similar pain in his leg and realised the other dog had joined the affray. *Why the fuck did he have to be the one to attract the fucking beasts?*

With his arm being yanked one way, his leg the other *and* the weight of two animals pinning him down, Gus turned his face to the side and yelled again. In the distance, two shots were fired. Gus' heart exploded into triplet time. More shots, this time to his right, near towards where the Harleys were lined up. The dogs made a whimpering sound and released their grip a little. Gus tried to yank his limbs away, but the animals' whimpering died in their throats as they refocussed on their prey. It was as if he was being tasered again and again. The pain ricocheted through his entire body and what had started as a trickle of blood hitting his face became a torrent. *Maybe the fucker had hit an artery.* His eyes began to flicker. Shit he was going to faint and then he heard a scream... a female screen... Alice! His eyes flickered again and his vision blurred. *A lot of fucking good Mickey's advice about wearing extra clothes had been—*

Chapter 82

00:30 Unknown Location

It is time. Much as I could hold off for a bit longer, it's too hard. Not knowing what's going on outside... it's killing me. Need to get it over with, and tonight's as good a night as any. Maybe if I'd had longer, I might have been able to get Matty onside and then I'd have had eyes on the outside. Hmm, on reflection though, Matty is a pussy. He'd be a liability in the end. No, it's better like this.

Bit of a rush getting this place kitted out at the end, but I managed. Okay, so a few more home comforts would've been better; I was more concerned about the end game. Nothing here should implicate me. Should have packed more food, though, and a little camping stove. That'd have been an asset as it would have given off some heat as well. Didn't reckon with the mind-numbing cold... or the loneliness... or the damn rain.

If that little foray on Monday night and then again on Tuesday morning hadn't nearly gone awry, I might have risked a couple more night trips. Found out what's going on, and that. Not worth the risk, though. Not for a bit of discomfort for a few nights. Shit, this is the important part. The bit I've been aiming for all along. A sighting of me would have messed everything up. The entire plan relied on me being missing. Bloody nosey bastard, rolling home from the pub half-pissed, he nearly spotted me. In the church van. He was more than likely too far gone to describe me with any credibility though – fucking old pisshead!

It'd been easy to talk Jenny into getting into the Reverend's old van. Stupid bitch took the Coke – drank it all. Never even tasted the rohypnol. Biker Joe had promised that they forget everything after that, so she wouldn't remember owt about me picking her up… or what I'd done to her.

She was a fucking interfering bitch, though. She deserved it all. Poisoning Ali's mind against me. I was the fucking victim, not Ali's mum or that other cow either. Then when Ali got drunk at my party and started dancing on the table – enough to make you think she wasn't a little fucking lezzer after all.

Frustrating though, not to know what everyone is thinking, how Mum and Dad are. Not that it matters… not really. Not out to punish *them*, but it does give me a hard-on thinking about my mother in bits and my dad trying to be stoic.

No, this plan was targeted at someone else entirely… everything else was just an added bonus. Sorting through the supplies in the corner of the cellar, I feel that familiar buzz. Electricity. My fingers aren't numb any more. It's like I'm sizzling… a bomb waiting to explode.

'Fireball explode, la, la, la. Fire ball burn high, da, da, da.'

Last leg of the journey. Home run. I can fool *everyone*… hell, I've done it before, haven't I? Why should this time be different? Do the deed, get back here and let the coppers follow the crumbs.

Chapter 83

01:35 Ilkley Moor

'A lot of bloody good you were. Might as well have left you back at The Fort if all you're going to do is sleep on the damn job!'

Gus opened his eyes and realised he was in the back of a police Land Rover with two paramedics working on him and a spotlight directed to his face. He blinked and moved his head but couldn't see the owner of the voice. *Shit, was he hearing things? Was Alice dead? Was he dead?* A wave of dizziness made his head spin and as his stomach lurched, he closed his eyes and tried to orientate himself. A sharp prick of pain made him open them again. He scowled at the paramedic who was working on his mangled arm. That was it. The dogs. The fucking Rottweilers. Demons from the bowels of hell.

He still couldn't locate the person attached to the Alice voice, so he assumed he'd been dreaming and wondered if he could summon up the courage to ask after her. He was reluctant to know the truth, yet he knew he must. The memory of that female cry was scorched into his mind. As he lay there, memories of the explosion, followed by his fight with the big biker and ending with the dog attack came back to him. The chaos of the events, the blurred figures running around, the acrid smell of explosive, the gunshots… it had all happened so quickly and he had no recollection of being transported to the vehicle.

A gurgle of laughter erupted from somewhere just outside his peripheral vision.

'That you, Al?' His voice sounded like the beasts had shredded his vocal chords not his arm.

'Who the hell else is it likely to be, you bloody idiot? Trust you to manage an encounter with Fluffy and Fido.'

Relief spread like a peanut butter sandwich after a long jog; all warm and oozing sweetness, in Gus' chest. *Thank fuck she's alright!* He spluttered, 'Fluffy and fucking Fido? You're kidding me, aren't you?!'

Alice's head appeared over the back of the front seats, 'Yeah. Actually, I think one was called Brutus. Didn't catch the other doggy's name. You look like shit.'

Gus studied Alice's face and thought the description could equally fit her. She had a whopper of a black eye and a long scrape across her forehead. 'Tell me!' said Gus.

Alice sighed, and lifted a bandaged hand to rub her cheek. 'I lost it.' She sounded deflated for a second, then her cheeks dimpled and she grinned. 'At least I stopped the fucker raping a comatose fourteen-year-old girl. Bastard!'

Ah, so that's what the disruption inside the clubhouse had been.

Trying to ignore the fact that he could feel neither his fingers nor his toes, Gus grinned back at her. 'Glad you're okay, Al. What about the rest of it? What was all the drama just before we stormed the place?'

'Well, in all the kerfuffle in the shit hole after I mouthed off, the giant fired that damn rifle into the air. He was *not* a happy bunny. Not one to take a telling from a woman, never mind one a fifth of his size. Mind you, from the holes in the ceiling, I got the impression he did that a lot... fired into the air, I mean. Anyways, all hell let loose. Everyone had guns, except the women, surprise, surprise. Guns were going off... this is what happened, here.' She pointed to the gash across her forehead. 'Just a graze, though. Then you lot must have triggered off an alarm, for at that moment a klaxon blared in the clubhouse and they all started to charge outside, chains, knives and guns in their hands.'

'Any injuries?'

Alice shrugged. 'A couple of minor ones on our side. The women were in a bad way and I'm pleased to say most of the bikers sustained, at the very least, a hard kick from me.'

'What about the stuff?'

'Hell yeah! Bloody bastards had dug out a cellar space that they hid with a mangy old rug. They found the guns and all, down there.'

'We get our two?'

Alice's smile nearly split her face. 'Hell yeah! Bastards are en route to The Fort as we speak.' Her gaze clouded. 'However, we're not getting to do the interviews. Nancy's passed it onto vice to deal with. Gives them greater ammunition if they tie the two together, but at least we know that two of them will go down for what they did to Jade.'

Gus closed his eyes. 'Thank God. At least Jade's parents will get some closure.' He waited a minute and then opened his eyes again, 'Al, do you think you could just have a look and see what's happening with my arm and leg.'

Alice snorted, 'Fuck's sake Gus. It's only a bit of blood.'

One of the paramedics pulled his mask down. 'Your arm's a bit of a mess, nothing a good clean and stitches won't fix. Your leg's only got a surface bite. You'll be right. Good job you wore some extra layers. That'll have helped a little.'

Gus scowled – it was only as an afterthought that he'd taken Mickey's advice and worn extra layers. Not that he'd tell her that, though!

Chapter 84

02:45 Bradford Royal Infirmary

Gus looked down at the useless pile of shredded clothes the doctor had cut off him so she could get access to his wounds. The twelve stitches to his swollen and bruised arm had increased the throbbing from dull to screeching. He was relieved when the doctor gave a morphine injection and handed him a container with some neurontin in it. The skin on his leg, though sore, wasn't broken and Gus was relieved to have only one addition to his scar collection. When the door opened, admitting Alice, he tried to pull the short hospital robe down to cover his thighs.

'Seen it all before, Gus, and believe me it's nothing to write home about,' she said, plonking down on the edge of the bed, causing it to bounce which, in turn, jolted his bruised body.

'Fuck's sake, Al, I'm the patient here. Can't you be a little less rough?'

She pointed to the butterfly stitches across her forehead. 'So am I. *You* don't have a monopoly on injuries tonight.' She ran her fingers over the stitches. 'You think I'll have a scar?'

Gus couldn't help grinning at the hopeful tone in her voice. 'Here's me wishing I had a few less war wounds and you're bloody gloating about it.'

Before Alice could respond, Gus heard a voice he recognised drift down the corridor outside. *Shit!* He glared at Alice, who was attempting to look innocent. 'Did you phone her?'

Shrugging, Alice picked at the bed sheet. 'The doctor wanted to discharge you and I reckoned you would want to head straight back to The Fort and wouldn't want to wear that thing.' She pointed to his lilac hospital gown. 'Appealing though you look in it, I thought you'd rather not give that knob Knowles any more ammunition to slag you off.'

She had a point, but Gus was damned if he'd admit it. As the door opened, he sent her a look that said, 'We're not done here' and pasted a smile on his face, as his mother bustled in, followed by his dad. Corrine McGuire reached over and cupped his cheek in her hand, inspecting his face before lowering her glance to his arm which, much to Gus' relief, was bandaged and in a sling, thus concealing the extent of his injuries.

'It's only a wee graze, Mum. Nothing to worry about and the skin on my leg's not even broken. They've just discharged me.'

His dad, holding a Kana Peena supermarket bag, stepped forward and dumped the bag on Gus' lap. 'Clothes!'

Gus frowned at his father's abrupt tone, but when he looked at him, he realised his dad's lower lip was quivering. *Shit!* Gus had been so worried about the effect this would have on his mum, he hadn't stopped to consider his dad might be affected too. He reached out a hand. 'I'm alright, Dad. Nothing a few days with my arm in a sling won't heal. I'm heading back to work in a minute, as soon as I can get dressed. The doctor's given me the all-clear.'

His dad took a large white hankie from his pocket and blew his nose, the sound as loud and discordant as a ship on the North Sea in the fog. 'I know you're fine, laddie. It was your mother who was worried. I've just got a bit of a cold, that's all.'

Alice, concealing her grin, winked at Gus as his mum tutted and set about pulling the clothes from the bag.

'I brought you jogging pants, Angus. Much easier to get on with one hand and they're fleece-lined so they'll be soft on your poor wee leg.' She pulled a large jumper from the bag and scrunched it up from the waist to the armpits before deftly putting it over Gus' head and easing it down so he could pull his injured arm from the sling and put it in first. His dad edged her out of the way and repeated the process with the bottoms. Gus, all too aware of Alice's amusement, scowled at her. He knew better than to try to do it himself. He knew that the best therapy for his parent's anxiety was to feel useful, so he'd put up with feeling like a five-year-old for a few minutes, if it made them happy.

He'd just, with his dad's help, managed to stand up, when the door burst open once more and his sister Katie walked through, out of breath and with a stethoscope draped round her shoulders.

'Shit, Gus, only just heard. You okay?'

'Course I am.' Truth was, he was knackered and sore, yet the sight of his family with their concerned glances, warmed him inside like nothing else could.

'Gabriella's on her way, too.'

'For God's sake, Katie, did you call Mo and Naila too? Talk about the bloody jungle drums beating. Who needs them when *you're* on the case?' He glanced up and saw his sister's sheepish look. 'Aw for fuck's sake, Katie, you did, didn't you? You called Mo and—'

The door opened and Mo, Naila and Gabriella piled into the room, all chattering at once and all fighting to get close to the bed.

'Right, that's it!' Gus raised his voice. 'It's nice of you all to come, but I'm busy right now. Got a murderer to catch and all that, so... I'll see you all later,' and with Alice trailing behind, he limped out of the room.

He'd reached the end of the corridor when his dad shouted after him, 'Wait up, Gus. Wanted to fill you in on the post-mortem on the girl found at Cottingley Ridge.'

Gus stopped and waited for his dad to catch up.

'Looks like you caught something good, Dad?'

'Whoever did this thought the bleach would be enough to cover his tracks... and it would have been, except for one very lucky break. The dozy bugger had traces of semen on his fingers, and when he strangled her, like so,' his dad made a circle of both hands with his thumbs to the front, 'traces of said semen transferred to the back of her neck, where, I surmise, her hair protected it from the bleach.'

'You're telling me you got enough for a DNA sample?'

His dad's grin told him he was right. 'Bloody brilliant, Dad. Just brilliant.'

'I've sent it to the labs and expedited it. Asked them to compare it to the semen found at the Proctor's house in case it matches with that.' His dad flung his arm round Gus' shoulders and gave a gentle squeeze. 'I'm glad you're okay. You gave us a fright and I could do without any more of those for the foreseeable future.'

Gus squeezed back. 'Me too, Dad, me too. Now, go and collect the troops and tell them all to go home.'

Relieved to take the weight off his leg, Gus leaned on the wall as the lift took them down to the ground floor. When the doors opened, Alice helped him on with his blood-stained fisherman's coat before they walked out into the night air. A freezing fog had descended, making the wheelchair users with their drip stands congregated in the smokers' shelter look like alien shadows against the backdrop of subdued hospital lighting, escaping through the ward curtains.

'Should have got you a wheelchair,' said Alice, eyeing him limp down the ramp.

Gus shook his head. 'Nah, it's—' but the sound of his phone ringing in his pocket interrupted him. With some difficulty he managed to locate it and answer.

He listened for a few seconds, before speeding up. 'Come on, Alice, looks like the Buttons' house is on fire. Let's get there now.'

In the distance he could hear the screeching of fire engines and, as they headed for the waiting car driven by a uniformed officer, two ambulances, blue lights blazing, exited the hospital car park and headed towards Frizinghall.

Chapter 85

03:35 Redburn Drive, Frizinghall

Despite the fog, Gus could see the lick of flames on the skyline as they approached Redburn Drive. For a second, he was transported back to the fire where Simon Proctor nearly lost his life and where Kyle Button's fiancée and unborn child died.

Before he'd even got out of the police car, smoke clogged his throat and his eyes started to water. Peering through the crowds of people, Gus looked for his team and located Sampson and Taffy setting up a boundary so the firefighters could work. As he approached, he saw that the paramedics were standing outside their ambulances, trollies and equipment at the ready. A row of firefighters were training hoses on the building, trying to damp the flames that were coming from a downstairs window. An explosive crash, followed by a roar of flames, halted Gus in his tracks. An upstairs window burst and flames escaped, reaching out like sparking fingers, roaring and ferocious. He hoped that Ali and her dad had managed to get out.

Peering through the smoke which competed in density with the fog, Gus, eyes streaming, grabbed Sampson's arm. 'Who's still inside?'

Sampson's face was streaked with soot, the whites of his eyes, in sharp contrast to his skin, seemed larger than usual. He turned to Gus and Alice, his shoulders slumped, and glanced towards the burning building. 'Both of them. The two firefighters who went in haven't come back out yet.'

Resting his hand on the younger man's shoulder, Gus squeezed. 'We've got a job to do, so let's do it.' He pulled Sampson away from the crowds and gestured for Taffy and Alice to join them.

'I don't believe in coincidences and this fire, coming hot on the heels of everything we discovered earlier, makes me suspicious. If this is arson, and I'm aware we don't know that for sure, however if it is, we need to be on the ball. We'll split into pairs and take a different section of the perimeter. Alice and Sampson, you're taking the front of the house. Start in the middle and one of you head one way, one go the other. Taffy, you and I will take the rear of the property. We're looking for any suspicious characters. I want you to photograph as many of the onlookers as you can.'

Taffy frowned. 'Why?'

Alice slapped him on the back. 'Because, my young Padawan, if this is arson, the tosser who set fire to the Buttons' house will be standing in a corner having a wank.'

'Eh?' Taffy cast a furtive eye round the crowds and Alice rolled her eyes. 'Not literally, idiot.' She tilted her head to one side. 'Well, I hope not, anyway. No, I meant figuratively. They get off on watching the fire and the fall-out scene afterwards. Look out for people who are recording the scene and also for those keeping themselves a little distant. Compo can use the images to get information on them.'

Gus headed for the back of the building by accessing a wide perimeter through the neighbour's garden. He'd directed Taffy to do the same on the left side. If anyone wanted to watch proceedings from a distance, the back of the property was the best bet for them. With the garden backing onto Heaton Woods, a voyeur could watch what was going on in private. If anyone was there, Gus wanted to be sure to get them.

On the other hand, a sensible arsonist would mingle with the crowd – but Gus was counting on the fire-maker, if it was a deliberately set fire, being Simon Proctor. Things were stacking up too conveniently against the lad and Gus wasn't about to risk losing him.

At the end of the neighbours' garden, Gus was relieved to spot a wooden gate leading into the woods. He carried his phone in one hand, while his other, released from its sling, was too tender to be up for anything strenuous. He stepped through the gate and found himself on a mucky path that led up through the woods to the top of Ashwell Road. Earlier in the year they'd found a body not so far from here.

He began to edge his way up the path, his eyes swinging from left to right. Behind him the fire crackled and spat noxious fumes into the air. The neighbouring houses, lit up like beacons, afforded a degree of light at the back of the property and cast moving shadows as the trees swayed in the gentle breeze. Through the foggy smoke, every tree took on a life of its own and Gus soon realised that even if he came across someone, he'd be unable to get a decent photo in the half light, so he slipped his phone back into his coat pocket and focussed on trying to discern any sudden movement in the trees.

The fire was concentrated to the front of the property, so Gus' hopes of seeing the arsonist in the woods diminished. He only hoped the others had more luck. A sudden increase in activity from the front of the buildings made him pause. Unintelligible yells, frantic and imperative, crescendoed over the fire's roar, sending shock waves through Gus' body. With his good arm, he yanked at the hedge that bordered the Buttons' garden and peered through. A dull orange glow became visible through the back-room windows, then, in a gust of flying glass and debris, the windows burst open and flames roared through.

Scorching heat blasted over him. The heat stung his face and the fumes engulfed his nostrils. If Ali and Kyle Button were still inside when that happened, Gus knew they'd be dead.

A figure approached, walking down the path. Gus tensed and stood still. His eyes were still reacting to the amber brightness of the flames and he had trouble focussing. The figure kept approaching and Gus reached for his phone. The figure continued at a snail's pace until, with a flurry of limbs, it pedalled the air and landed with a thud on the path. 'Fucking leaves.'

Gus grinned and returned his phone to his pocket. It was Taffy. He was about to yell to the officer, when movement in his peripheral vision, followed by a dull thump, had him spinning round. Still blinking against the orange dots that clouded his sight, Gus saw a figure balled up under a tree, about ten yards away from him. Whoever it was had jumped from one of the wide branches. As Gus stepped forward, it unfurled into a standing position, spun on its heels and took off into the woods.

Gus, hobbling, took off in pursuit. 'This way, Taffy.'

Within seconds Taffy had overtaken him and, with Gus lagging behind, hared off the track, between the trees. After a few metres, Gus admitted defeat. He wasn't fast enough in his current state and there was no guarantee that the person they'd chased had set the fire. Only too aware that there were many nefarious deeds one could get up to in Heaton Woods should you be that way inclined, Gus leaned against a tree, cradling his aching arm. Although the possibility existed that dodgy wiring could be responsible for the blaze, it would take a fully certified fire appraiser's report before Gus was convinced of that.

Taffy returned a few minutes later, panting and cross. 'Lost the fucker, Gus. Too damn dark to see a thing in among the trees.'

The pair of them, with Taffy lending a much-needed shoulder to Gus, headed back through the woods. The exertion had exacerbated both Gus' arm and his leg, so when Taffy suggested he slip his arm back into his sling, Gus did so with no demur. All he'd got for the exercise was more pain, streaming eyes and an annoyed Taffy. *Aw well, perhaps Sampson and Alice will have fared better.*

Chapter 86

04:15 Heaton Woods

That had been fucking close! I rub my hands together and blow on them. Fucking close! What a fucking buzz! My heart's pumping, entire body's thrumming. It's like I'm an extension of the fucking fire. *'you light my fire... fucking desire... you light my fire...'*

My nerve endings are as alight as the Button's fucking house. I pump my fist in the air, before flinging myself onto the grass under an oak tree. Too fucking wired to bother about the damp or the cold, too damn wired! Nearly couldn't run with my hard-on. Thought the fuckers were going to catch me for a minute. Shit, all the blood went to my todger and I nearly got caught. That would've been good, wouldn't it? Arsonist tripped up by his hard-on! Fucking ace!

Can hardly hear the fire noise from here, so I shut my eyes and replay it all, from the petrol through the broken windows, to chucking my bloody clothes in, to that feeling of power when I strike the match over the match box. *Aaaah, fucking good... aaah, beautiful.* Then the whoosh of flames, the colours, orange, blues, reds, yellow. Fingers of flame eating up the building, building up – spreading – faster... and the smell, petrol, smoke, burning toxic wood, *aaah*! *'Fuck that put me on fi...iiire!'*

I catch my breath, savour my heartbeat slowing down, the sweat drying on my forehead. Left a little gift for the woodland creatures, didn't I?

It had been so easy... almost too easy. I'd wondered if I'd have to wait for ages till they went to bed, but the lights were off when I got there… and the rest, as they say, was history. There's something so pure about setting a fire. I've always loved it, since I was a little kid and swiped some matches and made little fires from old porno mags round the back of the school. There's always loads of places you can find to make fire, so that's what I did. It's important to be able to control the fire… to master it… be the boss. Over the years there have been so many and I've never been caught. This one is the second biggest… the second most important. It's all about finishing the job… getting it done.

The first big one was great, but I misjudged that and nearly died. I'm not beating myself up about that, though. I were just a fucking kid. I've learned since then. Learned loads… honed my craft. I'd tried to be too smart with that one. Should have planned it different. Shit, I was only a kid then and I was angry. So fucking angry. That fucking bitch, Amina, betrayed me. Made me think she'd take me home with her and we'd be together… a family. For fuck's sake. Why would she do that to a child? Why would she destroy my hopes like that? Well, she got what she deserved, her and that stupid little bastard in her stomach. My only regret was that I missed seeing it. Missed the buzz of the flames licking the house, them bringing out the bodies… fucking bastard foster parents, fucking bitch social worker and fucking stupid fucking kids. Every one of them deserved it… deserved to die. No doubt about it.

After that, I was careful. My new mum and dad were easy to dupe. They never realised half of what I got up to and not once did they catch me out – idiots! The other fires were all smaller and, by necessity, less dangerous; old warehouses, the odd old mill, like the one in Thornton, a couple of houses… mind you, I couldn't risk doing that too often.

I'd wanted to hang around near the front of the house, but someone might have recognised me and that would have been the end of my big plan. When the cops and fire brigade started to gather, I headed to the side of the building and waited there. Was an alright view, I suppose... Not the best, not the worst. The old woman in the house next door was deaf, so there was little chance she'd come out and find me lurking in her rose bushes. When that stupid copper came round the corner, camera held out a foot from his face, I skedaddled into the woods. Knew it'd only be a matter of time before the fire reached the back of the building. I climbed a tree and waited. The through-rush of flames, when it came, was amazing. Lit up the entire sky. Brilliant.

I should go back to the cellar, bide my time... wait for them to rescue me. With all the stuff I've planted in Kyle Button's garage it wouldn't take them too long to figure it out; the knife I used on that bitch, the duplicate keys for the church van and the cellar, the bloody ropes. Nobody will believe his innocence... especially when they turn up and find me, near-hysterical, starving and filthy. Anyway, he'll be dead and that other cow Ali will be back in foster care. Hope she gets as royally fucked as I did. It's the perfect revenge... The perfect crime. In the end, Kyle and Amina didn't want me: still, I got the ultimate revenge.

Maybe just one last look before I head back. Just a peep!

Chapter 87

04: 45 Redburn Drive, Frizinghall

The scene in front of the Button's house had changed by the time Gus hobbled round with Taffy. Gus' first thought was how similar it looked to the fire scene in Leeds when Amina Rose died. The paramedics were working on a bundled-up sooty figure. Gus realised that it must be Ali Button, because her dad, in mucky wet pyjamas with a hypothermia blanket slung over his shoulders, was wringing his hands, his gaze never leaving the shape on the trolley.

Some of the firefighters were managing the last of the blaze now and the rest were sitting on the floor, leaning against the fire engine, their helmets and equipment discarded in heaps by their feet. None of them spoke. Most had bowed heads, a few rested their foreheads on arms supported by bent knees. Despite the sweat and filth, Gus saw the deep-etched fatigue on their faces.

He approached Alice, who stood, pale-faced, watching the medics administer to Ali. *Fuck's sake. Sampson should be here with Alice. What the hell's he playing at? He knows she'd been through a lot this week.* His tone sharper than he'd intended, Gus said, 'Where the fuck's Sampson?'

Alice, moving as if her body weighed a tonne, turned to Gus and held out one hand. It seemed that even that tiny effort was too much for her, because she dropped it to her side almost straight away.

Gus stepped forward and put his good arm round her shoulder. He'd get the paramedics to look her over when they'd stabilised Ali. Alice had been through too much all at once. Shock must be setting in now. Alice shrugged his arm off. 'He's gone, Gus. Sampson's fucking gone!'

Gus frowned. 'Where the hell's he gone? He should be here.'

Alice, bowed her head and began to weep. 'He's dead. He heard Ali yelling from the bathroom window at the side of the house and climbed up the drainpipe to get her. She must have frozen or something because next thing I see, he'd gone inside and he's helping her out, holding her till she caught hold of the drain pipe. Then, a rush of air or something went through the house and Ali was thrown to the ground, and–' her voice broke, 'Sampson's gone.'

Chapter 88

04:55 Redburn Drive

Skirting round the woods and entering the cul-de-sac through a garden half a dozen doors away was easy. I knew the fire was on its way out. Only an experienced fire-setter like myself could smell the change in the quality of smoke hanging in the air. The accompanying hustle and bustle of fire engines and so forth, is gone. I'm taking a risk, I know that, but I'm so buzzed, I don't care. I've always got Plan B to fall back on and I've been holed up in that fucking tomb for so long and this smoke-laden air is as fresh as it gets for me. I've waited so long for this... I deserve it.

I pull my hoodie right up and over my head. No-one will recognise me. I'll stay well back, anyway. I'll be careful, won't get too close. The first thing I see as I approach the cordon is an ambulance with its doors open. Fucking Button's standing outside it looking in. Fuck! Fuck! Fuck! I can almost feel the tension radiating off the man, but it's not E-fucking-nough.

I kick the fence and a bloke with a dog a few gates down glances at me and then wanders off, letting his dog pull him away. That were close. Need to keep a hold of myself. Get a grip. Button's still there, looking all sad and forlorn. Maybe Ali's dead... or her slut mum, maybe even both. I grin. That might work. First the bastard loses his fiancée and his bastard child, now he loses Ali. Win, fucking win! I want to punch the air, but stop myself. Need to blend in, not stand out like... a giggle at a funeral. Should have set fire to her sooner.

Maybe I will giggle at her funeral. That'll teach her. I'll piss on her grave for all the grief she's caused me.

Does it matter that *he's* not dead? *Come on, Simon, think.* Does it matter? He can deny everything, but what good will that do him? The stuff's still in his shed, and I'll still be locked in the cellar. When the idiot coppers finally trace the video footage it'll lead them to him. No, it's all good... cool. Well, not exactly cool... more scorching hot!

It's a disappointment, though. I wanted him to die. A dead man can't defend himself, after all. Suppose, though, I should celebrate. The more pain he has to deal with, the more pleasure for me to treasure.

A little away from the ambulance, a trio of coppers stand, huddled together looking like they've been slapped in the face. I screw up my eyes. The one with his arm in a sling might have been the one who chased me through the woods. Well, 'chase' is too strong a word. The idiot hobbled after me. If it hadn't been for the other bloke being a bit faster on his feet, I'd have enjoyed toying with him. Could have led him a merry dance, all over Heaton Woods.

I edge forward. Want to get a better view of Ali or her mum in the fucking ambulance. Why aren't they driving off. Must be serious. My heart speeds up, and I feel a familiar pumping on my veins. Even with the odd few slip-ups it's worked out well. A yell from my right jolts me. It's the fucker with the dog, pointing at me, shouting something. And he's with another bloke. I spin round, ready to run to the left, then my fucking hood slips off.

Chapter 89

04:55 Redburn Drive

It hadn't sunk in. How could it? Gus had only been gone half an hour. How could one of his officers have died whilst he was hirpling around the woods? Not minutes earlier, he'd cursed Sampson… now the lad was dead. The fire chief came over and expressed his condolences, but Gus wasn't listening, not properly. The chief had said something about retrieving Sampson's remains later in the day. Gus didn't want his remains. He wanted the quiet, dependable, slightly gauche lad back. He kept looking over at the smoking building, half expecting to see Sampson loping from the fire, his long-legged stride covering the distance to them in seconds. The desire to hobble over and into the building to look for Sampson himself was almost overpowering. The lad had been his responsibility. The only thing keeping Gus grounded right at that moment was his sense of responsibility for Alice and Taffy. He'd lost one officer, now he had to take care of the remaining two. Thank fuck Compo wasn't here. He'd be inconsolable. Alice looked like she'd never come round again. Her eyes were huge and staring. Taffy looked like he was about to cry, but was trying to keep a brave face. Although, Gus wanted this night to be over, he knew he wouldn't be going anywhere any time soon.

A glance at the cordon showed him that the vultures had already gathered. Jez Hopkins was talking to a man with a dog who was pointing beyond the ambulance. He'd be sniffing after a story, no doubt, and it wouldn't be long before Sampson's death leaked. Gus would have to make the death notice soon. Sampson's family needed to hear this from him before it became public knowledge. However, he didn't want to leave Alice and Taffy, not like this. He pinched this nose, just between his eyes. Shit. He'd have to tell Compo, too. Right now, the pain from his arm and leg seemed inconsequential. The death of one of his officers had created its own pain, right in his heart and Gus knew it would be a long time before it healed.

A yell from behind the cordon made him jump. He turned his head and saw Jez Hopkins moving towards a young lad in a hoodie, his cameraman following. 'Simon? Simon Proctor?'

The name hung on the air for a long second before Gus reacted. Ignoring the pain in his leg, he moved towards the lad. Hopkins overtook him on his right and then the bloke with the dog overtook on his left. Cursing his inability to move fast, Gus lagged behind. The lad had a head start and Hopkins was unfit so he trailed behind. Gus was soon making better progress than the journalist. Then, another figure, smaller and faster, came from behind Gus. Two figures were gaining on the lad, herding him down to the main road, away from the woods. One was Taffy, who ran with the determined ease of a sprinter, the other was the bloke with the dog. The dog, who appeared quite overweight, all of a sudden ground to a halt and collapsed on the path. Taffy overtook the exhausted dog and its owner by jumping over the dog's prone figure.

The hooded youth slipped on the slurry of foam that covered the road and landed on his back. Gus' heart pounded in his chest. Taffy was gaining on him. Surely, they'd catch him now. The lad jumped to his feet but Taffy had gained on him. Taffy was within arm's reach of Simon when he too succumbed to the slippery foam and fell forward, arms outstretched. As he fell, Taffy executed a rugby tackle that swiped the lad's feet from under him. Taffy landed hard on his front and crawled towards Proctor. Simon managed to grapple a few feet away from Taffy until he got purchase and then jumped to his feet and took off.

With his face uncovered, Gus saw that the person they were pursuing was indeed Simon Proctor. His frustration was palpable as he yelled into the air. Realising he had no chance of catching the lad, Gus stopped and did the next best thing. Pulling his phone out he dialled, and still panting after his exertions, yelped down the line: 'We need backup at the Button's residence right now. Simon Proctor has been sighted and is attempting to evade capture. If he gets into Heaton Woods, we'll need the canine division.'

Swerving to his left, Simon Proctor dodged into a garden and disappeared round the back of a house. Loud yells from the homeowner reached Gus' ears as he, phone call complete, tried to reach the property. As he approached, gingerly navigating his way over the stream of foam, the pyjama-clad owner blocked Taffy's path, gesticulating and apparently guiding Taffy away from the rear of the property where Simon Proctor had disappeared. Gus cursed and yelled, 'Move your fucking arse, this is police business.'

Meanwhile, Taffy feinted to the right and then to the left and, succeeding in evading the man, he continued his pursuit. Jez Hopkins and his cameraman caught up, camera rolling. Gus snarled at them. 'Turn the fucking camera off.' He took a warning step towards them. Seemingly realising that Gus was in no mood for an argument, the cameraman lowered the camera as Gus said to a uniformed officer who'd approached, 'Get any footage he's got. I'm not having them use anything till we've cleared it.'

Jez Hopkins didn't take the hint. 'What's he done? Is that Simon Proctor? Are you arresting him for Sue Downs' murder? Why is he here in the vicinity of this fire? Are the two incidents linked? Is this fire the result of an arson attack? Did Simon Proctor light the fire?'

Gus channelled every iota of anger, frustration and grief into the look he directed at the reporter. 'Back the fuck off. You want a statement from me, you get out of my hair right fucking now, okay?'

Hopkins looked chastened.

'In that case, get back behind the cordon and let us do our job.'

As Hopkins and his camera man sloped off behind the cordon, Taffy, heaving the struggling teenager in an uncompromising grip, came back round the side of the building. His expression was jubilant and Gus heaved a sigh of relief. *Thank fuck something's gone right tonight.* No sooner had the thought crossed his mind, when a figure in pyjamas hurtled past Gus. For a second, he thought it was the irate homeowner from earlier, but as the figure flung its entire bodyweight against Simon Proctor, pushing both the boy and Taffy to their backs on the footpath, Gus realised it was Kyle Button.

Kyle's face was contorted as he shrieked and pulled his fisted hand back. Taffy struggled to get to his feet and Gus limped towards them. *Fucking journalists, why couldn't Hopkins have kept his stupid questions to himself. Now look what he's started.*

With a tortured yell, Kyle punched the lad in the face. 'You little fucking bastard. You screwed my wife. You deserve this.'

Proctor, blood streaming from his busted nose, started to giggle uncontrollably and began to sing in an eerie high-pitched tone, ' *start to light my fi...re. Set Amina Rose on fii...re.... Kill your little bastard child... make a fucking funeral py...re...* '

For a second, Kyle sat on top of Simon's chest and then, as the words of the song sunk in, he raised his hand to his face, shaking his head as if they would dislodge from his brain. 'Nooooo!'

'Your fucking bitch girlfriend promised me she'd look after me, take care of me. Bitch deserved to die. She was going to leave me with some other foster parents who'd just screw me up the arse like all the fucking others. She deserved to die, and so did Ali.'

Before Gus or Taffy could stop him, Kyle grabbed Simon's head in both hands and began crashing it onto the road, punctuating each bang with a loud exhalation.

By the time, Taffy was on his feet and a firefighter had run over to pull Kyle Button off the lad, Simon Proctor lay unmoving, his eyes closed and blood pooling around him like a macabre halo. In the distance, another ambulance siren sounded. Gus looked up and saw Jez Hopkin's cameraman recording the scene, but before he could say anything, Hopkins, mouth curled up as if he had a nasty taste in it, said, 'We got Proctor's confession. The tape's yours.'

Turning to Taffy, Gus said, 'Book him.' He gestured at Kyle Button. 'Then get an officer to accompany him to his daughter's bedside.'

Much as he sympathised with Kyle Button, he also wanted to strangle the man. What he'd done to Simon Proctor had just sentenced him to jail time and Ali to yet another foster family. *What a fucking mess.*

He looked at where a firefighter and a paramedic were working on Simon Proctor's unconscious body. 'I know this is the last thing you want to do, Taffy, but I need you to accompany this fucker to the hospital and not leave his side till I get someone to relieve you. I need to go and speak with Sampson's parents and notify the Proctors.'

Gus moved away from the bloody mess that was Simon Proctor and peered towards the ambulance where he'd last seen Alice. She'd been near the ambulance. Where was she now? As his eyes raked the crowd; he saw two plain clothed police officers he didn't recognise, near the ambulance. Between them stood Alice, her face pale and startled, eyes staring at him. A viper's nest in his stomach writhed, releasing its venom into his bloodstream. The fireman who'd come to help Taffy, moved to his side and, without saying a word, put his arm under Gus' good shoulder and helped him over to Alice. Gus glared at the two officers. 'Can I help you?' They were clearly out for Alice's blood. Why else would they have turned up here to arrest her? They knew fine and well they could have got her just as easily on her return to The Fort.

The younger one flinched and looked away, but the older one held his gaze. 'We've got to take her in. She's been read her rights. She's been relieved of her duties and will be held in remand in Downview Prison in Surrey.'

'What?' The word exploded like a grenade form Gus' mouth, making the younger officer jump.

'They've got compelling evidence in the Sean Kennedy case. There's nothing I can do.'

Gus, firefighter at his side, edged closer. 'Well, the first thing you can fucking do is get those fucking handcuffs off her.'

'She's been classed as dangerous. Attempted murder of a fellow officer, the cuffs stay on.'

'She's just lost a colleague in that blaze. Give her a break.'

The younger officer smiled. 'Sure she didn't do him in? She's got form for that.'

Gus' fist clenched and as his hand drew back to land one on the smirking face, he felt a firm hand on his arm. Nancy kept her grip on his arm, but didn't meet his gaze.

She raised herself to her full height. 'It's customary for the DCI to be notified if one of her officers is to be arrested.'

The older man shrugged. 'Just carrying out orders, ma'am.'

Stepping forwards, Nancy put out her hands, one on each of Alice's cheeks. 'We've got this, Al. We'll sort this out. But, right now, my hands are tied.'

Seemingly responding to the human touch, a smile touched Alice's lips as she jiggled her handcuffed hands. 'Seems mine are tied too, boss.'

Nancy kissed her cheek and moved away to allow Gus to give her an awkward hug. Gus, ignoring the men on either side of her, saw that the glazed look had gone from her eyes. She looked frightened and there was a slight tremble on her bottom lip as she smiled. Gus had never seen her so brave. Unable to say anything, he hugged her in silence, but Alice took the opportunity to whisper in his ear. 'Sean's got mates all over the force. Loads of them must have been in his back pocket before. Half of them always thought I framed him. This could get mucky. Distance yourself from me, Gus. Don't tarnish your reputation by supporting me.' She pulled away from him. 'Tell Sampson's folks how sorry I am.'

His entire body rigid, Gus watched as Alice was marched towards the police vehicle. An elfin figure between two trolls. He'd have those bastards if they so much as put one of the hairs on her head out of place. For a moment all the activity around him merged into the background. His head was full of mince and his chest pounding like a death knell, ponderous and grim. He turned in time to see Jez Hopkins watching Alice being put into the unmarked vehicle. If Gus was in any position to judge he'd say that the look on the reporter's face was dismay. *Could he have feelings for Alice?* Gus studied the other man for a moment as the car pulled away and then said, 'Which one of my officers leaked information about this case to you?'

Jez, eyes still on the moving vehicle, said 'It wasn't Al, Gus. Never in a million years. It was an anonymous source, but, between you and me, I wouldn't look much further than Steven Knowles. Not that it'll do you any good. The bastard's as greasy as a mechanic's spanner.' Before Gus could reply, the reporter winked and moved away. Gus disliked Knowles intensely, yet he had nothing to pin this on him. Bloody git would get away with it… as usual.

Chapter 90

07:30 The Fort

When he walked back into The Fort, the weight of Sampson's family's grief was still with Gus and he wasn't looking forward to telling Compo that as well as losing one colleague, Alice had been arrested and was in a cell in Surrey awaiting trial for the attempted murder of her former lover and boss, Sean Kennedy.

On the way in, Hardeep, his expression grim, had handed him a bundle of newspapers. Leaning against the wall in the lift as it transported him upstairs, Gus had shuffled them under his arm and one-handedly opened *The Mail*. As expected, Alice was front page news on the national tabloids, whilst the local newspapers were full of the fire and Simon Proctor's brief resurrection.

Nancy had hotfooted it down south first thing and was calling in personal favours left, right and centre to find out what they had on Alice that was so compelling. What evidence would be enough to put Alice behind bars? It certainly wasn't the word of a crooked drug dealer who'd altered his story. Much as Gus wanted to storm down there himself, he'd have to trust Nancy to deal with it. He had enough on his plate right now, dealing with the Simon Proctor mess.

Proctor's parents had been taken to the hospital last night to see their son. In the short space of time that Kyle Button had access to Simon, he'd done a lot of damage and it was touch and go whether the boy would survive. On a personal level, Gus couldn't care less, however, on a professional level he wanted to see him tried and imprisoned for what he'd done. The boy had single-handedly been responsible for ruining a lot of lives.

Pushing open the door, Gus flinched. His team had been decimated. Someone had been in and cleared Alice's desk (for evidence purposes, no doubt) and Compo was in the process of packing all of Sampson's belongings into a cardboard box.

Compo's head jerked up when Gus walked in and Taffy, who was huddled behind a computer in the corner of the room, stood and moved over. The two young men looked at Gus as if he could solve everything. Their expressions were grief-stricken, yet hopeful.

Gus sighed. His head felt like it had swollen to twice its normal size and he wasn't sure he could hold it up for much longer. Tea sloshed around in his stomach, making it gurgle.

He'd never forget Mrs Sampson's face when he told her. Sitting in her living room, he was soon surrounded by Sampson's many sisters, and from every surface and wall, Sampson's smiling eyes taunted him. The lad had been in *his* care and he'd let him down. He should have taken better care of him. Refocussing his gaze on Compo and Taffy, he took a deep breath and exhaled. He needed to look after these two now. That's what Alice would have said, anyway. He squashed down his own tiredness and summoned a half smile. 'Look, we all need some sleep. Go home. Have a few hours and come back when you're rested.'

Compo, his tone ferocious, slammed down his box. 'We're *not* sleeping till we've got enough on that little piece of shit to make sure that if he wakes up, he *won't* see the light of day... not ever.'

Gus' eyes welled up. To hide the emotion Compo's words had ignited, he moved over to get some coffee, before saying, 'Okay, Compo. What have we got?'

Compo moved to his computer. 'Hissing Sid and co found a whole load of stuff in the Button's garage, which, thanks to the firefighters, was completely unburnt. Some of Simon's clothes, a bracelet belonging to Sue Downs and a ring of Jenny Gregg's. Alongside that was a printed scale drawing of the old St Augustine's Church which showed underground rooms; and an old key. We've already sent a team there and it's an interesting find. You'll want to head down there soon, Gus.'

Gus drained his cup and got to his feet with a reluctance born of extreme weariness. *No rest for the wicked.*

'Eh... Gus?' Compo shuffled his feet, 'We got some lab test results back on the girl found in Cottingley Ridge. Name is Julie Dyson, apparently, fifteen-year-old runaway.'

Gus sighed. With everything that had gone on in the past twelve hours, he hadn't even thought about that poor girl. With any luck it'll be a straightforward case of a pimp gone rogue and they'd be able to make an easy arrest. Seeing that Compo was waiting for permission to continue, Gus waved his hand at him.

'Well, when your da... I mean, Dr McGuire found the traces of semen on the back of the neck, he decided to see if he could lift any latents. He got an expert in and they got lucky. Found prints from a middle and index finger from each hand. They pulled up a match.'

Gus frowned when he saw that Compo's face had darkened to a deep beetroot colour. 'Well?'

'Steven Knowles.' Compo's shuffling was more frenetic.

'What?'

'Steven Knowles. The prints match the ones we have on record for him, I'm betting the semen will match him, too. Also, one of Julie's friends came forward and identified Knowles as having picked Julie up the night she died. Says he's a sleazy bastard, always after free blow jobs. Says Julie told her she'd been friends with Knowles' daughter. Shall I get someone to bring him in or wait till he turns up for shift?'

'Fucking hell!' The words spurted from Gus' mouth like shrapnel. 'Hopkins told me Knowles was our leak. I thought the bastard had got away with it. Well, he won't be getting away with this. Not a bloody chance. Get him brought in.'

Chapter 91

08:45 The Fort

Gus had planned it down to the last detail. He felt that not only did Julie Dyson deserve this, but the whole of Bradford Police did, too. Dirty officers were the bane of the service's life and this would give clean officers something back. Something to remember. It would also be a warning to any tempted to stray onto the dark side. He also wanted it for Alice. She'd hated Knowles, hadn't trusted him an inch and neither had Gus. Knowles deserved this.

Someone's phone buzzed. Gus glanced at Compo who nodded. Gus stepped forward and looked along the officers he'd directed to line up along the corridor. Apart from his own team, the other officers wore puzzled expressions. Some shuffled their feet, perhaps anticipating a rollicking of some description, others bounced on their toes, keen to get it over with and carry on with their workload.

Clearing his throat, Gus stepped forward, 'When that lift door opens, DC Steven Knowles will step into the corridor. He is under arrest for the murder of Julie Dyson. Earlier on, forensics confirmed his fingerprints were found around Julie's neck. I have also been informed that the leak to the press from this department lies at Knowles' door. As he walks past us we should all reflect on why we are here in this building; what our role is; and how it makes our job harder when officers like Knowles turn bad. No-one is to say a word to him, but as soon as he passes you, walk back into your offices and get on with the job we are honoured to do: keeping this city safe from predators like him.'

The lift pinged and the door swished open. All eyes were on the man who stood, an officer at either shoulder, at the lift's door. The silence was absolute. At a nod from Gus, the officers pushed Knowles from the confines of the lift. His eyes darted from side to side as he saw his colleagues lining the corridor before him.

'Move.' Gus didn't have to raise his voice to be heard, yet Knowles pulled back, jerking his arm from the officers who held him.

Gus repeated his directive, 'Move.'

Eyes swinging between Gus and the line of officers, each of whom held their gaze steady on Knowles, he paled and licked his lips. 'I'm not well. Need a drink… water.'

'The interview room's just at the end. There's water there. Move!'

Knowles took a single step forward, licked his lips again and hesitated. He held out a hand towards one of his friends. 'Fred? It's not what you think.'

Fred's lip curled up and he spun on his heel and walked back into his office, his absence leaving a thunder-like heaviness in the corridor. As if realising that drawing the walk of shame out would be worse, Knowles sped up, took three faltering steps forward and then collapsed on the floor, clutching his chest.

The officers watched him writhing on the carpet tiles, yet no-one moved. Gus stepped closer, then dropping to his knees, he began loosening Knowles' tie. 'Get an ambulance here now. The fucker's having a heart attack!' and without waiting to see if his orders were being obeyed, Gus began compressions, interspersed with mouth-to-mouth. 'Come on, come on! You… fucker… you're… not… going… to… die.'

All at once, Taffy was at his side. 'You do compressions, I'll do mouth-to-mouth, Gus.'

A single nod and Gus moved back, giving Taffy space, oblivious to the buzz of chatter around them. Working in tandem with Taffy, Gus put as much effort in as he could, trying to force life back into Knowles' dark heart. 'Not... fucking... here. Not... fucking... now. You're going to pay for what you've done.' Yet, somewhere deep inside, Gus knew that wasn't going to be the case. When the paramedics arrived minutes later, Gus' shoulders were aching and Taffy's face was red from exertion. They pulled Gus away from Knowles and slid onto the floor beside the dying man. Twice Gus heard the buzz of the defibrillator followed by a dull thud before the paramedics stood up, shaking their heads.

Gus' chest clogged up with the tension of the previous ten minutes. The bastard had denied them justice in the end. How could it be that Alice... quirky, gutsy, innocent Alice was locked up in a prison, when the real guilty parties had escaped justice?

Steven Knowles had abused his position and, it seemed, had escaped punishment for his deeds.

Simon Proctor had destroyed numerous lives, killed a lot of people and he, too, was escaping justice.

He didn't care for himself, no. Gus cared about the families who had to continue their lives, knowing that the person who'd killed their loved ones had escaped punishment. What sort of fucking justice was that? Hell, even Kyle Button would end up with a custodial sentence for what he'd done to his wife's killer and the upshot of that was that Ali had lost both her parents in one fell swoop and would end up back in foster care again. It was always the damn innocents who suffered.

Chapter 92

10:30 St Augustine's Church

Gus managed to hobble down the stairs into the deep recesses of the room which was part of the original structure of St Augustine's Church. Anthony Evans had known about it, but because it was so cold and so far under the church, he hadn't given it a thought in years. The entrance was at the bottom end of the old cemetery and had been far enough away from the preacher's new build to be almost private.

Evidence that Simon Proctor had been camping out there was everywhere, although the most damning evidence against him was the fact that Compo had managed to uncover the various encryptions on the video of Simon in captivity. Despite Simon's best efforts, Compo managed to bounce it all back to an old computer of Simon's that his parents thought he'd lost. Matty, when asked about where Simon might hide something like a computer, had gone down to his cellar and retrieved it. Simon had told him he needed a new laptop and wanted to pretend his old one had been left on the bus one day, so Matty had hidden it for him.

Gus had no doubt they'd find copious quantities of his DNA in the room. Not that they needed it to prove Proctor had been there. His own video footage did that. In one corner of the room was a rickety camp bed, it stank of sweat and excrement and the chemi loo was overflowing. When they'd examined Simon's rucksack they found a stash of money and jewellery. Gus reckoned that someone as devious as Simon Proctor would have had a backup plan, and he was sure it involved the money and jewellery. He reckoned Mrs Proctor would recognise most of the jewellery as hers.

Standing in the middle of the room, Gus turned in a slow circle. There was the camera the lad had set up himself. The rickety bed. What sort of person would make such an intricate and devious plan to get revenge on a man who'd already lost so much?

The psychiatrists would have a field day if Simon Proctor ever woke up. The diaries they'd recovered from his rucksack revealed the full extent of his crimes. Many deliberately set fires in the district could now be attributed to him, but what Gus found even more chilling was the account of a ten-year-old boy planning to kill the social worker he'd loved because he'd misunderstood her intentions when she'd said she'd keep him safe and get him away from his abusive foster parents. When she told him she was getting married and was having a baby, the ten-year-old Simon had been devastated and, already damaged, he planned a terrible revenge. If Amina Rose couldn't be his mummy then she would be no-one's mummy. Simon blamed Kyle Button for being the obstacle to his happiness. The almost inconceivable account of him locking his foster parents and the other foster children in the living room, and the social worker in his bedroom, was heart-breaking. If things had gone to plan, Simon would have escaped unharmed. His biggest gripe had been that his miscalculation of how fast the fire would spread had prevented him from having the satisfaction of seeing his own handiwork. He had been desperate to make Amina Rose's fiancé, Kyle Button, suffer.

Over the years since Simon had been with the Proctors, raising the occasional fire had sufficed, until he'd recognised Kyle Button. Seeing him with a new family had been the trigger for Simon to plan his revenge. Whatever it took, Simon was determined to deny Button any happiness.

What affected Gus the most, were the incoherent ramblings that interspersed completely lucid sections of writing. He suspected that should Simon Proctor recover enough to be held accountable for his actions, these rambling texts may be enough to put him in a psychiatric hospital rather than a young offenders' institution. Niggling at Gus was the question of how someone so organised could be so insane.

January 2018

Epilogue

13:30 HM Prison Downview, Surrey

She looked gaunt and tired and she held her entire body taut as if expecting to be attacked. Nancy had told Gus that Alice had already been attacked three times.

Prison was no place for a police officer and Gus was sure that Sean Kennedy would have put the word out that Alice was to be 'taken care of'. He worried about her. Nancy said she'd given as good as she got, but that wasn't the point. She didn't belong in here and it was taking too long to get her name cleared. Officers were crawling out of the woodwork in defence of Sean Kennedy and things were progressing too slowly. Alice's lawyers were 'hopeful', still Gus didn't trust them, 'hopeful' wasn't enough… not for Alice.

'Told you not to come, Gus.' Alice looked everywhere but at him.

Noticing her lower her eyes, he glanced over to where she'd last been looking. A tall woman with straggly red hair glared at him and then winked, before turning her attention back to her own visitor. Gus wondered if he'd endangered Alice even more by visiting. 'You okay, Al?'

A hard look came in her eyes and her chin lifted. She scraped her chair back from the table and took a deep breath. 'How many more times do I have to tell you to piss off? I'm not your fucking snitch. Go and swivel on a pointed pencil somewhere. Fuck off.'

She motioned to the guard, and without another look at Gus, walked away. Gus glanced round the room and saw that most of the inmates were smirking. Shocked by his own stupidity, he groaned. *What the fuck have I done?*

* * *

Don't know how I held it together when I saw Gus. All I wanted to do was throw myself into his arms and beg him to take me home. Right, like that would have worked. I did the right thing telling him to fuck off. Hairy Mary had her eyes on him from the get-go. Knew he was a copper.

I lower myself onto my bed. There's still a faint whiff of shit in the air from where they smeared my pillow. Must be imagining it. Thought I got it all. Lulu gave me a wet wipe to get it off my sheet. Don't get clean ones for another three days. I remade my bed. Put the bit with the cleaned off shit to the bottom, but it's still there.

Ribs hurt. One's broken, I'm sure of it. Maybe two. Don't think Gus could tell, though. Bitter sweet to see him. So much I wanted to ask. How was Sampson's funeral? Fuck, get a grip, Alice, don't let them see you crying. The funeral would've been grand. Gus would've made sure of that. Fucking little prick, Proctor. Hope he comes around soon, so he can get put away. My lawyer says the evidence against him is overwhelming. Now all we… they need, is to put the little bastard away. My lawyer also says the evidence against *me* is overwhelming. Fucking Sean Kennedy. What they need to do is find out what he has on all the witnesses who're lying to put me away… sooner rather than later, too. Don't know if I'll be able to last much longer.

* * *

Gus' heart was in his shoes making each step away from the yellow brick building heavier than the previous one. He'd made a huge miscalculation in visiting Alice and he only hoped her show of defiance was enough to keep her safe.

He walked over to Alice's aubergine Mini and walked straight into Patti Copley's arms. Breathing in her perfume made him flash back to Alice's pitiful figure as she'd stormed away from him. Who was offering Alice comfort? He'd left her back there in an environment that smelled of boiled cabbage and violence. He'd no business indulging himself with Patti, who'd refused to take no for an answer when he'd tried to shut her out after the case had been wrapped up.

Torn in two, his mind with Alice, his senses all too aware of Patti, he absorbed her strength for a long minute and then stepped from her embrace and tossed the Mini's keys to her. 'You drive, my arm's sore.'

Patti caught the keys and weighed them in her hand before tossing them back at Gus. Her voice was gentle but firm, 'She made *you* promise to look after it, not me. You owe her.'

A pulse throbbed at Gus' temple. Hell, he knew he owed her. Alice was not only his colleague; she was his friend. She'd stood by him when Greg died and when Gabriella walked out. She was always there for him. He gave an abrupt nod, Patti was right he owed Al, so he folded himself into Alice's Mini. She'd sent him a letter insisting look after her beloved Mini, and Gus, in the weeks since her arrest, had done so. 'Never even got the chance to tell her Minnie was okay,' he said, his voice gruff.

Patti turned to him. 'Tell me.'

'Nothing to say. Shouldn't have gone in. I've probably put her at risk. Looks like Sean Kennedy's got spies all over the joint.' He paused and ran his fingers through his dreads, 'She looked so diminutive and skinny. Life fucking sucks, Patti. Justice is a fucking myth… a joke.'

Coming Soon

DI Gus McGuire will return in Unspoken Truths, the 5th book in the series. Coming for you in Winter 2018 .
    Read on for an exclusive preview of Unspoken Truths

Unspoken Truths

Prologue

Tired and aching, her body pushed to its limitations, Alice left the prison gym with a cursory glance at the two other prisoners who also seemed to use physical activity to combat their demons. She never spoke to them, nor they to her, but, despite that, there was an unspoken bond between them. An appreciation of each other's determination and stamina. Her gaze shifted and all too aware of her 'stalkers' loitering by the exercise balls, two of them sprawled like beached whales on the mats, the other leaning against the wall, one foot resting on an inflated turquoise ball, rolling it back and forth, an unlit cigarette hanging from the corner of her mouth, Alice kept her gaze low as she entered the shower area. Until her imprisonment months earlier she'd only ever worked out in mixed gyms and the absence of testosterone in a gym where female sweat was regularly broken, never ceased to amaze her. Not that there was a lack of seriousness to the activity. No. Those who worked out, did so with a focus and determination akin to fanaticism. The gym was a basic, no frills joint, it's main aim being to dispel the 'stir crazy', and it worked. Well, it did for Alice. It was one of only two things in here that kept her sane.

She stripped her workout clothes off, flung them on the wooden bench and stepped under the shower head. Banging her palm against the button, she raised her hand to meet the lukewarm flow of water. One of the guard's should have accompanied her inside, but they'd been too busy huddled together gossiping. No doubt, they would notice her absence from the gym and catch up with her here in a minute but, for now, Alice welcomed being alone. She rested her head on the wall and savoured the water cooling her body, washing the sweat away. The door clicked open and a quick smirk tugged Alice's lips for a second. Big Brother was on her case!

As she pushed her forehead from the wall she paused, sensing movement behind her. A snigger, close by her ear had her ducking. Whirling round on one leg, the other bent at the knee, she saw a body mass before her it's arms extended ready to grab her by the throat. Alice extended her leg in a power kick that connecting with pink covered flab, eliciting an 'oomph' sound before collapsing in a curled-up position on the wet floor. Fists up, bobbing on the balls of her feet, Alice flicked water from her short hair. Eyes darting round the room she saw she had two more adversaries to face; Hairy Bloody Mary and her last remaining sidekick. Where was the guard? Surely, they'd noticed her absence by now? Alice sighed and weighed up the odds. Neither of her opponents was, what you'd call, in 'peak physical condition' so she reckoned she'd be able to dodge them. It all depended on whether the prison guard was actually going to put in an appearance, or, as Alice was beginning to suspect, had all too willingly turned a blind eye. She cursed herself. She should've known better than to sneak off on her own.

Narrowing her eyes, Alice relaxed her clenched fingers and dropped them to waist height, her palms towards the other two women. Wiggling her fingers in a 'come on then' sort of gesture she raised her chin and glowered at them. "What you waiting for? Better odds?"

Hairy Mary, her red hair ratted around her face like a henna-maned lion, took a step towards Alice, "Fucking got ya now, Cooper? Fucking got ya."

Ignoring her thumping heart and the transitory thought that being naked in a fight wasn't the best scenario she'd faced, Alice held her ground. Mary's pasty arms reached towards Alice, so Alice sidestepped which brought her closer to Mary's mate; the one Alice had named Haudit, a phrase borrowed from Doc McGuire. Daudit had already been disposed of and still lay in a heap on the ground moaning softly. A fleeting expression of wide eyed panic crossed Haudit's spotty face as Alice lifted her arms and stepped even closer. It was then that the slow clapping began. Alice halted. A huge grin replaced the earlier anxiety on Haudit's face. A quick glance showed that Hairy Mary's was grinning too – a Cheshire lion with spots and a minging mane. Alice looked to the right and her heart plummeted. How the hell had she not noticed Baby Jane (inflictor of pain) enter the arena? Not much bigger than Alice, Baby Jane, nonetheless, made Hannibal Lector seem sane.

Alice glanced around, looking for a way out. Wherever Baby Jane was, her goons wouldn't be far behind and Alice didn't want to wait around to see what the woman had in store for her. Taking a sideways step, Alice grabbed Haudit, and despite the excessive poundage the other woman carried, she managed to swing her round with ease before releasing her straight into Baby Jane. Not waiting to witness the impact, Alice dodged back, her eye on the shower room door. Within arm's reach of it, she felt a vice like grip on each of her upper arms as she was yanked backwards and slammed against the wall. A hand against her throat kept her in place, her toes only just skimming the floor. From what seemed like miles above her two cold eyes looked down at Alice. Aw shit, Baby Jane's enforcer was here. The colour drained from Alice face and after a couple of seconds struggling in vain, she went limp. Hairy Mary and her team had congregated by the door, guarding it, no doubt.

Baby Jane and her crew studied Alice as if she was a specimen. The enforcer released Alice's throat and, knowing better than to show weakness, Alice raised her chin and stared straight at Baby Jane, aware that, with Jane's thugs holding her arms by her sides, her options were limited.

Jane, eyes as blue as a summer's sea sent a shiver down Alice's spine. The smile on the woman's face didn't match with the emptiness in her eyes. This was a woman practised in feigning emotion. The only person, Alice had ever met with a similar expression was The Matchmaker and thankfully he was behind bars. Whatever Baby Jane wanted with her, Alice new it would not be in her best interests. Despite herself, she shivered and, apparently aware of it, Jane's enforcer released a yelp of pure gleeful excitement. It reminded Alice of the over excite reactions of hounds about to be let loose on a fox. Alice swallowed down the wave of nausea that engulfed her and did the only thing she could do …

Utilising the firmness of her attacker's hold on her arms, Alice waited till Jane was close enough to her, then in an instant leaned her weight against their grip, pushed both feet from the floor and, knees bent, before extending them and catapulting them at Jane's chest. Jane stumbled backwards a yowl of unadulterated rage hung in the cubicle and the smile was gone from her face in an instant. Her goons, increased the pressure on Alice's arms, forcing her back against the wall. As her head cracked against the tiles, Alice flinched, her eyesight clouded. She forced herself to shake her head, shake out the dizziness. Jane was coming for her, her arms raised like a banshee, her mouth open in a feral snarl. Alice backed up until the cold tiles pressed against her buttocks. There was nothing she could do, nowhere to go.

Jane breathing heavily smashed against her body. Alice breath poofed from her, her bones shuddered, then an agonising pain at her breast. Breathing in short pants, Alice's eyes flew open and she saw Jane dancing in front of her, something bloody gripped between her teeth, blood dripping down her skin. Her eyes fastened on Alice, she snarled, baring her teeth and then with one finger she pushed Alice's nipple into her own mouth and smiled. Two chews ... still grinning, she gave an exaggerated swallow and then opened her mouth wide in front of Alice , for all the world as if she was on *I'm a Celebrity Get Me Out Of Here.* 'All gone!'

Alice vomited, bile spewing down her chin and smacking onto the floor below. Jane leaned over and banged the button and a cascade of water spouted over them. "Let her go!'

Jane's goons released Alice and she fell to the floor as Jane straddled her, leaning in close. Alice, in a final act of defiance, stared her out. Jane extended a hand to one of her goons who place something in it. Jane took the pink Unicorn shaped toothbrush and studied it. The handle had been fashioned into a home-made Shiv, honed to a point with a blade inserted for good measure. Alice knew what was coming next. Sean had finally got to her...

The water pounded her body, warm prickles fading to cold. Curled in the foetal position, cowering, she shivered, watching trickles of pink tinged liquid flow towards the plughole where it swirled momentarily; a silent gurgle before eddying away. She was numb. The shiv had punctured her skin, created a wound that leaked her blood onto the shower room tiles, yet ... no pain. For the few moments after the shiv was pulled out, she'd waited, anticipating another thrust, but none had come. Just whispered words in her ear, a combination of foul smelling cigarettes, caffeine and the remnants of that evenings boiled veg concoction. It wasn't the foulness of her attacker's breath that made her blood run cold though, it was the husky words ... the threat.

Alice clutched her side. The strange discrepancy between her blood, warm as it left her body, and the coolness of the shower made her dizzy. She had to hold on. She had to survive this, for if she didn't, the worst thing imaginable would happen and she couldn't be responsible for that. She couldn't be responsible for more deaths. She needed to hold on. As her eyelids flickered and her hand, pressed to her side, weak and shaking, voices, hollow and echoey drifted above her. Shadows floated like phantoms around her and hands touched her skin. She clenched, trying to protest, then pressure was applied to the puncture site and gentle fingers skimmed across her forehead, she recognised the voice. Footsteps running, the shower's pounding stopped, softness replaced the hardness under her head …. then, nothing.

Chapter 1

10:40 Rural Rover train Manchester - Bradford

Jess sighed and directed her best school teacher frown at the young man sitting opposite her. It was irritating enough that this interminable train ride from Manchester to Bradford was running late, but being forced to listen to the thrum from the lad's headphones was just too much. The lad seemed oblivious to her annoyance, his head bopping in time to some annoying rhythm, no doubt filled with inane thoughts of sweaty encounters or scoring his next hit. She'd looked forward to having the time to read her book, but now he'd gone and spoiled it. No more than she'd come to expect from youngsters today. Resigned, she slipped a bookmark between the pages of her romantic novel and closed it. Leaning back against the head rest to watch the countryside pass by, she tried to ignore his blonde head bobbing at the edge of her vision. His extra-long fringe flopped over his eyes making her want to reach out and push it back behind his ears. His knee bounced and his hand drummed on the Formica table top and that combined with the train's persistent rattle, made his Costa cup dance across the table top. If it spilled on her new coat she'd be extremely annoyed.

Turning her head, Jess looked to see if she could move, but each table in the small carriage was occupied. She glared at the offending cup and then at the boy. His spotty face broke into a lopsided grin and he pulled his headphones off. "Just love that song." He leaned both elbows on the table and looked straight at Jess. "It's just pure brilliant. Sorted. You know?"

In the face of such enthusiasm Jess' earlier irritation faded as she risked a small smile in return. No point in being overly friendly, she didn't want to be engaged in a long blown out conversation with a teenager. "I probably wouldn't know the song, love. Nor the band, come to that."

"Course you would ... Everyone's heard of the Beatles." He laughed and raised his hand in the air to high five her.

Jess hesitated for a second. The song had been familiar, but she'd dismissed it as one of the latest radio favourites, played incessantly. Then, hoping no one was witnessing this strange encounter, she lifted her own hand to reciprocate with a small laugh. "Yes, you're right. Even *I've* heard of the Beatles."

The lad nodded, pulled his headphones on again and was soon lost in the rhythm.

As the train rattled towards Rawsforth, Jess hummed along to the now identifiable strains of *Norwegian Woods* fading into *Maxwell's Silver Hammer*.

Helen struggled to settle her two-year-old. Sammy had a slight cold and was tetchy. But she'd decided to brave the one and a half hour journey to her mums rather than be home alone with her husband away. Now, she wished she hadn't bothered. A fluey headache pounded at her temples, her sinuses were blocked and she was sure she'd caught it from Sammy. The only thing worse than trying to entertain a poorly toddler on a train was trying to do it when you felt poorly yourself. The only thing helping her to hold it together was the thought that when she reached Bradford, she could hand Sammy over to her parents until she felt better. Perhaps spending a few days with her parents wasn't such a great one after all. Maybe she should have struggled on at home on her own.

After tantrums and tears and grumpy throwing of toys across the carriage, Sammy's head drooped against her shoulder in a deep sleep, sucking on his dummy. Helen breathed a sigh of relief and for the first time glanced around at her fellow passengers. Her lips tightened when she noticed the young Asian man opposite, so engrossed on his phone. Would you bloody credit it? She'd left Bradford and moved to a rural village to get away from the Pakis and yet here she was, still in the leafy suburbs and she was surrounded by them. Well, ok it was only one of them, but still, they weren't in Bradford yet. Everything about the man annoyed her from his overgrown bushy beard down to his expensive trainers. God she hated them! Everyone knew you couldn't trust them but they were just too scared to say it out loud. Her grip on Sammy tightened a little and she angled him away from the lad and tried to look out the window to distract herself. God she felt rough.

Seconds later, she jumped when he muttered *Fuck* under his breath and threw his phone on the table. Almost at once, he snatched it up again and frowning, turned to glare out the window. Helen's lips tightened. Sammy was heavy and combined with the tension across her shoulders she thought her arms would break. Pulling her handbag onto her knee she edged closer to the edge of her seat. That's when she noticed the horrible black and white Paki scarf lying on top of his rucksack and images of the news feeds from the recent arena bombing played across her mind. She glanced anxiously at her watch; another forty minutes to go. Who knew what might be in that rucksack and why the hell was he fiddling with his phone so much. In a decisive move she stood up, hoisted Sammy up to lean on one shoulder and swung his changing bag and her hand bag onto the other. A quick glance round the carriage and then decision made she moved nearer to the exit, where the blind man and his dog sat.

Mike pretended to tap away on his laptop but all the while he was really eyeing up the woman opposite him. He'd noticed her at the station in Manchester and decided that she'd be a good person to chat to on the tedious journey to Bradford. Of course, her blonde hair, long legs and mini skirt had nothing to do with his decision to find a seat near her ... or so he told himself. Truth was, a bit of female company wouldn't go amiss. His wife was in one of her never-ending moods because the fertility treatment had failed ... yet again. Didn't she get it that it was hard for him too? All the jokes about his 'manhood', about 'firing blanks', his so-called friends who were already dads gloating and sneering, his boss tutting when he had to take time off for the endless appointments. It was ok for her; she got all the sympathy, all the kind words. Her boss was fine about the time off, but shit, if he lost his job they'd be in so much debt ... and now he wasn't even sure if he wanted a kid or not.

An hour into the journey and Mike was truly pissed off. Despite numerous smiles and many conversational gambits the blonde refused to be drawn into conversation. She was perfectly polite but each reply, though uttered in a sexy Eastern European accent, was monosyllabic. Her half smile was strained and her eyes seemed to focus somewhere above his left shoulder. *Bloody snooty cow! Sitting there gripping her laptop case like she thinks I'm going to snatch it and run.* As if – well she can swivel on one!

Jake sat near the carriage door. His guide dog Kipper lying by his feet, his head resting on Jake's knee, Jake was happy to listen to the activity around him. He knew exactly how many people shared the carriage and was content to pass the journey forming his own images of them in his mind. He knew that the young mother with the grizzly child had moved to sit opposite him. She seemed slightly breathless and he could hear her wriggling about in her seat.

Listening to the man with the expensive aftershave tap incessantly on his laptop and attempt to chat up the woman with the foreign accent in the high heels, Jake smiled. Despite her lack lustre responses, Jake knew that the young man would not give up. He was right. Laptop man persisted until, Jake heard her cross her legs and change position. He guessed that she'd angled her body away from her would-be suitor. Smile deepening, Jake turned his attention to the woman at the back humming gently to the tune that escaped from the young lads' earphones. He liked The Beatles too.

10:55

Paddy Toner's final words as the train hurtled relentlessly towards the lime green Toyota Corolla that sat abandoned in the middle of Rawsforth Level Crossing were;

"Fuck me! Who left that there?"

His final actions were to apply the brakes, close his eyes and cross himself.

His final memory was of his wife's flushed cheeks as she shuddered beneath him that morning.

His final thought before the train hit the car was that he'd never see her again.

The train's brakes squealed and the passengers screamed as they were sent flying from their seats, floundering helplessly like fish from an upended aquarium. The carriage began to tip to the right. The metal screeched against metal, sending amber and yellow sparks of amber. The train hit the car, followed swiftly by the explosion and overpowering burning petrol fumes. Then, nothing but silence

Acknowledgements

As usual, I have to give a massive 'shout out' to the incredible Bloodhound Books team. They are phenomenal and I'm proud to be part of their kennels. My editor, Clare Law, is indefatigable and always has her eye on the ball. As ever, my family have been with me on this journey and continue to inspire and support me. Thanks to Nilesh, Ravi, Kasi and Jimi.

The bloggers, book groups and reviewers humble me with their dedication to supporting and encouraging us authors. Love you all! My Leeds Trinity cronies are inspirational, awesome and damn hard taskmasters as is Martyn Bedford, who sits on my shoulder telling me to 'include more interiority' or 'not to dangle my modifiers' – cheeky!

The Barny Bunch make me laugh, keep me sane and more importantly keep me supplied with copious amounts of coffee and my friend, Toria, whose perception and thoughtfulness, combined with her energy and wit makes sure I'm on the right track – a huge thank you!

However, my biggest thanks must go to you, the reader, without whom writing would be an incomplete process. If you enjoyed *Uncommon Cruelty*, please leave a review. You've no idea how much we authors treasure your words of wisdom.

As ever any mistakes are mine and so I apologise in advance. I have taken odd bits of creative licence and created a few new places… forgive me… it was all in order to enhance the story.

Two delightful readers offered their names for my nefarious use; Amina Rose and Sue Downs. Thank you both. MIND charity, as ever, is grateful for your donations and will put the money raised in the raffles to great use.